Praise for the novels of Delores Fossen

"This is a feel good, heartwarming story of love, family and happy endings for all."
—*Harlequin Junkie* on *Christmas at Colts Creek*

"An entertaining and satisfying read...that I can highly recommend."   —*Books & Spoons* on *Wild Nights in Texas*

"The plot delivers just the right amount of emotional punch and happily ever after."
—*Publishers Weekly* on *Lone Star Christmas*

"Delores Fossen takes you on a wild Texas ride with a hot cowboy."
—B.J. Daniels, *New York Times* bestselling author

"Clear off space on your keeper shelf, Fossen has arrived."
—Lori Wilde, *New York Times* bestselling author

"This is classic Delores Fossen and a great read."
—*Harlequin Junkie* on *His Brand of Justice*

"This book is a great start to the series. Looks like there's plenty of good reading ahead."
—*Harlequin Junkie* on *Tangled Up in Texas*

"An amazing, breathtaking and vastly entertaining family saga, filled with twists and unexpected turns. Cowboy fiction at its best."   —*Books & Spoons* on *The Last Rodeo*

To see the complete list of titles available from Delores Fossen,
please visit deloresfossen.com.

DELORES FOSSEN

ALWAYS A MAVERICK

CANARY STREET PRESS

CANARY
STREET
PRESS™

Recycling programs
for this product may
not exist in your area.

ISBN-13: 978-1-335-00864-0

Always a Maverick

Copyright © 2024 by Delores Fossen

TM is a trademark of Harlequin Enterprises ULC.

Canary Street Press
22 Adelaide St. West, 41st Floor
Toronto, Ontario M5H 4E3, Canada
CanaryStPress.com

Printed in U.S.A.

ALWAYS
A MAVERICK

CHAPTER ONE

MAJOR BLUE DONNELLY forced open one eyelid, and he immediately closed it when the light came at him like a laser beam from hell. Man, it hurt. His head hurt, too. And his jaw. His shoulder as well.

When he realized the pain was pretty much everywhere, he quit naming off the parts of his body that were all throbbing like bad teeth.

He didn't attempt opening his eye again—he'd learned his lesson about that—but instead tried to tamp down the swarm of buzzing locusts in his head so he could figure out what the heck was going on. Was he hungover? If so, then it was the worst hangover in the history of such ailments. But no, it wasn't that. He hadn't had a hangover since his twenty-first birthday. Lesson learned there, too.

Maybe he was sick?

It could be a bad case of the flu that caused fever and body aches. Was that it? Or maybe it was worse than that. Had he been shot down?

Oh, crap. Was that it?

He was an F-22 pilot after all, and if the locusts in his head would just stop screeching and whirling around at tornado speed, he might be able to figure out if he'd been injured, then captured and was now in enemy hands.

"Major Donnelly?" he heard someone say.

That was his name, all right. Even the locusts and the god-awful pain couldn't cause him to forget that. However, the pain could apparently work together with his "yet to be determined" injuries to render him speechless. Blue tried to get his mouth working, but all he managed was a dry groan.

Despite the pain that cut through him with any movement of every muscle, Blue tried to sit up, but someone placed a hand on his shoulder to stop him. That kicked in his fight-or-flight response, and as usual, he chose the fight.

Or rather that was what he would have attempted had the world not gone dark on him.

Blue slipped into what he thought was a dream. He hoped it was, anyway. Because there were pterodactyls coming at him while he was in the cockpit of a fighter jet. He had to dodge a whole bunch of gaping, squawking beaks that seemed hell-bent on munching him to death. His feet were dangling out of the fighter, and a jumping T. rex was trying to chomp off his feet.

"Major Donnelly?" someone said, jarring him out of the dream. It wasn't the same voice he'd heard before. This was a man, and he thought the other had been a woman.

Again, Blue tried and failed to speak. He tried and failed to open his eyes, too. Since the pain was still there and seemingly even worse than before, he just groaned and listened, hoping whoever was saying his name would fill him in on what the heck was going on.

That didn't happen.

The dream snatched him back in, and this time it spun him into full *Jurassic Park* mode, complete with big trees, swamps and—

"Sheez, Blue," someone said. And this time, it was a voice he recognized. His kid sister, Captain Remi Donnelly. "That bruise on your jaw looks like a pig's butt."

"Remi," he tried to say.

He managed it in his head, but he didn't hear any sound come out of his mouth. But his sister's comment gave him hope. Well, sort of. If Remi was making fun of his bruise, then that probably meant he wasn't a POW or dying.

Probably.

That meant he could rule out two things that'd happened, so that left a quadrillion other possibilities for why he was…where? Judging from the scent, it was a hospital. There were also beeping sounds from monitors.

But why was he here?

Before he could try to locate any memories of that in the locust swarm of relentless pain, the darkness took him again.

No *Jurassic* deal this time, though. He was in the cockpit of an F-22 Raptor, and every inch was familiar to him. The sensations of the familiar grounded him and settled him down. Settled some of the locusts enough so he could see he was airborne, tearing across the cloudless sky and putting the Raptor through maneuvers that both he and the fighter jet could handle just fine.

He had the best job ever. The kind of job that slammed him with adrenaline and made him proud to wear the uniform. But there was something that didn't feel right. Something that wasn't routine. Something that he couldn't quite latch on to.

Blue cursed the darkness that closed in on him again, and he fought it. Mercy, he fought it. But it came, anyway, taking him out of the cockpit and dragging him down, down, down.

"Blue?" he heard someone say.

Not Remi this time or any of the other unfamiliar voices. This one he recognized. His big brother, Lieutenant Colonel Egan Donnelly.

Blue groaned.

If Egan was here, it had to be bad. Really bad. Egan was not only the commander of a fighter training squadron, he also ran the family ranch, Saddlebrook, in their hometown of Emerald Creek, Texas. Egan didn't have time for sibling visits unless things had truly gone to hell in a handbasket.

Blue got a flash of an image of being flung around, but it was just that flash before it vanished. Not the pain, though. It stayed right there with him, slamming into him, not in waves, but a constant smashing that seemed to be crushing his bones and scraping over every nerve in his body.

"Egan," he attempted and was surprised when he managed to say it aloud. Yeah, it was a croak and barely a whisper, but he got it out.

Even better, Blue got his eyes open. Well, one of them, anyway. The pain tried to make him pay for that small victory, but he fought that as well, and with some serious effort, he saw his big brother's face.

Egan was worried.

It didn't take a facial recognition expert to know that. His brother got up from the chair where he'd been sitting and took a cautious step closer to Blue, all the while studying him.

"Remi said the bruise on my jaw looks like a pig's ass," Blue muttered, and that was audible, too. More or less.

Egan made a sound of agreement and continued to stare at him with troubled blue eyes. "You remember Remi visiting a few hours ago?"

Hours? Heck, he'd obviously been out of it for a while. Blue tried to shake his head and stopped when the pain caused him to growl some raw profanity. He battled the pain and forced his eyes not to close.

"I remember some of Remi's visit." Okay, he only actually remembered the bruise remark that for some reason had stuck with him.

"She was in San Antonio for a physical," Egan explained. "But she couldn't stay. Once you were out of the woods, she had to leave for another deployment."

"Deployment," Blue muttered.

That made sense. His sister was a Combat Rescue Officer and was out of the country far more than she was in it.

"Out of the woods," he repeated when that registered. "What happened? Where am I?"

Egan drew in a long slow breath. The kind of breath a person took when this was not going to be a short, pleasant explanation. Then again, Blue had gotten an inkling of that already.

"You're in the hospital at Brooke Army Medical Center," Egan readily supplied.

Hell. This was serious, all right. Brooke Army Medical Center, or BAMC, was in San Antonio, and it was where the military took trauma patients. Serious trauma patients. Blue was stationed thirteen hundred miles away at Edwards Air Force Base.

"You were doing a demonstration flight at Lackland," Egan said, referring to the Air Force base in San Antonio. "You were going through maneuvers in a modified F-22 Raptor for a team of VIPs." He paused as if watching to see if that sank in or spurred any sort of memory.

It sort of did. Blue had no trouble recalling that he was a test pilot, an elite job that could be dangerous as hell. Hence, the adrenaline rush, and that rush was amplified when testing a modification to improve something on the Raptor. Sometimes, he also showed off those modifications with demo flights, and he had a vague—emphasis on *vague*—recollection of being scheduled to do the flight in San Antonio.

"Something went wrong with the demo," Egan continued. "They think it was a bird strike, and you must have decided it was too dangerous to eject and let the F-22 come down in such a populated area. So, you basically crash-landed." Again, he paused. Waited. Watched.

That rang some bells, too. That sense of being hurled around and out of control. Not with a T. rex below him, though, but rather in a fighter jet that was apparently about to crash and burn.

"More of a crash than an actual landing," Egan added in a mumble. "Uh, you were injured."

Blue didn't miss his brother's hesitation. That *uh* meant there was stuff Egan didn't want to spell out yet. Probably because he figured Blue already had enough to process. And he did. However, there were some things he had to know.

"How bad am I hurt?" Blue asked.

Egan paused again. "You want big picture stuff or details?"

"Details." Even though Blue thought this might be a situation of too many devils in the details, he still wanted to know what he was up against.

"A broken kneecap and two cracked ribs," Egan started, and he just kept on going. "A severe concussion. Some cuts, scrapes and various bruises, including the one that looks like a pig's ass. Your injuries weren't life threatening so you didn't have to go into ICU, but you're in an observation room because of the concussion."

Blue glanced around and saw that one wall of the room was clear plastic or maybe glass. All the rooms he could see were that way, and all were centered around a workstation filled with medical personnel.

"You're probably feeling woozy and out of it because of the sedation from the pain meds," Egan tacked on to that.

This was sedation? Well, flaming hell, it wasn't working. Even his toenails were hurting, and his groan must have conveyed that.

"I'll press this and it'll automatically deliver another

dose of pain meds," Egan said, pushing a button on a little remote on the bed.

Blue could have sworn he felt the meds immediately kick in. He welcomed the relief, but he didn't want to go under. Not yet.

"Why the *uh*?" he asked Egan.

Egan didn't give him a puzzled look or ask what he meant. His brother wasn't an idiot. And neither was Blue, though there were plenty who questioned the mindset of being a test pilot. What was the "right stuff" for some was "stupid shit" for others.

"Other than the obvious issue of the Raptor's crash landing, there were two other problems," Egan explained, using his commander's voice now as if giving a briefing. Maybe so he could keep the emotion out of it. "The bird strike damaged the bubble canopy, and that in turn caused some debris damage as well."

Okay. That explained the injuries. The cockpit of the Raptor was covered with a so-called bubble canopy, a polycarbonate shield that could withstand a lot. But not everything. And if damaged, then the cockpit and therefore the pilot could be damaged as well.

Blue tried to pick through the whirl of images and sensations in his head to recall the crash landing. Or anything else about the flight. But there was nothing. Maybe the head injury was to blame for that. Hell, he hoped that was all there was to it and that he didn't have brain damage. If he had, though, Egan probably would have told him. His brother hadn't had any trouble spelling out the other injuries.

Unless that was the "other problem."

"What else went wrong?" Blue asked, his words slow and slurred.

Egan didn't get a chance to answer, though, because at that exact moment, the sedating pain meds must have decided to kick in. The darkness came again and took him under. Not to a *Jurassic* world or even to one with memories. Blue just went away for a while.

When he surfaced again, the pain had lessened some and gone from sharp stabs to pulsing throbs. He opened his eyes, expecting to see Egan so he could continue to fill him in on what had happened. But it wasn't his brother. Nor was it Remi, but it was a woman standing at the foot of his bed. She had short, choppy blond hair and piercing green eyes.

Troubled, wary eyes.

She wasn't a nurse, or if she was, she was off duty because she wasn't wearing scrubs, but rather a gray shirt. Considering the reckless relationships he'd had when he had been on the rodeo circuit, Blue fought through the pain again so he could study her face to see if he recognized her. To see if she was one of those past reckless relationships.

Nope.

But despite the god-awful pain, he had to admit she would be his type if he were in any shape to do, well, anything. Athletic build and an interesting face. And there was some kind of…connection. Definitely not love at first sight, but something he recognized.

Lust at first sight.

Yeah, he was in no shape for that.

"Um, who are you?" Blue came out and asked.

She paused so long that he thought she might not answer. "I'm Marin Galloway."

Blue still had to go with a "nope" on this. The name didn't ring any bells. "Are you a doctor?"

She shook her head.

She didn't offer anything but just continued to study him as if he were a specimen under a microscope. "Oh, I get it," Blue grumbled. "You're a shrink of some kind. Maybe one of those PTSD counselors. Or a physical therapist here to—"

"I'm a natural horsemanship trainer," she interrupted. Then, she sighed a little when he gave her what had to be a flat look. "Also known as a horse whisperer."

Blue frowned. "Is this Remi's idea of a joke again?"

"No joke," the woman assured him. Her words were soft, barely a whisper, but Blue got the feeling that she'd wanted to yell that response at the top of her lungs. "You don't know me," she went on several long moments later, and she made a furtive glance over her shoulder. "And I don't have permission to be here. A former boss got me onto the base, and I lied my way to your room. I told the nurses I was your…girlfriend."

Blue hoped like the devil this woman wasn't hitting on him because despite the whole lust reaction, he definitely wasn't up for anything. "I'm guessing you thought it was important to see me, or you wouldn't have lied?"

Marin nodded. "When you're doing better, you'll get a visitor."

She took out her phone from her pocket and brought up a photo not of herself, but rather a kid. A boy who looked to be in kindergarten.

"See this boy?" she asked, but then didn't wait for an answer. "He worships you. He thinks you're the greatest thing since Nutella straight out of the jar."

Well, that was just plain confusing. Blue shook his head and regretted it. The movement hurt like the devil and didn't do squat to clear up the thick sludge in his head. "Who is he and why would he be coming to see me?"

"He's Leo Franklin, a good kid, and he...wants to meet you," she said, her voice like some kind of cautious plea.

Crap. Blue wasn't liking all these hesitations. First, Egan—and where the heck was he?—and now this woman who'd lied her way into his room.

"The meeting was supposed to happen right after your flight," she added to her explanation. "If you'd landed instead of crashed, that is."

Ah, a "meet and greet" deal. That sort of thing happened sometimes with demo flights, and again Blue tried the memory game. Nope. It still wasn't there. He couldn't even recall coming to San Antonio much less the crash and his trip to the hospital.

"The meeting is being rescheduled," she went on. "Your doctors were going to try to work that out once you're up and about."

She frowned, her gaze combing over his body. He was covered with a sheet from the waist down. Mostly. His left leg with his braced and bandaged knee was poking out, but there were obviously enough injuries from the waist up to give her some concern. She definitely didn't look to be on the verge of joking about the pig's ass bruise.

"Any idea of when you will be up and about?" she asked.

"Soon," he assured her, though he was basing that on absolutely nothing.

He felt like crap, obviously looked like it, too, and with all those injuries Egan had listed, Blue had no idea when he'd be able to walk out of here. He did know himself, however, and knew that would be as soon as possible.

"Leo will get that meeting with me," Blue added to the assurance. But then he stopped when he recalled something else about this weird conversation. "Why does the kid think I'm the best thing since Nutella straight out of the jar?"

It was a simple question. One obviously without a simple answer. Because the mysterious Marin muttered something he couldn't hear. Then, she muttered some profanity that he could hear. She followed that by shaking her head and glancing up at the ceiling as if the simple answer might be there.

She swallowed hard when her gaze came back to Blue's. "Because Leo believes you're his father."

CHAPTER TWO

IN HINDSIGHT, Marin realized she shouldn't have lied her way in here to the hospital. She shouldn't have thrown this at Major Blue Donnelly when he looked as if he'd been beaten to a pulp. But she'd given in to Leo's pressure.

Something she clearly did far too often.

Hard not to, though, after what the boy had been through, but with that hindsight awareness and after seeing the major's stunned expression, she should have waited a day or two. Maybe a week. Or even a month.

She watched, waited as the major's shock continued to register on his face. A face that she thought would be alarmingly handsome if it weren't for the world map of bruises, cuts and scrapes. Including the one on his jaw that sort of resembled a pig's butt, complete with a curly tail poking up.

"Father?" Blue repeated. And he repeated it a couple more times.

Oh, this was not going to be a short explanation, or an easy one, and Marin figured she was going to need short and easy since she was probably on borrowed time. In the fifteen minutes or so she'd been waiting for him to wake up, nurses had come and gone, and one of them would no doubt soon ask her to leave.

Marin started with a nod. Ended with one, too, because Blue apparently found enough mental footing to launch into some questions before she had the chance to begin an explanation.

"And why would he believe that I'm his dad?" Blue asked before she could say anything else. "Did you lie to him and tell him that I was? Or is he actually my kid?"

"No, he's not yours," Marin spelled out.

There. That was a biggie out of the way, and it obviously caused Blue more than a tad of relief. He blew out a breath and relaxed his head and shoulders against the pillow. Good thing, too, since this visit would end even sooner if his heart rate set off alarms and brought the medical staff running to see what had caused the spike.

"He's not my son, either," she went on. "But I believe you knew his mother, Justine Franklin?"

Judging by his huff, Blue knew her. And it wasn't an especially fond remembrance. "Jussie," he provided.

"Jussie," Marin verified. "From what I understand, she met you when you were still riding broncs in the rodeo. She was a self-proclaimed buckle bunny and your number one fan."

"I did have sex with her. Once," he admitted, and then he paused. "You're sure the boy's not mine?"

"Pretty sure. The timing doesn't fit for one thing. Leo's six, and from what I've read, you quit the rodeo and went into the Air Force ten years ago. You would have already been a pilot when Jussie got pregnant."

He paused again, maybe working out the math for himself. "But she told Leo that I fathered him. Why?"

Oh, this wouldn't be short and sweet, either. Heck, it would never be sweet. "I think a combination of wishful thinking and Jussie not wanting him to know who his real father is."

Marin got a flash of Brian Petty's twisted, angry face. If she'd been able to mentally share that image with Blue, he would have immediately understood why Jussie hadn't told Leo the truth.

"I'm so sorry about springing all of this on you today," Marin went on. "I wanted to wait, but Leo kept asking to see you, to make sure you were all right. He was watching when you crashed."

Marin got another image. Of the boy's horrified face as he'd seen Blue's fighter jet slam into the runway.

"Leo's wanted to meet you for a long time now," she added. "But you've been stationed in California, and before that, you were overseas. When he learned you were going to be in San Antonio—"

"If Leo was supposed to meet me today, then he would have found out I wasn't his dad," Blue interrupted.

She nodded. "I told him not to bring it up, that there'd be a lot of people around, and that it was something he could talk to you about later." She paused. "I'd planned on asking you for that *later* after I'd had my own chance to chat with you. Now Leo's worried you'll go back to California before he can meet you."

Marin had been concerned about that as well. Until she'd actually seen Blue. But now she didn't think he'd be going anywhere anytime soon with his injuries. She wasn't a nurse, but judging from the way his leg had been stabilized, he had a broken knee. His ribs had been wrapped as well so some of them were likely broken. Still, he was alive, and since she'd witnessed the crash, too, and the aftermath, Marin thought that was somewhat of a miracle.

Blue sort of reminded her of one of the wounded or rescued horses she worked with. Not his looks, of course. Those were more along the lines of a Greek god, rock star combo with some tall, dark and edgy thrown in. But he had that same traumatized look in his dark brown eyes, that same damaged vibe.

Marin wondered how much he knew about the crash. Maybe too much. Maybe not enough. Since she'd already doled out enough stunners for him today, she was glad she wasn't going to have to be the one to talk to him about that.

She took out a business card with her phone number and laid it on the bedside table next to his cell phone. "I'm hoping you'll be willing to talk to Leo. Obviously, not now, but after you've recovered. If you decide not to do that, just let me know and I can try to explain things to him."

"Explain to him that I'm not his father," he muttered. Not exactly a question, but he seemed to be asking something.

She nodded. "Yes, I am going to tell him the truth." Now she got another image she had to tamp down so she could continue. "The timing hasn't been good for that lately."

Blue studied her and was no doubt studying her answer, too. "Timing," he repeated, but he didn't question that. However, he did have a question. "So, are you Jussie's sister or something?"

"Or something." And once again, she had to fight that image of a sickly, frail little boy. "I was, uh, Leo's bone marrow donor, and Jussie and I got to be friends. Then, when she died six months ago, she left custody of Leo to me because she didn't have anyone else to take care of him." She waited, giving that some time to sink in.

"Jussie's dead," he muttered.

Marin nodded. "Cancer," she explained and left it at that.

"I'm sorry to hear that," Blue said. Then, he clearly shifted back to something else she'd told him. "Bone marrow," he repeated. "Leo was supposed to meet me. Like one of those Make-A-Wish things?"

Marin had to clear her throat before she could speak. "Something like that. Leo's fine, now," she added and prayed that was true. "But he was sick for a long time with aplastic anemia, and when he heard you were going to be in San Antonio, he asked his teacher to put in a request through the base liaison."

Blue opened his mouth, but then it seemed as if he changed his mind about what he'd been about to say. He ended up cursing instead. Marin was right there with him. She'd cursed plenty about Leo's illness.

"Where's Leo now?" Blue asked.

She opened her mouth, too, to let him know that the boy was back home with his sitter, but Marin wasn't able to answer because the door opened, and three people came in. Two men and a blonde woman. Marin could instantly tell from their uniforms that two of them were medical professionals. The third, however, was wearing jeans and cowboy boots, and he bore enough of a resemblance to Blue that she figured he had to be one of his brothers.

"I'm Lieutenant Colonel Milbrath," the man in uniform said, glancing first at Marin and then Blue. "I'm one of your doctors. And this is Captain Salvetti, one of the nurses who's been attending you." He tipped his head to the third man. "And I'm hoping you recognize this guy."

"I do," Blue verified. "Egan was here earlier. And my sister, Remi."

The doctor smiled. "Good. You do remember. Things can sometimes get a little fuzzy after your type of injury." He then shifted to Marin. "And you are?"

Judging from the way Egan and the nurse were now staring at her, they wanted to know the same thing. Marin figured she was about to be tossed out.

"That's Marin…" Blue said, hesitating, as if trying to recall her last name. "She's, um, my girlfriend."

Marin had no idea who was more surprised by that— Egan, the nurse or her. But Marin thought she won that particular title. Why the heck had Blue lied for her? Certainly, he didn't want her hanging around after everything she'd just told him.

Did he?

Maybe he just wanted to ask her more questions. Or because he hadn't wanted to get into who she really was and why she was there.

"I'm Egan Donnelly, Blue's brother," the man said,

extending his hand for her to shake while he also continued to study her.

Marin didn't think it was her imagination that he had plenty of doubts about her being Blue's girlfriend. Thankfully, doubts he didn't get a chance to express because the doctor went closer to Blue's bed.

"So, how are you feeling?" the doctor asked Blue.

Since this seemed to be the start of an exam, Marin started inching back toward the door and practically bumped right into the nurse.

"Lucky you," the nurse whispered while the doctor and Blue began to talk.

Jussie had certainly thought so. And yes, Marin thought so as well. Even if she had been interested in Blue, though, and she certainly wasn't, he would have been way out of her league.

Marin doled out a quick smile to the nurse and an equally quick goodbye to Blue. She also glanced at the card she'd left for him and hoped he would make use of it and call her when he could. If he didn't, well, she would need to have that talk sooner than later with Leo. She'd hoped to get him through his upcoming checkup. The one that had to confirm he was still in remission.

Had to.

That appointment was in a week, and once they celebrated the good news, she could tell him that Blue wasn't his father. Maybe, just maybe, the boy wouldn't want any actual details of who his real dad was, but those questions would no doubt surface soon enough. Maybe even surface immediately after she gave Leo the bad news about not having a hotshot maverick hero dad.

Marin was heading toward the exit signs when she heard the hurried footsteps behind her. She turned, spotted Egan. And silently groaned. It would no doubt come—the inquisition—where he'd reveal she was a liar. Then, he'd want to know why his brother had backed up the lie.

"Marin," Egan greeted once he'd caught up to her. "I'm sorry I didn't know about you or I would have called you after the crash. Did you fly in from California?"

Since she'd never been to that particular state, Marin didn't even attempt to lie about that. "No. I live just outside of San Antonio." She braced herself for questions about how Blue and she had met, how long she'd been his girlfriend, etc. And they came. Sort of, anyway.

"Are you stationed here at one of the bases?" he asked.

"No. I'm not military. I'm a horse trainer," she said, skipping the usual label, horse whisperer, that some people gave her. "I work mainly with rescues."

"Yeah," he muttered as if that rang some kind of bell. "I thought you looked familiar," he added.

That gave her a jolt of panic because she was certain she'd never met Egan, Blue or anyone else in his family. However, she did know that the Donnellys were practically ranching royalty.

"I'm the commander of the fighter training squadron at Randolph," he continued, referring to the name of the nearby base. "But I also help run my family's ranch, Saddlebrook. We haven't met, but I recall the ranch manager showing me your website when we were trying to figure out how to deal with a horse that'd been injured. We were going to hire you, but then the horse had a big setback and had to be put down."

With the size of Saddlebrook, it was understandable that from time to time they'd have difficulty training or treating horses who'd experienced some kind of trauma. And that such a horse might experience that kind of horrible setback. It was a little eerie, though, that she might have ended up working a job on Blue's family ranch.

Of course, depending on when this was, Marin might not have even known about Jussie or Leo. She'd met them three years ago. Sometimes, that felt like a blink of time and other times it seemed as if she'd known Leo his entire life.

"How is Blue? I mean, how is he really?" Egan asked, and Marin could both see and hear the worry.

"I'm not sure," she admitted and left it at that.

Egan sighed and scrubbed his hand over his face. "Did he ask about what happened with the crash landing?"

She shook her head and knew that Egan's worry was on several levels. Not just for his brother's physical injuries, but the mental ones.

"Blue doesn't remember the crash?" she asked. Why, she didn't know. She should be getting the heck out of there before Egan found out she was a fraud.

"I don't think so," Egan answered. "If he did, he'd… Well, he'll be an emotional wreck." He pinned his intense gaze to hers. "If he doesn't remember on his own, he'll have to know soon. I guess you didn't mention anything about it to him?"

Marin responded with another headshake. Paused.

And dived into questioning waters that she should probably just have avoided. Still, she wanted to know if Blue would ever actually be up to contacting Leo and her.

"How bad is Blue hurt?" she asked.

Egan sighed again. "The concussion and the knee are the worst of it. He'll need additional surgery and three to six months' recovery time." He hesitated. "And the recovery might not be a hundred percent."

Now it was Marin's turn to study him. Yes, genuine worry. "Blue might not be able to keep flying?"

"He doesn't know that yet," Egan confirmed with a mutter.

Well, crap. Marin barely knew Blue, but she'd heard plenty about him from Jussie and Leo, and if their accounts were anywhere near accurate, then being a test pilot wasn't just a job for Blue. It was his life.

"I asked the doctors if I could be the one to tell him," Egan went on. "I figured it'd be better coming from me. But I'm not going to say anything until after he knows about the crash landing."

Marin mentally repeated her, *Well, crap.* And here she'd dumped all this stuff about Leo on him.

A big mistake.

Yes, Leo had been through way too much, what with his illness and losing his mother. But Blue had been through the wringer, too.

"Blue has some tests and a meeting with the surgeon during the next couple of hours," Egan explained. "After that, I'll tell him before he hears anything from the media or anyone else."

That was a wise move on Egan's part. A hard one,

though, too. Still, something like this wouldn't stay under wraps for long.

Egan's gaze met hers again. "Once Blue knows the truth, he's going to have a tough time. A really tough time," he emphasized. "So if you truly care about Blue, just know that he'll soon be needing all the help he can get."

CHAPTER THREE

BLUE SAT UP in his bed. Well, sort of. He got semi-prone, anyway, so he was counting that as sitting up.

The maneuver was a huge accomplishment, considering it was something he hadn't been able to do in the past eight hours or so since he'd woken up in pain hell. He was still there in that particular pain dimension, mostly, with every movement of every muscle still hurting, but at least he wasn't flat on his aching back.

Now that the ceiling wasn't his primary view, he glanced around the hospital room and saw that except for him and the monitors, it was empty. It wouldn't stay that way, though; soon there'd be another wave of medical staff. More tests. Maybe more drop-ins from members of his family. They came and went, and some of the visitors he remembered better than others.

Like Marin.

Talk about a totally unexpected drop-in. Sheez. Could life possibly throw any more curveballs at him? He immediately withdrew that question, though, since he didn't want to tempt fate. Enough with the curveballs already.

Blue also recalled the meeting a couple of hours earlier with the surgeon who'd told him his knee was in bad shape, but that tomorrow's operation might be able to repair the worst of it.

Might.

Blue was ignoring that *might*, though, and believed that everything would be just fine. Because it had to be. It was the same for getting his memory back. All of it. He was getting there, piece by piece, and he could now recall coming to Lackland AFB for the demo flight. He could remember climbing into the cockpit and taking off. He could even recall some of the initial chatter from the command post and flight control center.

Anything after that and before waking up in the hospital was still a blank.

Some might think that to be a merciful blessing, but it wasn't. Blue wanted to recall every second of that flight so he'd know what had happened. And if he had done something wrong.

Now that he was sort of, almost upright, he could see the business card that Marin had left for him, and he debated what to do about it. He didn't have especially fond memories of Jussie. She'd been a "wild child, up for anything" partier. That had been a good description of Blue as well, back in those days, but he hadn't wanted to continue that rodeo life once he'd finally gotten his degree. He'd wanted to fly fighter jets and win a Top Gun competition so that had meant leaving the rodeo circuit and leaving people like Jussie behind.

It was a sad commentary on his life that he barely recalled having sex with her, and that had nothing to do with his concussion. He could recall the highlights of his life prior to the "hell in a handbasket" moments leading up to the crash.

But his sex memories of Jussie were thin at best.

However, it must have been pretty damn memorable for Jussie if she'd lied to her kid about him. Then again, maybe the lie had just been out of convenience since she likely knew he wouldn't be in Texas much after he joined the Air Force.

He risked reaching over to pick up Marin's card. Oh, he paid for it with his aching ribs and bruises that seemed to go bone-deep. While he was in that position, he got his phone, too. Not to start going through the texts and voice mails—crap, dozens of them—but rather to have it in case he decided to call Marin.

Blue thought of Jussie. Of the six-year-old boy who thought he was better than Nutella. Thought, too, of the lie that hadn't been the boy's doing. A boy who'd clearly been through hell, what with his illness and then the death of his mother. Blue wasn't sure he could give Leo one ounce of comfort or joy. Especially considering he'd soon have to know the truth about him not being his dad. But Marin had obviously thought a face-to-face with the kid would do Leo some good.

The guilt came. He didn't consider himself to be the textbook version of a decent human being, but he wasn't an asshole, either. With that reminder, he composed a text to Marin, telling her that she could bring Leo by the hospital for a short visit. Not that he was up to it. Far from it. But the non-asshole thing to do was see the boy and hope all went well.

He fired off the text, and while he still had his phone,

Blue did a search on Marin, just to make sure she was legit. It took him less than a minute to realize that she was. Well, she was a horse trainer, anyway, or rather a *natural horsemanship* trainer, obviously putting her degrees in psychology and animal science to good use.

Along with her website, there were at least a hundred articles about Marin and her training methods. There were also reviews, not just for her training successes, but also from students who she taught at the community college.

Blue clicked onto Marin's social media pages. He didn't immediately spot any photos of Leo, but she'd made some posts about how well he'd done on a particular school project or his love of Nutella. He scrolled back through some old pictures and saw one of her with Jussie. Not Jussie the wild child partier. No. Judging from Jussie's gaunt features, she was already battling whatever cancer had ultimately killed her.

He grieved for the "full of life, often pain in the butt" woman he'd known. Grieved, too, for the crappy life she must have had for her to lie to her son about his father. Blue grieved for the kid, too.

There was a tapping knock at the door right before it opened, and Egan came in. His brother first looked alarmed, probably because of Blue sitting up, and then he smiled.

"Feeling better?" Egan asked.

"Some." That was close enough to the truth.

"Good." He brought over a plastic container and set it on the table. "Maybell's triple chocolate cookies. Your favorite."

They were, indeed, and he thought of Maybell, the woman who'd been the cook at the ranch since before Blue had been born. "Tell her thank you for me."

"You might be able to tell her yourself. She and Grammy Effie will be coming to see you tomorrow after your surgery. Maybe Dad, too. He's on his way back."

Not a surprise, but Blue hated to worry his family like this. Especially his dad, who was dealing with his own medical issues. He'd had a massive heart attack just four months earlier and was recuperating in Washington, DC, where Blue's stepmother was stationed.

"Cal can't get away from work this week," Egan went on, sitting in the chair next to the bed. "But he'll come soon. He sends his best."

Cal, his other big brother who was also an Air Force officer and fighter pilot stationed in South Carolina. At least one of those voice messages and texts would be from him, and Blue made a mental note to call and reassure him there was no reason for him to come. Especially since Blue was hoping he wouldn't be in the hospital much longer.

Egan took out one of the saucer-sized cookies for Blue and then helped himself to one. "So, you want to tell me about Marin?" Egan asked. "I don't think I've ever heard you call anyone your girlfriend. And while physically she's what you usually go for, she doesn't seem your usual type. She's more grounded, less flashy."

All of the above was true.

But, no, Blue definitely didn't want to talk about Marin. However, there was something he needed to discuss. Or rather ask.

"What have the doctors told you about why I can't remember the crash landing?" Blue said for starters.

Egan shrugged, maybe a gesture meant to reassure Blue that it wasn't a big deal. They both knew it was, though. "They said that sometimes that's the way trauma manifests itself. The mind blocks out the trauma."

Blue shook his head, winced at the pain. "Along with winning a couple of Top Gun competitions, I'm a test pilot and have flown some dangerous missions. There's nothing that can happen that I'd need to block out. Nothing." He was well aware that his voice had gotten more intense and louder with each word.

Yeah, this was a big deal, all right.

"Did you see the flight?" Blue came out and asked, figuring there was a good chance he had since Egan was stationed only thirty miles or so from Lackland.

Egan nodded.

"Then, tell me what happened," Blue insisted. "Not the part you've already told me about the damaged bubble canopy or the likely bird strike."

Egan didn't groan, not out loud, anyway, but it looked like that was what he wanted to do. "It's still part speculation at this point. As you know, there'll be an investigation to determine what happened."

Blue's groan was out loud, and it was pure frustration. "Give me the speculation." It'd be fairly accurate since Egan himself was a former Top Gun and a fighter pilot.

Egan set the cookie back on the container and met Blue's gaze head-on. "When you crash-landed, debris flew off the damaged Raptor. And there were some injuries. It wasn't your fault," his brother quickly added.

Egan kept on talking, but Blue wasn't hearing him. He was cursing and mentally crashing and burning. Shit. Injuries. He'd caused people to get hurt.

"How bad?" Blue demanded.

"Some of the injuries were serious," Egan finally said. "But then so are yours. It wasn't your fault, Blue."

Despite the searing pain it caused, Blue lifted his hand to silence his brother. Because there was nothing Egan could say that would absolve him. He'd been the pilot, and the crash had hurt people.

He had hurt people.

Yes, he was a fighter pilot. But this wasn't war. This was a base in San Antonio where people weren't expected to get injured. Especially not by a pilot who should have managed to maneuver the Raptor away from them.

"Blue," Egan tried again.

But Blue shook his head. "Tell me about the injuries. How many? Who? And how bad?"

It didn't take a shrink for Blue to understand that Egan didn't want to dole out those particular details. But he would. Because Egan wasn't an asshole, either, and he'd understand Blue's need for the truth.

Even if the truth ripped him to pieces.

"Six people were hurt," Egan explained. "Three have minor injuries, cuts and bruises, that sort of thing. A sergeant on the maintenance crew got a broken leg and needed some stitches for a cut on his shoulder. Another sergeant was hit in the chest and like you, he's got some cracked ribs and a concussion. He's still in the hospital, but is expected to be released tomorrow morning."

Blue tried to wait out Egan's hesitation, but he finally gave up and prompted his brother. "You said there were six. What about the last one?"

"An airman, also part of the maintenance crew," Egan spelled out. "He's in a coma with a head injury."

"Shit," Blue spat out. Even though groaning and cursing caused him immense pain, he did it, anyway. In fact, he welcomed the pain. Because he deserved it.

"The airman's prognosis is yet to be determined," Egan went on, "but the initial signs are good. In other words, there's normal brain activity. The doctors are hopeful that he'll come out of the coma and make a full recovery."

"What's his name?" Blue snapped.

Egan sighed as if hearing the name wouldn't do any good, but he provided it, anyway. "Casey Newell."

Since Blue wasn't stationed at Lackland, he hadn't expected to recognize the name, and he didn't, but he wanted to know it. "I need to see him," he insisted.

There was no hesitation in Egan's headshake. "You can't. Even if you were in any shape to get out of that bed, he's in ICU. Only medical staff and immediate family can visit."

Blue would have demanded to find a way around that, but there was a knock at the door. "Come in," he practically snarled, though he wasn't in the mood to see anyone. Whoever it was, he'd get rid of them fast so he could work out how to see the airman he'd injured.

The door slowly opened, and he saw Marin peer in.

Blue wanted to curse himself for sending her the text. He especially wanted to curse himself when she stepped in with the little boy right by her side.

This had to be Leo.

The boy had brown hair and big green eyes. Eyes that shone at the prospect of meeting his hero. While Blue had never felt less like a hero in his entire life, he tried to shove that aside and not disappoint the kid too much.

Leo kept his attention nailed to Blue, and the only reason the boy seemed to be able to move at all was because Marin was urging him into the room. And that was when something else occurred to Blue. Crap. He'd forgotten just how bad he looked, and that could possibly scare the kid.

Except it didn't.

Leo came closer, this time moving of his own accord, and he stopped by Blue's bedside. "Aunt Marin said you got hurt," Leo said.

Blue nodded and studied the boy's face to make sure this wasn't too stressful for him. He didn't know many kids, but he'd thought a six-year-old would be bigger. And maybe Leo would have been had he not had to fight an illness.

"Will you be okay?" Leo asked.

That was the big question, and at the moment Blue didn't have an answer. He'd almost certainly recover from his injuries, but that wasn't a high priority for him. The priority was making sure the airman and the others recovered and that Leo didn't get his hopes dashed with this visit.

Egan stood, nodding a greeting at Marin, and then

he cleared his throat when he looked at Leo. "Uh, who is this?" his brother asked. His tone was friendly, and he was smiling at Marin as if waiting for her to make introductions.

The kid, however, spoke first. "I'm Leo," he volunteered, and then he pointed to Blue. "And he's my daddy."

CHAPTER FOUR

MARIN FINISHED PUTTING out the fresh feed and water for the horses she was currently boarding. A sweetheart Appaloosa, an elderly paint and an often surly bay gelding with the appetite and temperament of a teenager. She gave them all some back rubs and a few murmured reassurances that she'd be back soon before she headed out of the small pasture and toward her rental house.

Even though it was September and technically autumn, there was nothing autumn-like about the already ninety-degree heat. Typical for central Texas, and since she'd been with the horses for a couple of hours and therefore drenched in sweat, she headed straight inside and to the bathroom to turn on the shower.

While she waited for the water to turn hot, she checked her messages on her phone. Nothing from Leo's school, thank goodness. That was always her top worry, especially since he still wasn't anywhere near 100 percent. However, there was a text from Blue, letting her know that he had a photo that Leo had requested and that she could come by the hospital at any time to pick it up.

Marin frowned, a facial expression she'd been sporting a lot lately. Seeing Blue's name brought back the im-

ages of her visit with him five days earlier. A visit where
Leo had made that announcement to Blue's brother Egan.

He's my daddy.

Thankfully, Egan hadn't asked a lot of questions that
would have spilled the truth, but she was betting that
Blue had cleared up the matter with his brother as soon
as Leo and she had left after their short visit. So Leo's
illusion was intact for the time being, but soon, very
soon, some spilling was going to have to happen.

She sent a reply to Blue, thanking him for arranging
to get the photo that Leo had wanted of Blue in uniform. It was generous of him to go through with Leo's
request, especially since Blue had to have much more
important things on his mind. Like healing, for instance,
and coping with the horrific crash landing that had not
only caused his injuries but some others as well. She
didn't know Blue, not really, but she was wagering he
felt responsible for those others being hurt.

After checking the time, Marin added more to the
text and told Blue that she'd be at the hospital within
the hour. That way, she could get the photo, thank Blue
in person for all he'd done for Leo and let him know
that she'd soon tell Leo the truth about his father so the
boy wouldn't continue to press to see Blue again. She
could get all of that done and be back home with time
to spare to pick up Leo from school.

She showered and dressed in her usual jeans and a
work top, and Marin refused to worry about how she
looked. Or rather she wanted to refuse that, but her
lofty intention failed big-time. She fixed her hair and
even applied some tinted sunscreen, her substitute for

makeup. It was stupid for her to even consider looking her best for Blue, but apparently her body had decided it was a grand idea.

It wasn't.

Blue had the hard-and-fast reputation she avoided, and thanks to her old baggage with hard-and-fast men, Marin wasn't in the market for another one. She mentally repeated that to herself as she went to her truck and started the drive to the base hospital. She'd barely made it out of the driveway, though, before her phone rang, and she saw the familiar name on the dash screen.

Gina Kinney, her best friend. And an occasional pain in her butt.

"I'm not going on the date you set up for me," Marin greeted after she'd accepted the call.

"And how do you know I set you up on a date?" Gina answered without missing a beat.

"Because you're breathing." She waited for Gina to deny the date.

Of course, she couldn't. Gina might be a marriage counselor, but she had the heart of a matchmaker and believed she had superior skills in that particular area.

She didn't.

Case in point, Gina herself. She'd been seeing the same "commitment phobic" guy for eight years with no happily-ever-after in sight. Still, that didn't stop Gina from trying to arrange that blissful designation for others.

"This guy is perfect for you," Gina said, clearly jumping into her spiel. "A nonprofit lawyer who loves animals and candlelight dinners. And he's hot. I'll bet you'd have to look plenty hard to find one hotter."

An image of Blue flashed into Marin's mind. If she took Gina up on that bet, Gina would lose. Even with all his injuries, Blue was the supreme winner of hotness. Rather than confess about the man's hotness or listen to more about the date that wasn't going to happen, Marin volunteered something that would guarantee a change of subject.

"I'm on my way to see Blue Donnelly," she said. And yep, it caused some moments of silence for Gina.

"Why? Is he demanding you tell Leo the truth?" Gina asked, well aware of what Leo believed and what was fact. Marin had shared all of that with Gina. Well, all but Blue's hotness. No way would she mention that and stir up more matchmaking.

"No, he's not demanding that. Or anything else for that matter."

Which was, well, a shocker. Marin loved Leo, but Blue had only met the boy once. A boy who hero-worshipped the man he'd been told was his father. Marin wasn't sure how she would have reacted in the same situation, but she might have pressed for Leo to learn the truth since keeping up the facade would be hard.

"No?" Gina repeated. "Then, why are you going to see him?"

"Leo wanted a picture of Blue in uniform, and I'm going to pick it up." Now it was Marin's turn to pause. "That's probably not a good idea, right?" And the question was directed not to Gina her friend, but to Gina the counselor.

Gina's sigh came through loud and clear, emphasis on loud, and Marin knew why. A photo of Blue would likely strengthen Leo's fantasy about his perfect hero dad. "How were Leo's latest lab results?" Gina asked.

"Good." That was stretching it a bit. They were good-ish, but that was a huge improvement from his labs just six months earlier. And Gina knew what that meant. "I should tell him the truth now about his dad while he's feeling better."

"You should," Gina verified. "I can be with you for that," she immediately offered, not for the first time, either.

"Thanks," Marin muttered—again, not for the first time. When she did tell Leo, Marin thought it would be good to have a counselor on hand, especially a counselor who Leo already thought of as sort of an aunt. "Are you free on Saturday? I can tell him then."

"I'll be there," Gina said without hesitation. "Just text me and let me know what time."

"I will." She would, too. This way, she had a commitment to go through with it and wouldn't be tempted to chicken out at the last minute.

Every time Marin thought of telling Leo the truth, his image rocketed through her head. Not a good image of the happy smiling boy he was now but of the sick, colorless five-year-old child who needed her bone marrow to survive. That image was always a punch to the gut, but she had to get past it.

Somehow.

She had to focus on Leo's future, and that meant him learning the truth. A truth that she worried might crush his heart. It would certainly be a lot for a six-year-old to handle.

With that dismal thought now weighing down her mood, Marin ended the call with Gina and finished the drive to the base. Since she didn't have a military ID card and wasn't accompanied by a friend who did, she stopped by the visitor's center to get a pass. When she stepped into the building, though, she saw someone she hadn't expected to be there.

Lieutenant Colonel Egan Donnelly.

Today, Blue's brother was in a flight suit, and he looked every inch the Top Gun, commander in charge that he was. Judging from the way he got to his feet when he spotted her, he'd been waiting for her.

"Blue said you were coming," Egan greeted. "I figured I'd meet you in case there was a hitch with you getting a visitor's pass. I can drive you to the hospital and then bring you back here to your truck."

"Thank you," she muttered, but there was skepticism in her voice. No doubt in her expression, too.

Yes, it was possible there could be a hitch, especially if the base was on high alert, but Marin figured Egan also wanted the chance to talk to her. Maybe to warn her that she'd better not be trying to pull anything shady with his kid brother.

"I'm not after Blue's money," she threw out there as Egan ushered her out of the center and toward the parking lot.

He nodded. "I had a background check run on you."

She nearly tripped over her own feet but managed to stop walking and stare up at him. Marin felt the initial shock of having her privacy violated, followed by some "how dare you" anger. But the anger evaporated as quickly as it'd come. Because Blue did have money. Family money, that is.

Lots and lots of it.

And the reason she knew that was because she'd done her own background check of sorts on him and his family by combing the internet. Egan likely would have used a private investigator, but it made sense that he'd want to know all about a woman who'd shown up with a child claiming to be Blue's son.

"You have no criminal record," Egan supplied and got them moving again toward a sleek silver truck. "You have a small but solid business. There are no red flags to indicate you have ulterior motives for seeing Blue."

Marin had no doubts, none, that he knew her net worth. Which wasn't much. She was renting the ranch where she boarded horses, and the bulk of her income came from training emotionally and physically challenged horses. It made her enough to pay her bills and save for her own place, and thanks to Jussie's life insurance, she had enough to send Leo to a private school where he was in a small class. With his suppressed immune system, smaller was better.

"How is Blue?" she asked, because it occurred to her that Egan's interception could be because he wanted to give her a heads-up of some kind. Maybe Blue had taken a turn for the worst.

"His surgery went well enough, and he should be able to go home to the ranch in a day or two."

Some of the tightness eased in her chest. Good. If he

was going home, then that meant he had to be recovering. "But?" she questioned.

Egan glanced at her and drove out of the visitor's parking lot. "How much do you know about Blue's crash landing?"

The question threw her for a moment. Despite Egan's reassurance about her having no red flags, she'd been anticipating more questions about Leo and the daddy lie that Jussie had told her son.

"Only what's on the internet," she admitted. Marin purposely didn't add more or press Egan for why he truly wanted this time to chat with her. She just waited for him to continue.

He gathered his breath. "Six other people were injured. Blue's having a hard time dealing with that. He's also having a hard time dealing with his own injuries. Not just with the pain, but with the uncertainty of his career."

Marin had definitely gone there already. "The injury could maybe stop him from being a pilot?"

Egan shrugged, then nodded. "Possibly. But Blue's not ready to consider that yet. He might never be ready to consider it," he added in a mumble. "Right now, he's focusing on the guilt over the other injuries. Focusing, too, on Leo. Personally, I think that's his way of giving the guilt and worry a sort of rest."

Marin made a sound of agreement. "It's hard not to feel sorry for a little boy who's spent a good chunk of his life being sick." Heaven knew, she'd felt plenty sorry for him. "That's not why I accepted custody of Leo," she quickly informed him in case that was what

Egan was thinking. "I love him, and I wanted him once it became clear that his mom wasn't going to make it."

She waited again, figuring that Egan might have questions about her telling Leo the truth. But she was wrong.

"I'll bottom line this," he said, turning into the massive parking lot of the hospital. He pulled into a spot and turned to her. "Blue's going to need help recovering, and he won't agree to see a counselor. He won't even openly admit the possibility of not ever being able to fly again or that he'll have to deal with PTSD and the guilt trip from hell. The injured airman still isn't out of a coma."

Marin hadn't known that about the airman, but she'd guessed the other parts. Still, she had to shake her head. "What is it you think I can do to help?"

Egan didn't hesitate even a second. "I'm offering you a job. A really good one that involves you and Leo moving to Saddlebrook Ranch."

Once again, Egan had stunned her. That hadn't been anywhere on her radar. "What?" she managed and then tacked on a "Why?"

He met her gaze head-on. "Because according to my ranch foreman, you're damn good at your job, and we can use you. But that's secondary. A big secondary," he qualified, "but the main reason I want you and Leo there is because the only time my brother isn't in a dark pit of hell is when he's talking about Leo."

She had to shake her head again. "I plan on telling Leo the truth, that Blue isn't his father."

Egan nodded. "I suspect that won't be easy." He paused again. "I had background checks run on Leo's parents, too. His bio-dad is definitely no prize. But maybe Leo and Blue can help each other out with that. Blue can be around to soften the blow of the boy learning the truth, and in turn, it'll give Blue something else to focus on other than that pit of hell."

Marin couldn't deny that part about Blue maybe being able to help "soften the blow" for Leo. And that part alone made Egan's job offer tempting, but there were plenty of other things that made the job less tempting.

"Eventually, Blue will have to deal with whatever pit of hell he has to face," she pointed out.

Again, Egan nodded. "Yeah, and we'll cross that bridge when we come to it. I just need something to help him through the next couple of months. If you're as good as my ranch foreman says you are, the job will be yours well beyond that if you want, but we can start with a trial period."

Egan's words were whirling in her head, and she had to take a moment just to process the gist of it all. Once she had that down pat, she was able to see why the job offer wouldn't work.

"I have three horses boarded at the place I rent," she spelled out. "And Leo is in first grade at a private school nearby. Our life is there."

All right, that last part was a stretch since they'd only lived there six months and she wanted to eventually be able to buy her own small ranch, but still, it was their life, and it was just outside of San Antonio, not thirty miles away on Saddlebrook.

"I can have the boarded horses moved to the ranch

where you can still tend to them." Egan was so quick with that response that it was obvious he'd given this some thought. "As for Leo's school, I've spoken with the principal of the elementary school in Emerald Creek, and she can work with you to come up with the right class for Leo."

Clearly, the lieutenant colonel had gone well beyond mere background checks, and while she was trying to figure out how to nicely decline, Egan just kept on.

"There are guest cabins on the grounds of the ranch, and you and Leo can live in one of those rent-free while you're working for us. Added to that, my grandmother and longtime family cook live in the main house, and they've agreed to step in if you need childcare."

That gave her a mental stumble because childcare was a big problem for her. On the days that Leo was sick, she had to cancel training to be with him. Still, she didn't know either of these women, and it seemed way above the norm to volunteer to babysit.

Marin moved on to her next argument, and here she'd done some research, too. Saddlebrook raised both Angus cattle and thoroughbred Andalusian horses. Ones with impeccable lineages. These weren't animals meant for casual buyers, but rather for those interested in owning the best of the best.

"Your work hours can be flexible," Egan continued before she could speak. "I understand you'll need to work around Leo's school schedule, and that's fine. No time clock to punch. Just put in thirty to forty hours a week. You'll accumulate two days of sick leave for each month you work, but if you need more, just work it out with me or Jesse Whitlock, the ranch foreman. We both understand that quality training isn't based on hours."

Again, that was generous. "You can't possibly have enough troubled horses to justify hiring me full-time," she pointed out.

"At the moment, we have four." Again, no hesitation. "All came from a rancher who has what some would call a heavy hand. I'll just call it like it is and say he's a mean son of a bitch who shouldn't be allowed to own a pet rock, much less horses. He has other Andalusians I'd like to buy just to get them away from him, but I don't want to do that until I have the right trainer in place to deal with their recovery. Jesse and I feel as if you're the right trainer."

And here it came. That sickening dread anytime she heard about horses that'd been abused. It was her Achilles' heel. She'd never been able to resist helping hurt or troubled animals. Still, she was going to have to refuse this.

Wasn't she?

"I'll give you some time to think about it," Egan said, reaching in the glove compartment. He handed her an envelope. "That's a draft contract with salary and benefits. Look it over, and feel free to negotiate anything that doesn't work for you."

With that, Egan stepped out of the truck. Marin got out, too, but she resisted opening the envelope to look at the job offer—which she figured would be impressive. Too impressive when coupled with the whole Achilles' heel thing that was going on. She couldn't make a decision based on impressiveness and money.

"What does Blue think about all of this?" she asked as they walked into the hospital.

"He doesn't know yet."

That considerably slowed her step. "Then, Blue might not even want me there."

"He won't," Egan was quick to verify. "He'll think this is some kind of ploy for you to horse whisper him into healing." He glanced at her. "Those techniques won't work on him, will they?"

She sighed. "No."

Though she had no idea if that was true. She'd never tested them on a human. Well, other than using a reward-based system to get Leo to do his homework and pick up his toys. Still, she had no intention of trying it on a grown man who had reasons to wallow in whatever misery he was facing.

Egan shrugged and kept on moving, leading them toward Blue's room. "Anyway, Blue will resist, but if he agrees, I think his being around Leo will help."

"Because it will give him something else to focus on," she muttered, paraphrasing what Egan had said earlier. "But that's a big if. An if that could backfire."

Egan didn't argue with that, and she knew his silence was her out. Because it would be a "big if" for her, too, to uproot Leo and take him to a place where one of the ranch owners wouldn't make him feel welcome.

Marin didn't have a chance to voice that worry, though, because she realized they were at Blue's door. Egan knocked once, peered in and Blue must have been dressed because Egan opened the door.

Blue was indeed dressed, sort of, in a hospital gown,

and unlike five days ago, he was fully sitting up, and he had a laptop on the bed next to him. His face, *that amazing face*, still sported plenty of bruises, but they were now green and yellow instead of the vivid purple they'd been during her last visit.

"Marin," he greeted, and while it was friendly enough, there was nothing friendly about his expression. He was in pain and probably resisting meds.

"Leo's at school," she offered when Blue glanced at her side.

Blue nodded. "How is he?"

"Good," she answered.

And that appeared to be the extent of their conversation before it reached the awkward silence stage. Both Blue and Egan broke that silence at the same moment. Blue, when he reached for a picture on the bedside table and said, "This is for Leo."

Egan's words ran right into Blue's. "I've offered Marin a job at Saddlebrook."

That spurred another round of awkwardness with Blue volleying glances at both his brother and her.

"I told you about the horses I got from Clyde Canton," Egan added after some of those poke along moments. "Jesse and I want Marin to work with them, and the others I'll be buying."

Blue didn't ask for clarification about the horses, but he did fix his attention on Marin. She tried to pick through those bruised features to figure out how he felt about what his brother was proposing, but Blue clearly had a poker face. For this particular subject, anyway.

Though she thought that maybe his mouth tightened just a little when he finally shifted his gaze back to Egan.

"Well, Blue?" Egan prompted. "What do you think? Should Marin take the job and move to Saddlebrook with Leo?"

CHAPTER FIVE

BLUE SILENTLY CURSED. And he had plenty to curse about. Not just the hammering pain still going on in his head and the rest of his body. Not just the shitty hand he'd dealt out to the people he'd injured in his crash landing. Not just the worry about whether or not the surgeon had fixed him.

All of that should have been plenty enough to curse about, but now Egan had apparently decided to add something else to the mix.

Marin.

"Is this some kind of warped attempt to make sure I spend time with a woman?" Blue came out and asked. "Or do you think Marin can horse whisper me into healing?"

Marin laughed. Obviously, the reaction was as much of a surprise to her as it was to Blue because she quickly clamped her teeth over her bottom lip and waved her hand in a "forget I did that" gesture.

"Sorry," she muttered. "It's just earlier I spelled out to Egan that I wouldn't be able to, uh, train you."

"Good," Blue concluded. "I'm glad we agree on that." He looked at his brother again. "So, matchmaking, then?" But Blue stopped and silently waved that off, too. "Or a distraction. Yeah, that's it. You want to take my mind off my troubles by putting a cute kid around me."

Egan didn't deny it. "Partly. But I've also got four horses too afraid to take a piss because they've been whipped for anything and everything. Two have scars that'll never heal and another was nearly starved to death."

Marin made a sound, but this time it sure as hell wasn't laughter. She gasped, and her eyes teared up. She quickly tried to rein in her reaction, blinking hard to hold back those tears, but Blue could tell that what she'd heard had given her a hard knock.

"I want to buy the other horses from their asshole owner," Egan went on, anger twisting his features. All the Donnelly siblings had been raised to love and respect animals, not to beat them into submission. "But I need Marin to help with that."

That eased some of Blue's own anger about his brother wanting to bring in Marin and Leo to try to help him. *Some.* But Marin wasn't the only horse whisperer in Central Texas. Blue would have reminded his brother of that, too, but Egan's phone rang, and when he looked at the screen, he muttered something about having to take the call. He stepped out, shutting the door behind him.

Leaving Marin and Blue alone.

"The job wasn't my idea," she said right off the bat. She held up an envelope. "I haven't even looked at the contract."

He hadn't thought for a second that she'd put Egan up to it. No, this was a "big brother in charge" kind of thing. And technically Egan was in charge. Of the ranch, anyway.

"Look at the offer," Blue insisted.

Her eyes widened, and she hesitated. Man, did she. He could practically see her shuffling her feet. But then, she finally opened the envelope, and when she scanned over it, her eyes widened again.

"Holy crap," she muttered.

Yeah, and Blue knew that wasn't because it was a lowball offer, either. Jesse and Egan didn't operate that way. They brought in the best, not just for the cattle and the horses, but the best workers they could hire. It was one of the reasons Saddlebrook was so successful.

"Comprehensive medical insurance," she muttered as if that were some kind of holy grail. And for her, it just might be since she was responsible for taking care of a child with health problems.

She tore her attention from the contract and stuffed it back into the envelope. "Your brother obviously needs help with the horses, but I believe he also wants Leo and me there to get your mind off what happened."

"You can't get my mind off that," he quickly assured her just as she said, "I can't do that."

She nodded, clearly satisfied they were on the same proverbial page, and she stuffed the envelope in her jeans pocket. She tipped her head to the picture he was still holding. "You said that's for Leo?"

"Yes," he verified, handing it to her.

It was a shot of him winning the European Top Gun trophy. He was still in a flight suit, and both the suit and his hair were dripping with cheap champagne that his fellow pilots had spewed all over him. He was grinning in the photo and was spiked up so high on adrenaline that he looked, well, happy.

"My grandmother picked it out." Blue added that because he wanted Marin to know it wouldn't have been his choice. He would have gone with something less... wet.

"'For Leo,'" she said, reading aloud the inscription. "'Never throttle back. Angel.' Angel," she repeated. "Your call sign."

Even though it wasn't a question, Blue nodded. "A play on my name. I did an air show with the Blue Angels, the Navy's premiere demo fighters, and when I came back to normal duty, that's what everyone started calling me." He paused. "It's also blatant sarcasm since I'm not exactly an angel."

"No," she agreed, her response quiet but quick.

That likely meant she knew all about his reputation. Of course, she did since she'd been friends with Jussie.

"I didn't feel right signing it Dad or Blue," he added a moment later. "That's why I went with Angel."

She nodded. "Leo knows your call sign so he'll understand. He knows all your old rodeo stats, too."

Blue frowned. "Can he even read yet?"

"Some, but he's not allowed on the internet by himself so he has me hunt down articles about you that I can read to him. He has an excellent memory. For some things, anyway," she tacked on to that.

Yeah, he'd imagine a kid that age wouldn't remember to do a lot of things like chores or teeth brushing. And that mentally brought him back to what that contract offer would mean for Leo. Would it improve his quality of life to be on the ranch? It had certainly been an idyllic place for Blue to grow up, but he had no idea what kind of life Marin and the boy would be leaving behind.

"What will you do about that?" he asked, motioning to her pocket.

She glanced down at the contract that was sticking out and then looked at him. "I don't want to do anything until I've given it some thought. And until I find out how Leo and you feel about it."

Blue didn't know how he felt. Wait, yes, he did. He didn't want anyone seeing him on a daily basis until he was back to 100 percent. Of course, he couldn't avoid his family or Maybell. Probably couldn't avoid some of his friends, either. But he'd like to avoid this woman who seemed to send off heat vibes that struck home with him.

He didn't want heat vibes.

Didn't need anything that would blur his focus when it came to healing. Still, it seemed petty to deny Leo something good.

If that's what the boy wanted, that is.

He was about to tell Marin that she should talk to Leo about the job, but he didn't get a chance. There was another knock at the door, and Blue figured it was either Egan returning from his call or one of the medical staff. When the knocker didn't just open the door, Blue issued a "Come in."

The tall lanky dark-haired man who came through the door wasn't medical. At least he wasn't wearing a medical uniform. He was, however, military and wore BDUs with staff sergeant's stripes on the sleeves. Blue got an immediate jolt when his attention landed on the man's name tag.

Garcia.

As in Staff Sergeant Mike Garcia? One of the people Blue had injured in the crash landing. Probably. The sergeant had a few cuts and bruises on his face, and according to what Egan had told him, Garcia also had some cracked ribs.

Hell.

Blue had wanted to see the sergeant. And the others, too. But he hadn't steeled himself nearly enough. His pulse revved up. So did the guilt. It was one thing to hear or read about the injured, but it was a lot harder to meet them face-to-face. Especially when that face was carrying the proof of the damage that'd been done to his body.

"Sorry," the sergeant said, looking at Marin. "I didn't mean to interrupt anything. I can come back later."

"No," Marin said before Blue could issue the same response.

Marin glanced at both of them, and she must have figured out who this visitor was. She studied Garcia for several moments, making Blue wonder if she was trying to decide how this would all play out. Garcia didn't look pissed off or anything, though he had a perfect right to be.

"I'll be going," Marin insisted. She must have decided that Blue needed privacy for this because she immediately started for the door. "Thanks for the picture," she muttered, heading out.

The sergeant glanced behind him at Marin's quick exit. "I hope I didn't run her off."

"No," Blue nearly added some polite excuse, but he wasn't sure he could come up with anything. All his brain could focus on were those cuts and bruises.

"Major Donnelly," the sergeant greeted, and he plastered on a smile that was zinging with nerves. Blue was right there with him. Nerves galore. And he didn't even attempt a smile. "I'm Mike Garcia. One of the nurses passed along a message that you wanted to see me."

Blue nodded and dug deep for some of that steeling up he needed. "I wanted to say I'm sorry. So sorry."

Of course, the apology wasn't worth squat. Words couldn't fix this, and even if the sergeant's injuries hadn't been life-threatening, they had to have been terrifying.

"Thanks," Garcia said, clutching his uniform hat in front of him. Fidgeting with it, too. He was pinching the hat's brim. "How are you doing, Major Donnelly?"

"Call me Blue," he offered.

Though that wasn't military protocol. He was an officer, and as a sergeant, Garcia should address him by rank or sir. But that would feel like even more salt in the wound for Blue. Because addressing him by rank or sir would imply respect, and this man didn't owe him that. Not when he'd endangered the man's life.

"Blue," the sergeant said, and he was clearly uncomfortable with the informality. "How are you doing?" he repeated.

"I'm healing." Blue hoped if he said it enough, it'd be true. "And you?"

"I'm healing, too." Garcia attempted that smile again.

"I'll be off quarters tomorrow and will be going back to work. Light duty," he qualified. "I'm a crew chief."

Off quarters, as in no longer confined to home. But the light duty meant Garcia was still far from being able to do his usual job. Understandable since as a crew chief in tactical aircraft maintenance, he'd need to have full mobility. He likely wouldn't have that with cracked ribs.

"You were on duty during my demo flight?" Blue asked.

Garcia nodded and swallowed hard. Blue didn't have to be a body language expert to know that particular duty hadn't been a walk in the park for him. "I saw you come down and didn't think you'd be walking away from it."

Technically, Blue hadn't walked away. According to what Egan and the medical staff had told him, he'd been unconscious and had to be "extracted" from the cockpit.

"Was the landing gear damaged before I hit the runway?" Blue pressed.

The sergeant's forehead bunched up as if giving that some thought. "Um, I'm not sure. Probably. The accident investigation board hasn't released a report yet."

No, they hadn't, and Garcia would likely be questioned during that query where every aspect of the flight and crash landing would be analyzed. Where every move Blue had made would be studied, too. It was possible the board would come back with a conclusion of pilot error. But just the thought of it made Blue's stomach twist into a hard knot.

"You don't remember if the landing gear was damaged?" Garcia asked.

Blue had to shake his head. "Apparently, the concussion wiped my mind of what happened right before impact."

It was just a guess on his part, but Blue had lost a critical fifteen minutes. Not a huge span of time unless that span was when he'd been piloting a forty-three thousand pound fighter jet.

"Word is there was a bird strike," Garcia offered. "Since there was damage to the cockpit, it's possible the landing gear was compromised, too."

Yeah, possible. But not necessarily. And if the landing gear wasn't damaged, then Blue could and should have done more to make sure there were no injuries other than to himself. A bird strike was an unlucky shitstorm for a pilot, but it was the pilot's job to get out of the shitstorm with as minimal damage as possible.

Six injured people wasn't anywhere near minimal.

The door opened, and Egan stepped in. His brother obviously hadn't seen Marin leave or Blue's visitor arrive because Egan lifted a questioning eyebrow. Garcia had a totally different reaction. He practically came to attention, no doubt because of Egan's high rank.

"This is Staff Sergeant Mike Garcia," Blue explained, motioning for Garcia to relax. "This is my brother, Lieutenant Colonel Egan Donnelly."

Egan didn't ask who the man was, likely because he knew the names of the wounded as well as Blue did. "Staff Sergeant Garcia." Egan extended his hand in greeting. "It's good to meet you."

"Same to you, sir," was Garcia's formal response before he looked at Blue again. "Hope you're up and about soon." He started for the door, but then stopped. "Oh, and the apology wasn't necessary," he added before he walked out.

Garcia was wrong. It was necessary. A million apologies were. It was too bad, though, that saying I'm sorry didn't lessen one drop of Blue's guilt.

"You okay?" Egan asked him.

"Yeah," Blue lied.

Egan nodded and seemed to wait for Blue to add more. When Blue didn't, Egan asked, "Marin left?"

"She did when the sergeant came in." Blue paused. "She did look at the contract offer, though."

That obviously got Egan's attention off Garcia. "And?"

For a simple one-word question, it encompassed a lot. Marin hadn't spelled out much about her feelings over the job offer, but she had remarked about the medical insurance deal.

"And?" Egan pressed after more than a few moments had crawled by.

"If Marin accepts the job, then I'll be fine with it." And he would be, but Blue had to spell out something that he needed his brother and the rest of his family to understand. "I don't want you using Marin and Leo to try to fix me," he insisted.

And there was a damn good reason for that.

Because Blue was scared to the bone that nothing, absolutely nothing, could do that.

CHAPTER SIX

MARIN SAT IN the pretty kitchen at Saddlebrook Ranch eating a "to die for" chocolate chip cookie and listening to Leo gush about the cows and horses he'd seen on their drive to Emerald Creek. He, too, was eating a cookie and chatting with Blue's grandmother, Effie, and the cook, Maybell, as if they were lifelong friends.

The superior cookie coupled with the equally superior cup of tea were occupying Marin's mouth so she wasn't contributing nearly as much as Leo, but she was using the time to think and assess. The pretty kitchen in the pretty house on the pretty ranch where everything looked like a pretty postcard picture.

Blue's grandmother and Maybell fell into the "pretty" zone, too, both in looks and in their kind welcomes. Marin didn't know the women's ages, but Effie was probably in her eighties, and while her soft round face sported some wrinkles that came with age, there was still a quiet beauty there.

Maybell was younger than Effie, probably in her early to midsixties, and she was tall. At least six feet. She reminded Marin of a Viking warrior, what with her strong, sturdy build and the sharp but interesting angles of her face.

Both women had been generous with their kind welcomes and attempts to make this visit as pleasant as possible. They were succeeding and had clearly won over the "already won over" Leo, but their kindness, the ranch, the cookie and Leo's enthusiasm still weren't tipping Marin into making a decision.

She was waffling.

A word Marin hated. She had always thought of herself as a doer, an anti-waffler. Yet, here she was, still in the middle of decision purgatory even though Egan had given her the contract proposal three days ago.

Should she accept Egan's very generous job offer?

Should she stay put at the ranch she was renting?

Both came with consequences, but she thought the first had more consequences than the second choice. Of course, the first came with Blue, which could be trouble on several levels. Because along with anti-waffling, she didn't often lie to herself, which meant admitting she was attracted to the wounded fighter pilot cowboy. Attracted and frustrated since she didn't want the heat.

Hence, the continued dithering around.

Of course, Leo was totally on board with the new job and move, and at first, Marin had thought that was because of Blue. But, no, apparently Leo was seeing a bigger picture here. A picture of horses, cows and lots of space for him to explore. The boy had mentioned Blue some, but Blue hadn't been the main drawing card for Leo to say "please, please, pretty please" at least a hundred times to let Marin know he wanted this massive change in their lives.

It had even been Leo who'd reminded her that Blue

didn't live at the ranch and would be going back to flying when he recovered.

Marin had resisted the pretty pleases and the accompanying cherries on top, and she had extended the waffling by arranging this visit to Saddlebrook. She'd thought said visit would start with Egan ushering her around, clarifying her duties, maybe showing her the guest cabin he was offering as part of the contract package. But no. Egan had apparently been called to the hospital to pick up Blue and bring him home.

At the thought of Blue's homecoming, something Marin hoped to avoid, she finished the cookie and stood up, hoping it would signal an end to the chitchat. "Would it be all right if Leo and I walk down to the barn and corral to have a look around?" she asked.

"Of course," Effie assured her. She smiled again, the warmth rolling off her in waves, and she patted Leo's cheek. "There are treats in the barn for the horses."

That was incentive enough for Leo to wolf down the rest of his cookie, too, and he washed it down with a gulp of milk.

"Let me just wrap up some of these for you," Maybell offered, putting several of the cookies in a zipped plastic bag. She winked at Leo. "Might be able to talk your aunt Marin into letting you eat another one later."

Leo would, indeed, try. And likely succeed. There was always a hard balance with a child who'd endured a life-threatening illness. On the one hand, you didn't want to overindulge him, but Marin also wanted to give him at least some of the treats he'd missed out on during those months and months he'd been sick.

Marin thanked Maybell and Effie and was about to reach for the back door when it opened, and a blonde woman came in. She had huge canvas bags in both hands.

"Goodies from Blue's admirers," the woman announced, but then she stopped, her expression freezing for a moment when her attention landed on Marin and Leo. "Oh," she added like an apology. Then, she shrugged and met Marin's gaze. "Blue has lots of admirers."

Marin hadn't doubted that for a moment, and she was pretty sure this beautiful woman was carrying goodies from other equally beautiful women.

"I'm Alana Davidson," the woman greeted, extending three fingers of her right hand for Marin to shake. Three fingers was all she'd managed to free, what with the obviously heavy bags.

"Alana's a dietitian at the local hospital. She's also engaged to Blue's brother Egan," Maybell supplied.

At the mention of that, Alana shifted the bags, freeing her ring finger so that Marin could see what she presumed was the engagement ring. Not a massive diamond, but rather a brilliant ruby in what appeared to be an antique gold setting.

"Congratulations," Marin said, and she introduced Leo and herself.

Alana smiled, set the bags down on the countertop and stooped down to be eye level with Leo. "Hey, there are some ooey gooey chocolate caramel bars in one of the bags. Would you like me to snag one for you?"

"Uh, we have these," Marin volunteered before Leo

could take Alana up on the offer. She held up the plastic bag.

Alana grinned. "Those will be better than ooey gooey bars." She straightened upright and met Marin's gaze. "You're the horse whisperer?"

Marin forced herself not to roll her eyes. So, obviously Egan's fiancée knew about her and the job offer. Since she didn't ask who Leo was, Alana probably knew about him as well. Ditto for Maybell and Effie. Neither of them had mentioned a word about Leo believing Blue was his daddy. Thankfully, Leo had remembered not to mention it, too. Marin had asked him to hold off on saying anything about that under the guise of Blue maybe not having told them.

"Leo and I were just heading out to the barn and corral," Marin said to Alana. "It was good to meet you. And thank you again," she added to Maybell and Effie.

Marin took hold of Leo's hand and led him out onto the back porch. Or rather the back part of it, anyway since the porch wrapped around the entire bottom floor of the house.

Alana stepped out with them. "I hope you don't mind a little company," she said. "Egan had planned on being able to show you around, but when he got word that Blue was being released today, he headed straight to the hospital."

"It's okay," Marin assured her, frowning a little when Alana followed them down the steps and into the yard. Alana seemed friendly enough, but Marin had hoped to take in Saddlebrook…while she did more waffling.

"I can give you a tour of sorts," Alana said. "But a

disclaimer here. I wasn't raised on a ranch. I'm pretty much a 'Main Street, coffee shop within walking distance' kind of woman."

"Yet, you're marrying a rancher," Marin muttered before she could stop herself.

"I am. Love is blind and all that." Alana smiled, and Marin didn't need to hear the woman's internal thoughts to know it was genuine. "It was a long road for Egan and me to find our way to each other so I'll gladly give up Main Street and walks to the coffee shop to be here with him. What about you?" she tacked on to that.

The question threw Marin, and she wasn't sure what Alana was asking. She hoped it wasn't anything to do with Blue.

"I'm considering Egan's job offer," Marin settled for saying.

"Oh, you should. You should consider it and accept it. Come on, and I'll show you why Saddlebrook is so amazing. That's the main barn," Alana explained without pausing. She lifted her hand to the white barn dead center in front of them. "But there are three others."

Marin could see one of the three, but apparently the others were out of sight in the acres and acres of pastures.

"Cows," Leo blurted out, and he tore his hand from hers to go running toward the pasture fence.

"Be careful," Marin called out to him and kept her attention nailed to the boy.

"He'll be fine," Alana assured her. "Not much he can get into on this side of the fence."

No, but Marin's first instinct was to slow Leo down,

to try to hold him back before he could overexert himself. Again, that was the biggie when dealing with a child who'd been sick. She had to remind herself that he wasn't sick now, and he was clearly enjoying himself.

"I'm using highly technical terms here," Alana went on, pointing to the left, "but that side of the land where Leo is heading is usually for the cows and the cow thingy pens where they bring them sometimes for treatment and such." She pointed to the right. "They usually keep the horses on that side."

Marin could see several of the horses, some cropping grass in the front of the pasture. A pasture dotted with plenty of shade trees and huge troughs of water. Judging from the position of the main barn, the horses would have access to that if it got too hot or if the weather turned bad.

"Folks joke that Egan's dad and his ancestors didn't care for colorful critters," Alana explained. "The cows are all Black Angus, and the horses are all white Andalusians, but there are a few calico cats that frequent the barn. Hi, Jesse," she called out, again without pausing, and she waved at a dark-haired man who was in the process of trying to get some meds in a bull calf.

"Jesse Whitlock," Marin provided. "The ranch foreman."

"That's right. He looks more like a Donnelly brother, doesn't he? It's as if young Elvis and Marilyn Monroe decided to have a bunch of kids. All of them too hot for their own good," she added in a mutter and then winked at Marin. "I'm engaged but not blind."

Marin had good eyesight, too, and yes, the foreman

did indeed fall into the hot category, though, when she glanced around at the other hands she could see, she noticed they came in all ages, shapes, sizes. Some hot, some not.

"So, you don't necessarily have to be good-looking to live and work here," Marin remarked.

Alana laughed. "Nope, but I swear there are enough to fill three or four years of hot cowboy calendars."

Marin made a sound of agreement while continuing to keep watch of Leo. "Will it bother Jesse and the other hands if Leo asks a bunch of nonstop questions?" Because Marin was certain that was what he was already doing.

"Not at all. The local school brings classes out here all the time, and Jesse's good with them. Egan, not so much, but Blue is." The woman finally paused, and Marin didn't think it was simply to draw breath.

Alana was waiting for Marin to discuss Blue.

Since she didn't want this to be a long conversation, Marin went with the abbreviated version. "I'm not Blue's girlfriend. And he's not Leo's father, though Leo believes he is. I intend to tell Leo the truth soon."

"Yes," Alana said, and this time her pause was even longer as they made their way toward the right side of the pasture. "How is Blue? I mean, how is he really?"

Marin wondered if Alana knew that Egan had asked her the same thing. That'd been a little over a week ago, on the afternoon of Blue's crash landing. "I honestly don't know. In fact, I don't know Blue that well at all. Most of what I know about him came from Leo's mom, Jussie. She followed him around on the rodeo."

"One of Blue's admirers," Alana remarked with more amusement than judgment. "As I said, he has lots of them. Ones who bake him desserts with the words *sin* and *sex* in them. Women who'll wear their tightest push-up bras and shortest skirts when they visit him."

"So, a womanizer," Marin muttered.

"More of a charmer. I don't think he'd ever intentionally be reckless with a woman. That said, women are often reckless over him. They fall hard for him. Not you, though," Alana said.

Marin realized Alana was still walking, but also studying her, too. "Not me," Marin verified, hoping she would continue to feel that way if she did end up taking the job.

But the job was still a massive if.

And she would have no doubt lapsed back into waffling if she hadn't seen the horses. There were two mares in a fenced off area of the right pasture, clearly isolated from the other horses. After one look at them, Marin knew these were the two of the four that Egan had told her about.

One—the one that instantly crushed her heart—had deep scars on her flank and rump. From whippings probably. The other wasn't scarred nearly as much, but there were a few on her rump as well, and she was way underweight. The close proximity to the barn was probably so the hands could keep a watchful eye on them.

Both mares whipped up their heads, instantly alerted to what they wondered might be danger. Marin stopped, gently taking hold of Alana's arm to have her do the same.

"Going closer will alarm them even more than they

already are," Marin whispered. She volleyed glances at Leo to make sure he was okay. He was. And she continued to watch the horses to see how long it would take them to go off alert.

It took too long.

Minutes. That suggested a deep wariness and trauma since there was ready food and water for them to be chowing down on.

"That one is Cottontail," Alana said, whispering, and she pointed to the thin one. "The other is Pearl." She paused. "I have fantasies about castrating their previous owner."

And in that moment, Marin instantly bonded with her. Kindred spirits. "We could use a rusty knife or a dull rock."

Alana made a sound of agreement. "Egan and his dad both reported the owner, but nothing came of it. He's in the good ol' boy network and has enough money to keep off the heat and continue acting like a dickhead. The only bright spot is the dickhead is going to retire soon and wants to get rid of all his livestock. I'm holding out hope, though, that karma will take a good chunk out of his ass."

That was, indeed, a good thing to hope for, and Marin was thankful, so thankful, that Egan and his dad had seen the problem and were trying to fix it.

Alana tipped her head to the horses again. "Can you help them, or are they broken for good?"

"Nothing's ever broken for good," Marin heard herself say, though she knew that wasn't true.

But in this case, she wouldn't allow it to be anything but the truth. These beautiful mares could heal and might even be able to forget all about the bastard who'd done this to them.

"So, you'll take the job?" Alana asked.

Marin was about to say yes. The words were right there, ready to come out, but then she heard the sound of the approaching vehicle, and that stopped her. She turned and saw Egan. Not alone. He was helping Blue out of the truck.

Well, sort of helping as much as Blue would seemingly allow, anyway.

She was surprised that Blue wasn't climbing into a wheelchair, though there was one waiting by the truck. Blue also wasn't latching onto his brother for support. Instead, Blue maneuvered a pair of crutches in place and was clearly planning on using those to get into the house.

Marin wasn't close enough to hear whatever Blue said to Egan, but she could see the pain etched on his face. In a gesture that reminded her of the mares, Blue's head whipped up, and his gaze practically collided with hers.

Oh, mercy.

That kick of blasted heat came. Some invisible, unwanted magnetic force that caused her to lock eyes with him. And her heart did that little roll before she felt the crushing feeling in her chest.

Damn him.

It wasn't like the horses all over again, but it was close. Close and worse. Because she'd learned the really hard way that you couldn't fix charmers. That the charm didn't stop hearts from being crushed. Or stop people from dying.

Good grief. She couldn't do this. Could she?

"I'm going to needlepoint that on a pillow or something," Alana said, yanking Marin's attention back to her.

"What?" Marin asked.

"Nothing is ever broken for good." Alana gave her a reassuring pat on the arm and started toward Egan and Blue.

BLUE HADN'T EXPECTED to feel as if he'd been drop-kicked onto another planet. Not when he was surrounded by things as familiar to him as his right hand. Then again, his right hand was still bruised to hell and back so familiar things were all relative.

The ranch itself felt right. Like home. But then there was Marin and Leo. Not usual home things. Still, they weren't what was causing this feeling of drop-kicking and other planets. It was his own reaction to his home. Normally, he would have bounded—yeah, bounded— out of whatever vehicle he'd been in and he would have been eager to see everyone and everything. Grammy Effie, Maybell, his dad and any of his siblings who might be around. Jesse. The new horses. Heck, even the cows, though they were far from his favorite.

At the moment, he couldn't "bound" if his life depended on it.

Truth was he could hardly walk even with the use of the crutches. The physical therapist at the base hospital had told him he'd be on them for at least two weeks, but Blue was counting on shaving a lot of time off that.

"You're home," Alana said, hurrying to Blue and gently hugging him. Emphasis on gently. She was obviously being mindful of his injuries. "And Marin and Leo are here."

"I see that," Blue muttered, nodding a greeting to Marin as she approached. Not with Alana's speed or enthusiasm. There was a whole lot of caution in her expression. Maybe some dread, too. "Hello, Marin."

"Hello," she greeted back. She glanced behind her at Leo, who was at the corral fence watching Jesse.

"Good news," Alana announced. "I'm pretty sure Marin's taking the job. She might become my coconspirator in a castration, too. Not yours," she added, dropping a kiss on Blue's cheek. "The previous owner of those horses."

Blue looked at Marin and didn't have to ask if she'd personally seen the results of that previous owner. Her troubled eyes let him know that she had.

"Let's put castration plans on hold and get Blue inside," Egan suggested just as his phone rang. "It's Dad," he relayed.

"Tell him I'll call him later," Blue automatically said. He wanted to talk to him. His dad was another part of what made this place home. But he needed to steady himself before he had that particular conversation. His dad had his own health issues, and if Blue said the wrong thing, it would only cause his father to worry more than he already was.

"Need help getting into the house?" Alana asked while Egan stepped away to take the call.

Blue shook his head. "I'll just say hello to Leo first."

He wasn't sure who was more surprised by that, but Blue thought he might be the winner here. He actually did want to see Leo, and while that would delay the steadying time he needed, it would delay his having to deal with the troubled, poor pitiful looks he'd get from Maybell and Effie. They wouldn't mean to give him those looks, of course, but they also wouldn't be able to stop themselves.

Bottom line—he'd worried a whole bunch of people. Including himself.

"Uh, can you make it to the corral?" Alana asked.

"Sure," Blue insisted, but it was possibly the biggest lie he'd ever told. He wasn't sure he could make it two steps much less to the corral, but he was at least going to attempt it.

"I can have Leo come to you," Marin offered in a whisper.

Blue shook his head for that, too, and got moving at such a poky pace that snails could overtake him.

"I forgot something in the house," Alana said suddenly, and his "soon to be" sister-in-law hurried off at a pace the exact opposite of a snail's. Clearly, Alana thought he wanted some alone time with Marin.

He didn't.

Well, maybe he did. He wasn't doing a good job of steadying anything, including the thoughts crashing like waves in his head.

"So, are you actually taking the job or was that wishful thinking on Alana's part?" he came out and asked.

She paused for a long time. Long enough for him

to complete two whole steps. "I'm taking it if you're okay with it."

"Is Leo okay with it?" he pressed.

Marin nodded.

"Then, I am, too," Blue assured her. Again, that was a possible big-assed lie, but he didn't want to put Marin on a guilt trip about accepting what was probably a dream job for her.

Dream minus him, of course.

There was that wariness again. Probably an "old relationship baggage" kind of deal. Or maybe it was there because he'd had a one-off with Leo's mom, a woman who'd become her friend. Either way, Blue was counting on that wariness to stomp out some of this heat that was zinging between them. He wasn't in any shape for heat.

"Your parents and siblings will be okay with me working here?" she asked.

"They will be. Egan and Jesse are in charge of the hiring, and what they say goes." Blue didn't add that what they said was almost always gold, too. They didn't make many mistakes when it came to Saddlebrook. "My dad's more or less out of the picture these days when it comes to the ranch. He's with my stepmother in Washington, DC. My mom died when I was four, and Dad married Audrey four years later."

"Stepmother," Marin muttered. "I recall someone saying she's in the military."

"She is. Audrey's an Air Force two-star general. And yeah, it's okay to joke about me having to salute her."

But Marin didn't joke. The best she could apparently manage was to conjure up a small smile.

"I don't recall much about my mother," he went on. "Leo must, though, since Jussie died only a couple of months ago."

"Six months ago," Marin reminded him while they continued the same super slow, super painful pace. "Jussie had considered telling him the truth about you when she first got the cancer diagnosis, but she felt he had enough to deal with."

Yeah, he would have, considering the boy had been sick then, too.

"So, I take it Leo doesn't know yet about me not being his father?" Blue wanted to know.

She shook her head. "Not yet. I'd planned on telling him tomorrow, but I'll probably wait until after we've made the move to the guest cabin. I don't want to throw too much at him at once. It might take him a while to get adjusted here."

At that exact moment, Leo let out a cackle of laughter, and Blue saw that Jesse had allowed the boy to touch the bull calf through the slats of the corral fence.

"Maybe the adjustment won't be that hard for him," Blue concluded. Hell, he hoped so, anyway. Jussie's kid had already been through way too much.

Jesse continued to let Leo in on the petting, and Blue could hear Jesse giving Leo a warning about not going near the livestock, especially the bulls, unless an adult was with him. Good advice. Blue recalled a particularly nasty incident when he'd been eight or so and tried to play matador with one of the bulls. He hadn't been hurt, but he'd had to scramble to get over the fence before the bull could trample him.

"And what about you?" Blue added to Marin. "How okay are you with all of this?"

He thought she might give him a pat answer, something along the lines of her being fine as long as Leo was. Which would no doubt be true. But instead of patness, Marin looked at him. This time the wariness wasn't there, but he did see a whole lot of what he thought was resolve.

"Three years ago, I got involved with the wrong man," she said.

Bingo. He'd been right about that old relationship baggage. "And you're spelling out that you won't be getting involved with me."

"I can't," she muttered.

Not *won't* but *can't*. There was a big-assed difference in those two words.

"I don't think I'm wrong that you feel guilty about those people injured in the crash landing," Marin added a moment later.

Blue managed a nod. Didn't, however, manage to buffer the metaphorical fist punch that the reminder gave him.

"Well, I know all about that kind of guilt," she insisted. "Except in your case, it wasn't your fault. In my case, it was."

And with that, Marin hurried ahead of him to go to Leo.

CHAPTER SEVEN

MARIN STOOD STOCK-STILL in the shaded pasture with the two mares. Cottontail and Pearl, the ones she'd first seen five days earlier on her visit to Saddlebrook ranch. Then, she hadn't even been sure she would accept the job Egan had offered. Now, here she was, not only on her first full day of work, but Leo and she were settled into the guest cabin.

Well, more or less settled.

Marin figured it was going to take a heck of a lot longer than five days for her to feel at home here. Egan and the rest of the ranch crew had been generous, what with helping her move and relocating her boarded horses to the ranch. Alana, whose aunt was the principal at the local elementary school, had also been generous in working to get Leo into a "small class" situation where Marin hoped he would fit in. There'd likely be adjustment pains for both of them, but for now, everything seemed to be in the "so far, so good" category.

Again, that was more or less true.

One of her biggest obstacles and objections in coming here had been Blue, and she hadn't seen much of him at all over the past five days. She had heard talk, though, from the other ranch hands that he was being driven to the base hospital daily for physical therapy on his knee. There'd been no talk, however, about how he was recovering.

Marin took another small step closer to the mares and then stopped again, measuring their response to her. As with the other steps she'd made in the past half hour or so, they looked at her with wariness, the muscles in their necks tensing. Their nostrils flared, and Cottontail snorted. When Marin didn't pose whatever threat they feared, they relaxed.

Another "more or less" applied here.

The pair wouldn't totally relax since they'd learned the hard way to fear humans, but the plan was they would eventually let her get close enough to touch them. Right now, she was still twelve feet away from them. Within the hour, she hoped to reduce that distance by half. Then, she'd call it a day for these two and shift over to working with the other two mares who were in a different part of the pasture.

Since this particular part of the training meant taking baby steps and then standing around a lot, it gave her some time to think. A blessing and a curse. Normally, she could fill her mind with thoughts of Leo or maybe her favorite movie or books. She could fantasize about a dream vacation on a tropical beach.

Not today, though.

And she could put the blame for her troubling thoughts squarely on her own shoulders. After all, she'd been the one who'd blabbed to Blue and opened a can of worms from the past that she should have never opened.

Well, I know all about that kind of guilt. Except in your case, it wasn't your fault. In my case, it was.

Why, why, why had she volunteered that? Because she'd been trying to spell out to Blue why she couldn't get involved with him. But she should have found another way of making her point instead of baring the most wounded, painful part of her soul.

Silently cursing herself, Marin tried to level her mood since the mares would likely pick up on it. When she thought she had her mind under control, she took another step. And this time she forced herself to focus on Leo. That little face always lightened her mood, and today was no different. He was in school now, probably spreading his infectious enthusiasm despite having been uprooted just days earlier. Then again, the boy had been doing a lot of uprooting lately, what with Jussie's death, his move to Marin's rental and then the move here.

Marin's job contract was for two years with no penalty if she terminated it early. A long commitment, but she was already thinking about what she would do down the road. Since she wasn't having to pay rent and her salary hit the amazing mark, she might be able to save enough in those two years to put the down payment on her own place. That would give Leo some stability that Marin desperately wanted to give him.

Stability that started with Leo learning the truth about his father.

That was on the agenda for tonight, and Gina had agreed to come to the ranch for that particular conversation.

Marin took another step and was pleased with the

mares' reaction. They still tensed and Cottontail still snorted, but their wary response time was significantly less than with her other steps. Marin didn't speed things up, though. She waited and took the final step of the day, putting herself close enough to the mares for them to get a good look at her. A good sniff, too. It was obvious from their body language that they still didn't trust her, but their fear levels had dropped some.

Calling it a day with the pair, Marin slowly retraced her steps, walking backward until she made it to the fence. Still keeping her movements slow, she turned to climb over.

And realized she had an audience.

Jesse, Egan. And Blue.

They were standing beneath one of the massive oaks in between the house and the barn, and they'd obviously been watching her. Since this stage of training didn't seem like much, not on the surface, anyway, Egan might be wondering why they heck they were paying her such a high salary to take steps and stare at the horses. Jesse might be wondering the same thing.

She didn't want to speculate about what Blue was thinking.

But she did plenty of speculation about him.

He looked good. Very good. *Too* good. The bruises were all gone from his face, and he wasn't using crutches. However, he was wearing some kind of complicated-looking splint on his injured knee.

Marin climbed over the fence, grabbed a thermos she'd left on the ground, and while gulping down some water, she made her way to them, ready to explain what she'd been doing with the mares. But Jesse spoke before she could say anything.

"They didn't bolt away from you," Jesse pointed out. "That's a good start."

Marin nodded and adjusted her attitude. She often had to justify the training. Obviously not, though, in Jesse's case.

"Tomorrow, I'll try to get close enough to touch them," she explained, drinking more water. "It might be another day or two, though, before any actual touching happens. Once they're comfortable with that, then I'll start bringing in a saddle so they can get used to being around one. None of this will be a fast process," she added.

"Didn't figure it would be," Egan said.

Blue made a sound of agreement that had her glancing at him. Oh, yes, he looked too good, and he smiled at her. One of those charmer smiles that was a quick reminder of why he'd earned his reputation.

"You're up and about," she said, silently groaning at stating the obvious. "How's the physical therapy going?" she risked asking.

"Good," he said, but for reasons she wouldn't push, she thought he might be lying.

"How's Leo?" Blue asked.

"Good," she repeated, but hers wasn't a lie. "He's at school." She studied Blue's eyes to see if he was also silently questioning if she'd told Leo the truth or not, but she didn't see anything to indicate he was thinking that. "He wants to learn to ride," she added a moment later.

"Well, plenty of opportunities for that around here," Egan remarked. "How about his room in the cabin? Is that okay? It obviously wasn't originally set up for a boy, but Maybell and Grammy Effie tried to add some touches."

"They succeeded," Marin assured him, and that wasn't lip service. "I need to thank them again for that."

The cabin was on the small side, two bedrooms, two baths, but Maybell and Effie had brought in all sorts of books and games that they thought would be suitable for a six-year-old boy.

Egan opened his mouth to say something else, but the sound of an approaching vehicle cut him off. "He's here."

"A new stallion," Jesse supplied to her, also turning his attention to the shiny black truck and horse trailer that was making its way to the corral.

Both Jesse and Egan started toward the trailer. Blue took a hobbled step, too, but then stopped. "Best if I don't tackle that slope yet," he said, motioning toward the incline of the yard. "But go ahead if you want. He's supposed to be a blue-blooded rock star of the Andalusia breed."

Marin stayed put in the shade, drinking more water and watching as the stallion's handlers led him off the trailer. A rock star, indeed.

"His name is Iceman," Blue provided. "The name speaks for itself, huh?"

"It does. He looks impressive and cocky."

"My dad and granddad didn't approve of artificial insemination for the breed stock," Blue went on. "They preferred live covering of the mares in either the breeding barn or the pasture."

His father wasn't alone in that particular practice. In fact, Marin had always thought live covering fit better with her natural training techniques. There could still be injuries to a mare during the coupling process, but it paired better with the mare's instincts.

"My dad tried to buy Iceman a few months back when he still ran the ranch, but he couldn't quite manage to close the deal," Blue added. "Egan picked up on the negotiations where our dad left off, and he managed to finalize the purchase. Iceman will be able to pass on those superior genes to the next generation."

Marin mentally squirmed a little since they were talking about sex. Yes, it was horse sex, but it was still uncomfortable with Blue standing right next to her. But she rethought that. Maybe Blue was no longer feeling anything sexual for her after she'd spilled her confession.

Well, I know all about that kind of guilt. Except in your case, it wasn't your fault. In my case, it was.

Oh, yes. That could put a man off, all right. But then, Blue looked at her. Just a look, coupled with the barest hint of that damnable smile that qualified as intense foreplay. And in that look she saw the attraction.

Felt it, too.

So, apparently her mysteriously worded bombshell hadn't caused the attraction to vanish. Neither had the "snap out of it" lectures she'd had with herself. At least a week ago, she could have used Blue's injuries as a reason for her not to have the hots for him, but he seemed to be healing just fine.

Rather than continue to lock gazes with him—something that was fanning the heat—Marin glanced at Cottontail and Pearl to see if they'd noticed what was going on with the stallion.

They had.

The mares had inched closer to the fence and were having a look at the new guy on the ranch. Marin was afraid she might be projecting because of her attraction for Blue, but she thought that Cottontail and Pearl were very interested in what they saw, and it was that interest/projection that caused her to mutter some profanity under her breath.

Profanity that obviously she hadn't muttered softly enough because Blue heard it, or rather she assumed he had because he chuckled.

"Do you plan on giving them a warning about Iceman?" he asked.

"I would if I thought it'd help," Marin admitted. "Or if I thought they'd actually want to listen to me about that particular subject."

But then she shrugged. A warning might not be necessary since it was possible the mares would be as leery of the newcomer as they were of everyone and everything else. And if they weren't, if they were indeed receptive to being live covered by an arrogant cocky equine rock star, then that would give the ranch a start on that next generation of champion bloodlines.

"So," Blue said, breaking the silence that'd settled between them. "Should I ask what you meant by your guilt comment? In other words, do you want to compare guilt trips, or would you rather just get a closer look at Iceman?"

Marin didn't curse, groan or lecture herself, though

that was what she wanted to do. She debated how to go about this. It was possible some of this was in the background check that Egan had run on her. Not all, though.

Because other than her, there was no living person who knew *all*.

And there was a reason for that. Simply put, it'd been just too painful to talk about. If she did a tell-all now to Blue, it also might make things worse for him and the guilt trip he was going through. If she clammed up, it might make him so curious that he did some digging to find out what she was hiding. She didn't want her past to become a quest for him.

Decisions, decisions.

She went with a very sanitized, very scaled-back account. "Something bad happened three years ago. Nothing to do with Jussie or Leo," she quickly added. "I didn't know them then." She paused. "I was a bone marrow donor for my sister who had leukemia. And she died."

"Shit," he spat out. "I'm sorry." He repeated his *shit* and looked at her. "You don't blame yourself for the bone marrow deal not working, do you?" Blue didn't wait for an answer. "Three years ago," he repeated, obviously working out something in his mind. "So, if you hadn't donated marrow to your sister, you wouldn't have been in the system and been a match for Leo."

She nodded. There was that. It was something she held on to when the darkness threatened to eat her alive.

"Silver linings," she muttered.

"Yeah. A whopping big one. You saved his life."

Marin winced because Blue made it seem so heroic. It hadn't been. She'd been in the right place at the right time, and she'd done what Marin believed anyone else would have done to keep a child alive.

"My bone marrow saved him," she said. "DNA to the rescue."

He shifted his attention back to her. "Does that mean Leo's related to you in some kind of way?"

She shook her head. "Strangers match all the time, but plenty of the matches come from family members. The flip side to that is family members often aren't matches for their own kin."

Marin left it at that, and she waited. When Blue didn't ask for more info, she guessed he must have assumed her sister, Selene, had died from the leukemia. No. She'd died because of that something bad that'd happened three years ago. DNA hadn't been at fault then. Nor had the leukemia. That'd all been on Marin because if she hadn't started the "something bad" rolling, then Selene would still be alive.

And here it came.

The guilt so strong that she felt the old familiar feeling of being swallowed up. No way could she fight that now. Not with Blue right there next to her. Besides, she still had work to do, and the mares would almost certainly pick up on anything negative that was going on in her head. Best to switch subjects, finish her break and get back to work. Thankfully, she had a good subject switch. Good for her, anyway because it was something she truly wanted to know.

"How are you, really?" she asked, drinking the last of her water.

Blue took a deep breath. "Well, I no longer have a

bruise that resembles a pig's ass on my cheek so that's something."

She made a show of studying his face. Not the smartest idea she'd ever had because, hey, she was now looking at him. "Yes," she verified. "It's gone. And the rest of you?" she pressed. "How are your other injuries?"

His forehead bunched up. "According to the doctors and physical therapists, I still have a long way to go. The ribs are healing, and now I only scream a little bit when I cough or sneeze." He grinned. "That's progress."

Yes, it was, and she was relieved the pain had lessened.

He paused again, his expression turning serious. "The kneecap fracture was what they call complex. I guess that's easier than saying there's no easy fix. But I'll get there," he insisted. "I'll finish my PT and get back in the cockpit."

She believed him. And that gave Marin an unexpected feeling of…sadness. Which was stupid. Of course, she wanted Blue to heal. She wanted him to go back to doing what he loved, and that meant not being here at the ranch 24/7, but at whatever military base he happened to be stationed.

"The airman I injured might not get that chance," he added in a mutter.

She nearly corrected him with "the airman injured in the accident," but Marin knew that wouldn't do any good. The blame and guilt were there, and words weren't going to fix it. Even if she had plenty of personal knowledge about accidents and such.

"He's still in a coma," Blue explained, and cursing,

he scrubbed his hand over his face. "I've been in to see him. He's young. Too damn young, and he's supposed to have his whole life ahead of him."

Oh, there was so much pain in Blue's voice. So much guilt. "Nothing is ever broken forever," she blurted out and immediately wanted to slap herself. Crap. Had she really gone there?

Yep, she had.

Blue looked at her with a whole lot of skepticism. And rightfully so. Marin had said that about the scarred mares, but that'd been more like a promise to herself to help them, to make their lives better. Blue wasn't a damaged horse, and it was entirely possible for some things to be broken for good.

Blue frowned. "Did Alana tell you that?"

"Uh, no. Actually, I said it to Alana. Why? Did she mention it?"

"She put it as the screen saver on her laptop and then left her laptop in a spot where I was sure to see it." Judging from the way his mouth tightened, he hadn't been pleased about the overly optimistic message.

Marin supposed that was akin to needlepointing it on something. "Sorry."

He shrugged. "Alana's worried about me. They all are." Blue drew in a long breath and glanced back at the house. Sure enough, both Effie and Maybell were looking out the window at them. "I guess I'd better go in and eat some sin cookies or sex cake. Apparently, there's something called Fine Ass buns. Want any?"

Despite the super serious conversation they'd just had, Marin had to smile. Had to also ignore that kick of lust when he reached into his foreplay arsenal and grinned at her again.

"No, thanks," she said. "I have to get back to work."

"For another round with Cottontail and Pearl?" he asked.

"No. I'll move on to the other two horses, Dolly and Princess." She paused, though. "Did their previous bastard owner give them such sweet names?"

"Not a chance. According to Egan, they were being called…other things. My sister, Remi, was here when the four mares arrived, and she named them. Normally, she goes with more kick-ass ones like Kara after the first female fighter pilot. Or Katniss. There's even an Annie Oakley around. But for these four, I guess she figured they deserved a little pampering."

"They do," she agreed, and she recapped her thermos to get ready to leave. She'd refill it in the barn before heading out to the pasture.

"Hey," Blue said, stopping her. "I'm sorry about your sister, and I'm sorry I asked about it."

He wasn't just blowing smoke. She could tell he was sincere. Probably because he knew what it was like to have someone pick at an old wound. And her sister was a wound, all right, one that wasn't going to heal. Yes, there were definitely things that were forever broken.

Marin headed to the barn, refilled her thermos and was about to head to the pasture when her phone rang. Her heart thudded when she saw the name on the screen. Emerald Creek Elementary School. Marin bobbled the thermos and nearly dropped it when she rushed to answer the call.

"This is Marin Galloway. Is Leo okay?" Marin immediately asked and hoped she would hear a quick reassurance that all was well and this was just a routine call about school supplies or something.

It wasn't.

"Miss Galloway, I'm Pamela Marino, the school nurse."

"Yes, I remember you." Marin had spoken with her at length. "Is Leo okay?" she repeated with even more urgency and concern this time.

"You asked me to call if there were any indications Leo was sick. I think you should come to the school right away."

CHAPTER EIGHT

BLUE FIXED HIS GAZE—which was narrowed and pissed off—out the window of the truck. He wasn't seeing the scenery and definitely wasn't listening to the young ranch hand, Chad Haney, go on about ranching shit that Blue didn't want to hear.

He appreciated the ranch hand driving him to and from his appointment at the base. Something that Blue still couldn't do for himself, but he wished he had a mute button so he could wallow in quiet misery. Still, Chad was better than Egan, Maybell or any other friend or member of his family since they would have pressed Blue to tell him how the follow-up appointment had gone with the surgeon.

It'd gone shitty.

And Blue definitely didn't want to be pressured into talking about it.

At the moment, the follow-up was just another item on a long-ass list of things that had pissed him off and sent his mood plummeting below rock bottom. Plenty of items that made him want to curse fate, the universe or whatever the hell it was that people cursed when dealt a shitty hand. It wasn't only his hand, though, but rather Leo's that was at the top of the list.

A cold.

Normally, something like that was a mere inconvenience for most people, but it had sidelined the kid and for the past three days had put the look of sheer terror on Marin's face. She hadn't spelled out any worst-case scenarios, not to him, anyway, but Blue had filled in some blanks. With Leo's compromised immune system, anything, including a common cold, could be life-threatening. So far, though, that worst-case scenario shit hadn't kicked in, and according to all accounts, Leo was recovering.

Blue couldn't say the same for himself.

Or rather the surgeon hadn't been able to say so. Oh, yeah, there'd been progress with his knee, the surgeon had said, but that'd been only to sugarcoat the bottom line. That the progress wasn't nearly good enough for Blue to be taken off medical leave. The surgeon wouldn't even venture a guess as to when Blue could return to the cockpit.

Reliving those words, even the sugarcoated ones, had Blue cursing. Not just in his head this time, either. He growled out enough words that had Chad hushing and muttering an "Are you okay?"

Blue didn't even attempt a lie. He just waved Chad off, and since he was mentally going over the list of things that had sucker punched him into this god-awful mood, he went to the next item.

Another biggie.

In fact, even worse than Leo's situation. Leo was recovering, but Airman Casey Newell wasn't. He was still in a coma and had been for sixteen days now. Even

though the medical staff hadn't been willing to speculate on his prognosis, Blue had done his own internet
searches and knew that each and every day in the coma
lessened the chances he would come out of it. Especially come out of it with all his brain functions intact.

That was on Blue.

It would always be on him.

While Chad kept on driving toward the ranch, he re-
started his conversation, and this time his chosen subject was Marin and the progress she was making with
the four mares.

"She throws saddles at them," Chad said, shaking
his head in disbelief. "Never heard of such a thing."

Blue frowned. He'd never heard of that, either. "Marin
actually throws saddles at the horses?" he asked because
that didn't sound like a part of her "gentle training" approach.

"Well, not at them exactly, but she sort of tosses a saddle on the ground near where the mares are. Then, she
stands there and waits for a while for them to quit snorting and rearing before she picks it up and tosses it again."

Blue wasn't a trainer, but he guessed that was some
kind of desensitization technique. That made sense because all four of the horses were wary and distrustful.

Which sort of described Marin herself.

After their "guilt trip" conversation three days ago,
Blue had vowed not to question her anymore about
her sister or the reasons she felt as if the "something
bad that'd happened" had been her fault. He followed
through on the no questions, but he'd failed big-time to
control his urge to do internet searches on her.

He hadn't needed the info in the articles to know she was a superstar in her profession because Blue had personally seen the progress she was making with the mares. Still, he'd read through those trying to get to the gist of what had happened to her three years ago. And he'd found it.

Sort of.

There were accounts of her sister's tragic death in a car crash three years ago when Selene had only been twenty-five. So, she was Marin's younger sister since Blue had also looked through Marin's employment contract and knew that she was thirty-two, two years younger than he was. That meant if the age was right in the articles, that Marin was four years older than Selene.

So, Selene had been her kid sister. Something that Blue knew about since he had one himself. He would do anything to save Remi even if she often was snarky and a pain in his ass. She was also a decorated Air Force Combat Rescue Officer who'd sacrifice her own life for others. The latter wasn't the reason he loved her and would do anything for her, but it didn't hurt.

Yeah, he'd do anything to save Remi, all right. And if the "anything" failed, he'd blame himself just as Marin was apparently doing. But Blue hadn't been able to find anything to point to why Marin put herself on that particular "guilt trip" road. Marin hadn't been the driver of the car that'd crashed and killed her kid sister. The driver had been a guy named Drew Carson, a DJ, who'd apparently sustained only minor injuries despite the fact that neither Selene nor he had been wearing seat belts and the car had been exceeding the speed limit.

Of course, Blue had dug into Drew Carson and there'd been a lot more on him than on Selene or even Marin. Judging from the sheer number of posts and pictures, the guy loved social media. He clearly loved himself, too, because there was picture after picture of his various exploits from trips to exotic beaches to mountain climbing.

There were enough photos to cause Blue to conclude the guy was an adrenaline junkie. A good-looking one who, again judging from the pictures, attracted plenty of women. And that might explain why Marin didn't want to act on the obvious attraction between them. If Selene had been involved with this guy, and he'd turned out to be bad news, then that could be messing with Marin's head now.

Blue couldn't blame her. All sorts of things could mess with your head, and in his case, the lack of memories about that crash landing were wreaking havoc with him.

Chad finally made it back to the ranch, and he pulled into the side driveway, probably because there weren't as many steps here as there were on the other portions of the porch. Fewer steps, less pain, but Blue didn't want the shorter, less painful route. After he thanked Chad for the ride, he limped his way to the front porch and climbed his way up, up, up. If his knee and ribs could talk, they'd be flinging f-bombs at him right about now.

He cursed the flight suit he'd insisted on wearing. He'd put it on, not easily, since it had been like squeezing his still swollen knee into a sausage casing. But he had refused any other clothing choice. No way was he, a test pilot, going to show up at the base in civvies. Besides, the uniform had a way of grounding him.

Usually.

It hadn't especially worked this time, but he was reasonably sure if he'd donned those civvies, he would have been feeling even crappier.

Breathing hard and hurting a hell of a lot more than he wanted, he stepped into the cool AC of the foyer and immediately heard laughter.

Correction: he heard giggling.

Specifically, Leo's giggles.

Blue had intended on going straight to his room—which meant more stairs—so he could brood and possibly even sulk, but instead he limped his way toward the sound in the kitchen. Not an especially short trek, but that could be said about any room in the massive house. When he'd been a kid, Cal and Egan had convinced him that more rooms grew overnight, springing up like magic, and that he'd never be able to find them all. Part of Blue still believed that might be possible.

He paused a moment, then two, outside the kitchen so he could level his breathing, and then he stepped in. Yep, Leo was there, all right, with Grammy Effie and Maybell. Not a big surprise since he'd been spending time with them while Marin worked.

Leo beamed out a big smile to Blue. One of those hero-worship smiles that made Blue squirm. The kid really did need to know the truth about him. Though Blue had to admit, he would miss being looked at as if he were the greatest thing since Nutella. Still, the talk needed to happen once the boy was well.

"I'm sick," Leo announced, chowing down on a chocolate chip cookie that was practically as big as the kid's head.

Blue had a déjà vu moment of his own childhood illnesses where he'd been pampered with chicken noodle soup and cookies right here in this very kitchen and with these very women. Leo was in mighty good hands.

"How sick are you?" Blue asked, and he snagged a cookie for himself.

Thankfully, the pain hadn't dulled his appetite. Then again, there probably wasn't anything that could put him off one of Maybell's cookies. Apparently, Leo had a fondness for them, too.

"A little bit sick," Leo admitted. He pointed to a small chocolate blob in the cookie. "Maybe that little."

"Good." Still, Blue studied him and was relieved when he didn't see any signs of the cold that'd sidelined him.

"Leo's been hanging out with us in the kitchen," Effie explained, "and testing out some new recipes."

Blue glanced at the counter and spotted some homemade pizza, nachos and, yeah, homemade chicken noodle soup.

"I ate some of all of it," Leo proudly announced, "and then I got a cookie. After this, I gotta get back on the computer and do the rest of my classes."

The boy didn't seem disappointed about that, but it was possible he was used to doing virtual classes.

"Grammy Effie's gonna help me with homework if I need it," Leo added.

Blue met Effie's gaze to see if she objected to Leo calling her Grammy. Apparently not, even though both

Effie and Maybell knew the boy wasn't Blue's. Still, it could be like an honorary title.

"Are you going to help Aunt Marin with her owie?" Leo asked.

Again, Blue glanced at Effie to see if there was something wrong. "One of the mares had a little problem about fifteen minutes ago," Effie said, her voice and expression unruffled.

But Blue thought that unruffled stuff was all for Leo's sake. Hell. Had Marin been hurt? He wanted to know, but Blue also didn't want to alarm Leo. That was why he kept his "question" to a long look that he aimed at Effie.

"Marin's fine," his grandmother assured him. "Maybell saw her go into the barn, and she texted her to make sure everything was okey dokey. It is."

"Okey dokey?" Blue repeated.

"It's funny sounding," Leo said, giggling. "Sounds like donkey."

Yeah, it did, but since Leo was laughing, it meant he wasn't worried about Marin. That was good because Blue knew for certain that Marin wouldn't want the boy upset over something that'd happened to her.

"How'd your appointment at the base go?" Maybell asked, pouring Blue a glass of milk to go with his cookie.

"Great," Blue lied. "I'm only a little bit hurt now," he said, paraphrasing Leo.

Clearly, neither Maybell nor Effie believed him, but Blue was hoping if he said it enough, it would become true. Or at least the perceived truth so that Maybell, Effie and his family didn't look so damn worried about him.

"Where is Marin?" he asked. His question was two-fold. He wanted to get off the subject of his appointment, and he truly wanted to know if she was okay.

"She's probably still in the barn," Effie replied. "Maybe putting some ice on her foot. Have her come in if it's giving her trouble."

Blue opened his mouth to ask what the heck had happened to Marin's foot, but he decided to see for himself. He issued an "I'll be back" at Leo, and Blue took his milk and cookie to head to the barn. He grabbed another cookie for Marin. It wouldn't be a cure-all for an injury, but he figured it wouldn't hurt, either.

This time, Blue went down the slope. And nearly landed on his ass when he stumbled. Since he also spilled some milk, dumping a large portion of it onto his flight suit, he downed the rest of the milk and set the glass on a chair beneath a towering oak, then he went to the barn with his one and a half cookies in tow.

He stepped in, immediately getting hit with the smells of saddle soap, leather and the horses. Definitely not a bad combo but one that always steadied him. Just as his uniform usually did.

As usual, the barn was a whole lot cleaner than most other barns with nothing, including hay, strewn on the floor. And it was relatively cool compared to the outside temps. That was thanks to the industrial fans that had been built high into the walls. It wasn't quite as effective as air-conditioning, but it gave the hands and horses a break from the heat.

Apparently, not today, though.

There wasn't a hand or a horse in sight. No Marin,

either. So Blue went to the back where there was a break room with a fridge and coffee maker, and he found her hopping around like a bunny. His first thought—a bad one—was that she'd broken her foot, but then he saw that one of her boots was off and on the other side of the room by the well-worn leather sofa. She was apparently hopping to get to it.

She was wearing her usual jeans and a gray work shirt. No hat, though. It was on the sofa. And it appeared she'd been shoving her hands through her hair or something since parts of it were standing up in damp spikes.

Her head whipped up when she spotted him in the doorway, and she looked up at him, surprise in her eyes. Then, she muttered what he was pretty sure was some profanity born out of frustration. He was guessing that frustration was because she hadn't wanted anyone to see her hobbling. He *totally* got that.

"I brought you a cookie," he said, trying to ease some of that frustration. "It won't cure a limp. I'm proof of that. But it's a gazillion calories of goodness."

Sighing, she took the cookie he offered and then continued toward the sofa where she plopped down and pressed a handful of wet paper towels to her foot. Even though this room was relatively clean, too, Blue could see what had gone on here. There was a wad of wet paper towels in the trash can under the sink and some water drops on the floor. Marin had probably removed her boot, gone to the sink to wash her foot and get more paper towels before she had then done the hopping.

"I told Jesse and the other hands I was fine," she said like a challenge for Blue to dispute that.

He intended on disputing nothing right now. He hobbled to the sofa, too, and sank down next to her so he could get a better look at her foot. It was bruised, and Blue had some more déjà vu.

"Looks like the horse stepped on you," he remarked. "Been there, done that. Is it broken?"

"No. It's fine. It'll be fine," she amended. "I made a stupid rookie mistake. I was working on Pearl, trying to get her used to the saddle so she wouldn't shiver and rear when she caught sight of it. Cottontail no longer has a problem with the saddle, but she went into the 'monkey see, monkey do' mode and panicked when Pearl did. Cottontail stepped on my foot before I could get out of the way. Rookie mistake," she repeated in a mumble.

"Ranch hands get stepped on all the time," Blue pointed out.

"But good trainers don't," she concluded like gospel, but then she shrugged. "I don't usually get stepped on."

Blue couldn't fault her for those high standards, but he felt compelled to point out something. "According to what I've seen when I've watched you from my bedroom window, you've made solid progress with Pearl and Cottontail."

After he heard those words come out of his mouth, he realized just how creepy and stalker-ish they sounded.

"Sorry," he tacked on to that. "It's just that part of the pasture is in the direct line of sight from my window." Well, it was if he leaned all the way to the left side. Which he'd been doing. "Solid progress," he emphasized.

"I'm doing my job," she muttered. "Or rather I *was* doing it."

"Will this put you out of commission for a while?" he risked asking.

"No." She managed to keep the paper towels in place, hold on to her cookie and check the time on her watch. "I'll consider this my lunch break. Then, I'll pop some ibuprofen, check on Leo and go back to work."

"I just saw Leo. He's doing great. And FYI, that's not the kind of *great* that needs to be put in air quotes. He's having a blast with Maybell and Effie. Now, I will put air quotes around the word *blast*, because it involves a bit of a food and a sugar high. They're keeping him well-fed, and I can guarantee you that both women are loving every minute of it."

Marin sighed and took a bite of the cookie. She made a "mercy, this is good" sound that reminded him of sex. Then again, a lot of things reminded him of sex whenever he was around Marin.

"I feel like I'm imposing on them with the babysitting. I asked them for recommendations for sitters, but they said they'd be happy to do it."

"You're not imposing. You're giving them a chance to relive their glory days of when me and my siblings were kids." He paused, rethought that. "Okay, maybe not glory since there were four of us, and I wasn't living up to my call sign of Angel then, but they love cooking, baking and taking care of people."

"They're both very good, very generous women." She took another bite of the cookie, made another of those pleasure sounds.

"Yeah, they are," Blue was quick to agree. "Grammy

Effie moved here after my mom died, and Maybell started shortly thereafter."

"Effie said it was okay for Leo to call her Grammy. Is it?" Marin wanted to know.

"It's all good," he assured her and was relieved that seemed to settle her a little. He couldn't say her expression was frustration-free, but he thought both the conversation and the sugary chocolate were helping.

She took another bite and then looked at him as if truly seeing him for the first time. "You're in uniform. Because of your doctor's appointment at the base," she concluded. "Do you want me to ask how that went?"

"No." Blue couldn't say that fast enough. "But if Effie, Maybell or Egan asks, tell them I'm okey dokey."

She frowned. "You want me to use those exact words or something more manly like A-okay?"

"Use okey dokey. It'll amuse them for a second or two while you change the subject. And speaking of a subject change, what can you tell me about Leo's father?"

Obviously, she hadn't been expecting the chat to go in that direction, but Blue hadn't been able to research the man since he hadn't known his name. And there'd been nothing about him on Jussie's archived social media pages. No mention of him in her obituary, either.

"Well, like I said, there was a reason Jussie never told Leo about his real father, Brian Petty. The man's an asshole."

The name sounded familiar. "Did he ride rodeo?"

She nodded. "Bulls, but I don't think he was very good at it. Jussie hooked up with him at the rodeo, though. They were together a couple of years, but never married," Marin explained. "And when she told Brian she was pregnant, he up and left. He showed up twice in the time I knew Jussie, and both times it was to try to borrow money from her. He never once asked about Leo, and he wouldn't even test for the bone marrow registry when Leo got sick."

Asshole was too kind of a term for a man like that. So, yeah, Blue could see why Jussie had lied to the kid.

"When you tell Leo the truth, will you also tell him about the asshole?" Blue wanted to know.

"I'm debating that. But probably not. Leo would likely want to try to research him or hear stories about him, and I don't know any good stories about the asshole. I think I'll just tell him that you're not his father and then will use a kid-friendly way of telling him that his asshole sperm donor isn't around. I'll make sure Leo understands that's the asshole's loss so he doesn't feel abandoned."

Even though there was nothing about this conversation that was funny, her repeated use of *asshole* made him smile. And Marin noticed, too.

"What?" she asked, her back going up a little.

"I'm just glad Leo has you on his side," he settled for saying.

Marin relaxed and even did a little smiling herself. She also locked gazes with him. That caused the smile to vanish, but the eye lock stayed in place.

Blue could see the battle she was having with herself over resisting every inch of him. And it was a battle he thought she could win. Not him, though. Nope, and he couldn't even blame a fuzzy head because of the pain.

He had pain, all right, but at the moment it wasn't nearly enough to cause him not to make the bad decision he was about to attempt.

"I want to get something straight," he said. "I'm not your boss. You report to Egan or Jesse. I'm not in your chain of command."

"Okey dokey," she said with a whole boatload of caution. "Why are you telling me that?"

Blue went with it, spelling it out for her. "Because I want to kiss you, and that wouldn't be appropriate if you worked for me."

She made a small sound of startled surprise. Not a huff, though. It was more like the sound she'd made when she'd discovered the cookie was as good as he'd claimed. What she didn't do was tell him to go to hell or move away from him.

Gazes stayed firmly connected.

He heard the change in her breathing. Quicker now. And he thought that might be a whole bunch of heat he saw in her eyes. Still, he didn't move in on her mouth. He wanted to give her that chance to put a stop to this before it even started.

But she didn't stop it.

Marin uttered a single word of profanity, leaned in and did something that Blue certainly hadn't seen coming.

She kissed him.

Her mouth—which he noticed right off was warm and soft—landed against his. Not some "hungry, I need you now" contact. It was testing. Gentle. But then, she groaned, cursed again and pressed harder.

She tasted good. Of course, she did. But he didn't

think it was all the chocolate chip cookie's doing. Even beneath all that caloric goodness, he could still take in Marin's taste.

And yeah, she lived up to the expectations.

The hunger came. Man, did it. That pressure kicked up a whole volcano of heat that made him want to take this kiss to the next level. But he still didn't push despite his body yelling at him to do just that.

Marin finally pulled back, meeting his gaze head-on again. Judging from her glazed eyes, flushed face and quick jerks of breath, the kiss had lived up to her expectations as well. Had maybe even exceeded them. Still, it didn't surprise him when she said what she did.

"We shouldn't do that again," she muttered.

Yep, he was right there with her. But Blue knew something else. That *shouldn't* didn't always behave itself.

He cursed, too, because he knew that his life, and Marin's, had just gotten a hell of a lot more complicated.

CHAPTER NINE

MARIN SILENTLY CURSED herself again, something she'd been doing for the past two days since the curse-worthy event had happened. She had kissed Blue. Kissed him.

On the mouth. On the very mouth that she should have been avoiding. Yet, she hadn't, even though he'd given her ample time to move away from him after he'd spelled out his intentions to kiss her.

Not only had she not put a stop to it, she'd initiated the kiss.

Talk about a rookie mistake. The bruised foot was a drop in the bucket compared to kissing a man she should be... Marin stopped the mental lecture. Not the silent cursing, though, because it was a waste of energy to lie to herself and say it wouldn't happen again.

It would.

Blue and she were apparently stupid when it came to each other. Strange, since she was normally a non-stupid person. Or least she hadn't been since Selene's death, anyway. And she thought Blue might not fall into the reckless category, either. A risk-taker, yes, but even he had to know that kissing or anything else between them was a really bad idea.

Blue was a fighter pilot, a guy who gobbled up dangerous duty and relocated every two to three years. She was grounded here in Texas with Leo. A grounding she wanted. She truly did. And that caused her to dole out more mental cursing. Because there was no need for her to spell out why things wouldn't work between Blue and her. Especially work out to the point where one of them would need to give up their wings or their roots. Nope. The most that could come out of this deal with Blue was sex.

That mentally stopped her.

Her brain should have been flashing huge warning signs about risking her heart to have sex with Blue. It wasn't. And she could blame the kiss for that. Kissing broke down barriers and made all things seem possible. Or at least incredible for a moment or two. But incredible stuff could come with a massive price tag, and she didn't have the mental energy for another broken heart.

Trying to put that thought aside and the incredible sensation she got from the memory of the kiss, Marin forced herself to get back to work. Not with the Andalusians this afternoon, but rather with the three boarded horses that'd been moved to Saddlebrook. They had a much better setup here than at the rental place. No surprise there. It was like moving from a cheap economy car to a Ferrari.

There was no need for Marin to check the feed and water supply since Saddlebrook had automatic systems in place for that. She did, however, clean out the small barn, even though Jesse had assured her the ranch had crews to do that. These three horses weren't Saddlebrook's responsibility. They were hers, and she was being paid to take care of them. For now, anyway.

With the generous salary Egan was giving her, she really didn't need to supplement her income, and while she loved tending horses, the boarded ones did take time. Time away from Leo since she didn't come to the small side pasture with the boarded horses until she'd finished for the day with the Andalusian mares. Since this job at Saddlebrook seemed to be working out for both Leo and her, she'd soon talk to the owners of the boarded horses about making other arrangements for them.

She would also need to have that chat with Leo. The one to tell him the truth about Blue. She'd put it off because he'd been sick, but it had to happen soon.

Marin finished cleaning and washed up using the faucet and hose on the side of the barn. It was almost five o'clock, which meant she had to be getting back to pick up Leo from the main house where Marin had dropped him off after she'd picked him up from school. It was an arrangement that Effie and Maybell had insisted on. Marin had agreed, for now, anyway, but she was still doing phone interviews with sitters who could not only pick up Leo from school, but also be with him on sick days.

Thankfully, Leo had quickly recovered from his cold, and there hadn't been any complications. But he was a kid and would get other colds. Marin didn't want Effie and Maybell to have to be nurses along with what they were already doing.

She started toward the gelding she'd ridden out to the boarded horses, and she caught sight of a white stallion and rider coming across the pasture toward her. Lowering the brim of her hat to shield her eyes from the sun, she took a longer look and saw that it was the new arrogant stallion, Iceman. Not in a gallop, though she suspected that was the stallion's preferred gait. The rider had Iceman in a controlled trot. Then, she made out the face of the rider.

Blue.

What the heck was he doing? She hadn't heard any gossip about Blue being cleared to ride. Just the opposite. She'd heard murmurs about him not healing as fast as he'd expected or wanted. Yet, here he was on the back of a magnificent stallion that had the personality of a wild mustang.

Of course, the same could be said of Blue.

Oh, mercy. He looked good. Of course, that was the default look for Blue. Good and hot. No flight suit today. He was all cowboy in his jeans, hat and boots. He was still wearing the brace, though, on his knee.

"Should you be doing this?" she had to ask when he reined in next to the gelding.

"Riding doesn't make my knee hurt." Blue grinned. "Getting in the saddle was no fun, though. I had some help. But it was worth it to take Iceman out for a test flight."

Iceman didn't look so appreciative, and Marin thought the stallion might be giving the gelding a high and mighty look to establish his dominance. The gelding didn't bite, not literally or figuratively. He just continued to munch on some grass.

Blue tipped his head toward her foot. "How's the bruise?"

"Walking doesn't make it hurt," she settled for saying, though it was still there and gave her twinges when she moved wrong. It hadn't stopped her, though, from doing any parts of her job. "I was about to head back to the main house to pick up Leo."

"I'll ride back with you." Blue gave Iceman's neck a long stroke. "I didn't give him as much of a workout as he wanted, but he'll enjoy eyeing the mares. I think he fancies Cottontail."

"It's mutual. Cottontail fancies him," Marin was quick to say, and while she dreaded getting into this next part with Blue, it was something he should know. "Cottontail has shown some initial signs of going into heat," she said, climbing onto the gelding. "It's often hard to tell that with a mare from her circumstances since the abuse and neglect have similar symptoms to the heat."

Blue nodded. "Increased anxiety, unpredictable behavior and an interest in stallions?"

Yes, this wasn't a comfortable discussion. Especially since Marin knew those symptoms applied to her and her reaction to Blue. Anxiety, unpredictability and an interest in him.

Like now, for instance.

She glanced at the fit of his jeans and felt herself go warm in all the wrong places. Good grief.

"Anyway," she went on, "if Cottontail truly is in heat, we'll know in a day or two." She kept the gelding at the slowest gait possible to minimize the jiggling movements for Blue's knee.

"Is Cottontail anywhere ready to be covered by Iceman?" Blue asked.

Again, an uncomfortable subject, and while Blue didn't smile, he did seem to have a glimmer in his eyes to confirm this conversation was happening on more than the surface level.

Marin's response wasn't going to help matters.

"The urge for Cottontail to mate could be a temporary cure for what ails her," Marin explained. "Temporary," she emphasized. "She'll probably be receptive to the stallion and will go through with what her body is urging her to do. But afterward when the basic instinct is sated, she'll probably revert to her old self."

Blue stared at her. And stared. "Those basic instincts can, indeed, fix a whole bunch of stuff." He chuckled. "I'm going to need a cold shower when I get home."

She nearly blurted out that she'd be taking one as well, but that gave her a flash of a naked Blue being doused with water. Yes, Cottontail wasn't the only one showing interest in a daredevil.

They continued along at their slow, leisurely pace that was in contrast to the thoughts and heat that had kicked up inside her. Thankfully, though, she had something to cool her down and bring herself back in check.

"I have a friend coming over later," Marin said.

Something else flashed in Blue's eyes. Jealousy, maybe? Again, maybe a projection on her part. It occurred to her, and not in a good way, either, that she had a similar reaction when women came to visit Blue. And there was a steady stream of them. That one kiss had clearly broken down barriers that should have stayed in place. In this case, though, there was no reason for jealousy.

"Gina Kinney," Marin explained. "She's a friend and also a counselor. The plan is for me to order pizza and then tell Leo the truth about you not being his father."

A different sort of emotion flashed through his eyes. "I saw Leo at the house before I went out for a ride, and he seems good. Is he?"

Marin nodded. "No trace of the cold, and his lab work came back with no red flags." The blood tests had been standard for someone with his medical history. "I doubt there'll ever be an ideal time to tell him, but I think tonight will work. He loves pizza and Gina so that'll put him in a good mood."

"You said before that it'd be okay for me to be there when you tell him," Blue reminded her. "Is that still true?"

"It is." She sighed and looked at him. "But if it's something you want to skip, I'll totally understand. I'm not sure how he'll react. There might be tears or even a tantrum—"

"I want to be there," Blue insisted. "What time?"

She checked the time again. "I told Gina to be here at six, so in about an hour." That would give Marin enough time to pick up Leo, shower and for the pizza to be delivered. They could eat together, and then she could tell Leo.

Somehow.

Marin still wasn't sure exactly what to say to him when she delivered this bombshell that would change his life forever. Again. A tantrum was possible, though she'd never experienced one of those with Leo. When he'd been a toddler and therefore in the potential tantrum stage, he'd been too sick for such things.

Blue and she continued their ride, and as they got closer to the barn, she spotted both Pearl and Cottontail. And the mares spotted them. Both trotted toward the fence to admire the horse hunk that Blue was riding. Iceman confirmed that Cottontail and maybe Pearl were in heat when he did a classic flehmen response of lifting his head and curling his lips.

Marin sighed. Heat would only last about six days, and she'd have to talk to Egan or Jesse sooner than later about whether or not they wanted to test out if the mares were ready for Iceman. She really hoped, though, if horse sex did happen that Blue wouldn't be around.

When they made it back to the barn, there was a ranch hand/groomer, Elsie Granger, waiting to take the horses. That, too, was the norm at Saddlebrook, however Marin preferred to tend to the horses herself. She didn't now, though, since the clock was ticking on that conversation she needed to have with Leo.

"I'll take care of them," Blue told Elsie.

"Oh," the groomer said and then blinked. "You're sure you can manage that?"

"I'm sure," he insisted, and this time he sounded more like a boss than a cowboy who'd just taken a superstar stallion for a ride.

Blue didn't budge until Elsie was out of the barn, and then he looked at her. "I can handle the horses," he repeated. "Just not sure, though, I can get out of the saddle without a whole lot of wincing and grunts. If you'd rather not be around for that, you can head on to the house."

"No. I can help you." At least she thought she could. She climbed down out of the saddle and to Blue. "What should I do?"

"If you can, just kind of cushion my landing," he muttered.

That sounded easy. It wasn't. Because it involved some maneuvering. First, for Blue who had to swing his injured knee over the top of the saddle while putting the foot of his uninjured leg into the stirrup. He ended up in the more traditional dismount position with his rather superior butt sliding against her breasts as he made his way down while she put her hands on his waist and abs.

Marin felt herself react. A bad reaction. Because she was still zinging from memories of the kiss, touching Blue caused all sorts of fresh heat to spring up. Hot, scalding heat.

He moved slowly, so slow—the body slide lasted for what seemed long enough for at least a dozen orgasms. He continued the slow pace when he anchored his good leg on the ground and then eased down his injured one. He stumbled just a little, enough for Marin to tighten her grip on him, but she also tried to be mindful of his cracked ribs.

Blue turned, and she saw no signs of pain on his face. Just the opposite. He was clearly just as aroused as she was, and Iceman must have picked up on it because he snorted. That should have been Marin's cue to get moving, but she stayed put, debating if she should go ahead and screw things up six ways to Sunday by kissing Blue again.

She didn't get the chance, though.

Marin heard the sound of approaching footsteps a split second before Gina said, "Well." Her friend was there, right in the barn door where she'd no doubt had an excellent view of the foreplay dismount. "Did you two have a nice ride?"

It wasn't even a veiled question because Gina was smiling and loaded her tone with, oh, so much amusement and teasing. Since Marin didn't want said teasing to continue, she let go of Blue—and felt her body immediately whimper in protest. Then, she went to Gina and purposely pulled her in for what would be a sweaty, smelly hug.

"Ewww," Gina protested in a whisper.

"Serves you right," Marin whispered back, and she turned around to face Blue again who appeared to be enjoying his own moment of amusement and teasing. "Blue, this is my friend, Gina. Gina, this is Major Blue Donnelly."

"Blue," he automatically said, and he shook Gina's hand when she offered it. "It's good to meet you. Don't worry, I'll shower before we talk to Leo."

"We?" Gina asked, glancing at Marin.

Marin nodded. "Blue wants to be there for the talk."

"A great idea," Gina concluded. "How are you with outbursts from kids?"

"No experience whatsoever," Blue quickly answered.

"Good." Gina patted his arm. "Then you'll do just fine. We'll expect the best and deal with the worst if it happens. Experience might have led you to forget how to expect the best."

Blue nodded, looked at Marin. "I'll deal with these horses, put Iceman in the pasture so he can, well, do stallion stuff, and I'll be over at your cabin after I've showered. Want me to bring anything to go with the pizza? Maybell made fresh cookies today."

Until he added that last part, she'd been about to say no, but Maybell's cookies had a therapeutic effect. Hard to be pissed off, crushed or throw a tantrum when eating one of those.

"That'd be nice, thanks," Marin told him, and she hooked her arm through Gina's to get them moving.

Gina didn't say a single word until they were out of the barn. "Great day, he's hot. How the heck can you focus on work when surrounded by all that hotness?"

"It's a challenge," Marin admitted. No way, though, would she tell Gina about the kiss because the queen of matchmaking would spring into action.

"So, how good of a kisser is he?" Gina asked as they made their way to the big house.

Marin groaned. At times, she could swear that Gina had been issued ESP with her counseling degree. "Good. Though we haven't actually kissed." She felt Gina's gaze slide to her. "Well, it wasn't a long kiss. Just a lapse of judgment on my part."

"So, you initiated it. Good for you." Gina gave her a little poke with her elbow.

Marin repeated her groan. "Blue will be leaving the ranch as soon as he's able to return to duty."

"And in the meantime, you can play around with

him," Gina was quick to point out. "Nothing that would risk your heart. Or his. Though he might already have his heart under control."

Marin suspected he did and hoped it was true. She was already acting irrationally enough around him, and it was best if Blue didn't jump on that irrational train along with her.

"It's risky to play around with one of the owners of the ranch where I want to continue working," Marin pointed out, which she wanted to serve as a reminder to herself.

"He's not your boss," Gina said with complete authority. "He is." She tipped her head to the back porch where Marin saw Egan pacing while talking to someone on the phone. "I met him when I got here and was looking for you."

"Yes, he's the boss," Marin verified. "But all the Donnelly siblings co-own the place."

Marin didn't get a chance to make sure that was crystal clear to Gina so all matchmaking would cease and desist because Egan finished his call, spotted them and came down the porch steps to meet them.

"Good," Egan said. "You found her." He turned to Marin. "I was just on the phone with the abused mares' previous owner. Figured I'd better take the call out here in case it involved some curse words that I'd prefer my grandmother, Maybell and Leo not hear."

Marin totally understood that. She wouldn't be able to get through a conversation with the asshat without profanity.

"Anyway, I closed the deal on the sale," Egan went

on. "That means we'll bring in six other horses within the week. Four mares, a gelding and a stallion. I don't expect you to work with all of them right away, but I want them here at Saddlebrook so we can get them out of their current hellhole and then assess their needs. If the assessments go the way I think they will, then some of them will be under veterinary care for a while."

Mercy, it hurt to hear that, and it would no doubt send her through a heart wrenching when she finally met them. At least there was a solid bright light at the end of this particular tunnel. The horses would soon get help and start to heal.

Marin nodded, trying to keep the emotion out of her voice. "I'll help in any way I can."

That might include training at least one of the other hands in natural horsemanship techniques, but that could be a good thing, too, in case she ever had to take any time off because of Leo's health.

"I did a progress report on Pearl, Cottontail, Dolly and Princess and sent copies to Jesse and you," Marin explained after Egan nodded in response to her assurance of help. "Have you had a chance to read it?"

"I have. You're doing good work. Damn good." His phone rang again, and after glancing at the screen, he didn't answer it. Egan pinned his attention back to Marin. "You were riding with Blue?" Egan asked.

"Uh, not really. He took Iceman out for a test ride and ended up at the area with the boarded horses. We came back together."

"Did Blue do okay on the ride?" Egan asked, but

then he immediately waved that off. "It'd be better if I asked him myself."

Marin's sound of agreement was quick and certain. And the truth was, she didn't know how Blue had done. He hadn't complained much about being in pain, but it was possible that the ride had been excruciating. Well, except for that dismount. She definitely hadn't seen any misery then.

"Have a good evening," Egan said to them, and taking out his phone again, he made a call while heading to the barn. No doubt to check on Blue for himself.

Marin took a step toward the house, but Gina tightened her grip on her arm to keep her in place. "Just hold on a second before you go in and get Leo," Gina said. "There's something you should know." Gina definitely had no teasing or amused expression now.

Sweet heaven. What now? "What's wrong?" Marin immediately began to mentally flip through the possibilities. Leo was fine so it wasn't that. Well, hopefully it wasn't. And Marin didn't have any family to speak of so it wasn't that. But that left Gina herself. "Did something happen to you?"

Gina shook her head. "I'm fine." Then she paused, letting Marin know that all was not well. "I got a call earlier. From Leo's dad."

That sure as heck hadn't been on Marin's radar. "Why would Brian call you?"

"Apparently because he didn't have your number." Gina paused again, then sighed.

And that was when Marin knew what this was all about. "Does Brian want money?"

"Probably, but he didn't come out and say it. He said he'd seen an article about you coming here to work at Saddlebrook, but he didn't want to bother you." Gina rolled her eyes. "I think bothering you was exactly what he had in mind, but he's too much of a chickenshit to leave a message for you at the ranch. So, he remembered we were friends, and he called my office instead."

Gina was right about the chickenshit part. Brian was a classic bully. In other words, a coward. No way would he want to risk locking horns with Egan. Both Egan and his dad had a tough reputation and that would have come through loud and clear in anything Brian read about Saddlebrook.

"Brian wanted to know if you had Leo with you," Gina said, causing Marin's heart to stutter for a few beats.

"Shit," Marin muttered.

"Yeah, my sentiments exactly. I lied to him," Gina quickly assured her. "I said I didn't have a clue where Leo was." She looked Marin straight in the eyes. "But I have to tell you, I don't think that's the last we've heard of the chickenshit."

No, Marin quietly agreed. It wouldn't be the last.

CHAPTER TEN

BLUE TRIED NOT to wince too much when he stepped from the shower. His knee was doing a whole lot of protesting by throbbing like hell, but Blue didn't regret the ride on Iceman. He'd needed it because it was part of his normal life when he was at Saddlebrook.

Normal was his goal, not just for the ranch, but for everything else in his life.

He had to get back in the cockpit, and yeah, that caused him a twinge or two of a different sort. Because it would mean leaving Marin and Leo. But leaving was normal, too. He'd done it for years with his family, first with the rodeo and college and then with the Air Force. He always got those twinges when he said goodbye, but he'd never gotten them with anyone other than family and close friends.

Apparently, Marin and Leo were in the "close friends" category now, too.

So, twinges would happen, but he would cope the way he always did. By throwing himself into work and staying in contact by text and the occasional calls. He wasn't sure about Leo's current texting skills, but the kid would get better as he got older.

And that reminder caused Blue to frown.

Not about the "kid getting older" part, but that Leo might not want much of anything to do with him once he learned the truth about Blue not being his father. Leo certainly wouldn't look at him with that hero worship in his eyes. That caused Blue some twinges, too, and added another level of dread to this pizza party at Marin's that wouldn't be a party at all.

Blue dressed in jeans and a black tee. Not easily. Nothing was easy breezy these days. For some reason, that caused Marin's face to pop into his mind. Not her expression when she had her guard up around him. But the one right after she'd pulled back from that kiss where she'd been all rosy and flushed with arousal. With her lips slightly parted, her eyes issuing all sorts of invitations.

Yep, there'd be twinges when he left her.

Possibly regrets, too. Not having sex with her might make it worse. At least that was what the brainless part of him behind the zipper of his jeans was telling him. That part was insisting that if the sex didn't happen, then Blue would only lust after Marin even more. That she'd stay in his system a lot longer than his actual lovers had.

That was bullshit, of course.

Sex with Marin would almost certainly lead to both him and the brainless part wanting more, more, more. And more could not only complicate the hell out of both their lives, it could cause her to get hurt. Blue didn't know all her secrets and what had put that haunted look in her eyes, but he was dead certain he didn't want to hurt her.

He'd already caused too much of that without adding more.

That reminder brought on a different flash in his head. Of Airman Casey Newell. Since Blue checked often, he knew the airman was still in a coma and had been for eighteen days now. Not exactly a good stat, but according to one of the nurses who was giving Blue reports, the family hadn't given up hope. Blue prayed that hope didn't get crushed as the hours and days lingered.

Remembering Casey had Blue cursing his own throbbing knee. A bashed knee was small in the grand scheme of things, and he felt guilty as hell for being able to walk, or rather semi-walk, when Casey couldn't do anything but lie in a bed and when his family could do nothing but wait.

With that dismal reminder dragging him down, Blue checked the time and was pleased that it'd been a full hour and fifteen minutes since Marin and her friend Gina had left him in the barn, which meant he should be right on time for pizza delivery followed by the dreaded talk with Leo.

Blue snagged the cookies that he'd already put in a plastic container and said a quick goodbye to Maybell and Effie, who were having their dinner in the kitchen. Then, he headed out to yet something else he dreaded. It was nowhere at the level of dread as the talk with Leo, but it was a compromise.

A big-assed one as far as he was concerned.

He went to the side area where the ranch vehicles were parked and immediately spotted the rental truck that he'd had delivered earlier in the day. It had an automatic transmission, something his dad would have never purchased for any of the ranch vehicles. Blue much preferred the old-school manuals as well, but since his knee couldn't handle a clutch and he was tired of being chauffeured around, the automatic had been the compromise.

Blue got in and was thankful that nothing hurt when he drove. Nothing other than a few protests from his ribs when he hit a bump on the narrow road that led to the cabin, but even that pain was nowhere near the level it had been two and a half weeks ago.

He parked outside the log and white stone guest cabin that had once been his. Marin probably didn't know that, but his dad had had cabins built for all four of his kids as they'd each turned eighteen. Blue figured that was his dad's way of giving them all their own space to encourage them to come home.

No encouragement had been needed, though.

Blue and the others came home as much as their military commitments allowed, and while Blue had stayed in his cabin a time or two, he preferred his old room in the main house. That way, he could chow down on Maybell's superior cooking without having to make a drive. His siblings must have felt that way, too, because they pretty much did the same.

After a couple of years of the cabin staying empty, Blue had offered it up as guest quarters to be used whenever by whomever. He was pleased that Marin and Leo had been the *whoever*. Not only because Marin was doing a good job with the training, but also because Blue liked having Leo and her around.

Before Blue even made it to the front porch, the door opened, and Leo greeted him with a big smile and a hug. Yeah, he liked having the kid around, all right, even when there was a possible crap storm on the horizon.

"You brought cookies. And you rode Iceman," Leo announced with a pre-sugar high sort of glee. He took hold of Blue's hand and pulled him in.

"I did," Blue verified.

"Did you get to go real fast and jump over things?"

Blue didn't think the kid was referring to a reaction to the sugar high from the cookies. Nope, this was about riding Iceman, and he had to shake his head. "Not this time. I took it slow."

Some of the kid's glee vanished. "'Cause of your sore leg?"

"And because Iceman and I were just getting to know each other. I'll soon get him to go real fast and maybe jump over things if he's in the right mood."

That last part was a massive exaggeration since Iceman wasn't a show horse, but Blue was glad to see it caused the kid's smile to return. Good. He wanted all the smiles possible since Blue figured there wouldn't be any after the chat.

Since the cabin had an open-concept floor plan, it wasn't hard for Blue to spot Marin and Gina in the kitchen. There were two boxes of pizza and soft drinks on the counter.

"You made it," Gina said, smiling, but not in a flirty kind of way. No, this was more of a "I know Marin and you have the hots for each other" sort of thing. That made Blue wonder if Marin had told her, or if Gina had picked up on it all on her own.

The latter, he decided, when he recalled that Gina had walked in on Marin and him in that touchy, huggy moment in the barn when she'd been helping him down from the saddle.

"And you drove here yourself," Marin added, glancing out the window at the truck.

"I did. Small victories." Even if this victory had an asterisk because of the type of transmission. He added the cookies next to the stash. "For those in need of massive amounts of sugar."

"Me!" Leo announced.

"Later," Marin announced right back, stopping the boy from snagging one then and there. "Thanks for the cookies," Marin added to Blue, handing him a plate. "Help yourself."

Marin's eyes met his. No bouncy glee there. She was dreading this.

Like Blue, she'd obviously showered, and her hair was still damp. Even over the aroma of the pizza, he caught a whiff of her soap, not the flowery, perfumy kind, but the basic stuff that just smelled clean.

And she looked amazing.

Then again, she always did, and Blue had to rein in the lust. It was a seriously bad time to be mentally undressing her and hauling her off to bed.

"Leo's already gotten started on the pizza." Marin tipped her head to one of the plates on the table that had a half-eaten slice of pepperoni. "That's his second slice."

"I was real hungry," Leo explained. "You don't have

to eat the one with olives and gunk on it," he added in a whisper to Blue.

Blue smiled, and even though he did like olives and gunk—aka peppers and sundried tomatoes—he went with a slice of the pepperoni and a Coke. As soon as he had the pizza on his plate, Leo tugged on his tee to lead him to the table.

"Kyle at school eats dirt," Leo announced. "Dirt pies he calls them. And Francie says it's disgusting, that he'll get worms. Will he?" Leo wanted to know, and he apparently thought Blue was the expert on that since the question was aimed at him.

"I don't know, but I'd rather eat pizza than dirt."

Judging from the boy's reaction, that was a darn good answer. Then again, Leo seemed to be impressed with whatever Blue had to say. Blue was hoping that would help the rest of the evening go better. Because Leo just might need some soothing after he knew the truth.

Marin and Gina joined them at the table where Leo continued to give them accounts of his fellow classmates and their more disgusting habits. It was obvious that Leo was the only one of them who actually had a good appetite, but the adults made a show of enjoying themselves for his sake.

"I like this," Leo announced when they were nearly done. "It's like what families do."

It was, indeed, and that must have been Marin's cue to move on to the hard part of the evening. "Let's have cookies for dessert and talk," she said.

Because of the small space, all she had to do to reach the cookies was lean over a little bit and pick up the container. She doled out a cookie for each of them, and then refilled Leo's glass of milk. Blue didn't think it was his imagination that Marin might have wanted a shot of something stronger for herself. Still, she settled for a sip of her ice water before she folded her hands on the table and looked at Leo.

"There's something I have to tell you," she said. "And, I'm sorry, but it's not something you're going to want to hear."

While chowing down on the cookie, Leo looked at her. Frowned. "We're not gonna have to move again, are we? Because I really, really, really like it here. We're not going to have to move, are we?" And he directed that one at Blue.

"No," Blue, Gina and Marin all said in unison.

It was Marin who continued. "We aren't moving, but I need to tell you something about Blue. About your father."

Leo's eyes widened, and he looked at Blue again. "Are you sick like I was?" the boy wanted to know.

"No," the three repeated again.

Again, it was Marin who carried through on the rest. "But Blue isn't actually your daddy."

Leo glanced at all of them, and his mouth quivered as if fighting back a smile. "'Course he is. Mama said."

Marin pulled in a long breath, nodded. "Your mother told you that because she wanted to make you feel good. She didn't want you to be upset because your real dad wasn't around."

Leo shook his head, and this time when his mouth quivered, it darn sure wasn't to fight any smile. "But my real dad is around. He's right here." He dropped the cookie on the table to take hold of Blue's hand.

Marin tried again. "Blue and your mom were friends, and she liked Blue a lot. That's why she told you what she did. But he's not your father. Your real dad couldn't be with you."

Leo's bottom lip trembled even more, and tears welled up in his eyes. Hell. Blue could face down enemy fire and fly straight into combat, but he wasn't sure he could handle this kid's tears. Still, he fought to steel himself up because it wouldn't do Leo any good if he lost it.

"It's true?" Leo asked him.

Blue nodded. And left it at that, mainly because he didn't want to say the wrong thing. Plus, he had a lump in his throat and his voice likely would have come out in a croak.

"Blue still loves you," Marin insisted. "So do Gina and I."

Leo stayed awfully quiet for what seemed way too long, and one of those tears slid down his cheek. "We have to leave now that you're not my dad," he insisted, and he bolted out of his chair and ran toward one of the bedrooms.

Marin was right behind Leo and made it to the room a split second before Leo slammed the door. That didn't stop her. She went right in, no doubt ready to dole out whatever reassurance and comfort she could give him.

"Shit," Blue grumbled, and he scrubbed his hand over his face.

"Yes, shit," Gina echoed. She went to the fridge and poured herself a glass of wine. "Want one?" she offered.

Tempting, but he shook his head. It'd been nearly two weeks since he'd taken any of the prescription pain meds that the hospital had given him, but he didn't want alcohol in his system if the pain turned so god-awful that he had to pop one of them.

Blue listened for any sounds of Leo's sobbing, and his stomach twisted when he heard it. "Shit," he repeated, and he dropped back down into the chair. "What can I do to help?"

"He'll no doubt want to talk to you," Gina was quick to answer. "After Marin settles him down, Leo will almost certainly want you to confirm she's telling the truth. Because he won't want it to be true," she added. "You'll have to assure him that it is, but that he's still going to be all right."

Gina made it seem simple and straightforward. It wasn't. "How the hell do I do that last part?"

She gulped down some of her wine. "Be a soft place for him to fall, but not a fake one. If you have his back, then let him know that," she continued when he gave her a "say what?" look. "Just try to assure him that Marin and others, like me, will be there for him. If you decide you can't be there for him, then don't promise Leo you will be. He doesn't need fake soft falling places because his dick of a birth father has already crapped out on him."

Blue appreciated the plain speak, and it was certainly food for thought along with being a "slap in the face" realization. "I'm normally at the ranch only three or four weeks out of the year," he spelled out.

"Then tell him that. Heck, he might already know

because he's had Marin and me read him some articles about you. Still, spell it out. And if you think you won't be able to spend time with him during those three or four weeks, then promise nothing. Absolutely nothing. Understand?"

Clearly, that wasn't a counselor's tone. It was more of a protective aunt who didn't want to see a child hurt again.

"I won't promise Leo anything I can't deliver," Blue assured her.

Gina stared at him. And stared. Finally, her expression softened. "Do me a favor, and do the same thing for Marin. I don't think you're dicking around with her, but she's been burned to hell and back. Don't be the one who burns her again."

And that was the tone of a protective friend. One who obviously knew what Marin had been through. Blue nearly pressed for more info, just so he'd know what he was up against with Marin. But he decided any and everything about Marin's past should come straight from her.

Leo's bedroom door opened, and a very pale, very shaky Marin came out. "How is he?" Blue immediately asked, and Gina uttered a version of the same.

Marin made a so-so motion with her hand and looked at Blue. "He wants to talk to you." She eased the door shut behind her. "Please don't promise him anything you can't deliver."

"I won't," Blue assured her. "Gina's already gone over that with me."

Marin nodded, but stayed put in front of Leo's door,

blocking Blue from entering. "And that part I said about you loving him. Maybe you can let him down gently if he comes out and asks if that's true?"

"I won't say or do anything to hurt him," Blue insisted, and he had to figure out a way to make sure that was true. People called him a charmer, and he was usually good at making people feel better. He really needed to amp that up with Leo.

Marin finally stepped away from the door, and she kept her gaze locked with Blue's as he walked forward. Blue considered saying something light, or giving her a quick kiss, to try to lift her mood, but he doubted anything was going to work on Marin right now.

Gathering his breath, Blue went inside.

Leo was on the bed, not face down and sobbing, but rather sitting on the edge, silently crying and staring at a framed photo that was on his nightstand. Blue thought it might be a picture of Jussie, but as he got closer, he saw it was the one of him that he'd given Marin to pass along to Leo.

Hell. That was another gut punch, but it wasn't the only one. Blue looked around and realized he was a prominent fixture in the boy's room. Someone, Marin probably, had printed out other pictures of Blue that had been posted on various sites. Most were of him in uniform, but there were a couple from his rodeo days.

There was also one of Jussie and him that Blue thought had been taken shortly after they'd met. Blue was wearing his rodeo gear, and a beaming Jussie was leaning against him. It, too, was framed and was on top of his dresser, which was positioned toward the foot of the bed. It meant it'd be the last thing Leo saw when he was falling asleep and the first thing when he woke up.

Yep, another gut punch.

"It's my favorite picture," Leo muttered, his voice barely louder than a whisper, and Blue realized the kid had followed his gaze.

"It's a good one. I liked your mom a lot," Blue said.

It wasn't a lie. He had liked Jussie. He just hadn't been able to care for her as much as Jussie had obviously cared for him. That was obvious in the picture. Jussie was looking up at him with proverbial stars in her eyes. While Blue was indeed smiling, there wasn't a single lovestruck star aimed at Jussie. He couldn't regret that. He would have been leading her on had he given Jussie a look like that, but it still twisted away at him that he couldn't give Jussie's son more than he'd given her.

Blue went closer and sat on the bed next to Leo. "How you doing, kid?" he asked.

Leo didn't give him a pat answer. He wiped his eyes with the back of his hand and turned to Blue. "You're really not my daddy?"

And wham, another gut punch. "I'm not, and I'm really sorry about that."

Leo nodded, and while he didn't start crying again, his chin and shoulders sank even lower. "Then, who's my real dad?"

Blue would have bet his favorite horse that the boy would ask that question, and Blue had already decided to go with a pat but truthful answer. "I don't know. Did you ask your aunt Marin?"

"She said he wasn't around." Leo's sigh was long and weary. "Is he?"

"I don't think so." Considering what little he knew about the man, this next part of the response was going to be hard because Blue was going to give the jerk far more consideration than he deserved. But the response wasn't for the jerk. It was for Leo. "I'm guessing he had to go away and couldn't come back."

"Because he didn't like me?" Leo quickly asked.

Blue couldn't say what he wanted to say because it would have involved the words *asshole sperm donor* so he went with a milder response coupled with a big-assed lie. "Of course, he loved you. But sometimes people can't be around even when they love somebody."

Leo seemed to give that some thought. "Like you when you have to fly."

"Like me when I have to fly," Blue verified.

"So, is my real dad a pilot, too?"

"I'm not sure," Blue settled for saying. He considered mentioning that his dad had been in the rodeo, but decided against it. That would just open up a whole boatload of other questions, and any answers should come from Marin or Gina, not him.

Leo stayed quiet, clearly processing all of this and maybe trying to wrap his head around this nameless, faceless man who'd fathered him. It was a lot for a six-year-old to take in.

"So, do we have to leave the ranch?" Leo asked out of the blue.

Thank God that was an easy answer. "Absolutely not. You don't want to leave, do you?"

"No," Leo was quick to say.

All right. So that was a good assurance for both of them. Even if Blue wouldn't be around much, he liked the idea of Leo and Marin being here when he came home.

Leo took hold of Blue's hand while he stared at the photo of him on the nightstand. "I know you're not my dad, but will you still do some dad things with me when your leg is better? I mean," he added before Blue could say anything, "Francie in my class has a stepdad and they do things together. Sometimes, he brings her lunch to school."

Blue had to swallow the fresh lump in his throat before he could answer. "Absolutely."

Leo smiled. It wasn't a beaming kind of deal, but it was there, and he gave Blue's hand a squeeze. "Good. And maybe you can teach me to ride when your leg gets better? I know Aunt Marin said she'd do that, but I'd rather it was you. I mean, since you rode broncs and all in the rodeo."

"I'll teach you to ride," Blue assured him. He didn't think Marin would object to that.

Leo's smile got a little wider. For a moment, anyway. But then his face turned serious again. "Will you still love me even though you're not my dad?

Oh, man. The biggest gut punch of them all, and he had no trouble remembering what Marin and Gina had warned him about. For him not to make any promises he couldn't keep. An answer to that question would either have to be a lie or a promise.

Blue went with the promise.

"Yeah," Blue told Leo. "I do love you, kid."

It was love, all right, and in that moment Blue knew something else. That he'd do anything, *anything*, for this boy.

CHAPTER ELEVEN

MARIN'S NERVES WERE way past the jangling stage. And for the first time in three days, the nerves weren't for Leo. He was doing great, something she hadn't thought possible when he'd sobbed in her arms after she'd told him the truth about Blue. But after Leo's conversation with Blue, the boy had done a complete one-eighty and was his usual happy self.

She owed Blue big-time for that.

Especially since he'd carried through on doing some "dad" things with Leo. On the day after the chat, Blue had taken him on his first fishing trip at one of the creeks that threaded through the ranch. This morning, he'd driven Leo to school with plans for them to stop along the way for a breakfast sandwich at the bakery. Blue wasn't back yet, but that was fine with her.

So, no nerves for Leo. These were all for Cottontail and what was just about to happen. Or rather what might not happen. Jesse and the other ranch hands had followed her instructions to a T when it came to Cottontail's "romantic encounter" with Iceman, but that didn't mean the mare would go through with it.

Per Marin's instructions, Iceman was in the corral and would be harnessed until Cottontail went to him.

Jesse was taking care of that. Marin had taken care of getting Cottontail into the pasture area just outside the corral. Once the mare had sight of Iceman, Marin had backed away and opened the gate.

And now the wait was on.

As expected, Iceman lifted his head and curled his lips, which meant he'd obviously caught Cottontail's scent. The stallion snorted, pawed at the ground and tried to bolt from the restraint on him, but Jesse held on and did his level best to steady the massive animal. Hard to keep a leash, though, on the animal's over-whelming instinct.

Marin suspected that Cottontail's heart was going a mile a minute right now, but she wasn't backing away in fear. That was a good sign. Another good sign came when the mare stepped closer. Certainly, not at an eager "I'm doing this now" pace, but rather a slow, cautious one, as if she knew the risk she was about to take was huge.

Iceman continued to snort and pull. Cottontail continued to mosey forward until she was fully inside the corral and only about twenty feet away from Iceman. Marin checked carefully for any signs that the past trauma was getting to the mare. But it wasn't. Cottontail continued to close the distance between her and the stallion.

"You can let Iceman go," Marin called out to Jesse, and she held her breath, hoping like the devil this wasn't a mistake. Another round of trauma could erase the progress they'd made and set the mare back for weeks.

Marin did her own stepping—away from the corral. She walked backward, her attention pinned to the mare, and she moved under one of the trees so she could continue to watch.

Iceman didn't charge at Cottontail. No surprise there since this wasn't his first rodeo so to speak. The stallion sauntered—there was no other word for it—toward Cottontail, first to get a better whiff of her and then to touch his nose to hers.

"That's almost romantic," someone said.

Marin barely stopped herself from letting out a yelp of surprise, and then she silently groaned. Because Blue was here. And she didn't especially want to witness this with him around. She immediately glanced at him to make sure Leo wasn't with him. He wasn't.

"I took Leo for breakfast and then dropped him off at school as planned," Blue let her know.

That was awesome. What wasn't awesome was the hot Blue stepping up beside her. She caught his scent, much as Iceman was now doing to Cottontail, and he smelled all leather and male. An incredible combo, and it was a powerful mix, what with the fit of his jeans and shirt. Simply put, Blue managed to look even more cocksure and impressive than the rock star stallion.

"Did you get Leo a reasonably healthy breakfast?" she asked, trying not to notice the human rock star, Top Gun, cowboy beside her. In the corral, Iceman and Cottontail were still sniffing each other.

"Not especially," Blue answered, and from the corner of her eye, Marin could see he was watching the equine couple. "No sugar in it, but lots of bacon and cheese."

"Good," Marin muttered.

"Good?" Blue questioned.

"I think Leo needs indulgences from time to time. Thank you for giving him that. Actually, thank you for the way you've handled him."

She managed to keep her voice level enough. Hard to do, though, once she saw that Iceman had finished with the foreplay and had moved to mount the mare. Cottontail stood firm, not panicking when she took the weight of the stallion and not doing anything other than what a mare would do under these circumstances. Not that Marin had witnessed a lot of horse sex, but so far she was pleased with Cottontail's response.

Iceman finished the job, dismounted, and in true rock star fashion, he moved away from the mare. He moseyed back to Jesse, no doubt so he could remove the harness. Cottontail stood shivering and shuddering for a moment before she went back out into the pasture. She trotted away, maybe to join Pearl and do some horse girl talk about what had just happened.

"Lust can apparently overcome all sorts of obstacles," Blue remarked.

Marin felt the blush rise up on her neck and cheeks, and she so didn't want to acknowledge the truth of that. Well, the truth when it came to horses, anyway.

And to her.

Apparently, it applied to her, too, and that was why her sound of agreement just wasn't a bright thing for her to do. Neither was her looking at Blue. Though that was exactly what she did on both counts.

"You gotta feel good about how Cottontail handled that," Blue said.

It sounded innocent enough and prompted her to make another sound of agreement. But there was nothing innocent about this. The heat levels were sky-high right now.

"I do." Marin cleared her throat. It didn't help. Her voice carried the heat and the silk, and even to her own ears, it sounded like a sexual invitation. "Pearl's in heat, too, but I don't think she's ready yet. I'll lead her closer to Iceman tomorrow and see her reaction."

The corner of Blue's mouth lifted, and Marin knew the smile had absolutely zilch to do with the horses. No, this was about them. About that kiss and all the lusting they'd been doing.

"Want to go on a date?" he asked.

She blinked, even though she'd sort of suspected things would move in this direction. With all the scalding looks they were giving each other, however, she was surprised he hadn't asked if she wanted them to go to her place.

And, mercy, she wouldn't have said yes, but it would have been darn hard for her to turn him down.

"A date?" she questioned.

He nodded, grinned. "Dinner. Or maybe lunch while Leo's at school."

"This is about sex," she blurted out.

"Damn straight it is," Blue admitted right off. "But first of all, I think you'd prefer at least some wining and dining. And before you say no, consider this. My bum knee is more or less a chastity belt. So, while I'd like for sex to stay on the table, it probably can't happened for at least another week or so."

Marin thought that timing might be wishful thinking

on Blue's part. He was still limping. A lot. Still, wincing some, too, when he moved wrong and aggravated his cracked ribs.

"So, just lunch or dinner," he went on. "We can eat and continue to torture each other with something we can't have. Not yet, anyway."

She sighed, and while this wasn't ideal timing for a heart-to-heart chat, Marin went with it, anyway. "How much research did you do on my sister's death?"

Blue pulled back his shoulders. And winced. Apparently, that was a wrong move for him. "As much as I could find," he confessed.

Good. Because it meant she wouldn't have to get into the specifics of the car crash. "Well, the reason I avoid men is because I screwed up big-time with my last boyfriend. It was a hard lesson to learn, but I learned it, and it's why I can't risk getting involved with you."

Blue frowned. "Involved with me," he repeated. "But what you wanted to say was involved with *men like me*."

Marin had to nod. "It's not exactly an insult." It was, though, and that made her curse under her breath. "In many ways, you're nothing like that wrong man. I've seen that with the way you interact with Leo. You care about him, about this place." She fanned her hand over the ranch. "About your family."

"But?" he pressed when she stopped.

She sighed again. "But I can't just leap into bed with you. You aren't that wrong man, but you aren't the right one, either, Blue. You'll be leaving soon," Marin was quick to add. "And at best, you'll only be back for a couple of weeks out of the year."

Blue stayed quiet a moment, and she hated that she'd probably hurt his feelings. "So, you're looking for the right guy?"

"No," she said a little faster than she'd intended. "Right now, I'm focusing on Leo and my new job." Now it was her turn to stay quiet a moment, and she continued with the explanation she'd already botched. "I'm also not sure I'm ready to risk being involved."

"Because of the wrong man," Blue concluded. "He broke your heart."

"Not in the way you think." She gathered her breath and just went with it. "He killed my sister."

Obviously, Blue hadn't come across a hint of that in his research on Selene. "What?"

"He didn't actually murder her," Marin explained. "But he's the reason she's dead. And I'm the reason he was in that car with her."

"Drew Carson," Blue provided. "He was the driver of the vehicle."

Marin nodded. "He was." And she had to pause again. "Drew was a charmer, and while I knew the charm covered a bad boy, I didn't resist him. We had a hot summer fling, and he didn't take it well when I ended things with him." She saw the muscles in Blue's jaw tense. "No stalkings or threats. Drew went in a different direction, using his charm skills."

"On your sister," Blue said, filling in the blanks.

"Yes." Marin tried and failed to tamp down the horrific memories. The guilt. "Selene was young and very naive, and he convinced her to go out with him. Drew told me himself that he wouldn't have done that if he and I had still been together." Oh, another wave of guilt rolled over her. "Selene wouldn't have been in that car with him, wouldn't have died, if I'd never gotten involved with Drew."

Blue stepped in front of her, forcing eye contact. "Bullshit."

That wasn't the reaction she'd expected. Marin had thought Blue would go into the "now, now" mode of trying to dole out some comfort.

"Bullshit," he repeated, enunciating each syllable. "First of all, from everything I read, the accident was just that, an accident. And your sister could have met him even if he'd never gotten involved with you first."

"But she didn't meet him through other means," Marin argued right back. "Drew was in her life because of me."

Blue opened his mouth, no doubt to drill home the point about it being an accident, but Marin could see the exact moment when he mentally backed down. And she knew the reason for that. He was no doubt recalling that the crash landing had been accidental, too, but that didn't make him feel less responsible.

"All right," Blue finally said. "I get it. I really get it. And while I wish I didn't, I can understand why you feel the way you do." He paused a heartbeat. "I'm still asking you out on a date. And I'm still doing this."

He leaned in and surprised the heck out of her by brushing his mouth over hers. And nearly melting her where she stood. The lust slam was hard and fast, but Marin still managed to be aware of where they were.

She glanced around to see if anyone noticed, and the answer to that was thankfully no.

Well, other than Iceman.

The stallion seemed to be smirking at her, but Marin admitted that was probably her imagination.

"Even after everything I just told you," she managed to say, "you can't believe it's a good idea for us to go on a date. Or do this." In a "turnaround is fair play" move, she brushed her mouth over his. And could have sworn the heat took off the top of her head.

"Oh, I don't," Blue readily admitted. Then, he grinned. That cocksure grin that reminded her just how damn irresistible he was. "But I'm hoping you'll say yes, anyway. Who knows, it might be a way for both of us to put a temporary mute button on our guilt trips."

Judging from the look in his eyes, Blue knew even temporary might be impossible. Especially for him. She'd had three years to dive into the guilt pool, but it was still relatively fresh for Blue.

"So, will you go out with me?" Blue still pressed.

"Interrupting anything?" someone called out before Marin even had a chance to answer.

Her first thought was that it was Egan, and there was no way in Hades she wanted her boss to witness anything that'd happened between Blue and her for the past ten minutes or so. The voice certainly sounded like Egan. But it wasn't, not unless he'd grown a couple of inches.

The man who walked toward them was wearing a flight suit and grinning. His demeanor seemed to be a mix of both Blue's natural charm and Egan's confident air of authority.

"I'm Cal Donnelly," he said, extending his hand for her to shake. She did, after going on autopilot. "And I'm guessing you're Marin. I've heard lots and lots of good things about you."

While she managed to mutter and nod a thanks, Cal turned to Blue and gave him a look that only an older brother could have managed. "I've heard things about you, too." He slid glances between Blue and her. "Not this, though," he added before he pulled Blue into a hug.

"Good to have you home," Blue told him.

And that was Marin's cue to get moving so the brothers could have their reunion. She made it just one step before Cal spoke again.

"I can step aside and wait if you want to give Blue that answer about that date," Cal offered.

She shook her head. "It can wait." Wait until she at least had a good answer. Which probably should include turning him down.

But she wouldn't.

Dang it. She wouldn't.

It didn't have zilch to do with pausing a grief button, either. Not for her, anyway. But it might work for Blue, and that, in turn, worked for her. Because she owed him for the way he'd handled things with Leo.

And she wanted him.

That was the real bottom line here for her, and no amount of logic was going to convince her to steer clear of him. She wanted Blue even if it screwed up her life all over again.

Even if she ended up with a ton of regrets and a broken heart.

Which she would almost certainly get.

Cursing herself for that "screwing up her life all over again" that was practically a 100 percent guarantee, Marin muttered a quick goodbye, "it was nice to meet you" to Cal and headed to the barn. She could burn off some of her frustrations by saddling a horse and riding out to the other two mares to do some training. Then, she could do the same to Cottontail and Pearl. It was best if she spent as much time with them as possible since the new horses would be arriving soon.

Marin made it all the way to the barn, mindful that Blue and his brother were likely watching her exit. She didn't have time, though, to get to the tack room before her phone vibrated. She'd put it on silent so as to not startle Cottontail, but she'd set it to vibrate in case Leo's school tried to get in touch with her.

But it wasn't his school.

In fact, she didn't know who it was because it said Unknown Caller on the screen. Figuring it was spam, Marin didn't answer, and a few seconds later, she saw that the caller had left a voice mail. She pressed it to listen.

And instantly went stiff.

"Marin," the man greeted.

It was a voice she knew all too well, even though she'd only met him once. It was Brian Petty, Leo's asshole dad.

"It's me," the message said. "Been trying to get in touch with you, Marin. We need to talk. And I want to see Leo," he added as an afterthought. "Don't try to dodge me, either, because you're gonna want to listen to what I have to say."

That was it. Just a handful of sentences. But Marin knew a threat when she heard it.

Hell.

What did Leo's father want now?

CAL DONNELLY STOOD at the corral fence, drinking his coffee while he watched Marin do her thing with the two mares. She was good. Damn good.

He'd been around trainers most of his life and hadn't needed Jesse, Blue and Egan to confirm that for him. But now he was seeing her in action for himself, and he seriously doubted Egan would ever want to let go of her. She'd have a job here at the ranch as long as she wanted.

From what little he'd overheard of her conversation with Blue the day before, Marin had some troubles. Some guilt even. Well, she was in the right place because the whole ranch was swimming with guilt right now. It even extended to another time zone and another continent, what with his sister in on the guilt stuff as well.

Everybody wanted to help.

Everybody had other commitments.

Remi was on deployment somewhere, so she hadn't been able to pitch in much other than a quick visit to Blue right after he'd been hurt. Added to that, she wasn't just an ordinary officer. She was a Guardian Angel also known as a Combat Rescue Officer. She saved lives and was needed where she was.

Their dad hadn't wanted to tell Blue, but he hadn't

been medically cleared to travel and come to the ranch to try to lend a hand. That left Cal, and that guilt-swimming was way deep with him. He needed to be here. He needed to make sure the legacy of Saddlebrook lived on without metaphorically breaking Egan's back from the workload.

But he wasn't sure what the right fix was.

He had fourteen years in uniform and had made rank early enough that people were muttering the *G* word around him. As in *general*. He had the right stuff for it, too. A good record, a high-risk job and a couple of mentors who would work behind the scenes to make sure his right stuff earned him those general stars.

Cal wasn't sure he wanted them, though.

Unlike Blue, he didn't have the "need for speed" by being in the cockpit of a fighter jet. In fact, he wasn't even sure what his needs were, but he had to admit that every time he came back home, it was harder and harder to leave.

The guilt was playing into that, all right, but so was the ranch itself. He might not have a need for speed, but he sure as hell had a need to be here in the place that always anchored him.

He turned when he heard the footsteps behind him and expected to see Blue, even though his little brother definitely wasn't a morning person.

But it was Leo.

The boy was eating a breakfast burrito and wearing his backpack. Cal automatically checked the time. It was just past eight o'clock, and he'd heard Effie and

Maybell say the car pool parent would get there at about eight thirty to take Leo to school.

"So," Leo said as if they'd already been having a conversation, "Blue's not my daddy-daddy, Aunt Marin told me that, but Blue said he can be my bonus dad. Does that make you my bonus brother?"

"Or bonus uncle. Which would you prefer?" Cal asked.

Leo's face screwed up in thought. "Uncle. Can I tell the kids at school that?"

"Absolutely. And I'll call you my bonus nephew."

Though Cal currently didn't have any actual nephews or nieces. He suspected that was about to change since on his way out to the corral, he'd heard Alana puking in the downstairs powder room. Of course, she could just have some kind of stomach bug, but he was thinking Egan had probably knocked her up.

Cal smiled at that thought. They'd be damn good parents.

"So, are you a cowboy or a pilot?" Leo asked, pulling Cal's attention back to him.

"A pilot, but I'm a bonus cowboy."

Leo grinned at that. "Then, I can be a bonus cowboy, too."

"Absolutely," Cal assured him. "Have you learned to ride yet?"

"A little. Aunt Marin took me out on a horse named Marshmallow. Blue let me sit on one named Sugarfoot."

Cal knew both mares and they were as gentle as they came.

"Is Blue gonna be real sad if his leg keeps on hurting?" Leo threw out there a moment later.

The answer was a whopping big yes, but Cal thought it best not to spell that out. "Blue's going to the doctor to make sure it heals." It was a cop-out response, but he didn't want the boy to worry.

Leo nodded. "And then he'll be leaving. I'll be sad when that happens."

Cal couldn't come up with a reassurance for that other than, "When Blue gets leave, he'll come back home."

Another nod, and Cal realized Leo had his attention pinned to Marin. "I was hoping Blue could make my aunt Marin happy. Because she's sad a lot and doesn't want me to know."

Cal frowned. He'd definitely picked up on the sad/guilt thing the day before. No way, though, could he give Leo any hope that Blue would be able to fix whatever was wrong with her. Especially not when Blue was dealing with so much sadness of his own.

"I think Aunt Marin is sad because of me," Leo added a moment later.

"No way," Cal was quick to say. But then he drew a blank as to what he could add to try to convince the boy of that.

Leo shrugged as if there could definitely be a way. "I think it's because of my dad-dad," Leo said. "Not bonus dad Blue, but my real one."

That got Cal's attention. He'd yet to hear Blue mention anything about Leo's birth father other than he was out of the picture.

"Why do you think your aunt Marin is sad because of your dad?" Cal asked.

"Because I heard her talking to Miss Gina about it.

That's her friend, and Aunt Marin told Gina that my dad might cause some trouble." He looked up at Cal. "I don't want trouble so could maybe you and Blue fix it so Aunt Marin isn't so scared?"

Well, crap. Cal definitely hadn't seen that coming.

At the exact moment Leo asked that question, a van pulled into the driveway of the house, and the driver honked the horn. The car pool, no doubt.

"Bye," Leo said, and he ran off, leaving Cal to stand there and wonder what the hell he was going to do now?

CHAPTER TWELVE

BLUE HADN'T ESPECIALLY wanted a babysitter for this particular trip to the base, but he hadn't been able to shake Cal. Probably because Cal knew that Blue wasn't being up front about his recovery.

But Blue didn't want to be upfront.

There was no need to hash and rehash that his recovery wasn't going as well as the surgeon had hoped. It sure as hell hadn't gone as well as Blue had thought it would. But it wouldn't do any good for Cal or the rest of his family to know that. It would only cause them needless worry, especially since Blue still expected to make a full recovery. Once he was anywhere near enough to pass a flight physical, he'd take it.

And he'd pass.

Because in his mind, there wasn't another option. He'd need to ace that physical before he could get off medical leave and return to the cockpit.

Since Cal's arrival at the ranch two days earlier, Blue had had some chats with his brothers. Chats that'd stayed on the surface when it came to the injuries—both Blue's and the others'. Cal hadn't pushed too hard there.

Not yet, anyway.

Nor had Cal pushed hard when it came to Marin. A

surprise since Blue had filled him in on Leo. Maybe Cal had held back because he didn't want Blue to do a turnabout and pester him about his love life. Or lack thereof. At the moment, Blue was partially in the "lack thereof" category, but he was hoping to change that by getting Marin to agree to go on that date with him. That would be a start. Possibly a stupid one for both of them, but Blue didn't see any turning back now.

He focused on that, on Marin, as he heard what the surgeon had to say after his latest poking and prodding, and Blue tried not to curse when the doctor said to make a follow-up appointment—another one—for two weeks out. Two more weeks before there was even the possibility of Blue getting the go-ahead to take that physical. During that time, he'd also have to continue with physical therapy.

Thankfully, Cal hadn't actually gone into the exam room with Blue, but his brother was right there, waiting for him when he came out.

"Well?" Cal asked.

Blue gave him a thumbs-up. "The knee's coming along just fine," he lied. "I might be good to go as soon as two weeks from now."

Of course, that vocal reminder made him question, again, why he'd pressed Marin for a date. He shouldn't have. Not with him possibly leaving so soon. He wasn't sure, though, that he could stop himself from testing those particular waters.

Blue checked the time. It was almost noon. "You have time for lunch before I take you to the airport?"

"I do," Cal said, walking out with him.

Blue tried not to limp, but it was impossible. All that poking and prodding had stirred up the pain. Thankfully, though, only in his knee. His ribs seemed to be behaving themselves.

"I'm going to fly into DC and see Dad before I go back to Shaw," Cal said, referring to Shaw AFB where he was stationed. "Dad will want to know how you're doing. What should I tell him?"

"That I'm fine," Blue insisted.

Cal sighed. "So, I'm to lie."

"I'm fine," Blue insisted a little harder, trying not to lapse into the territory of "doth protesting too much." But his dad would press Cal to try to find out if Blue's recovery was coming along as well as Blue wanted them to believe. "If you need to shift the subject with him, let him know how well Egan's doing, what with handling the ranch and commuting to work."

But Blue immediately rethought that.

"Just don't gush about it too much," Blue clarified. "I don't want Dad to think Egan's replaced him."

"He has," Cal was quick to point out. "But, yeah, I get what you're saying. Best to leave that opening in case Dad wants to come back and pick up where he left off."

That was what they all had hoped for. And they'd all been shocked when that hadn't happened after their dad's heart attack. Blue had never thought in a million years that Derek Donnelly would relinquish the reins to Saddlebrook, but he'd seemingly done just that and was now living happily with Audrey. Not only that, their dad had indicated he'd be accompanying Audrey on her next assignment, which would almost certainly be overseas.

"I wish Dad would come back, at least part-time," Blue muttered. "Egan's got a lot on his plate right now, and I suspect when Alana and he get married, they'll start a family."

Cal didn't disagree with any part of that. "I have a long leave coming in a few months. I can put in some more hours at the ranch then."

Egan would appreciate that, but it was still just a Band-Aid fix. Their big brother had strong shoulders, but he was carrying a heavy weight right now. Blue had tried to help with that, too, by taking over some of the paperwork. A chore he hated. But figuring Egan hated it, too, he'd pitched in and done what he could.

Again, though, that was just a Band-Aid that would have to work for the next two and a half years. That was when Egan could retire from the Air Force and work the ranch full-time. His brother would still need help, but that would lighten Egan's load some.

Blue and Cal walked to the elevators that would take them to ground level and the parking lot. And Blue sort of froze. Even though he didn't particularly want an audience for the visit he was thinking about making, he decided to just go for it. He pressed the floor where Airman Newell was still hospitalized and in a coma.

"Do me a favor and don't ask about this," Blue told Cal.

Cal didn't. Not verbally, anyway. But his brother wasn't an idiot so he probably knew what this was about. It was about picking at a wound that wasn't going to heal. Because even if Airman Newell made a full recovery, he'd still lost all this time. Weeks of his life.

They rode the elevator up to the floor and got off. Blue didn't have to ask for directions since he'd come to the room twice before after he'd gone to his own appointments. No one questioned him as to why he was there, but Cal's uniform and rank might have helped with that.

As he'd done on his previous visits, Blue stopped outside the airman's room and peered at him through an observation window. He was still hooked up to a ventilator and other machines. This time, though, there was a woman sitting next to his bed, and she appeared to be reading to him. Judging from her resemblance, she was probably Newell's mother.

Blue definitely didn't want to speak to her, but fate must have had a different notion about that because the woman spotted him and immediately got to her feet.

"Shit," Blue muttered under his breath.

Cal didn't echo the same, but Blue could practically feel him bracing for whatever the woman said or did. Blue didn't want to brace. He wanted her to unleash all the anger she must have for what he'd done to her son.

"Major Donnelly," she said, her voice soft and tentative. Not the shout or profanity Blue had been expecting. "Cal," she added, shifting her attention to his brother. "It's good to see you again."

"Again?" Blue questioned, and he hadn't missed the woman using Cal's given name.

Cal nodded. "I dropped by the hospital two days ago before I went home. I met Mrs. Newell then."

"Maria," the woman corrected.

This was the first Blue was hearing about the visit, but judging from the woman's friendly attitude toward Cal, it had obviously gone well enough. Maria wasn't exactly smiling when she shifted her attention back to Blue, but she wasn't hostile, either.

"I was just reading to Casey," she said, holding up a science fiction paperback. "I think it helps."

Blue had to fight just to keep his throat from closing up. "How's he doing?" he finally managed to ask.

"Good. I think good," she amended a moment later with a little less enthusiasm. "I'm glad you came to see him."

Blue had been before, but he didn't mention that. Instead, he went with something he needed to say. "Mrs. Newell, I'm so sorry."

Tears shimmered in her eyes, but she still smiled and patted his arm. "I'm so sorry you were hurt, too. I hope you're recovering."

That wasn't what Blue wanted to hear. He wanted the anger. The raging. The accusation that he should have done more to make sure her son wasn't lying in a hospital bed in a coma.

But she didn't do any of that.

"I'm recovering," Blue muttered.

She smiled again and gave his arm another pat. "I hope you'll visit Casey when he's awake. I'm sure he'd love to meet you."

Yeah, meet the man who'd nearly killed him. Blue doubted there'd be much love in that meeting, but if Casey woke up, Blue would absolutely visit him if for no other reason than Casey would have a chance to do that ranting and raving.

Blue searched through the pockets of his flight suit and came up with a piece of paper and a pen. He jotted down his number and gave it to Maria. "Call me if you need anything. Or if you just want to…talk," he settled for saying.

"Oh, I will." Her smile was even broader this time. "Hope to see you both soon," she added before heading back into her son's room.

"Shit," Blue repeated after she was out of earshot. Cal and he went back to the elevator. "You didn't mention you'd visited."

"No," Cal was quick to admit. "I just wanted to see Casey for myself, but I didn't think it'd help if you knew."

It wouldn't have helped. Then again, Blue could say that about pretty much anything. Well, unless Casey came out of the coma, that is. If that happened, maybe Blue could find his way out of the dark hole that was closing in around him.

Once they were outside the hospital, Blue hobbled his way to the truck in the massive parking lot. Massive, which meant he hadn't been able to park close to the clinic for his appointment. Still, he tried to convince himself that all this pain was good, that it was a sign the muscles were healing.

He got in the truck, and as Cal and he were buckling up, his phone rang, and he saw an unexpected name. Marin. Rather than answer on hands-free for Cal to hear, he started the truck to get the AC going and answered the call the old-fashioned way.

"Is everything okay with Leo?" Blue immediately had to ask.

"Yes," Marin was just as quick to let him know. "He's fine and everything's fine at the ranch and school. Ditto for Pearl. She did great with Iceman so the ranch might soon have the next generation of Andalusians."

Blue was sorry he'd missed that. Though missing it was probably a good thing. He was already having trouble keeping his hands off Marin, and a discussion about sex, even horse sex, wouldn't have helped with that.

"How'd your appointment go?" she asked.

Blue repeated her "Fine" and hoped that her responses had been more truthful than his. He wouldn't mention the meeting with Casey's mom or what the surgeon had said to him about his slow progress. He damn sure wouldn't say a word about the look in the surgeon's eyes that'd conveyed he was concerned about Blue making a full recovery. Which he would make.

No, there was no need to get into all of that.

"I should probably have my head examined for this," Marin continued after a long pause, "but I'm saying yes to the date."

Wow, he definitely hadn't expected that, but he felt some of the tension ease in his chest. Hell, he even smiled. "When?"

"Well, tonight at six-ish if you're free. Leo's going to have a movie night with Maybell and Effie at the main house so I could fix us something here. But if you want to be with Cal, I'll totally understand. Effie said Cal was leaving to go back to his base today, but I wasn't exactly sure when he was doing that."

"He's leaving soon," Blue provided. "And I'll be there."

He had no doubts about that, either, even though he, too, should probably have his head examined. Especially since he was planning on passing that flight physical sooner than later. Still, there was no way he was going to talk himself out of seeing Marin.

Apparently, he also wasn't going to talk himself out of wondering why she'd caved and wanted to go through with the date.

Blue wanted to ask if she was sure nothing was wrong. Because there just might be if Marin was willing to risk being alone with him in her cabin. Still, he didn't plan on pressing her for anything that would make her change her mind.

"See you later," Marin murmured.

Yeah, she would, and Blue ended the call in a whole lot better mood than he'd started it with.

"A date with Marin?" Cal asked.

"Yeah." And he went through another round of dread over the lecture he figured his brother was about to give him.

But Cal didn't say anything close to what Blue had expected.

"Yesterday morning, I was at the corral and Leo came down to see me before he left for school."

Blue nodded. "Yeah, I saw him with you when I went into the kitchen to get some coffee. I was on my way out there when his ride showed up. I'll bet Leo asked if you'd be his bonus uncle?"

"You'd win that bet, though he offered me either bonus brother or uncle status," Cal verified. "Leo also said he was worried about Marin, that he thought she was scared because of something his real dad was doing. He wanted you and me to fix it. Know anything about that?"

"No," Blue could honestly say. Marin hadn't said a word about it. "As far as I know, Marin hasn't had any contact with Leo's dad in ages. Leo actually said Marin was scared?"

"He did." Cal blew out a long breath. "I considered just going straight to Marin to tell her what Leo had said, but then I figured that conversation should come from you. I would have told you sooner, but you've been tied up with ranch stuff and Leo since I got here. No complaints about that," Cal quickly assured him. "I was just looking for the right time to talk to you about it."

Cal was right about them not having much time together. Even on the drive from the ranch to the hospital, Blue had spent the bulk of his time arranging for the pickup and delivery of those other horses that Marin would be working with.

Well, crap. This explained why Marin had agreed to the date. Maybe it did, anyway. It was possible she wanted to talk to him about some trouble Leo's birth father was causing, but he'd been hoping that the date would be a blissful distraction from all the other stuff going on. Apparently not, though.

Blue considered phoning her back here and now, but it was best to have this conversation in person rather than over the phone. Added to that, he got another call as he took the turn toward the airport. He got another gut punch of concern when he saw the name on the screen, too.

Colonel Rafe Artis.

Blue's commander.

It wasn't the first time the colonel had called him in the past month. There'd been plenty of initial contact when Blue had still been in the hospital, but that had tapered off to weekly emails that had a "just checking on you" tone.

"Colonel," Blue answered, taking the call hands-free. "How are you doing, sir?"

"I was about to ask you the same thing. I recall you're supposed to have a checkup today."

"Just finished it." Blue paused. Then, silently cursed. He wouldn't lie to his commander, but he was going to be a hell of a lot more optimistic than the surgeon had been. "Everything's healed but the knee, and I'm making slow but steady recovery there. I have another appointment in two weeks, and I plan on asking to have my medical hold lifted."

"You're doing that well?" the colonel questioned.

"Well enough," Blue insisted.

Not a lie. He might still be in pain and limping all to hell and back, but he had recovered enough to at least ask for the medical hold to be lifted. Even if he couldn't immediately return to the cockpit, Blue could request DNIF status. Duties not involving flying. Being DNIF sucked, but it would put him one step closer to returning to his normal life.

One step further away from Marin and Leo, too.

But he wasn't going to think about that right now.

"It'll be good to have you back," the colonel concluded, but there was a hesitancy in his tone. Maybe because he was holding back, waiting to read the report from the surgeon.

The colonel wouldn't actually get a copy of Blue's medical records, but the surgeon would provide a summary of the checkup to the flight doctors at Edwards Air Force Base. Blue was certain that info would get passed along to the colonel.

"I called to find out how you're doing," Colonel Artis went on. "But I also have some news. The accident investigation board finished looking into your crash landing, and I just got their report."

Oh, that gave Blue a nasty jolt. Not just of the handful of things he could recall about the incident but also the whole shebang of an aftermath. The injuries. Airman Newell's coma. The soul-crushing pain and guilt.

Cal didn't say anything, but Blue could feel his brother staring at him. Watching to see how this was all mentally playing out for Blue. Well, it wasn't playing out well, that was for sure.

"The board concluded the crash landing wasn't your fault," the colonel went on.

Artis paused, probably to give Blue a moment for that to sink in. Maybe a moment for him to cheer or at least blow out a breath of relief. But there'd be no cheering or breathing in relief. Because while the crash landing itself might not have been his fault, the location of that landing was. And simply put, he should have brought down that Raptor in a spot where no one should have gotten hurt.

"The board concluded that you risked your life to take measures to save others," the colonel spelled out for him. "I'll be putting you in for a meritorious service medal."

"I don't want it," Blue blurted out.

He wished he'd toned down the intensity and volume of his voice. Wished, too, that he could explain why he didn't want a medal, an explanation that wouldn't get into that whole "soul-crushing guilt" stuff.

"I don't want it," Blue repeated, somewhat calmer. "But thank you for considering it." He didn't add that he should have done more. So much more that would have spared the six from being injured.

"All right," the colonel concluded. "No medal. But I will give you a handshake when I see you."

"I'll take that." Again, not because Blue thought he deserved any kind of thanks or recognition, but because a handshake would mean he was back on duty.

"Good. I'm about to email you a copy of the report," Colonel Artis went on.

"Thank you, sir," Blue said, but Artis immediately interrupted him.

"Don't thank me yet, and I'm going to ask you to do me a favor. There's an attachment to the report. Footage of the actual crash landing. It's pretty ugly, Blue, and you'd be doing yourself and me a favor if you didn't watch it."

Blue heard everything the colonel had just said, but he latched on to one word. *Footage.*

"Thank you, sir," Blue repeated, and he left his commander with the impression that he wouldn't look at the recording.

But he would.

And even though Blue still didn't have memories of it, he'd finally be able to see his screwup in all its glory.

CHAPTER THIRTEEN

MARIN DEBATED WHAT she had set in motion by inviting Blue over for dinner. Then again, debating it was something she'd been doing nonstop since the idea had first planted itself in her head.

Probably a really bad idea.

But she needed to talk to Blue about Brian's phone call, and she didn't want to do that in front of Leo. No sense risking Leo overhearing any part of that. Marin didn't even want to mention the sperm donor to Leo much less let him think this man could now be some kind of threat.

Marin had nixed the idea of telling Blue, too, when there'd been the possibility of ranch hands being around Which was most of the time. She had obviously not kept her secrets so secret with Blue, but she also wasn't ready to have her fellow ranch hands tuned into her personal life. Still, she'd wanted to tell Blue to feel him out and see if he thought this was a potential problem she should report to Egan or Jesse. After all, if Brian knew how to contact her, then he almost certainly knew the location of Saddlebrook.

She took the lasagna from the oven and frowned at the little spots on top where she'd let the cheese get too brown. She considered scraping them off, but it was probably best to let Blue learn upfront that she wasn't a stellar cook. That way, he wouldn't expect any future home-cooked meals.

But there were probably other kinds of expectations on both their parts. Expectations that were risky since being alone with each other could lead to more kissing, all the while knowing he'd be leaving soon. In some ways, his leaving would make it easier for her because then she'd know that this heat between them was just temporary.

Scalding hot, but temporary.

But each day he stayed, each time she kissed him, she knew she was risking her heart more and more. Too bad Marin didn't have a clue how to stop the attraction because she was certain that even without any more kisses, her heart was still about to be crushed.

Yet, she wasn't doing anything to stop it.

In fact, she seemed to be playing along, not just by offering this meal but based on the fact that she'd dressed as if this was an actual date-date. She'd put on a dress for one thing. Not a fancy one, but a loose comfortable green cotton dress. She still hadn't gone beyond the tinted moisturizer routine for her makeup, but she made sure her hair was as fixed as it could be.

She got the full jangle of nerves when she heard a vehicle pull to a stop outside the cabin. Marin glanced out the window, saw Blue, and her nerve-jangling went up a whole bunch of notches. Not because she dreaded this visit but because he was his usual hot self.

He was the cowboy this evening. Those great fitting

jeans, a black tee and a face that made her want to throw every ounce of caution to the wind and greet him with a French kiss. She wouldn't, of course. She would resist the overwhelming temptation of his mouth.

Marin opened the door.

And she failed in the resisting.

Then again, Blue clearly failed, too, because he went straight to her. He slid his hand around the back of her neck, and in the same motion, he pulled her into his arms. And he kissed her.

His mouth landed on hers, pressing hard. Taking. Giving, too. He was definitely doling out some giving. He kissed her as if there were no tomorrows, no consequences and as if he had a pocket filled with condoms. It was hot, deep and long, and the meaning behind it wasn't subtle. This was a kiss that started the need for that stash of condoms.

But Marin was the one who made it French.

Yep, she clearly had no willpower whatsoever. She kissed him right back, tasted and sent the lust skyrocketing. Seriously, there wasn't a meter or scale to measure this kind of lust.

With her body threatening to combust on the spot and with every part of her begging to haul Blue off to bed, she had to work hard at it, but Marin managed to pull away from him. She had to do that while gasping for breath and no doubt looking completely stunned at what she'd just done. But she maneuvered back enough to get a good look at his eyes.

Mercy, no.

"What's wrong?" she demanded.

He didn't tell her. Blue simply sighed, dropped another quick kiss on her mouth, and taking hold of her arm, he led her inside.

"I think we both have some crappy news to tell each other," he said, mentally throwing her for another loop. Did he know she wanted to tell him about Brian, or had he simply known something was up because she'd accepted his date?

Maybe.

But that left his crappy news. Considering he'd had a doctor's appointment earlier, that meant it probably hadn't gone well.

"I just wanted to start things off with a positive spin before we started talking," he explained. "Was it positive for you?" he asked, and he almost managed one of his cocky grins.

Almost.

"What's wrong?" she repeated.

"You first," Blue insisted.

He glanced around, spotted the bottle of red wine on the counter, and he poured glasses for both of them. Not halfway, either. He filled them practically to the top, an indicator that they were both probably going to need it.

Marin took a long sip. "Leo's dad called me yesterday. I didn't take the call, but he left me a voice mail." She took her phone from the pocket of her dress and played it for him.

"Been trying to get in touch with you, Marin. We need to talk. And I want to see Leo. Don't try to dodge me, either, because you're gonna want to listen to what I have to say."

Blue cursed, but didn't seem especially surprised. "Has he tried to call you since this message?"

She shook her head. "But he probably will. If he knows I'm working here at the ranch, he's probably after money."

Except there was no *probably* to it. Brian had tried to use Jussie as his cash cow for years, and if he got the chance, he'd attempt to do the same to Marin.

"I can call him," Blue suggested.

Marin didn't even have to think about this. "No. Because if he knows that any of the Donnellys have a personal connection to Leo, or me, then he'll be pressing you for money."

Blue gave her a level look. "He can press all he wants, and then he'll see what he's up against." Then, he paused. "Does he have any kind of legal claim to Leo that he can use as leverage?"

"No," she was quick to say. "Nothing legal. After Jussie was diagnosed with cancer, she got him to sign away his custodial rights by paying him off. She didn't want Brian to try to come after Leo for life insurance money or anything. I have legal custody of Leo."

That didn't mean, however, that Brian wouldn't try to stake a claim on the child. Not because he loved him. Nope. The man had never shown one ounce of interest in the boy. Well, except for the one sentence Brian had left in the voice mail.

And I want to see Leo.

Brian had no doubt added that, though, as a threat to her. A threat that he would, indeed, try to go after Leo if she didn't hand over some money.

"FYI, Leo is aware that something is up with his bio-dad," Blue threw out there. "He believes you're scared."

Marin felt her mouth drop open. "What? How?"

"Don't know, but he talked to Cal about it."

She groaned and pressed her fisted left hand hard against her temple. "Leo must have heard me talking to Gina about it."

Marin cursed herself, and she tried to go back through her phone conversation with Gina. It had happened when Leo should have been asleep in his bedroom. But what exactly had she said that he could have overheard? Most likely some anger and cursing.

But also possibly some fear.

She wasn't actually scared of Brian since he'd never been physically violent with Jussie or Leo, but Marin hated that the man could try to drop into their lives this way. A drop-in that could end up hurting Leo because it would be damn hard to explain to the boy that his bio-father was basically a moneygrubbing scumbag.

"I'll let Jesse know just in case the asswipe shows up at the ranch," Blue insisted. "There are no signs or such to point him to this cabin, but if he asks around town, somebody might tell him."

Her stomach sank. Because yes, someone would. Folks were probably gossiping about the new horse trainer who'd moved to Saddlebrook.

"Jesse and the hands obviously won't be able to keep watch 24/7," Blue went on. "But someone would hear an approaching vehicle. I'll let Grammy Effie and Maybell know, too, just in case."

Again, she wasn't going to turn that down, but it

made her feel sick to involve Maybell and Effie in this. "Thank you," she told him.

His eyes met hers again, and even though she was still battling jangled nerves, the scalding heat and the anger about Brian, Marin shoved all that aside and focused just on Blue.

"What's your crappy news?" she came out and asked, and her gaze flickered down to his knee.

"It's not that," Blue volunteered. "The appointment with the surgeon went…well enough."

Marin was glad he hadn't gone with a blatant lie and gushed about his recovery. Then again, the "well enough" could be a lie, but even if it was, it still hadn't qualified as his crappy news.

"After the appointment, though, I dropped by Airman Newell's room, and his mom was there," Blue said.

She held her breath because this could definitely have ended up as crappy news. "I'm sorry," she said, knowing there was no way a visit like that could go well for Blue since she was almost certain the airman was still in a coma. If he'd come out of it, Blue would have told her.

"His mom didn't yell at me," Blue said. "She should have, but she didn't." He paused again, drank some wine. "In fact, she said she was glad to see me, glad that I'd visited."

Marin immediately understood why that would have eaten away at Blue. The yelling would have been easier for him to take because he believed he deserved it.

"Airman Newell isn't improving," Blue went on, his voice a low whisper now. "His mom was reading to him when I got there, but there's been no improvement."

She didn't repeat her apology. No need. And even though this was an emotionally charged moment, she took a risk.

Marin set her wine aside, went to him and pulled him into her arms. Not for one of those mind-blowing kisses. Not for anything sexual. She just hugged him while being mindful of his still-aching ribs, and she hoped that the contact gave him some measure of comfort.

"I must look pretty down if you're giving me a pity hug," he muttered.

"I don't do pity hugs," she insisted. "Well, not for you, anyway. I do hug Leo when he's gotten a boo-boo." She eased back, keeping her arms around him, and she even managed a smile. "Though you do look pretty down. I probably should have taken a page from one of your admirers and baked something sugary."

"You left out the part about the sugary baked something having a name that's akin to a sexual invitation." He managed a smile, too.

"No. I just didn't think bringing it up was a good idea while I've got you in my arms."

His smile stayed in place for a few more seconds, and then he sighed and pressed his forehead against hers. "After my appointment and the visit with Airman Newell's mom, my commander called to let me know the accident investigation board finished their review of my crash landing," he said.

Oh. Well, that caused another round of stomach-tightening. She certainly hadn't forgotten about it, but it hadn't been in the front of her mind, either. She'd been far more worried about Blue's injuries than she had about anything that might come out in a report. But clearly something had been in that report that had put that dark look on his face.

"It's not too late for me to bake something," Marin offered, knowing that her attempt to make this light would fall flat. It did.

"My commander said the board had exonerated me for the crash," he added a moment later.

Instant relief, and Marin was ready to launch into a mental happy dance. "That's great news—"

"What my commander said isn't true," Blue interrupted. "Not completely, anyway. I read the entire report, and yeah, the board concluded that I mostly did my job by not crashing into a large city and killing a whole bunch of people."

There was a massive amount of sarcasm in his voice now. Not the joking, jesting kind, either. But the kind that told her this was a huge part of his crappy news.

"Mostly," Blue emphasized. "The board further concluded that out of all the options I had after the bird strike, the decisions I made were adequate. Not textbook. Not totally right. *Adequate.*"

Groaning, he moved out of her grip, turning his back to her. "According to the report, the bird strike shattered the canopy bubble of the Raptor I was flying," he explained. "That sent fragments into the number two engine, causing it to fail. I don't remember any of this, by the way," he added, giving her a quick glance. "But apparently, some of those fragments that took out the engine also slammed into my helmet."

That explained his head injury. It probably explained, too, why he had no memory of the incident.

"Now, here's where the *mostly* and *adequate* come into play," Blue continued. Bitterness and hurt had replaced the sarcasm. "Seconds after the impact with the bird—which by the way, the bird didn't fare so well, either—I executed a turn that caused the Raptor to lose speed and lift."

She had to shake her head. "I don't know what that means."

"It means if I hadn't executed that specific turn, I could have maybe found another way to avoid crashing into the base or the city. It means I could have maybe found a way to land without hurting six people."

In that moment, her heart broke for him. Marin went back to him, stepping in front of him so she could make eye contact.

"I heard all of those maybes," she pointed out, taking hold of his shoulders so he couldn't move away from her again. "Will you curse at me if I remind you that you saved a lot of people that day and that maybe the decision you made with the turn was the best thing you could have done under the circumstances?"

"Yes, I'll curse at you," he snarled.

But then he shook his head and cursed. Not at her. But at himself. Blue was harsh on himself, too. Not a surprise, considering how the rest of this conversation had played out.

"The board gave me the benefit of the doubt and said the maneuver could have been a reflex action," he continued a moment later. "Could have been caused by my head injury. Hell, it could have been caused by the pieces that were flying off the damaged Raptor. But it was a maneuver I made. *I. Made. It*," he spelled out. "And it's possible if I'd done something different, then Airman Newell's mother wouldn't have to be sitting by his bedside reading to him while he's in a coma."

Marin had no idea what kind of decisions a fighter pilot would have to make under those circumstances. She had no idea how to help Blue deal with this, either. It was a nasty what-if loop that he would likely have to deal with for the rest of his life. She knew all about nasty what-if loops because of her sister. And that meant she knew there was absolutely nothing she could say to Blue to fix this.

"There's more crappy news," he said while she was still mulling over if there was any way possible around her inability to fix him.

Marin went stiff. Sweet mercy, not more. Blue had already had more than enough. "What?" she finally managed to ask.

"There's footage of my crash landing," he explained, and she thought he was making an effort to keep the emotion out of his voice. "It was attached to the report from the accident investigation board. My commander advised me not to look at it, but I'm going to watch it, anyway."

"Why?" And she wished she could immediately come up with a solid argument to stop him.

He shrugged, but there was nothing casual about the gesture. "It might jog my memory."

Yes, and it might also give him a lifetime of nightmares. Especially if there were any images of the six people who got injured.

"I figured I'd watch it after our date," he added.

Again, she pressed for an argument that would talk him out of this, and she rattled out the first thing that popped into her head. "Some of the horses I work with seem to have amnesia. For instance, they forget what a saddle is. Or maybe they've just blocked it out. I don't try to get them to remember old memories. I just work to give them new, more positive ones."

And, of course, that was a lousy example. No way would it convince him not to look at that video. Except Marin figured he wouldn't just look at it. Blue would study it frame by frame, and she was convinced there was nothing he'd see in that footage that would ease this guilt inside him.

"I could watch it with you," Marin tried again. It wouldn't be a boatload of fun for her, either, but at least she could look at it with some objectivity. A little, maybe.

But Blue shook his head. "That's something I'd rather do alone." He tipped his head to the lasagna. "In the meantime, we can eat, maybe drink another glass of wine. Then, maybe push some limits with another kiss."

She quickly did the math. Eating and drinking another glass of wine would take at least twenty minutes. Probably more since Blue would almost certainly initiate some kind of small talk to try to take her mind off all this rotten stuff they'd been discussing. Since the lasagna would be so-so at best, and the wine wasn't doing anything for her, then the "pushing the limits" kiss was the only bright spot ahead.

So she sped right past the main course, the wine and went straight to the dessert. And she did that by kissing Blue again.

That wouldn't fix anything, either, but it might get his mind off his troubles for a few seconds, anyway. He cursed again, and this time she thought it might, indeed, be aimed at her. But he didn't move away from her.

Just the opposite.

He hauled her to him, taking her mouth as if it were his for the taking. Which, at the moment, it apparently was.

The heat came, of course. No way to avoid that, but there was a different level to it. The hunger whirling around with the need for comfort. This wasn't the kind of kiss that could happen between two people who'd just met. Or between two people who didn't have a connection. No. The connection was there. The hunger was there. And it was now a potent mix that confirmed to Marin that she would end up having sex with Blue. Maybe not tonight.

But it would happen

Did that stop her from kissing him? Nope. Not only that, again she was the one who deepened the kiss, which was akin to giving Blue the biggest, brightest green light imaginable. The only thing that would save her from hauling him off to bed was his injuries. Though sadly, they could probably figure out a way around that if the hunger won this particular battle.

His mouth moved over hers. His tongue moved over hers, too. Not in an aggressive way like some other guys were prone to do. Blue was clearly accomplished in this area, and using that finesse and experience, he knew how to make her burn. How to make her want even more than he was already giving her.

He tasted like the hot cowboy pilot that he was, and despite his injuries, he managed to press his body against her. Pressing in all the right places. His muscled chest against her breasts. Her breasts, and especially her nipples, thought this was a stellar idea and welcomed even more pressure. Some possible touching, too, which meant they were going to jump ahead a couple of bases on the making-out scale if something didn't cool them off soon.

She gave a whole lot of thanks for breathing because it was the need for air that finally caused them to break the mouth-to-mouth lock. They both gulped in some oxygen, but the body-to-body contact stayed firmly in place.

Because she now had her arms around him, she could feel the muscles strain in his back. And his breath, that slight heaving of his chest, was providing even more pleasurable torture for her breasts. So, while their mouths weren't racing around those make-out bases, the rest of them certainly was.

"Thanks, I needed that," he said, and again, his breath kicked up the heat. It brushed across her cheek and earlobe almost as effectively as his mouth. Almost. "It's sort of like an anchor."

There weren't many clear thoughts in her head right now, but she couldn't quite figure out what he meant by that. "Kissing me is an anchor?"

He nodded. "A good one." The corner of his mouth

lifted in a smile. "Maybe a bad one too, though, because kissing you stirs up a whole lot of heat."

"It does," she admitted. "I want to be sorry that I'm the one who started it. I'm having a hard time, though, working up any regret."

Blue chuckled, and then sighed. He managed to make both sounds as sexy as hell. Sheez, if she could bottle him, she could make a fortune. Or keep it all for herself and be an incredibly satisfied woman.

"I'd hoped that I'd get to kiss you again," he continued.

This time, it was his thumb that performed a little sexual magic. Blue ran it over her bottom lip, sliding it through the moisture that had gathered there. Then, as if sampling one of those indulgent sex desserts, he flicked his tongue over his thumb, apparently savoring the taste of her.

"I considered more than a kiss," he went on, his voice now a low seductive drawl. He was reeling her in. And she was willing to go wherever he was taking her. "That's why I purposely didn't bring a condom with me."

That stopped the reeling in, and even though her mind was still clouded with heat, that got through. No condom. Which meant no sex.

She repeated that to herself.

Multiple times.

Her body started a whine fest, but the small logical part of her brain that was still lurking about whispered that this was good. That even if Blue was physically ready for sex—and his erection pressing against her proved that he was—they shouldn't just jump into this.

"Two things," Blue added a moment later. "I didn't bring a condom tonight because I wanted to give you some time to think it through. At least a day or two of thinking time. I don't like to leave things unsaid."

"And what you're saying is that anything between us would be temporary," she finished for him. "Something more than a one-off, but less than a fling."

"Oh, I don't know. I might be up for a fling." He smiled, winked at her. Then, his expression turned serious. "But I don't want you hurt, and if you think you can't walk away from this unhurt, then this is as far as it goes."

Her body practically screamed out a *no*, and that small logical part of her brain suddenly turned mute. Her brain gave her no advice. No flashes of the past to make her ever so wary about jumping into a fling. The only thing that came through loud and clear was that at the end of that day or two of thinking time, there'd be only one conclusion she would reach.

She was going to have sex with Blue.

CHAPTER FOURTEEN

BLUE COULDN'T REMEMBER another time when it'd been so damn hard to walk away from someone, but this was apparently a night of firsts for him. And it wasn't over. Not by a long shot.

Two hours earlier, he'd poured out his heart and fears to Marin, though that sure as hell hadn't been the plan. He had intended to give her a sanitized version of things. Just the basics while he added a smile or two to let her know that all was well. But all wasn't well, and Marin had seen that right from the get-go.

After the heart pouring, Blue had screwed up and kissed her. And kissed her. And he probably would have kept on kissing her, probably would have hauled her off to bed, too, if he hadn't been wise enough not to bring a condom with him. Of course, the brainless part of him behind the zipper of his jeans was saying that hadn't been a wise move, but rather a stupid one.

Blue was going with the wise because this way Marin had that time to think. That day or two where she could decide if anything more was going to happen between them. The brainless part was hoping beyond hope that she'd just go for it, but Blue had told her the truth when he said he didn't want her having any regrets about this.

He'd already caused enough regrets without adding her to the heap.

With that dismal thought doing a tap dance in his throbbing head, Blue drove back to the house, thankful that Maybell, Leo and Effie were still in the family room. Maybe still watching a movie and pigging out on junk food, but it was just as likely they had all fallen asleep. Before he went to bed, he'd check on them to see if he needed to cover anyone up or carry Leo to the guest room.

Before bed, though, Blue had a big chore to do.

He had to look at the footage of the crash landing.

No pigging out on junk food for this particular viewing. In fact, he suspected his stomach would be churning so much by the end of it that he'd regret the lasagna and the two glasses of wine. Kissing Marin, though. He didn't think there was anything that would cause him to regret that.

He powered up his laptop, and foregoing any chance of painkillers tonight, he poured himself two fingers of whiskey from the small bar area in his room. He locked the door—no way did he want anyone walking in on this—and he settled down at his desk in front of the laptop screen. The moment he had the video attachment downloaded, he hit Play.

And tried to steel up every part of his body capable of steeling.

The start of the video was fairly clear, and he realized it'd likely been taken by a base photographer who was there to document the demo flight. The photographer had even managed to zoom in on Blue's face as he'd been prepping for takeoff. Blue had flashed a big smile, a wave to the crowd and a thumbs-up.

Leo was somewhere in that crowd. Marin, too. And he wondered what they'd been thinking as they'd seen him. In Leo's case, probably some giddiness because he thought Blue was his dad. For Marin, though, she was likely dreading it since the plan had apparently been for Blue to meet Leo after he'd landed. She would have been worried that Leo was going to blurt out that part about believing he'd just watched his daddy fly.

Of course, then Blue wondered what he'd been thinking since seeing himself hadn't jarred any memories in that particular department. He probably hadn't imagined that his life and others were about to change in a flash.

There was audio with the footage. Again, no surprise because Blue would have had contact with the command post who would have provided any and everything he'd said to the accident investigation board. The board had almost certainly analyzed his every word, but for the moment he wasn't saying much. Well, nothing that didn't just seem overly damn cocky.

"Hi-yo, Silver, away!" he'd called out. A nod to an old TV show that his grandmother loved. *The Lone Ranger.*

The photographer had managed to shoot Blue's takeoff. It looked textbook to Blue. No obvious hitches. No visible birds. Just the Raptor knifing through the air as it lifted off the runway.

The quality of the footage changed. No surprise there. Blue could see that he'd stayed low-level, but he'd still gone with some speed. Nowhere near the top speed, though. A Raptor was capable of hitting fifteen hundred miles per hour, but that wouldn't have given the crowd much of a show. More like a shiny blur.

Blue watched as he'd gone through what he called the "ooh and aah" maneuvers. Some rolls, some climbs, flying upside down while he shouted out an occasional "yeehaw" and even attempted a lyric from "Sweet Child of Mine," a song that he recalled his mother listening to when she'd been so sick. It was a rare memory that he pulled out while hotdogging it for the crowd.

Even though his brain knew what he was doing in the cockpit to make all those things happen, seeing it didn't do the job of breaking free any of those memories.

The time lapse was ticking off in the right hand corner of the video, and at seven minutes and twelve seconds, he saw the first signs that something was wrong. The Raptor turned sharply to the left. Definitely not part of the demo. No, this had likely been the point of impact with the bird, and Blue had probably reacted out of instinct to try to avoid it.

Clearly, he hadn't been able to.

He listened carefully to everything he said. "Bird strike," he'd relayed to the command post, and he'd followed it by reporting a litany of the damage. There was no fear in his voice. Only focus. Which clearly hadn't done as much good as Blue had wished it had.

The seconds spun off after that, and he saw the bank, aka the turn, that the accident investigation board had mentioned. Yep, it would have slowed him down, and at this point, he probably wouldn't have been thinking about damage or ejecting. He would have put the bulk of his focus on not crashing into a city with millions of people. That would have been flashing like a damn neon sign in his head.

More seconds spun off, and Blue watched as the Raptor approached the runway. Not with the finesse and speed of takeoff. Just the opposite. The landing gear was clearly damaged, something he would have known, and at that moment, he might have considered an ejection while letting the Raptor crash onto the runway. Obviously, though, he'd decided to ride it out.

Crash landing was a good term for it. He'd gotten the Raptor on the ground, but pieces of the landing gear and jet went flying all to hell and back. Or rather went flying into the crew who clearly hadn't expected things to end this way.

Because of the smoke and debris, Blue couldn't see much after that, but on the video he could hear the wail of the emergency responders. Lots of movement. Lots of horrified sounds coming from the crowd.

The recording ended before the responders got to Blue. Probably for the best. He didn't need to see them haul his bloody, unconscious body from the cockpit. Didn't need to see the others who'd been injured, but he had no trouble imagining them. Because while the responders had been extracting him, others would have been hurrying toward the crew. All hell would have been breaking loose, and Blue still didn't have any memories of it.

"Shit," he snarled, tossing back his whiskey.

He would have gone for another shot to get him ready

to watch the footage again, but his phone dinged with a text.

Marin.

Of course, she'd be worried about him and probably wanted to try to talk him out of watching the video. He clicked the text, and instead of prepping to tell her he was fine, he raised an eyebrow instead.

Want to see a picture of my breasts? she'd messaged.

Since he was a guy who was seriously attracted to her, he couldn't type, Yes, fast enough. He'd been giving a lot of thought to her breasts. And the rest of her.

A few seconds later, she sent the picture, and laughter burst from his mouth. Because it was a photo of a pack of chicken breasts.

Yummy, huh? she asked.

I'll bet yours are better, he responded.

Part of him wished it had been the real deal photo, but that wouldn't have made him laugh. His body would have had a totally different reaction. Maybe even an instant hard-on. But the laughter felt damn good.

Thanks, he added. That helped.

Did it? she quickly responded.

Yeah. No lie there. It had. Leave it to Marin to accomplish the impossible.

Are you okay? she texted a moment later.

Yeah, he answered, and that time, it was indeed a lie. Maybe a permanent one. Because Blue had to wonder if he'd ever be truly okay again.

"GREAT," BLUE MUTTERED as he watched the ranch hands unload the horses. "Damaged, hurt horses."

Not exactly a way to lift his rock-bottom mood. A mood he'd been in since watching the footage of the crash landing the night before. Then again, the horses hadn't had an easy go of it, either, so he had no right to complain. Still, it'd be damn hard to see them and know how much they'd suffered.

Damn hard for Marin, too.

She was right next to him beneath the oak, both of them staying back so they wouldn't spook the horses more than they already were. Jesse was dealing with the unloading on his own. A slow process that allowed Blue and Marin to get a look at each horse while Jesse led them from the trailer to the corral.

Jesse had asked Marin if she'd wanted to be part of the unloading, but she'd declined. For apparently a good reason, too. She didn't want to be part of the horses' trauma, and this transfer would, indeed, be traumatic. That way, she could approach them with a "clean slate" of sorts.

"Four mares," Marin muttered after Jesse had the first group in one of the corrals. "I don't see any visible scars, do you?" she asked.

"No." But they were skittish as all get-out, and all four of them were underweight. Not starved exactly, but clearly not cared for, either.

Jesse led out the gelding next, and Marin gasped. Blue didn't have to ask why. This one had scars, but he wasn't particularly skittish. There was arrogance in him, a gladiator spirit that the previous asshole owner hadn't been able to break.

"He might give you trouble," Blue remarked. "But trouble in a good way."

She looked at him, smiled a little, and even though Marin didn't come out and ask, she probably knew that, yeah, he could also be a good kind of trouble. And just like that, some of his lousy mood lifted. It wasn't a picture of chicken breasts, but her faint smile had done the trick.

Her smile faded, though, when she turned back to the horses, but there was also some relief, too, when the stallion made an appearance. He didn't have Iceman's or the gelding's arrogance, but he appeared to be unharmed. Maybe the previous asshole owner had had a higher tolerance for a horse with balls. That still didn't earn the asshole any brownie points with Blue. Just the opposite. He was still pressing to have charges brought against him, and it was the reason he'd asked Jesse and the veterinarian to document every single scar.

"Showtime," Marin muttered when the stallion was put in the corral away from the mares and gelding. She shifted a backpack off her shoulder and unzipped it to take out a bunch of bananas and some butterscotch candy. "Treats," she explained.

"Bribes?" he wanted to know.

"Absolutely. Right now, Jesse's the bad guy for hauling them here. I'm the good guy for bringing treats."

She started toward the corral, but then stopped and gave him a once-over that was similar to what she'd just given the horses. "You watched the video of the crash landing, didn't you?"

"I did," he confirmed. "It didn't jog my memory."

She stayed quiet a moment, obviously giving that some thought. "I'm not sure if that's good or bad."

Maybe it was both. But he didn't voice that. Nor did he voice that at this point, the memories weren't going to help. What was done was done, and this aftermath stage was just another level of hell.

Marin plucked out one of the butterscotch candies from the backpack and handed it to him. "There are too many ranch hands watching, but use your imagination. Because I just gave you a long French kiss to cheer you up."

He smiled. Man, he didn't know how she managed to do that, but he could have sworn he felt that imaginary kiss in every part of his body.

Blue watched as she made her way to the corral. And, yeah, he watched the way her jeans pressed against her butt. Of course, now he was fantasizing about both her breasts and her ass, and it might be a while—or never— before he ever got to see her completely in the buff.

That brought on the stirring of an erection so he popped the candy in his mouth, hoping the brainless wonder would be satisfied with a sugar high instead. Nope. The sugar didn't help, but what did was the sound of the approaching vehicle. He nearly swallowed the candy whole when he saw the SUV pull to a stop.

And his dad stepped out.

For weeks now, his dad had been saying he was going to make this trip home, but there'd been no firm plans. Blue suspected that was because his dad had been waiting on the okay from his doctors, but no one had spelled that out for Blue. Probably because of his own recovery, Blue was still in the category of "people walking on eggshells around him."

His dad stretched and flexed his shoulders as if getting out the kinks from the ride, and he made a sweeping glance around the ranch. Probably looking for any signs of change since he was last here. When he spotted Blue, he waved, and they started making their way toward each other.

Blue tried not to react, but seeing his dad was a hard gut punch. He'd never seen him look this old, this frail. Shit. The heart attack had really taken a toll on him.

His dad wasn't alone. Blue's stepmother, Audrey, stepped out from the driver's side, and nothing about her looked old or frail. There were a few threads of gray in her dark hair, but that only added to her air of being in charge. She waved at Blue, too, but instead of coming to him, she opened the back of the SUV and was about to pull out a suitcase before one of the housekeepers, Reba Neumann, hurried out to help with that.

"Blue," his dad greeted, and he pulled Blue into a hug. Blue hugged right back, and he hadn't known just how much he missed having his father around until just this very moment. "You doing all right?"

Blue nodded. "Still limping, but I'm getting there. I should be off medical leave soon."

"Yeah, that's what Effie told me. You look good, son. In fact, everything looks good."

There was possibly some bullshit mixed in with that observation, but Blue would take it.

"That's the horse whisperer I'm hearing all about?" His dad tipped his head to Marin who was now at the corral with the mares. She tossed in the treats and then immediately moved back. The mares went for it and began inching toward the goodies.

"Yes, that's Marin Galloway. FYI, if you call her a horse whisperer, she might roll her eyes. Well, she did when I called her that, anyway. She prefers natural horsemanship trainer."

"Horse whisperer," his dad repeated. "I can handle the eye rolls. Is she as good as Egan claims she is?"

Blue had to clamp down a laugh when he thought of the photo of the chicken breasts. "She's as good as Egan claims."

Clearly, Blue hadn't totally muffled the near laugh or else there'd been something in Blue's tone that had his dad turning toward him. His father cursed. "Hell, boy. You're not stirring up stuff with her, are you?"

"I am," Blue admitted, figuring that would earn him a lecture. He loved his dad and had always put him on a really high pedestal, but Derek Donnelly could be a hard-ass when needed.

"Well, at least she fits in better here than most of the ones you've dallied with over the years," his dad grumbled.

She did, indeed. And she fit Blue better, too, but that didn't give him much comfort. Just the opposite. Because that walking away without any hurts and regrets could play out both ways, and it could end up being mighty hard to leave a woman who cheered you up with photos of poultry.

His dad shifted his attention back to the corrals, and

Marin was now standing back from the mares as they chowed down on their treats.

"This is a good move for the ranch," his father said. "It's the right thing to do, and it'll give Saddlebrook some positive publicity. It might make people forget that I could be a tough son of a bitch when it came to deals."

Blue couldn't dispute that "tough son of a bitch" part. Or the part about this being "positive publicity" or "a good move for the ranch."

"There are always plenty of horses around who need rescuing," Blue commented.

His dad made a sound of agreement. "That's job security for the horse whisperer. Egan mentioned she has custody of a little boy?"

"Leo. He's six."

"Good. The ranch needs kids. I figure Egan and Alana will help with that soon. Probably not Cal, Remi or you, though."

Blue echoed his dad's earlier sound of agreement, and he wouldn't mention that he thought Alana might already be pregnant. That was news best coming from Egan and Alana if it turned out to be true.

They watched as Marin approached the gelding who challenged her by pawing at the ground and snorting. She didn't back away, but went ahead and put two bananas and some candy just inside the corral fence. The gelding pawed a few more times, but he, too, obviously had a sweet tooth because he went after the treats.

Marin didn't move back as she'd done with the mares. Maybe because the gelding wasn't cowering in fear. Just the opposite. After eating the candy, he went closer to her and had a sniff. She said something to the gelding that Blue couldn't hear, but he could have sworn the gelding smiled. She gave the gelding a little rub on his neck and moved on to the stallion.

"Yeah, she's definitely not your usual type," his dad confirmed again.

His dad patted him, much as Marin had just done to the gelding, and they turned, walking toward the house. It definitely wasn't a speedy pace, what with his dad's obvious weakness and Blue's limping. Still, speed didn't seem to matter since his dad clearly had other things he wanted to discuss.

"How's Egan doing?" his dad asked. "How's he holding up under the pressure of the job and running the ranch?"

Tough questions, but Blue attempted an answer that he hoped wouldn't end up pissing off Egan if it got back to him. "He's managing just fine, but he could use some help." He left it at that, to see how his dad would respond.

"I won't be returning to the ranch, not anytime soon, anyway," his father admitted. "I think I've come to the end of this particular trail. I'm not dying soon or anything like that. I just need to take it easy. That last coronary I had did a lot of damage to my heart. Not much energy these days." He patted Blue on the back again. "Besides, it was time for me to step aside for the next generation."

Yeah, but too bad the next generation wasn't around. Well, none of them except for Egan, who was carrying the load for all of them.

"Nearly dying put a lot of things in perspective for me," his dad went on, looking at him again. "Did it do the same for you?"

It might if Blue could actually remember nearly dying. Then again, he didn't want to remember if it caused him to be at the end of this "particular trail." Yeah, he had a ton of guilt over those injuries he'd caused, but he was certain it wouldn't help rid him of that guilt if he never returned to the cockpit.

He walked with his dad to the back porch and opened the door for him so he could go inside to Maybell and Effie, who were waiting to greet him. Blue would have gone in, too, but Audrey stepped out.

"Got a minute to talk?" she asked, sounding very much like a general and not a stepmom.

Blue didn't mind, though. He figured Audrey was a little reserved with him and his brothers because she didn't know where she stood with them. She might even consider that they believed she'd replaced their mother and now had "lured" their dad away from the ranch. But Blue didn't blame her for either of those things, and while he figured they'd never be best buds, he didn't mind being around her.

"Sure," he answered.

"Thanks," she muttered, but didn't say anything else until they were off the porch. Blue and she ended up under the same shade tree where he and his father had just had their chat.

Marin was still by the corrals and had doled out some treats to the stallion who was far more receptive than the gelding had been. She looked back over her shoulder at him, maybe checking to see if he was still watching, and she did seem a little puzzled that he'd traded off conversational partners.

"Are you about to tell me to make sure Dad doesn't overdo it?" Blue came out and asked Audrey.

"No," she was quick to say. "And I won't be telling you not to overdo it, either. You're both grown men and can make your own decisions." Though she did glance down at his knee. "Should I ask about your recovery?"

"No," he was equally quick to say.

She nodded. Then, paused. It was that pause that caused Blue's breath to go a little thin. Hell, this wasn't a lecture, but judging from Audrey's expression, she had something bad to tell him.

"Just spill it," Blue insisted. Because his mind had already made the leap to a couple of worst-case scenarios. Like Remi being hurt or his dad's condition being worse than Blue had been led to believe.

Audrey nodded again and surprised him when she cursed. Not only that, she pulled a cigarette from her pocket and lit up. Blue hadn't been around her much over the past decade or so, but he had thought she had given up smoking. Apparently not.

"I allow myself one a week," she said. "It settles my nerves."

That notched up the worst-case scenario stuff. "Spill it," he repeated.

She didn't, not right away. Audrey looked at him, and he recognized mental fidgeting when he saw it. "It's not about your dad," she finally said. "Or Remi, Egan, Cal or you."

All right, that eliminated plenty. Not Audrey, though. "Is something wrong with you?"

"Nothing medical. I'm as healthy as a horse," she muttered.

A bit ironic since the corrals were now filled with horses that weren't exactly healthy.

"It's about something that happened thirty years ago," Audrey finally said, causing Blue to frown. "And for the record, you aren't going to like hearing this."

"My mom died thirty years ago," Blue was quick to point out.

"Yes. And in a roundabout way, it's about her."

Shit. Blue definitely didn't need a gut punch from the past when he had so many more recent ones. "Are you going to tell me that something could have been done so she didn't die?"

Audrey looked at him, the smoke from the cigarette creating a filmy curtain around her face. "No. Nothing could have been done. Your mom had terminal cancer." She paused again. "I knew her, knew Ella," she said, using his mother's given name. "She was a little older than me, but before she dated your dad, she went out with my brother…"

She stopped, cursed, dropped the cigarette and stomped it out. Blue still didn't know what Audrey was trying to tell him, but he was now 100 percent sure he wasn't going to like it.

"No sugarcoating," she muttered as if reminding herself. "I went to your mom's funeral, and for the next couple of weeks, I reached out to your dad to lend a shoulder, that sort of thing. It led to sex."

Blue stared at her. And stared. When he finally got his mouth to working, he did some cursing, too, and he didn't hold back, either. "What the hell?" he managed to say.

"I could go on and on about how it wasn't planned, how your dad was wracked with grief, et cetera, but I don't expect you to understand."

"Good, because I don't," Blue spat out. The anger built. Not for himself, but for his mom. And WTF had his dad been thinking? "My mother had just died, and your go-to response was to have sex with her widower?"

Her mouth tightened a little. "It happened, and as I said, I don't expect you to understand." She took something else from her pocket, and for a moment he thought Audrey might pull out another cigarette. It wasn't. It was some kind of printout.

"Now, what?" Blue snarled when Audrey tried to hand it to him.

He glanced at it and saw it was from a genealogy website. In fact, it was a site that provided DNA test kits, and since Remi had given him one of the kits for a Christmas present, it was the very one that Blue had used.

Blue cursed again. A single word of profanity when he realized what he was looking at. A man identified as Rowan4321 was a 25 percent match with Blue. Twenty-five percent. Not enough for a sibling. That would have been in the 50 percent range.

But it was enough for a half sibling.

"Yours and dad's child," Blue spat out.

"Your dad doesn't know," Audrey was quick to say. "He, uh, regretted having sex with me so when I found out I was pregnant, I didn't tell him. I had the baby and gave him up for adoption. I've never done my own DNA test because…I wasn't sure he'd want me to try to find him."

Blue had so much to process. So much anger and shock to deal with, but he started with one simple question. "How did you get access to my DNA matches to find this?"

"Remi," she said on a sigh. "She set up the account for you, using her email so she's the one who gets the matches, and she forwarded this to me to ask what it meant. She doesn't know about the child I gave up," Audrey added in a whisper.

The anger was still building inside Blue. "So, why tell me?" Blue demanded.

"Because I want your opinion. As I said, your dad doesn't know, and I'm not sure there's a reason to tell him unless Rowan4321 actually wants to have contact with us." She paused.

He couldn't even think of an opinion, not one that didn't involve a whole lot more cursing. Not just aimed at Audrey, either, but his dad. What the hell had his dad been thinking to land in bed with his dead wife's friend?

Blue didn't even get a chance to consider the answer to that, though, because of the vehicle that turned into the driveway. An old pickup that had probably once been red, but now it was scabbed with rust, and the red was more of a dull pink. He didn't recognize the truck, but he sure as hell recognized the man who stepped out. Not because Blue personally knew him, but because he'd seen a picture of him on the internet.

"Shit," Blue spat out.

He thrust the paper back at Audrey and headed toward the truck. Because the visitor was Brian Petty, Leo's dad.

CHAPTER FIFTEEN

MARIN HADN'T HEARD anything to send alarm bells ringing in her head, but from the corner of her eye, she saw Blue move away from his stepmother. Not an easy, limping gait, either. He hurried, probably ignoring the pain.

And that was when Marin got those alarm bells.

Hooking her backpack over one shoulder, she moved quickly away from the corral and up the slope. Her concern soared when Audrey called out to Blue.

"You want me to get Jesse?" the woman asked, and the urgency in her voice indicated she had a good reason for the ranch foreman being around. Maybe because there was something going on that she didn't feel Blue could handle solo.

"No," she heard Blue answer in response to his stepmom's question. "I'll deal with this."

Marin still didn't know what "this" was, but she soon made it to the top of the slope and saw where Blue was heading. He was making his way toward a beat-up truck that was now in the driveway. It took Marin a couple seconds more to spot the driver who was still by the truck door.

Brian.

That gave her a nasty jolt of adrenaline, and she

broke into a run. She didn't quite catch up with Blue, though, before he made it to Brian.

Brian didn't look disheveled as he had the other time she'd seen him. He was wearing khakis and a green collared shirt. He'd obviously cleaned up for this visit. Probably because he thought it would earn him some respect. It didn't.

"What do you want?" Blue demanded, and Marin had no trouble hearing that. No trouble hearing the menacing tone in Blue's voice, either. He obviously figured this would not be a pleasant visit.

Brian lifted his hands and said, "Whoa," as if Blue's demand and movement forward were too aggressive. "I'm just here to talk to Marin, that's all. I don't want any trouble."

He would see it that way—not wanting any trouble. But that just likely meant he wanted her to hand over some money without giving him any lip about it.

Marin very much intended to give him some lip.

"You left me a threatening message," she was quick to point out to him.

Brian's eyes widened, and he said another "Whoa. That wasn't a threat."

She yanked out her phone, located the message and hit the play button. It took only a couple of seconds before his voice oozed through the air.

"It's me. Been trying to get in touch with you, Marin. We need to talk. And I want to see Leo. Don't try to dodge me, either, because you're gonna want to listen to what I have to say."

Brian smiled in an aw-shucks kind of way that didn't

cause Marin's anger to ease up one bit. Apparently, others at the ranch had picked up on the vibe, too, because Audrey had joined them, and Blue's dad and Maybell were coming out the front door.

"I didn't mean that as a threat," Brian insisted, and he tried to turn that aw-shucks expression toward the others. Marin figured, though, that beneath the surface, the man was doing anything but trying to play innocent. He was probably pissed to discover that he hadn't caught her alone so he could try...well, try to do whatever the heck he thought he could get away with that would make her fork over some money.

"I'm sorry," Brian went on. He repeated that a couple more times, making eye contact with Audrey, Derek and Maybell. "I really didn't threaten Marin."

Marin held up her phone again. "Should I replay it? Because the threat is definitely there."

Brian lost a bit of his composure, and he shook his head. And sighed. Obviously, he'd decided to go for a different tactic. "I was upset when I left that message, and now that I've heard it, I can see how it might have upset you. I'm sorry about that. I just got to missing my boy so much, and I wanted to see him. I still want to see him," he said, glancing around. "Is he here?"

"No," Marin and Blue said in unison. Neither of them volunteered, though, that Leo was in school.

Brian shifted his attention to Blue, and he extended his hand. "I'm Brian Petty, by the way. No need for you to introduce yourself. You're Major Blue Donnelly. You used to ride in the rodeo. And I saw your picture on the news sites. You crashed a jet in San Antonio."

Blue didn't respond, not verbally, anyway, but he was giving Brian the glare from hell. But Marin had to wonder if that "crashed a jet" had hit home with Blue. It was still a very sore subject.

"What do you want?" Blue repeated, the menace in his tone going up a whole bunch.

When Blue didn't shake Brian's hand, he lowered it back to his side and took a deep breath. "Like I said, I want to see my boy."

Marin tried to match the glare Blue was giving Brian, and she must have succeeded at least somewhat because Brian finally shifted his gaze and muttered something under his breath.

"All right, I deserve to be treated like this," Brian admitted. "I've been a shitty father who spent more time drinking than I did with my son. I regret that." He put on a "sad dog" face. "I regret it to the bottom of my soul."

Marin mentally rolled her eyes and bit off making some snarky comment about hearing violins playing.

"What do you want?" Blue said again, and Marin wasn't sure how he managed it, but Blue's intensity continued full throttle and then some.

Brian sighed again. "I'm a changed man. I've been clean and sober for forty-one days now. Not a drop to drink." He lifted his hand in a scout's honor gesture. "Once my mind cleared from the haze of the booze, I realized I wanted something more than my next drink. I wanted a fresh start. A fresh start where I get to see my son and tell him I'm so sorry I haven't been around for him."

Marin could have verbally slung so much at him.

Like a reminder that he'd never paid a penny of child support. Another reminder that he'd hounded Jussie for money when she was alive and hadn't been around a single day when she was dying. But she had the cream of the crop comeback.

"You signed away your parental rights," Marin spelled out for him. "For money," she emphasized.

Brian closed his eyes a moment and shook his head as if hearing the truth hurt. Or maybe he just wanted to make it seem as if it hurt. She wasn't sure if he was playing or not. And that wasn't just about the "clean and sober" part, but about truly wanting to see Leo.

"I made so many mistakes," Brian finally said, his voice a hoarse whisper. He turned pleading eyes on Marin. "I want to see Leo and tell him how sorry I am."

She wasn't totally immune to the man's begging. And some small part of her had to acknowledge that he might be telling the truth. But even if he was, that didn't mean she should let him see Leo.

Did it?

Was it fair to Leo to keep his dad from him, especially now that he knew Blue wasn't his father? Marin debated that a few seconds. And then she recalled the yelling, raging man who'd demanded money from Jussie.

"Are you in AA?" Marin asked him.

Clearly, Brian hadn't been expecting the question, and he seemed to do a mental double take. "Yes. And I'm doing well. Everyone says—"

"I want to talk to your sponsor," she insisted, talking right over him. "I want to ask him or her about your progress. Then, if he or she gives you stellar praise, emphasis on stellar," she added, "then I'll talk to a counselor about the possibility of Leo having a supervised visit with you."

And there, she saw it. That flash of anger. Oh, so much anger. This was not how he'd wanted her to play the game he was trying to set into motion.

"Sponsors aren't supposed to talk about the people they're helping," Brian said, and he made a visible effort to try to tamp down that anger.

But it was too late.

Marin had already seen it, which meant she was wise to him. That supervised visit with Leo was looking like a dim possibility right now.

"Sponsors can and do talk if the people they're helping give them permission to talk," Marin said.

"They absolutely do," Audrey was quick to confirm. She used her general's tone, too.

Again, the flash of anger came, but this time Brian had to fight even harder to rein it back in.

"All right," he said through partially clenched teeth. "I'll have my sponsor call Marin, but I'm not going to give you his name. I want to protect his privacy, too."

"No deal," Marin insisted.

"Agreed," Blue said. "Because without a name, I can't have a PI verify that the person is actually a sponsor and not just someone you put up to making the call."

Brian opened his mouth, and it was obvious from his expression that he was about to snarl out something. But once again, he pulled back. He closed his mouth and seemed to rethink what he'd been about to say.

He looked at Marin. "You've got a cozy setup here

on this big ranch. But this conversation we're having should be private. Just you and me."

Blue stepped to her side. "Not gonna happen."

Brian flicked Blue a look that could have frozen hell. Blue flicked him one right back.

"All right," Brian repeated, and this time there wasn't much of a leash on that temper of his. "Just know this, Marin." He said her name as if it were some kind of nasty fungus. "I need to see my son. I don't want to go through legal channels to make that happen, but I will. I swear to you, I will."

And with that threat, Brian jumped back in his truck and sped off.

THERE WERE THREE reasons why Blue figured this visit to see Marin was a big-assed mistake. Reason number one—she was probably working, especially since a storm had moved in and was dumping so much rain and lightning that any training had become impossible. So, like pretty much everyone else on the ranch, she'd decided to do reports and such at home.

Reason number two—since Leo was at school, it meant Marin was alone, and that would give them privacy that could turn into a temptation they couldn't resist. It was the reason Blue purposely hadn't brought a condom with him. This visit wasn't about sex. Of course, it could be about that, but he'd told her to take at least a day or two to think it through, and so far, she hadn't given him any indication that the thinking was over and done.

Reason number three—his mood was rock bottom and his knee was throbbing. Added to that, he hadn't been able to get his mind off what Audrey had told him. A secret that was going to knock his dad for a loop once he found out. Blue wasn't sure his dad could handle being knocked for a loop.

So, not exactly a sunshine combination for a visit.

Still, he hadn't had a chance to talk to Marin since their encounter with Brian the day before, and he wanted to check on her.

Blue figured she was worried sick over the man's threat. Immediately after Brian had left, Blue had assured her that he would get a PI if the asshole managed to come up with an actual sponsor. Blue and his dad had also told Marin they'd make sure to keep Brian away from the ranch and that she could use the attorney they kept on retainer if it came down to any kind of legal fight.

Assurances, though, wouldn't mean squat right now since she was probably terrified of Brian going after Leo. Blue wasn't exactly calm as a lake about the prospect of it, either. Brian might never get his greedy, lying hands on Leo, but he could try to stir up trouble.

Blue had sent Marin a text to let her know he was on his way over. He hadn't wanted to frighten her if the storm let up enough to allow her to hear an approaching vehicle. He didn't want her to think it was Brian making a return visit. She hadn't responded with a willy-nilly kind of answer like "thanks, but I'm fine." Marin had instead gone with an, Okay. Not exactly an enthusiastic reply, but since it wasn't a "no, don't come," Blue had braved the storm to go to her.

Braved in this case meant getting wet.

The wind had made it impossible to use an umbrella, but thankfully his hat had stayed on, so at least one part of him didn't get soaked when he'd hurried out of the house and to the truck. The rain didn't let up one bit on the drive, and he got another soaking when he did more hurrying to get to her front porch.

Blue had barely made it to the top step when Marin opened the door and immediately offered him a towel. Blue took it, dried off a little and then pulled her into his arms to kiss her.

Another big-assed mistake.

But he didn't care. Marin just looked so irresistible, and she didn't hold back in her response to the kiss, either. With the storm lashing at his back, they stood in the doorway and kissed as if big-assed mistakes weren't even a possibility.

She tasted more than good. As usual. A taste that was familiar to him now, but the familiarity didn't lessen the punch it gave him. A punch that made him want to take more, and he might have gone in the more mode, but the rain was slanting in and was giving his ass a good soaking.

"You're getting wet," she muttered. "Wetter," she amended, and Marin stepped back, tugging him inside.

She shut the door, but that didn't do anything to muffle the sound of the rain since the cabin had a tin roof. It was as if someone had cranked up one of those soothing sound machines.

He'd been right about her doing work. Her laptop was open and positioned on the desk in the corner. Next to it was a notepad that he'd seen her use to jot down something after a training session.

"FYI, I think kissing should be our customary greeting from now on," he said, keeping his voice light. It wasn't hard, either. The kiss had gone a long way to helping with his dark mood.

"That might cause some gossip if we *greet* each other while your family or any of the ranch hands are around," she pointed out, putting *greet* in air quotes.

It would, indeed, but Blue figured the gossip was already going. Anyone who saw Marin and him together had likely seen the heat between them, too.

"Speaking of your family, how's your dad doing?" Marin asked, going into the kitchen.

She offered him a cup of tea by holding up a kettle, but Blue shook his head. She made herself a cup, though, and the scent of apples and cinnamon instantly filled the cabin.

Blue considered her question and decided there was no reason to pull back on the truth. "I think he's scared spitless and thinks if he makes one wrong move, that it'll be his last."

That put some alarm in Marin's eyes. She stopped dipping the tea bag and looked at him. "Is his heart condition that bad?"

"Possibly. Audrey says he's improving, but maybe it's like those people who fall off a horse and never get back on."

At the mention of his stepmother's name, he thought of Rowan4321. No way did he want to dump all of that on Marin. She had enough to deal with. Plus, Blue hadn't wrapped his own head around it enough to have a discussion about it. That said, though, if he was going to talk to anyone about it, it'd be Marin. She'd be a hell of a lot more objective about it than Egan, Cal or Remi. Eventually, though, his siblings would have to know.

And his dad.

Hell, his dad would have to know. And Blue didn't want to guess what that would do to him and to his relationship with Audrey. He doubted his dad would be pleased about having been lied to for the past thirty years.

"When do Audrey and your father go back to DC?" Marin asked.

"Not until Sunday." Which was still two and a half days from now. "We're doing a big dinner on Saturday night. Well, sort of big. Alana's supervising the menu so it'll be healthy for dad."

Since Alana was a dietitian, the dishes might not contain enormous amounts of fat and sugar, which were staples when Maybell cooked "big."

"Would you like to come and bring Leo?" Blue asked.

She was quick to shake her head. "No. But thank you."

He understood. It was a family deal, and while every single member of his family would have likely welcomed Leo and her, Marin probably wouldn't feel comfortable.

Still trying to dry himself off with the towel, Blue went closer to Marin to try to ease the traces of alarm that were still in her eyes. That was when he saw the papers on the kitchen island.

"It's an affidavit of voluntary relinquishment of parental rights that Brian signed," she explained. "The affidavit was used in the court order that terminated his parental rights."

Since the papers were on top of a file folder, it was obvious that she'd taken them out and been reading them. Of course, she had. Brian's visit had shaken her to the core.

"I spoke to the lawyer who Jussie used for the court order and for setting me up with custody of Leo, and the lawyer insists it's airtight, that it'll hold up in court," she added and then paused. "But that doesn't mean Brian won't try to fight it."

No, it didn't. And Blue understood there was nothing he could say to her that would take all the alarm out of her eyes. Because it wasn't just for Leo's dad.

It was worry over Leo.

A kiss wouldn't fix this, but he went to her, anyway, set her tea aside and pulled her into his arms. Nope, it wasn't a fix for worry, but it felt damn good.

Now he didn't just have to smell the amazing scent of the apples and cinnamon, he got to taste it, too, and combined with Marin's own natural taste, it certainly packed a wallop. Then again, that always happened with Marin.

Not exactly a comforting thought.

Because he had to wonder if she had now become the benchmark for all future kisses. If so, he was screwed because no one else was going to live up to this.

The sound she made yanked his attention back to her. Not that his attention had strayed too far. But she made the sound that was a unique mix of silk and intense pleasure. Again, that would become a benchmark.

The kiss lingered on and on, and Blue had no intentions of stopping. Marin apparently did, though. She pulled back, and this time when she looked at him, there was something else in her eyes.

A storm of a different kind.

And yeah, he recognized the signals. She wanted more. Hell, he wanted that, too, and was mentally cursing himself for not bringing that condom.

"We never did talk about whether or not we were having sex," he said.

"Let's talk about it now," she countered.

She pulled him back to her, the new kiss immediately notching up the heat by a thousand degrees or two. That brought on more mental cursing because it was obvious this was going to get out of hand in the next couple of minutes.

But he was wrong about that.

It got out of hand *now*.

Marin saw to that by moving her grip down to his still-wet ass and giving him a push so that their middles landed against each other. It was a mind-blowing move that gave him an instant hard-on. Of course, he'd already been heading in that direction, anyway since the kissing had fired up every inch of him.

Every inch of him wanted yet more firing up, and that came through loud and clear. Not only did Blue deepen the kissing by lowering his mouth, and his tongue, to her neck, he did some adjustments of his own to deepen the contact. He hooked his arm around Marin's butt, lifting her off the floor so that his erection had just the right contact with her center.

She made that sound again.

And cursed him.

It was a good kind of cursing, too, to let him know he'd hit the right spot. And, of course, that only escalated things even more. The heat rolled through him. Hungry and insatiable. Well, insatiable with only kisses and touches. This kind of heat demanded sex. Right here on the kitchen floor. Definitely a now, now, now urgency.

Which couldn't happen.

Blue mentally repeated that to himself, and somehow he managed to convince his mouth to hit pause on the kiss just so he could speak. "I don't have a condom with me," he managed to tell Marin.

He watched her process that. Not easily. Probably because her brain was just as clouded with lust as his. But he knew the exact moment when it sank in because she cursed again. This time, though, it definitely wasn't because he'd hit the right spot.

But he could do something about that.

Maybe it wouldn't appease his brainless hard-on, but it would hopefully give Marin some release from this pressure cooker of heat.

He didn't let go of her, and with her feet still several inches off the floor, he moved her toward the kitchen table. "Let's play a game," he suggested.

Clearly, she didn't like that idea, and the frustration—lots and lots of frustration—fired up in her eyes. Some of that went away, though, when he kissed her again. A full-on deep kiss that made it impossible for her to voice any of that disappointment. It likely robbed her of her breath. It had certainly done that to Blue, and he had to fight hard to make sure it also didn't rob him of at least a shred or two of common sense.

A shred that would prevent them from having unprotected sex.

"This game is called red light, green light," he said, sitting her on the table and moving in between her legs. He lowered his mouth to her jaw. "And the rules are simple. Say green if you like what I do. Red, if you don't."

Blue launched right into it by tongue kissing her neck while he lowered his hand to her right breast. He swiped his thumb over her nipple.

"Green," Marin said, the word rushing out with her breath. "But if you don't have a condom, we probably shouldn't be doing this."

She was right. Playing with fire always posed a risk, but Blue proceeded, anyway. He kept his mouth on her neck, trailing down while he eased up her top. When the trailing down and easing up met, he kissed the top of her breast. Then, tongue-kissed the front of her bra and her nipple.

"Green," she was quick to say. "Yes, green."

That was a good sign so he kept going. Kept up the playing with fire by lowering the cups of her bra. Even though there'd been just a millimeter or two of fabric between his mouth and her breast, it was amazing just how much better a deep kiss could be with that millimeter removed.

Much better for him, and apparently much better for Marin because she gushed out another "Green."

Blue considered this the liftoff stage. He was off the runway and had Marin soaring. But he wanted to take her a lot higher than this. Even if this playing around was causing his erection to ache in protest.

He pulled off her shirt and unhooked her bra so he could do some soaring with her breasts. No simple nipple kiss this time. He lingered. Tasted. Savored. And apparently hit just the right level.

"Green," Marin said, and there was a whole lot of fresh urgency in her voice to let Blue know he would have to move to the grand finale soon.

But not too soon.

With her breasts now bare, he yanked off his own shirt to give them both some skin to skin. Yeah, it was amazing, and the rain actually worked for him. His wet chest created a slippery effect that had them sliding against each other and creating the best kind of friction.

Definitely amazing.

Blue would have gutted out his own "green" if Marin hadn't beaten him to it.

She beat him to something else, too. Apparently, the slippery sliding gave her some ideas, and she slid the palm of her hand over the front of his jeans. His eyes crossed. His heart missed a couple of beats. And he saw stars. Not the same kind of stars people saw with pain. But the opposite. This was pleasure, all torturous pleasure.

That couldn't continue.

Well, it couldn't unless he was willing to risk having sex. And he wasn't. Hopefully, he'd continue to think that way.

Blue eased her hand away from his crotch and went

after her jeans instead. He kissed her while he lowered her zipper. And eased his hand into her panties.

He had to pause then. Had to rein in a whole bunch of demands from his dick that was alerting him to the slippery heat that his fingers located.

"Green," Marin managed, though there wasn't much sound. It was mainly breath and need.

The wind and the rain lashed out against the windows and the roof, and Blue's heartbeat seemed to pick up the rhythm of it. Fast and hard. Which was what he wanted to be doing to Marin right now. Not with his hand, either. But this would have to do, and it would no doubt become a cautionary tale for him to bring a condom with him the next time he paid her a visit.

He slid his fingers into her, touching and teasing. Helping her climb higher and higher. This was as much of a "full throttle" mode as he could manage without having full-blown sex.

"Green," she muttered.

He upped the pressure of his touch. Upped the speed some, too. While he anchored her with his free hand on her back. He kissed her breasts again, taking her nipple into his mouth while he kept touching. Kept his fingers sliding through all that wet heat.

"Green," she repeated.

Then, he went for the skies. More pressure, more speed. More, more, more. Until he felt the climax start to ripple through her.

"Green, green, green," Marin murmured as he sent her flying.

CHAPTER SIXTEEN

"DO STARS HURT when they're in your eyes?" Leo asked.

That yanked Blue out of the fantasy he'd been having about Marin. A fantasy that hadn't involved marriage. But rather sex. An ill-timed fantasy, considering Leo was with him, and they were riding the two-seater ATV back from their latest fishing trip.

Blue frowned. "Uh, why would you think that?"

"Because I heard Miss Maybell telling Grammy Effie that you had stars in your eyes over Aunt Marin, and that she has stars for you, too," Leo was quick to explain. "And I just wondered if they hurt."

Since Leo was seated beside Blue and therefore couldn't fully see his face, Blue's frown deepened. Not because what Maybell said wasn't true. It probably was. But he preferred not to have the attraction discussed in front of Leo.

"No, it doesn't hurt," Blue settled for saying, hoping that would be the last of it.

It wasn't.

"What does it mean to have stars in your eyes?" Leo pressed.

Blue didn't have a clue how to answer that. He didn't want to say anything about liking Marin. Definitely nothing about the heat that had nearly gotten out of control two days ago on the kitchen table. Nope, he wasn't going anywhere near that topic.

"Your aunt Marin and I are friends," Blue finally responded, though talk about a lame-ass answer. They were more than friends. Even more than friends with benefits, though there actually hadn't been any full benefits between them. Not physically, anyway, but in his head, Blue had had sex—damn amazing sex—with Marin multiple times.

"Good," Leo concluded. "I'm glad you're friends."

Blue blew out a breath of relief and hoped that was the last of that particular topic. They were only a minute or two out from the cabin where Marin was working on some reports, and even though Leo and he did "catch and release" with the fish, he'd be eager to tell Marin all about the bass he'd managed to reel in. It would get the boy off the subject of friends and stars.

"Are you friends with my real dad?" Leo asked.

That threw Blue for another mental loop, and he hoped like the devil that Maybell and Effie hadn't been discussing that, too. "No, I'm not. Why do you ask?"

Leo lifted his shoulder. "I just wondered. Aunt Marin doesn't like to talk about him so I don't think they're friends, but if you're his friend, I thought I could maybe ask you stuff about him."

Blue cursed, but he managed to keep the profanity in his head. "What kind of questions?"

"Lots of them," Leo said. "I mean, I know what he looks like since Aunt Marin showed me pictures. That's how I knew who he was when I saw him."

Blue's head whipped toward Leo so fast that his neck popped. "You saw your dad?"

Leo nodded, clearly not picking up on the "holy shit" look that had to be all over Blue's face. "Yesterday, at my school. Well, across from the playground when I was out for recess. I waved at him, and he smiled and waved back."

It took a moment, a couple of them, for Blue to get his teeth unclenched. "Did he say anything to you?"

"Nope. But he smiled," Leo repeated, grinning as if that were the best thing since…well, Nutella straight out of the jar.

Blue wasn't jealous, but he was damn concerned. He tried to keep that concern out of his voice, though. "Tell you what. Why don't I drop you off with Miss Maybell and Grammy Effie so you can have a snack, maybe even go through some of the new books that Grammy bought you."

There were at least a dozen of them. Plenty of stuff for snacks, too. And that should keep Leo entertained enough while Blue told Marin about Brian being near the school.

After Blue had stopped the ATV, he fired off a quick text to Maybell to let her know that Leo would be heading into the house soon. Maybell didn't question why, she just came back with a triple happy face response.

With that done, Blue walked Leo to the back porch, and the moment the boy was inside, he called Marin. She answered on the first ring.

"I'm on my way to the cabin," he said, heading toward the truck. "Leo just told me that Brian was across from his school yesterday. Did he mention it to you?"

Though Blue already knew the answer. If Leo had, Marin would have passed along that info to him.

"No," she said, and she sounded as stunned, and worried, as Blue was. "What did Brian do?"

"Nothing other than smile and wave. Leo saw him and knew who he was. Leo's with Maybell and Effie right now, and I figured I'd go have a chat with Brian. Do you want to go with me?"

"You bet I do." Some of the shock and worry were gone, and now there was quite a bit of anger in her voice. Then, hesitation. "But I don't know where he lives."

"I do," Blue answered. "The ranch keeps a private investigator on retainer, and I had her do a thorough background check on Brian. He rents an apartment in San Antonio, but he's been staying at a motel just off the interstate. About fifteen miles from the ranch."

Blue hadn't wanted to give Marin that information over the phone. But this way, she could maybe be over the initial shock of what she'd just heard and be ready to confront this asshole who'd bothered Leo, but had never been anywhere close to a father to the boy.

"I'll be at the cabin in a few minutes," Blue added to her. He ended the call, hurried to the truck and started driving.

There was no storm messing with the roads today so he made it to the cabin in record time. As expected, Marin was already on the porch, and she had her purse hooked over her shoulder, clearly ready to go. She still had her hat on when she jumped into the cab of the truck with him.

"Leo didn't say a word about this to me," she muttered. "Why wouldn't he have told me?"

"I don't think it occurred to Leo to tell anyone. It just came up in conversation on the way back from the creek."

Blue already knew the way to the interstate and the motel so he didn't bother to put the address in the GPS. He just started toward what felt a whole lot like a showdown. A showdown that would take at least twenty-five minutes since he had to travel on a narrow country road to get to the motel.

"You swear to me that Leo wasn't upset?" she pressed.

"I swear. He didn't seem the least bit bothered by it." Then, Blue paused. "However, he did want to know if having stars in my eyes hurt."

Marin gave him a blank look. "What?"

Blue sighed. "Apparently, he heard Maybell and Effie talking about us having stars in our eyes over each other. I thought you should know in case it comes up in conversation."

"Thanks for the heads-up," she muttered.

She probably would've been a whole lot more bothered by that if she weren't so worried about Leo and Brian. Later, though, it would probably sink in and she wouldn't be too pleased to know that they were the subject of gossip. Then again, Marin and he had done plenty to initiate that gossip. That whole stormy "make out" session had certainly been gossip-worthy, and while no one else had personally witnessed it, anyone who saw his truck at her cabin could have guessed what was going on.

They were still about nine miles out from the motel when Blue's phone rang, and he saw Egan's name on the dash display. Blue debated letting it go to voice mail, but Egan may have seen him speed away from the ranch and would be worried.

"What the hell is wrong?" his brother immediately asked.

Yeah, Egan had seen him, all right. "Marin and I are going to pay Brian a little visit because he was near Leo's school Friday. Leo's not with us right now so feel free to curse," he added to his brother.

Egan took him up on that. He cursed. "Where are you right now? Because I want to be in on that meeting, too."

"We're headed to the motel out by the interstate, but there's no need for you to be with us on this visit. I just want to make a few things clear to Brian."

"That's what I'm afraid of," Egan grumbled. "I'm on my way to meet you there. Any chance I can get you to hold off talking to him until I arrive?"

"Not much of a chance," Blue admitted. "Emotions are running pretty high right now."

Egan's next sigh was even louder. "All right, then, just be careful," he insisted. "And while you're driving, you can tell me what's going on with Audrey."

Blue had a moment of brain freeze, not the kind you got with eating something cold too fast, but rather the kind that came when he didn't know how the heck to respond.

"What do you mean?" Blue asked. Plain and simple, it was a cop-out, but there was no way he wanted to get into the details about his conversation with Audrey over the phone.

This time, Egan didn't sigh. He huffed. "Maybell said she saw you talking to Audrey and that the conversation looked pretty intense. It doesn't take a psychologist to see that Audrey has been out of it. She's definitely not her usual self, so using my amazing powers of deduction, I can guess that something is wrong. What I want to know is if she talked to you about it? Is she worried about Dad?" Egan tacked on to that before Blue was forced to answer.

"She is worried about him," Blue said, and that wasn't a lie. They were all worried about his dad.

"Does Dad have some health problems she's not telling him about?" Egan pressed.

"Not that I know of. That's the truth," Blue added when Egan huffed again. "She's worried about him, but she didn't get into any specific details about his health or lack thereof."

The silence came, and Blue could almost see his brother thinking this out. Blue was doing some thinking about it, too, and he made a mental note, another one, to do more research on this Rowan4321.

"All right," Egan finally said. "I'll see you at the motel in a few minutes."

Blue ended the call, and he glanced at Marin, who was looking at him. She didn't come out and question him about the way he had responded to his brother, but he could see the question in her eyes.

Even though they would arrive at the motel in under fifteen minutes, Blue went ahead and launched into an explanation. "Audrey's conversation with me wasn't about Dad. It was a confession. Apparently, thirty years ago, shortly after my mother died, Audrey and my dad had a one-off."

Marin's mouth didn't fall open, but it was close. "Wow," she said, letting him know that she clearly hadn't expected that. Blue sure as hell hadn't expected it, either, when Audrey told him.

"According to Audrey," he continued, "the one-off happened as an 'intense grief' sort of thing, something that neither of them had planned. Or wanted."

Since Blue had gone this far, he continued with the rest of it.

"Audrey got pregnant but didn't want to tell Dad because she thought it would only add to his grief. So, she broke off things with him, making sure he didn't see her when she was pregnant. She had the baby and gave him up for adoption. That would have been near the early days of her career so she probably thought it wasn't a good time to be raising a child."

Blue couldn't resent her for thinking about how a baby could affect her career. But he could damn sure resent that she hadn't told his dad about the baby.

"I didn't ask for specifics," Blue went on, "but I'm guessing the adoption was private since Audrey had no idea what his name was or where he is now. Or rather she had no idea until she found a DNA connection to me on one of the ancestry sites. The percentage of DNA in common means the person is likely the kid she gave up for adoption."

"Wow," Marin repeated. "What did she want you to do? Get in touch with him?"

"She wanted to know if she should tell my dad. I didn't get a chance to tell her hell, yes, before Brian showed up." Blue paused. "Now, I'm glad I didn't insist she tell him because I'm not sure he's healthy enough for news like that."

Marin made a soft sound of agreement. "So, what will you do? What will Audrey do?"

"I'm not sure about her, but as for me, I'm thinking about sending this guy an email. I don't know his name. He's using Rowan4321 for his contact on the genealogy website. But I could email him, and in a casual way I could just ask if he knows how we're related. It could turn out to be nothing other than a cousin marrying a cousin kind of deal that ended up giving me and this guy twenty-five percent DNA in common."

She nodded. "But if he comes back and asks you if you're his half brother, what will you do?"

"I don't have a clue," Blue said.

And he didn't. Any contact with the guy could result in some communication that would lead him to the ranch. Then, his dad would find out what Blue was worried he might not be ready to hear.

Blue shoved all thoughts of that aside, though, when he pulled into the parking lot of the motel. He immediately spotted the beat-up truck that Brian had driven to the ranch, and it was parked in front of room 112. The very room where the private investigator had said he was staying. So, obviously the man hadn't checked out yet.

"I'm not going to ask you to wait in the truck," Blue told her. "But if you get the urge to punch him, you might want to hold off on that. It would only end up hurting your hand, and it probably wouldn't accomplish much."

Heck, talking to the asshole probably wouldn't accomplish much, either, but Blue intended to try.

Marin didn't stay put, of course. She got out of the truck when Blue did, and together they walked to the door. Brian didn't answer on the first two knocks so Blue knocked even harder. Finally, the door opened.

No khakis and cleaned-up look for the man today. He was sporting some scruff on his face and was wearing ratty jogging pants and a stained T-shirt. At first, some alarm went through Brian's bloodshot eyes, but that was soon replaced with a smirk.

"Are you here to make arrangements so I can see my son?" Brian asked.

"No," Blue and Marin said in unison. It was Blue who continued. "We're here to tell you to quit skulking around Leo's school. Along with just being plain creepy, that's also stalking."

Brian rolled his eyes. "Leo is my son," he said as if that excused everything bad he had ever done.

"He's your son in DNA only, "Marin was quick to point out. "I shouldn't have to remind you that you signed away your rights."

"DNA is a biggie, and Leo will always be mine," he argued. "And as for signing away my rights, well, I've changed my mind about that."

"It doesn't work that way," Marin insisted. She shook

her head and Blue didn't have to guess that it was a headshake of disgust. "What is it you really want? Because I'm not buying that you actually want to see Leo after all this time."

Brian stared at her. And stared. His mouth tightened with each passing moment. That tightening didn't improve much when Egan pulled up and barreled out of the truck.

"Great," Brian grumbled. "Reinforcements have arrived." He turned an icy gaze on Marin. "You think you're so special," he spat out. "So much better than me. But you're not. Working at a big fancy ranch doesn't make you better than me."

"No, not being an asshole jerk makes me better than you," Marin fired back, and it nearly made Blue applaud. "What do you want?" she repeated, emphasizing each word.

Brian volleyed more of those icy glances at all three of them. "I've already said that I want to see Leo."

She shook her head. "No, that's not it because if it were, you would've already produced the name of that sponsor that you were bragging about. That was the condition for me to consider letting you see Leo, and that consideration would have happened only after I spoke with the sponsor to confirm what you said."

"And after I had the sponsor investigated to make sure he wasn't a fake," Blue added, causing Marin to give a confirming nod.

Marin followed up that nod with a huff. "Just cut to the chase, Brian. You came to the ranch to ask for money."

Blue hadn't thought it possible, but Brian's eyes narrowed even more than they already were. And he remained silent for several long moments. "Yes," Brian finally snapped. "I need money, and I think it's only fair that you should pay me since you got the privilege of raising my son."

Talk about idiot logic, but Blue had expected no less from this moron. Apparently, neither had Marin because her sigh was long and loud.

"I'm not paying you one cent," she insisted. "And you will leave Leo alone."

Brian looked ready to challenge that, but then he made another glance at Blue and Egan and must've decided this wasn't a time to increase the idiocy. "I'll have my sponsor get in touch with you," he spat out. "And when you're finished with the verification, then I will see Leo."

"Maybe," was Marin's response. "A really big maybe. And in the meantime, you'll stay away from him."

"Or what?" Brian challenged.

"Or I'll get a restraining order," Egan was quick to say. "I won't have any problem getting one."

"Because you're a big man with money." Brian's tone was mean and chiding, but he took a step back into his room when Egan moved closer. "Did Marin tell you that her boyfriend killed her sister? Did she tell you that, huh?"

Marin reacted fast. Not to throw a punch at the asshole. But to stop Blue from doing it. "I've told Blue everything about that," she said, meeting Brian's gaze head-on. She took hold of Blue's arm. "Stay away from

Leo," she added in warning to Brian before she started back toward the truck.

Blue wanted to stay put. He wanted to throw that punch. But unlike Brian, he wasn't an idiot. It was probably what Brian wanted him to do so that he could in turn use it to get money. Neither Marin nor he needed to give this asshole any kind of fodder that could be used against them.

"Restraining order," Egan repeated as a threat to Brian before he went back to his own truck.

Brian slammed the door so hard that Blue was surprised it didn't fly off the hinges. So much anger. So much slime. And Blue was afraid they hadn't seen the last of him.

"If he produces a sponsor," Marin said once they were back on the road, "I want him vetted."

"Absolutely," Blue assured her.

"And I'll pay for it. I'll pay for it," she repeated when he groaned.

"Don't you dare say this is your problem," he was quick to point out. "Because it's not. You and Leo are part of Saddlebrook now, and that means if you need help, you get it." He had to tamp down more of his anger before he could get out the rest. "I want to help you."

She looked at him as if trying to decide why he'd added that last part, but there was not just one thing. It was the whole package. His feelings for Leo. For Marin. Wanting to protect them and keep them safe. And yeah, the attraction to Marin was probably playing into some of that.

"Egan pays me well," she added. "But thank you, not

just for the offer, but for going with me. Brian would have tried to toss a whole lot more at me if I'd been alone. He's a coward. But he has a sharp tongue." She paused, groaned. "I don't know how he found out about my sister."

"He's an asshole who's willing to use anything or anybody to get what he wants," Blue pointed out. "I'm sorry he used the memories of your sister to try to hurt you."

And that convinced him even more that they needed to go through with the restraining order. That way, Brian could be arrested if he showed up at the ranch or at Leo's school. With the man's track record and rap sheet, it shouldn't be hard to get one, especially with Egan pushing for it.

Marin stayed quiet, no doubt trying to process all of this. Probably while also trying to tamp down the crappy memories Brian had stirred up. Blue reached for her hand and managed a gentle squeeze. Just as his phone rang. He was surprised when he saw the name on the dash display.

Remi.

He'd thought his sister was deployed somewhere to a classified location, and it was a rarity for her to call when she was on the job.

A rarity unless it was some kind of emergency.

Blue couldn't answer the call fast enough. "What's wrong?" he immediately demanded.

"I was about to ask you the same thing," Remi fired back. "What the heck is going on? And who is Rowan4321?"

CHAPTER SEVENTEEN

Marin had no trouble hearing what Blue's sister had just asked, not with Remi's voice pouring through the truck. She also had no trouble recalling who Rowan4321 was since Blue had told her about it on the drive to the motel.

That was the identity his half brother was using.

"Well?" Remi pressed when Blue didn't say anything. "Who is he?"

"Where are you?" Blue asked.

"On my way to the ranch. I got a couple of days' leave, and I just flew in. I checked my emails after I landed, and I got a notice from the ancestry site that I had a strong relationship match. It took me a while to figure out that the match was for the test I gave you for Christmas, and I forwarded the report to Audrey since I didn't want to bother Dad or you with it until you were both healthier. So, who the heck is Rowan4321?"

Blue groaned. "How soon will you be at the ranch?"

Remi wasn't quick to answer. "That bad, huh? So bad that you don't want to tell me over the phone?"

"How soon will you be at the ranch?" he repeated.

Remi muttered a single curse word under her breath. "I'm about fifteen minutes out. How about you?"

"Five minutes out. Don't mention this to anyone else before we talk," Blue tacked on to that.

More muttering from Remi. "Too late. I texted Grammy Effie because I figured it could be a close cousin connection, but she didn't know anything about it. The DNA percentage is right for either Cal or Egan to have a kid out there we don't know about. Or some kid mom or dad had with someone else."

"Shit," Blue said on a groan.

"That bad," Remi concluded again. "See you in a few, and I'll expect a full explanation. Oh, and hello, Marin."

"Hello," Marin answered back. "How did you know I was here?"

"Blue would have cursed a whole lot more if he'd been alone or with Egan. Besides, Grammy said you two had driven off somewhere together and that Leo was having a playdate with a friend. By the way, I didn't explain the Rowan4321 issue."

Yes, Leo was at a playdate, and he still had another four hours before the friend's mother would be bringing him home. Since Remi knew Leo's name, then someone had clearly filled her in on things. But not on Rowan4321. That would not be a fun conversation.

"After we get to the ranch, I can use one of the other vehicles or an ATV to go to the cabin," Marin offered after he said goodbye to his sister and ended the call.

He glanced at her and muttered more of that profanity that Remi had been so sure he wouldn't say with her around. "I don't intend to tell my dad. That means when I talk to Grammy, I'll have to give her a bullshit answer, something along the lines of I got a message from the ancestry site about some wrong results being sent out. That'll settle things down long enough for you to meet Remi."

Marin shook her head. "This could be a really bad time for introductions."

"Yeah, and I'm sorry about that, but if Effie told Remi about us heading off, then my grandmother will want an explanation about that, too. Especially since Egan did some 'heading off' as well. If you leave immediately after we get back, then Effie's going to be worried."

Marin so wished she could argue with that because she didn't want to be anywhere in the vicinity when Blue was having to tap-dance around his stepmother's secret. Still, Blue had stood up for her against Brian, and that meant she could do the same for him with his family.

Blue turned onto the ranch road, and before the house came into view, he pulled off onto the shoulder and motioned for Egan to go past him. His brother did, but not before giving them a long look as his truck crept by them. Egan probably figured they still had to discuss their meeting with Brian.

"I just need a minute," Blue said, throwing the truck into Park. "And I need this."

He leaned over, pulling her to him as much as the seat belt would allow, and he kissed her. Oh, she hadn't seen that coming, but she had no trouble feeling the instant heat it created.

Her body reacted to that heat. Mercy, did it, and her

mind went straight back to what had happened in the kitchen of the cabin. Not having a condom had prevented Blue and her from having full-blown sex, but he'd still managed to make it memorable. And very, very pleasurable. Her body urged her to do the same thing for him as soon as they could manage it.

Of course, with everything happening, managing it might take a while. So, this kiss might have to hold her over—that was why she made the most of it. Despite all the other messes happening, Marin poured herself into that kiss and savored it as if it were the last one she would ever get.

"Thanks," Blue drawled in that voice that was pure sex. "Like I said, I needed that."

"I needed it, too," she muttered. It was a huge deal to let him know that. Well, maybe it was. And it was just as likely that Blue already knew she'd fallen hard for him. Yes.

He smiled in that hot way of his that was just as sexy as his drawl. And his kiss. Both the moment and the smile seemed to freeze, and their gazes held. A dozen things seemed to pass between them. Worry, for sure because neither one of them was in a stellar place right now. Lust, that was for sure, too, because the heat was always there between them. But there was something else, something she didn't quite get a chance to wrap her mind around.

Because his phone rang again.

"Shit, what now?" he grumbled. "Is the sky falling?"

Marin nearly laughed. Because fate really did seem to have it in for them today.

The number that popped up on the dashboard screen didn't have a name associated with it as Egan's and Remi's calls had. This one had some kind of initials that Blue must've recognized because he answered it right away.

"This is Major Donnelly," Blue said, letting Marin know this was an official call.

"Major Donnelly," the caller greeted. "I'm Captain Carswell, and I'm calling about your appointment. From what I understand, you're interested in taking a flight physical as soon as possible."

Definitely an official call. Marin knew what that meant, too. A flight physical, or rather Blue passing one, would return him to duty.

"Yes," Blue said. He sounded a little hoarse. As if his throat had tightened. Hers was certainly tightening, too. "That's right. I want a flight physical."

"Well," the captain responded, "I can schedule one for 0930 Wednesday of next week if that works for you."

Wednesday. Only five days from now.

Blue paused. But not for long. "Schedule it," he said.

"Done, I'll send you a confirmation email with the date and time of the appointment, and if you have to cancel, the instructions will be in the body of that email." With that, the captain signed off.

Again, Blue paused, staring at the dash screen, and this time the pause was a whole lot longer than the other one. He was clearly trying to process what had just happened. Marin was processing it as well, but she already knew what Blue needed from her. Not a kiss this time. That wasn't going to work. She needed to give him the words.

"This is good," she managed to say.

She repeated it, and this time she thought she sounded certain of what she'd just said. She was certain, all right, this was the right thing for Blue. But, mercy, her heart was already aching. No way, though, did she intend to let Blue see that.

He started driving again, and the moment she saw the house, she also spotted Egan, Effie, Maybell, Audrey and Blue's dad all on the porch. Marin quickly checked if there were any "doom and gloom" expressions, but she didn't see any. So maybe they had all gathered out there anticipating Remi's arrival. The glasses of iced tea they were all drinking seemed to be an indication of that.

Blue pulled to a stop, and Marin heard him take a long, deep breath before he stepped out of the truck. She stepped out with him, and she had to rethink the absence of those "gloom and doom" expressions that she had missed with her first glance. Effie was definitely sporting some concern.

"What happened? Why did all of you drive off like that?" Effie asked, directing her questions at Blue.

Maybell added, "Is Leo all right? He's not sick again, is he?"

Egan launched right in with a response. "I was just about to explain that we went to have a chat with Leo's bio-dad. We told him to stay away from Leo and the ranch so if anyone sees him around, you need to let Jesse or me know right away."

"Is that man going to give you some trouble?" Blue's father asked. He got a variety of answers.

"Not if I can help it," Blue snarled.

"I don't plan to let him get close enough to Leo to cause any trouble," Egan contributed.

"I hope he doesn't," was the best that Marin could say. But it wasn't the best she could do. If Brian came after Leo, she would stop him. She didn't know how, but she would.

None of what was said alleviated the concern for Blue's dad, but it seemed to appease Effie. For the moment, anyway.

"Good news," Effie said, smiling now. "Remi will be here soon."

"Yes," Blue verified. "She called me on the drive home."

"I'm so glad she'll get to see her dad and Audrey before they have to head back to Washington," Effie gushed. "Did Remi manage to ask you about that Rowan4321?"

Blue didn't groan or curse, but Marin figured that was exactly what he wanted to do. Good grief. No way did Blue want to deal with this now. She could say the same for Audrey because the woman lost nearly every drop of color in her face.

"Who?" his father asked. "Is that some guy from a dating site or something?"

Effie shook her head, and she clearly hadn't picked up on Audrey's and Blue's expressions of dread. "No, Remi thought it might be a cousin because he came up as a DNA match on that site Blue used," Effie explained.

"You remember the gift Remi gave Blue for Christmas? Well, you get matches of relatives, and Blue got one."

His father looked at Blue who hadn't gone pale like Audrey, but it was obvious to Marin that Blue was having trouble coming up with what to say.

"Is he a cousin?" his dad came out and asked. "Because I don't remember any cousin on my or your mother's side of the family named Rowan."

"Oh, that might not be his real name," Effie was quick to explain. "I've got a friend who did the test, and she used Tater Tot for her ID. She didn't want to say who she really was because she didn't want to get spam."

Derek looked at Blue again, and unlike Effie, he seemed to be clueing into the fact that this topic was making his son very uncomfortable. "So, who is this Rowan4321? Did you find out? And just how close of kin is he?"

Marin wanted to curse when she looked at Audrey and saw the tears shimmering in her eyes. Tears that Audrey quickly blinked away, though, and she pulled back her shoulders. It was as if she were trying to put on her general's facade and gearing up for battle.

"It's okay," Audrey said to Blue, and then she turned to her husband. "Derek, we need to talk."

Derek shifted his attention to Audrey, and he took his time studying her face. "What is it? What's wrong?"

Audrey drew in a breath, the kind of breath a person took if they were about to launch into a long explanation, but then she glanced around. This definitely wouldn't be a private conversation, what with Egan, Maybell, Blue, Effie and Marin around.

Marin wished she could just turn and run or have a big hole swallow her up. She shouldn't be here, not for what was a very personal family matter. But when she started to move away, Blue caught onto her hand. He glanced at her, and even though he had to know how uncomfortable she was, Marin knew he was silently asking her to stay. Maybe because he would end up telling her about it, anyway. Or maybe because he just needed her there. Either way, she stayed put.

"We should probably talk inside," Audrey muttered, but then she groaned, stepped away from Derek and went to the far end of the front porch before she turned and came back. "Everyone will end up knowing about it, anyway."

"Knowing what?" Derek pressed, and this time there was even more concern in his tone.

Audrey didn't pace away again. She stood firm and looked her husband straight in the eyes. "I believe this Rowan4321 is our son." That was it. All she said.

"Your son?" Effie questioned, glancing at both Audrey and Derek. "What do you mean..." But her voice trailed off, and she shook her head. "You don't mean that. Derek and you didn't have a son."

"We did," Audrey answered, still keeping her attention on her husband. "I'm so sorry I didn't tell you, Derek. So sorry." The tears had returned, and Audrey was having to battle them back.

"No," Derek muttered. "No."

"Yes," Audrey insisted. "I got pregnant that time we were together." She paused, obviously giving him a chance to absorb that.

Maybell, Egan and Effie were trying to absorb it as well, and judging from the glance Egan gave Blue, he had figured out that Blue had already known about this. Marin was betting that would soon lead to an intense brotherly conversation.

"What time were you *together*?" Egan wanted to know.

"Shortly after your mother died." The response came from Derek, not Audrey. Derek groaned and scrubbed his hand over his face.

Egan and Blue both went to their dad, probably because they were afraid this would lead to another heart attack. But Derek didn't look ready to collapse. However, he did look thoroughly stunned. And pissed off.

"Explain," Derek demanded, and his gaze had taken on some fire. Marin got a glimpse of the man's former self. Not the man who'd experienced a life-threatening heart attack, but rather the "tough as nails, formidable" rancher.

"I got pregnant," Audrey repeated, and even though it looked as if she wanted to take a step back, she didn't.

Derek's jaw turned to iron. "And you didn't tell me?"

"I didn't," Audrey confirmed. She paused, muttered some profanity. "I intended to, but when I came to see you, you were an emotional mess. Ella had been dead less than two months, and you were grieving. We talked, remember?"

"Of course, I remember," he snapped. "I'm not senile. I remember every one of those days after Ella died."

Audrey nodded. "You were trying to hold yourself and your family together. We talked for a long time, and during that conversation you said you needed to focus on your kids to try to get them through the loss."

"I said that," Derek agreed. "But that didn't mean you shouldn't have told me you were carrying my child." There was so much anger in his voice.

"I made the decision not to tell you," Audrey spelled out. "It felt like the right thing at the time."

"Well, it wasn't," Derek snapped. He kept his stare on her. "What happened to our son? What did you do to him?"

Audrey squared her shoulders again. "I gave birth to him, and because I wasn't in a good place to raise him myself, I placed him with an adoption agency."

Oh, that didn't help with Derek's anger. "Again, without telling me. And what excuse do you have for not telling me after we got married? What excuse, Audrey, because I'd sure as hell love to hear it."

"Dad," Egan said, touching his father's arm. "Why don't you sit down?"

"I don't want to sit down." He aimed an accusing finger at Audrey. "I want her to finish telling me a truth that she shouldn't have kept to herself for thirty years." Derek stopped and looked at Egan. "Or did she tell you?"

"She didn't," Egan said.

"She told me," Blue volunteered.

"Yesterday," Audrey supplied. "I wanted his advice as to whether or not I should tell you."

Derek aimed some of that anger at Blue. "And you kept that to yourself."

Audrey jumped right in on that. "It's not Blue's fault.

It was my secret, not his. And for the record, he was just as stunned as you are now."

"Stunned doesn't even begin to describe what I'm feeling," Derek snapped, returning his attention back to Audrey. "Now, explain why you didn't tell me about our son after we got married? He would have been… what…three? I could have had all these years with him if you'd told me."

"He'd been adopted by then," she reminded him. "And if you recall, before we got married, you and I talked about whether or not to have kids. You said you didn't think it would be a good idea for us to have children since it might be hard for Egan, Cal, Blue and Remi to have half siblings introduced into their lives. I agreed with that," she added to Egan and Blue. "You had a difficult enough time losing your mom and dealing with a stepmother."

No one disagreed with her, but the tension was still thick and drenched in shock and anger.

"Where is he now?" Derek spat out. "Where is Rowan4321?"

"I don't know. That's the truth," Audrey insisted when the anger intensified in Derek's eyes. "I saw the DNA match just a couple of days ago and was deciding if I should contact him or not. Even if I do, it's possible he won't respond. He might not even know he's adopted."

Derek opened his mouth as if to cut her off, but he didn't say anything. He just stared at Audrey for several moments before he cursed. He might have said whatever he'd intended, but an SUV pulled into the driveway. A tall woman with dark auburn hair stepped out.

Remi, no doubt.

She wasn't in uniform, but rather jeans, combat boots and a tee. Her gaze immediately went to them, and she must have figured out what was going on. Her dad obviously filled in some blanks, too.

"Remi knows, too?" Derek demanded.

"No," Audrey insisted. "Remi got the initial DNA report because she was the one to set up the account on the ancestry site, but she didn't know what the report meant. Blue was the only one I told." She paused. "It's possible, though, that Rowan4321 figured it out. I mean, he would have seen the DNA he has in common with Blue and probably at least wondered about it."

But Audrey was talking to Derek's back because the man had already turned away from her. He stormed inside, slamming the door behind him.

CHAPTER EIGHTEEN

"Shit," Blue snarled just as Remi said the same thing.

Normally, that would have earned Remi and him a stern scolding from Effie and Maybell, but the women were clearly too worried about Derek to dole out any criticism. Besides, they might be doing some silent cursing of their own because of the bombshell they'd just heard. Especially Effie.

After all, she had another grandson out there.

One that she and his father had never seen.

"Derek won't want to talk to me," Audrey muttered. "Check on him, please," she added, glancing at Blue, Egan and then Remi. She didn't wait to see if they would comply. Audrey started walking, heading for the barn.

Blue looked at Marin to apologize for keeping her in place so she'd had to hear all of this, but she waved it off. "It's all right. Go to your father."

Marin started walking, too, in the direction of the ATVs that were in the large parking area on the far side of the house. He'd need to see her later, and, well, he would just need to see her. Especially after he tried to deal with the emotional wringer his father was no doubt going through.

Audrey would be going through it as well, but she

wasn't Blue's priority right now. She hadn't recently had two life-threatening heart incidents or been shaken up by Leo's asshole sperm donor.

It was the reminder of his dad's heart problems that got Blue moving quickly into the house. He wasn't alone, Egan and Remi were right behind him, and Blue paused long enough to give his sister a welcome home hug. Even though this sure as hell wasn't much of a welcome.

"Do either of you know anything about this Rowan4321?" Egan asked, glancing at both Blue and Remi.

They both shook their heads. "I only have the email address he set up with the ancestry site," Blue provided as they made their way up the stairs toward the master bedroom where Blue figured their father would be. "I'd have to send him an email and wait for a response."

Egan seemed on the verge of saying "do that" but then he hesitated. Just as Blue had done when he'd debated how to go about this. Because contacting their half sibling could have some bad consequences. As Audrey had pointed out, Rowan4321 might not know he was adopted. Then again, if he'd seen the DNA results, he should have likely figured it out.

"Let's first see if Dad wants to get in touch with him," Egan decided.

Blue was all for that. Mostly. Though he did have to wonder about this half sibling he had out there. Did Rowan4321 know anything about them? If he had connected the dots with Blue's DNA, then maybe.

Egan knocked when they reached the bedroom door,

and even though their dad didn't tell them to come in, Egan opened the door, anyway.

"We're worried about you," Egan said right away, which let Blue know that his dad was, indeed, in there.

Egan stepped in, moving to the side so that Remi and Blue could enter as well. Blue spotted their father, who was at the window, but he didn't turn to face them. He just kept staring out.

"Dad, are you all right?" Remi asked. But his sister immediately waved that off. "Of course, you're not actually all right. No way you could be. But are you having chest pains or anything?"

"No chest pains," he answered in a mutter. That was all he said for several seconds. "If Audrey is with you, you can tell her to leave."

Hell. There was so much bitterness in his father's voice. The bitterness was deserved, but he hated to see his father hurting like this. Heck, he hated knowing that Audrey was hurting, too.

"What can I do to help?" Blue asked.

Again, his dad wasn't quick to respond, and he finally shook his head. "I'm not sure if anything can be done. I have a son out there who might despise me because he thinks I abandoned him. So, even if I find him, he might want nothing to do with me. My own son might want nothing to do with me."

Despite everything that'd just happened, his father sounded stronger than he had in a long time. Ironic, since he'd just been dealt a hard emotional blow.

"I can try to find him," Blue offered. "I can try to talk to him."

His father lifted his hand in a "hold off on that" gesture. "Give me a little while to think about it, and I'll decide what to do." He looked back over his shoulder at Egan. "Do we still have the PI on tap?"

"We do," Egan verified.

His dad nodded. "Good, because we might end up needing her. For now, though, I want just a little time to myself."

He went to them and pulled Remi into his arms for a hug. Then, he did the same to Blue and Egan. His father wasn't much of a hugger so when he did it, it always packed a solid emotional punch.

"I'm sorry, Dad," Blue muttered.

"I'm sorry, too," his father repeated. "You kids have had some bad turns in life. You're still dealing with some of those bad turns," he added, glancing down at Blue's knee.

His dad moved away from them and walked back to the window. "You must hate me for what Audrey and I did so soon after your mom died."

"No," Blue was quick to say, and his siblings were equally fast in echoing the same. "I don't hate you."

Blue could even understand why it happened. People didn't always do rational things when dealing with pain and grief. Of course, most people didn't have to deal with consequences like his father and Audrey were, but Blue wasn't about to blame either of them for finding comfort in each other's arms.

That said, Audrey still shouldn't have kept the pregnancy and the baby a secret. No, it wouldn't have been easy to deliver news like that to Derek, but he should have known. Blue suspected that despite the hell his father had been going through at the time, he would have offered to marry Audrey so they could raise the child together. At the very least, he would have paid child support and been a part of his son's life. His dad might have been a hard-ass when it came to business, but he'd always been there for his kids. This Rowan4321 would have been no different.

"I'd like that alone time now," his father insisted. "I'll be down in a couple of hours to talk to Maybell and Effie. They're probably reeling from everything they heard, and I'll need to settle nerves there."

His dad hadn't mentioned Audrey, and neither did Blue, Egan or Remi. They all walked out, closing the door behind them. In the hall, they stood and stared at each other a few long moments, even though there really wasn't much they could say. At least there was nothing they could say that would fix this, anyway.

"I'll call Cal and tell him what's going on," Egan volunteered. "I don't want him blindsided by anything Effie might say if he calls her."

"Agreed," Blue couldn't say fast enough. Then, he paused. "I need to make sure Marin is all right," Blue muttered, and he headed out.

Each of them, including Effie and Maybell, would need that thinking time, but he wanted to do that with Marin. So, he got in his truck and drove to the cabin.

Of course, it was a bad time to come see her. That was the norm between them, though. The heat always created an intensity, and now it would be coupled with the punches of adrenaline, and the inevitable adrenaline crashes.

That didn't stop him.

He checked the time as he drove and calculated there were still two and a half hours before Leo would get home from his playdate. That was good. Blue loved being around the kid, but for now he just wanted to be with Marin alone.

Marin opened the cabin door before Blue even brought the truck to a stop, and she hurried out to meet him when he got out.

"How's your dad?" she asked, and her voice and expression verified what he already knew. That her nerves and worry were stretched to the limit, too.

"I'm not sure," he admitted.

She nodded, studied him. Marin looped her arm around his waist and led him toward the cabin. "And how are you?"

Blue had to go with a repeat of his answer. "I'm not sure. How about you, how are you?"

Marin didn't answer. Not with words, anyway. The moment they were in the cabin, she closed the door, pulled him into her arms.

And she kissed him.

MARIN DIDN'T EVEN try to talk herself out of what she was doing. Because she didn't want to be talked out of it. She wanted Blue, and even though there would be hell to pay, she was willing to pay it.

She didn't start out with a comforting kiss. Even though both of them could've probably used some comfort, Marin thought they could use some thing a whole lot more.

This insatiable heat.

This need that just wouldn't go away.

Since it wasn't going away, Marin decided to do something about it, and she put all of that need and heat into the kiss. If Blue had not known her intentions when he first arrived at the cabin, he certainly knew them now.

Blue returned the kiss with the same intensity and that same maddening need. He cupped both of his hands around her face, anchoring her to him, though she had no intentions of going anywhere.

The kiss started out scalding and just escalated from there. It was long, deep and carried with it the promise that there was a whole lot more to come.

Marin made sure that "whole lot more" got started fast.

"I ordered condoms," she managed to say, though the kiss had robbed her of most of her breath. "They arrived this morning."

"I brought two with me," he let her know.

Good. They were on the same page, and she hoped they stayed there until they finished this. Maybe even finished it twice since it might take more than once just to scrape off the surface of the need.

Marin didn't forget about his injuries, couldn't, and she took care when she pulled his shirt off over his head. She wanted her mouth on his chest so that was where it went, and she kissed him there. Tasted him. Wanted him even more.

Blue clearly wanted her, too, because he went after her top as well. He had it off of her in no time, and the battle began. He clearly wanted to kiss her breasts as much as she wanted to kiss his chest.

Both of them succeeded because they took turns.

He rid her of her bra and used his clever mouth on her breasts and her nipples. Until she was, indeed, breathless. Until her back bowed from the pleasure.

Blue touched her as well, proving that he was a stellar multitasker. He slid his hand down her back to cup her butt And then moved her against him.

Until they were center to center.

Until she could feel his erection pressing in exactly the right spot.

She hadn't needed anything else to fire her up, or to increase the urgency, but that did it. Feeling him there was the ultimate reminder of where she wanted him to be. And where she wanted him to be was inside her.

Without saying anything, they started toward the bedroom at the same time. It wasn't a flawless trip. Definitely no graceful movements since they were basically groping each other. Finesse groping, anyway, on his part. Blue managed to touch her in just the right places. Managed to kiss her just the right way. Until he had lit one very large, very hot fire by the time they made it to the bedroom.

The urgency made her want to fall onto the bed with him, but despite the hazy mind caused by lust, she took care with his injury. Still kissing him, Marin eased down with him onto the foot of the bed.

Blue continued to kiss her breasts, continued to torture her while she went after his jeans. Again, not an easy task. Her eager hands were trembling a little. Heck, she was trembling all over from the need, but she steadied herself enough to get him unzipped. And she did a little turnabout fair play torture by sliding her hands into his boxers.

He cursed her when she wrapped her fingers around his erection. But Marin only smiled and added some neck kisses to the mix. Not for long, though. He clearly had his own ideas about torture, and he eased her back onto the bed so he could go after her jeans.

Blue succeeded, too.

He got them off her in record time, shimmying them off her legs. Sliding off her panties as well in the same motion. And when he was done, he claimed his reward for getting her stark naked by giving her a kiss in the center of all that heat.

Oh, yes. He was very good at this torture stuff.

Marin made a sound, part protest, but mostly pleasure. In fact, 99 percent of it was pleasure. Hard not to make that sound when he was using his mouth to drive her up, up, up. He nearly had her at the peak before she remembered that she wanted them to make this particular journey together.

It took a lot of willpower to move him away from her. To lose the heat and pleasure from his mouth. But she knew there were other pleasures awaiting them. First, though, she had to get him out of his jeans.

She couldn't go the "quick and fast" approach that he had done when undressing her, so she took things slow. And had some fun along the way. She lowered his jeans and boxers to his ankles, revealing the rest of his amazing body.

Of course, she saw the scar on his knee. And it caused her stomach to tighten before she realized he was watching her reaction. She reined in the tightening and brushed a gentle kiss over the scar.

Before she took his erection into her mouth.

Two could definitely play this torture game.

Blue cursed her, making her smile because she knew what this was doing to him. Like her, though, he obviously had other plans for how they were to finish this.

He rifled through his pocket and took out a condom before he yanked off his jeans and boxers and tossed them on the floor. He hurried. Everything felt hurried right now. The heat and the intensity had built up in them for so long, and neither of them had any intentions of waiting any longer.

The moment he had the condom on, he eased her onto his lap. The position put them face-to-face. Chest to breast. Mouth to mouth. All good, and it was especially good that this way might keep the pressure off his knee.

He didn't kiss her. Blue's hot gaze locked with hers and stayed locked when he pushed inside her.

Marin went still. She had to. No other choice. The pleasure had robbed her of movement, of speech, of breath. But she could feel. Mercy, she could feel, and the sensations going through her hit well above the amazing mark. There was no pleasure scale for this. Blue was creating a whole new scale of his own.

With his hands on her hips, he started the thrusts inside her. More pleasure. So much more. And with each thrust, he carried her higher and higher to that peak. She wanted to hold on, she wanted this to last so much longer. But again, the need and intensity were calling the shots here. Blue and she were just going along for the ride.

And what a ride it was.

The thrusts became harder, deeper, faster. Until that peak came at her so fast and so hard that Marin couldn't hold back a second longer. She gave into the climax, latching on to as much of the pleasure as she could.

Blue did the same.

And after she had made it to the peak, Blue followed right after her.

CHAPTER NINETEEN

BLUE STILL HAD a buzz going. The kind of buzz that came with really great sex. And the sex with Marin had been just that. Really, really great. So great that even now, nearly twenty-four hours later, his body was still humming. He could still taste her. Still feel her.

And he had some flashes of her amazing naked body as she'd straddled him.

He figured he wouldn't be forgetting any of that soon, but for now, he had to at least put the thoughts of her on the back burner while he did something that almost certainly wouldn't land in the "really great" category. But it was necessary.

Because he had to talk to his dad.

He had to see how he was doing.

Even if his father had made it crystal clear that he wasn't ready to talk to anyone just yet. His dad had done that by keeping his door shut and not even coming down for breakfast. Instead, he'd asked one of the housekeepers to bring him up something. Or rather he'd asked her to bring up "anything." Blue figured it wasn't a good sign when you didn't care what you ate.

Blue finished up some ranch paperwork for Egan along with answering some emails of his own and then headed out of the office to his dad's bedroom. But there was already someone standing outside his door.

Audrey.

She wasn't knocking. She was just standing there as if trying to figure out what to do.

"Blue," Audrey muttered when he approached her. Man, she looked shaky, definitely not her usual general-like self.

"Is Dad in there?" he asked, though he already knew the answer. If his dad had left his room, Maybell or Effie would have let Blue know since they were all so worried about him.

She nodded. "I, uh, need to get back to the Pentagon. And, yes, it's Sunday, but I've got to prep for a meeting I have first thing in the morning. I'm leaving in a few minutes."

Her departure didn't surprise Blue. Audrey had an important job, and her visits normally only lasted a day or two.

But this wasn't a normal situation.

"Would you let your dad know..." she started, but then stopped. "Please let him know I'm going and to call me when he can."

Audrey was clearly hurting, and while Blue and she hadn't always seen eye to eye, he hated to see her like this. He walked over to her and hugged her. She went stiff, probably because there hadn't been a whole lot of hugs between them, but then she sighed and returned the gesture. Audrey kept the contact short, though, and when she pulled away from him, it was obvious she was having to fight to hold on to her composure.

"I'm sorry," Audrey muttered, and with that, she turned and started down the stairs.

Blue did his own sighing and knocked on the door. "It's me," he said, hoping it would prompt his dad to answer. "I need to talk to you."

Silence. For way too long. "Come in," his dad finally said.

Blue was relieved that this hadn't turned into a battle of wills. A battle Blue would have to win since he had to see how his father was doing.

His dad was standing at the window again, but Blue spotted the breakfast tray that Reba, the housekeeper, had brought up. It wasn't untouched, thank goodness. His dad had eaten most of it.

Blue joined him at the window and realized this was a good spot for seeing all sorts of activity on the ranch. For one thing, Marin was in the front pasture, working with Pearl. Not her usual working day since it was Sunday, but the weather was amazing, cool and dry, so she'd texted him earlier that she was going to put in a few hours while Leo was making cookies in the kitchen with Maybell.

But Marin wasn't the only person Blue could see. Remi was at the pasture fence, watching the training that apparently involved Pearl actually being saddled today. Jesse was by the barn, watching as well. Maybe watching Remi, too, since Jesse and his sister had once had a thing for each other a few years back. Blue didn't know what'd happened to drive them apart, but he hadn't missed that they usually avoided each other.

Just as his dad was now doing to Audrey.

Audrey was in view from the window, too. She was in the process of putting her suitcase into the back of the rental SUV.

"You don't want to say goodbye to her?" Blue asked his dad.

"No," he was quick to answer.

Blue sighed again. "I saw her in the hall a couple of minutes ago. She wanted me to let you know she was leaving and that she would like for you to call her when you can."

His dad nodded in a "message received" kind of way. But that was it.

"Will you call her, or are things over between the two of you?" Blue came out and asked.

His dad finally tore his gaze away from the window and looked at Blue. "I'll call her. When I'm sure I can have a civil conversation with her. Right now, it might not be civil."

Blue could see that. His dad was still plenty pissed off, and any chat he had with Audrey right now would likely just turn into an argument. That might not be so bad since it could lead to a good air-clearing, but Blue wasn't sure an air-clearing was even possible.

"What will you do?" Blue pressed.

His dad didn't scowl and didn't dodge the question. "I'll stay home for a couple of days, spend some time with Egan, Remi and you. And I'll do some thinking. One thing I've already thought enough about is Rowan4321. I'd like for you to go ahead and send him a message. Something along the lines of you saw the DNA connection and you'd like to know who he is. Don't give away anything yet in case he doesn't know he's adopted. Will you do that?"

Blue nodded. He'd already done a draft of the message and had run it past Remi and Egan who'd approved. Blue had just been waiting to get the nod from his dad that it was okay to send it.

"If you don't get a response from him," his dad added, "then, use the PI to try to track him down." He paused. "I'm still thinking about how to handle things when we do find him."

Not *if* but *when*. That meant his dad had no plans to stop looking. Blue couldn't blame him. If he had a kid out there, he'd want to find him as well.

"You can also let Maybell know that I'll be coming down for lunch," his dad added. He met Blue's gaze. "It'd be nice if Remi, Egan, Alana, Marin, Leo and you could join me."

Blue smiled. "I think I can arrange that," he let his dad know, and Blue headed out, feeling a whole lot better than he had when he came in.

The good feeling didn't last, though, when he took out his phone and scrolled to the message that he had already composed to Rowan4321. Blue hit the send button and tried to tamp down that sinking feeling in the pit of his stomach. He only hoped that whatever happened, it wouldn't crush his father or Audrey. That it wouldn't crush anyone else in the family, either.

He put away his phone and made his way to the kitchen. The moment he stepped in, he smelled the cookies. And even though he'd had a good breakfast, he was suddenly hungry.

"We're making gooey, gooey cookies," Leo announced. He was at the table with Effie and Maybell, and they were rolling out dough balls that seemed to contain both chocolate and peanut butter chips.

"Sounds gooey, gooey delicious," Blue said, making Leo giggle. He glanced around and didn't see any of the finished products, though.

"The first batch will be ready in about eight minutes," his grandmother relayed to him.

That should give him just enough time to go out and pass along his dad's invitation to Remi and Marin. For now, though, he'd tell the group in the kitchen.

"Dad said he would be down for lunch and would like for all of us to join him," Blue told them.

He instantly saw plenty of relief and smiles on Maybell's and Effie's faces. Leo grinned, too.

"We can all have cookies for dessert," the boy announced.

"Sounds like a good plan to me," Blue assured him, though he figured Leo would be consuming at least one cookie before lunchtime.

Blue paused a moment, and looked at Effie and Maybell. "Dad also wanted me to send the message that we've been talking about."

Both women nodded, and even though that didn't cause them to smile this time, Blue thought he saw some relief in their expressions. His dad was moving on to the next step, and while that step might be rocky, Blue thought it was a necessary one.

With the assurance that he would be back soon to test one of those cookies, Blue headed out the back door and toward the pasture fence where Remi was standing. His sister immediately looked at him, studying his face.

"Audrey left to go back to the Pentagon," she said. "Does Dad know?"

Blue nodded. "He said he would call her soon." And he left it at that. No need to speculate as to how that call might go. "Dad's also coming downstairs for lunch and wants all of us there."

As Maybell and Effie had done, Remi smiled. "Well, that's a good start."

Blue agreed, but it was still just a start. Again, that rocky road was ahead. "I also sent the message to Rowan4321."

His sister stayed quiet a moment. Then she sighed. "Another brother. Why couldn't dad and Audrey have given me a kid sister? I missed that whole deal of being able to braid hair together and try on makeup. Plus, I didn't get anyone to boss around like Egan, Cal and you did to me."

Now Blue smiled as well. Remi was going to be okay.

They both turned their attention back to Marin who had successfully gotten the saddle on Pearl. Great progress on a different front. Marin didn't keep the saddle on the mare for long, though. This was all about conditioning, and Blue knew Marin would continue, extending the time of the saddle being in place until the mare was eventually ready to ride. After that, Pearl might never completely get over the trauma, but she'd be able to have a somewhat normal life.

Blue continued to watch as Marin began walking back toward them. He got more of those flashback memories. The good ones. The ones where she was naked. Marin looked at him, too, and she smiled in such a way it made him think she was having some good flashbacks of her own.

Remi cleared her throat, and when Blue looked at her, he realized that she had noticed the little smiles going on between Marin and him. "Why don't I go inside and see if those cookies are ready?" she said and didn't wait for him to answer. "That way, you two can discuss whatever is on your mind." She winked at him and headed for the house.

Blue would have, indeed, liked to discuss what was on his mind. Heck, he would have liked to kiss Marin, but just because his sister was no longer around, it didn't mean they had privacy. He doubted that Marin would appreciate the gossip that a hot kiss would create. Besides, he did have some things to discuss with her that didn't involve kissing. Well, not kissing at this moment, anyway, but he was hoping to do some of that with her later.

"I hope I didn't run Remi off," she said, coming to the fence.

"Nope. The first batch of cookies should be coming out right about now, and Remi has a sweet tooth. I hope you do, too, because it's what we're having for dessert. Or rather it's what we will have for dessert if you can join Dad and the rest of us for lunch. Dad wants Leo there, too."

Marin smiled. That seemed to be the going reaction for the day, and it was a hell of a lot better than some of the other reactions they'd been having since his crash landing, almost a month ago.

"I'll be there," Marin said. "So, your dad and you had a nice talk?"

"Nice," Blue verified. "Not perfect, but it's a start. I have more good news. I just got a text that Clyde Canton has been arrested." There was no need for him to spell out who that was. Marin knew it was the asshole rancher who'd abused the horses that she was now training.

"For real?" she asked, dropping the saddle at her feet. "But you said he had a lot of powerful friends."

"He does, but the Donnellys have powerful friends, too. One call from Dad tipped the scales in our direction. Of course, there'll be a trial, but you've got good documentation of the condition of the horses when they arrived. Canton will be facing a hefty fine and some jail time."

Marin made a giddy sound before she flung her arms around him and yanked him to her. The fence was between them, but that didn't stop her from giving him a celebratory hug.

A hug that led to a kiss.

It was just a little one, hardly more than a peck, but having her in his arms again kicked up those memories, and Blue made it a whole lot more than a peck. He kissed her the right way. Which involved plenty of heat and some serious hungry contact.

Obviously, having sex hadn't cooled them down one bit. In fact, it seemed to have only escalated the heat and need. Not good because now Blue was kissing Marin in plain sight and wanted nothing more than to haul her off to bed. Or the barn since it was closer.

"Are you sure you're not gonna get married or something?" Blue heard someone ask.

Not just any old someone, though. Leo.

That got Marin and him flying apart. And banging their elbows on the fence. Both yelped in pain, and Blue barely managed to bite off the profanity he normally would have spewed after hitting a funny bone that clearly wasn't funny. Still, he managed to gather his composure as quickly as he could so he could face the boy and attempt to answer the question.

Marin beat Blue to a response, though. "No, Blue and I aren't getting married. We were just celebrating because we got some good news."

Leo's eyes brightened. "Good news about the cookies? Because I'm supposed to tell you they're ready."

"Good news about the cookies," Marin confirmed.

Still rubbing her elbow and licking her lips as if trying to erase any evidence of that kiss, she climbed over the fence and dropped down next to them. She stooped down so she'd be eye level with Leo.

"But I meant it when I said Blue and I aren't getting married," she explained. "Sometimes, adults kiss, that's all."

"They kiss when they like each other." Leo's eyes brightened again. "Maybe when they like each other enough to get married."

Marin sighed. "Remember, Blue will be leaving to go back to work soon. He's already got an appointment for a checkup, and the doctor could tell him he's ready to fly again."

Blue certainly hadn't forgotten about that, but with

everything else going on, it had gone on the back burner as well. Which was somewhat of a miracle. He'd been obsessing about a physical since he'd gotten injured.

"You know how much Blue loves flying," Marin added to Leo. "So, going back to work will make him very happy."

It would. But Blue felt himself frown. Heard the profanity that he let loose in his head. He had to get back in the cockpit, period, but that sure as hell didn't mean it wouldn't be hard for him to leave Marin and Leo behind.

"Maybe Aunt Marin and you can come and visit me at the base in California," Blue suggested, and he hoped it sounded like more than a suggestion. It was an invitation. "And I'll get some leave, too, and be able to come back to the ranch to visit."

That wouldn't happen for a while, though, since he had already been on medical leave for nearly a month. A long, very intense time of pain and upheaval. Of grief. Surprises.

And pleasure.

No way could he forget the pleasure with Marin. But it was more than that. Hell. It was much more than that. Before Blue could try to wrap his mind around exactly what the "much more" included, her phone dinged with a text.

"I don't recognize the number," she muttered after looking at her screen. "Oh," she added, the alarm creeping into her voice. She stood and patted Leo's head. "Why don't you go ahead to the kitchen and pick out which cookies you want Blue and me to sample?"

Leo was clearly all for that, probably because it meant he'd get to do some sampling as well, and he took off running.

Marin showed Blue the text, and he frowned when he saw the name of the sender. Gregory Riddle. Blue only had to read the first line before he cursed.

Miss Galloway, I'm Gregory Riddle, attorney at law, and I've been hired by Brian Petty to assist him. Please contact me as soon as possible so we can arrange for Mr. Petty to see his son. Mr. Petty will be fighting your claim on his son and will be seeking custody.

CHAPTER TWENTY

MARIN WOKE UP next to a naked man. A really hot naked man who'd sneaked into her room the night before after she'd put Leo to bed. Blue had shown up with a smile and a bottle of wine. They hadn't gotten around to the wine, but had instead started a kissing frenzy that had led them straight to her bed. She hadn't expected him to stay the night, but this was a bonus.

It was also plenty comforting.

Something she very much needed.

Not only was she still reeling from the threat from Brian's lawyer they'd gotten two days ago, but today was also when Blue would be seeing the doctor and taking that physical. That was still a few hours off since it was barely five in the morning. But Marin figured those hours would just fly by. Then, Blue would soon be flying as well.

Maybe.

She had no doubts, none, that he'd be returning to duty, but Marin figured he'd want to deal with Brian's lawyer first. There'd been no further contact from Gregory Riddle or from Brian himself, but Blue had told her if the contact came, that she was to refer any communications to the ranch attorney.

Marin had plans to do just that. Along with the plan of letting Blue know she could handle it so he could return to duty with a clear conscience. She dreaded dealing with Brian, but this wasn't Blue's problem. It was hers, and she would do whatever it took to make sure Brian didn't get his hands on Leo.

Beside her, Blue stirred and groaned, which somehow managed to sound as hot as the rest of him. And the rest of him was definitely plenty hot. The sheet was covering the lower part of his body, but thanks to the thin light that was coming from the slightly open bathroom door, she could see his toned chest and abs.

Yes, definitely plenty hot.

He opened his eyes, which were hot in their own right, and even in the barely there light, he had no trouble snaring her gaze. He smiled. Mercy, that smile would always get to her.

Blue would always get to her.

That wasn't exactly a comforting thought, not with him leaving soon, but Marin refused to think about that now. She likely only had a day or two at most with him, and she didn't want to spend that time thinking about what the future might hold.

Of course, that wasn't a sensible way to go about this. But her heart was firmly at the controls right now. Well, that and apparently some other parts of her body because she turned all warm and soft when Blue reached out and pulled her down to him for a kiss.

It wasn't the lusty kind of urgent kiss that had gone on the night before, but it was just as potent. Just as effective.

"Leo's still asleep?" he asked.

"Yes. He won't be up for at least an hour and a half."

Just in case, though, she checked the monitor on her nightstand. Most parents gave that up once a child reached Leo's age, but with his history of illness, Marin had wanted to be able to look in on him throughout the night. She looked now and saw he was still sacked out. No surprise since it was so early, but if he didn't wake up on his own, she'd have to get him up in about two hours for school.

"He's asleep," she verified.

Blue kissed her again, and since he was smiling when he did it, she was able to taste that cocky grin. It fired her up just as much as the kiss itself.

"I think I can figure out a way to pass the time before I have to sneak out of here," Blue remarked.

Marin had no doubts about that. But she also had her own ideas about how to use the time. And she started using it by closing in on his mouth and deepening the kiss that he had already started.

Just like that, the heat began to blaze. It was especially fast, especially hot since they were both already naked. A bonus since she didn't have to undress him before she could touch. And touch. And touch.

She started with his chest, sliding her hands over all those muscles, feeling them stir beneath her fingers. This was a pleasure all on its own, but she knew there was so much more to come. Literally.

Blue didn't shy away from deepening the kiss, either. His mouth was clever. So was his tongue. And those parts of him were especially potent when he combined them with some touches of his own. To her breasts. Then to her nipples. He put his tongue and mouth to use on both of those.

Marin's breath caught in her throat as the pleasure flooded through her. So much pleasure, and Blue was just getting started. He trailed some kisses from her breast to her stomach, and he likely would have turned this into an orgasm with his mouth, if she had not wanted him inside her.

And she wanted that now.

Apparently, her body had decided there had been enough foreplay. For now, anyway. But since it was the now that counted, she threw the sheet off him and straddled him. Marin might have immediately taken him inside her if Blue hadn't caught onto her hips to stop her.

"Condom," he said.

She groaned and cursed this heat that could make her senseless. Thankfully, there was a condom nearby, though, and Blue snagged it from his jeans pocket. Those few seconds that it took for him to get it on felt like an eternity. Then, he thrust inside her, and the feeling of eternity vanished. The only thing in her head now was the intense heat and finding a way to sate it.

This wasn't a slow, leisurely pace. They were well past the point of that, and even though they had had each other just hours earlier, their bodies seemed to insist that everything had to go fast. Everything had to happen now.

Marin went with that.

She quickly upped the pace and intensity. Blue made no objections whatsoever. In fact, he picked up the rhythm as well and managed to torture her breasts and nipples while she rode him hard.

Of course, it didn't take long for her to feel the climax closing in on her. But Marin slowed down in her mind enough to savor every second of this. To savor every bit of Blue.

He continued his own savoring as well, but when she was right at the edge of the climax, he took hold of her chin, spearing her gaze with his. And it was his face, his mouth, his eyes that she saw when the climax claimed her. It was her face, her mouth, her eyes that Blue saw when he found his own release.

Marin collapsed on top of him. Sated, buzzing and with the possibility that all her bones had dissolved. She certainly wasn't capable of moving, and Blue seemed just fine with that. With his own breath gusting, he wrapped his arms around her and held her close.

The moments slid by as they lay there. Heart to heart. But Marin silently groaned at that last thought. Yes, it was a romantic notion, but she couldn't spin any fairy tales about this. She had to put on a brave face and hope that it wouldn't take too long for her to get over the broken heart she would almost certainly get when Blue left.

Blue stirred beneath her, reminding her that she had gotten plenty of pleasure to go along with the whole heart-breaking.

"I need to sneak out of here before Leo gets up," he reminded her in a whisper.

He groaned. So did Marin. And they kissed again before she rolled off him so he could get up, gather his clothes and head to the hall bathroom. She got a nice bonus when she was able to watch him walk away. The man had a superior butt to go along with the rest of that superior body.

Even though she doubted Leo would be up anytime soon, Marin climbed out of bed, too, and headed to the en suite bathroom. She didn't shower. She'd do that after Blue left. After she kissed him goodbye. But she grabbed clean clothes from the closet and threw them on. She had every intention of walking Blue to the door for that farewell kiss, and she preferred not to do that in her gown.

By the time she came out of the bathroom, Blue had already dressed and was drinking something. Water, she realized. Not his usual coffee.

"I might have to do lab work before the physical," he explained, "and I don't want to eat or drink anything that could screw up the results."

"Of course," she muttered, pouring herself a glass of water as well. Blue was apparently more effective than caffeine since she was already wide-awake.

And already dreading him leaving.

That brought on a mental lecture, and she told the dread to take a hike. For one thing, she didn't want Blue to pick up on that dread, and for another she didn't want it to spoil this moment. Instead, she slipped her arm around Blue as they tiptoed toward the door. He opened it, the cool air washing over them. And he kissed her.

Marin felt herself melt again. That wonderful sensation of heat and pleasure. The even better sensation she got when she ran her hands over his back and pulled him closer. The kiss would have almost certainly gone on for a while if Marin hadn't heard the sound of someone clearing their throat.

Blue and she whirled toward the sound and saw Remi sitting in one of the porch chairs. She was in her Combat Rescue Officer's uniform and was drinking what smelled to be a mug of coffee. She was also smiling at them.

"Sorry," she said, her tone teasing. "I'm not interrupting anything, am I?"

"You are," Blue snarled, and he surprised Marin by going back to her mouth to finish the kiss they'd started. It didn't have the same melting effect as usual, though, because Remi was right there.

Blue finally eased back from the kiss, and he smiled at Marin. The smile went south, though, when he turned his attention to his sister.

"What are you doing here?" he asked.

"My afternoon flight was canceled, and they put me on a much earlier one," Remi said with a yawn. She got to her feet. "I have to be at the airport in an hour and a half, and I didn't want to leave without saying goodbye."

Marin saw Blue's tense muscles relax, and he went to his sister, pulling her into a hug.

"I did check your bedroom first," Remi added, "but when you weren't there, I drove down. I shut off the headlights when I got to the cabin because I didn't want to wake Leo. I figured if you weren't trying to sneak out of here before I finished my coffee, that I'd leave you a note."

"I'm glad you didn't leave a note," Blue told her. He hugged her even harder. "Can you tell me where you're heading?"

"I don't know, but I'm sure that somewhere in the world someone needs rescuing. I'll be in touch," Remi assured him. "I might not be able to respond right away, but you'll let me know how things go."

There was certainly a lot she could be referring to, but Marin thought Remi was specifically talking about Blue's physical.

"I will. Did you say goodbye to Dad?" Blue asked.

Since this was a family goodbye, Marin tried to inch inside the cabin, but Blue caught onto her hand to stop her. Maybe he was planning on another kiss after Remi left. She wouldn't say no to that.

"I did," Remi answered. "Dad was apparently up at zero dark thirty. Once a rancher, always a rancher," she muttered. "Anyway, he says he's going to stay at Saddlebrook for a while and deal with the paperwork and such for Canton's arrest and trial. He wants the bastard put away for a long time."

"And so say all of us," Blue immediately responded.

Marin agreed. Knowing the rancher would be punished for what he'd done made it easier for her to work with the rescues that Canton had abused.

"I called Audrey last night," Remi continued a moment later. "She said Dad hadn't gotten in touch with her."

"No," Blue concurred. "I spoke to him about that last night, and he says he's not ready yet to talk to her." He paused. "And no, I still haven't heard anything from Rowan4321."

Remi nodded, but Marin thought she saw disappointment in her eyes. There was probably some uncertainty, too, but none of the Donnelly siblings seemed to be the type to bury their heads in the sand.

"Any idea what you'll say to him if he does reply?" Remi wanted to know.

Blue sighed, shook his head. "I didn't put my phone number in the message that I sent him, only my email." He took out his phone and started scrolling through what appeared to be his inbox on his email app. "So, he won't be able to call me, and if I actually do get a message from him, then I can take some time to figure out what to…" His words trailed off. "Shit."

Everything inside Marin went still. "He sent you a message?"

"What did he say?" Remi immediately wanted to know. She hurried to Blue's side and peered at the screen. "That's not from Rowan4321. It's from the PI."

That got Marin's attention. She hadn't known the PI was involved yet with the search for Audrey and Derek's son.

"And it's not about Rowan4321," Remi muttered. She lifted her gaze to Marin. "It's about Leo's dad."

That sent Marin hurrying to Blue as well, and she saw the message from Kathryn Fulton, the private investigator. According to the date and time, the email had been sent at nine o'clock last night, about the time Blue would have arrived at her house. That explained why he was just now seeing it.

Just to let you know what I found out, the PI had emailed, Gregory Riddle is, indeed, a lawyer.

Marin knew that name. It was the attorney who Brian claimed he had hired. The one who'd texted.

I spoke to Mr. Riddle earlier, the PI's email continued. It took a little pushing, but when I explained that someone was using his name to toss around threats, he fessed up that Brian Petty had never been a client of his. I suspect Petty got the name from an internet search since Mr. Riddle does handle family law cases. Don't have a clue who Petty hired, though, to text you and claim he was Mr. Riddle. The PI ended her email with, Let me know how you'd like me to proceed with this.

"Brian was trying to scam us," Marin spat out.

And that both pissed her off and gave her loads of relief. She was furious that Brian was continuing to play these sort of mind games, but she was also glad that it'd been an empty threat.

"I'll handle it," Blue responded.

"I don't want you to go see Brian again," Marin was quick to insist. "Even if you had time, which you don't, he's not worth it."

Blue looked her straight in the eyes. "Oh, he's worth it because I want him off your back. I'll start with a phone call. If that doesn't do the trick, then I'll make time to go see him again."

Marin still didn't like any part of this, but Blue apparently wasn't going to be talked out of it. Blue closed the email app, and he put his phone on speaker and made the call to Brian.

Or rather he tried to make the call.

The phone rang. And rang. Brian must not have had the voice mail function set up because it continued to ring. He continued not to answer. Then again, it was early.

Blue didn't give up, and Marin lost count just how many times the phone rang before someone finally answered it.

"What the hell?" Brian demanded. "Do you know what the hell time it is?"

Clearly, Brian was pissed off, but since he didn't ask the name of the caller, she guessed that he had programmed Blue's number into his phone.

"Yes," Blue said, his voice a calm contrast to Brian's. However, there was no calmness in his eyes. "This is the time when I tell you that your lie didn't work."

Brian cursed, and it was vicious. "What are you talking about, Donnelly?" he spat out.

"I'm talking about the fact that you lied about having a lawyer. By the way, I wouldn't be surprised if the actual lawyer, Gregory Riddle, isn't really pissed off about that. You might even be hearing from him, and that would be hearing from him in a bad way."

Brian cursed again. What he didn't do was try to lie his way out of this and say that the attorney had been wrong, that this was all a big misunderstanding.

"I'm in the process of getting an attorney," Brian finally said. "I plan to fight that bitch Marin for taking my son."

The weariness and frustration was like an avalanche. She was so tired of dealing with this lousy excuse for a human being, and it made her feel even sorrier for Jussie who'd had to deal with him for years.

"No more calls," Blue insisted. "No more threats. And you can keep your name-calling to yourself, too. Just stay out of our lives. Leo deserves a hell of a lot better than you, and he's got it."

Brian didn't jump in to argue that, probably because he knew that last part was the truth. However, Marin could almost feel his rage seeping from the other end of the phone line, and that kind of rage didn't just go away.

"You want me gone," Brian finally snarled. "Well, there's a surefire way to do that, and it's not a restraining order. That only limits me to personal contact. I can still be around. I can still make sure Leo catches sight of me."

That wasn't an empty threat. The restraining order would keep Brian at a distance, but it wouldn't keep him away.

"Here's my offer, Donnelly," Brian continued. "Give me fifty grand. That's chump change for someone like you. And your fifty grand will buy you plenty."

Marin was shaking her head before Brian even finished. Blue clearly saw that headshake, saw that she was completely against paying this piece of dirt one penny.

Every muscle in Blue's jaw turned to iron. "Really?" Blue challenged. Not a challenge aimed at her. But rather Brian. "Fifty grand?" he questioned.

"That's what I said and I didn't stutter," Brian fired back. "Give me the cash, Donnelly, and I'll be out of Leo's life for good."

With that, Brian ended the call.

CHAPTER TWENTY-ONE

BLUE SAW THE intense argument in Marin's eyes before she even had a chance to respond to what Brian had just demanded. She was furious, and he wouldn't have been surprised if little cartoon puffs of smoke had come out of her ears. He was having a similar reaction, but he wanted to try to calm her down.

"You're not paying him a cent," Marin snapped.

"Couldn't agree more," Blue said, but that didn't calm her down nearly as much as he'd hoped.

"How dare that son of a bitch," Marin went on, pacing on the porch. Not that she could pace that far because the porch wasn't that big. "This is extortion, right? It means I can have him arrested."

"In theory, yes." Blue put his phone away, went to her and took hold of her arms to stop her so he could make eye contact with her. "But it was a phone conversation, and Brian would almost certainly insist that we misunderstood him. Or that he didn't say it at all."

"But we heard it." She motioned toward Remi. "We could be witnesses."

Blue didn't repeat that *in theory, yes*. It could work with Marin and Remi giving a statement about what they'd heard. *Could.* But without tangible proof of the money demand, Blue figured the odds were slim to none that Brian would actually be arrested.

For now, anyway.

"I'll call Sheriff Watson and let him know what's going on," Blue spelled out to her, and somehow managed to stay calm while doing it. Hard to do that, though, when he was riled to the bone that this asshole was putting Marin through the wringer. "I'll ask him about recording any future calls Brian might make so they can be admissible if it goes to court. The sheriff can even go have a chat with Brian, and that might get him to disappear. Brian wants money, but he doesn't want to end up in jail."

That seemed to steady Marin some, but she shifted from really pissed off anger to a weary sigh that put a choke hold on his heart. Yeah, he hated what this asshole was doing to her.

Blue brushed a kiss on her cheek, and then he took a "what the heck" attitude and really kissed her despite Remi standing right there. He doubted it mattered since Remi had already witnessed them in a lip-lock and because she'd also seen Blue sneaking out of the cabin before dawn.

And speaking of dawn, Blue couldn't help but notice it would be happening soon. The horizon was already starting to light up a little with the approaching sunrise. That was his cue to head out. Too bad the heading out meant Marin being alone to mentally process what had just happened.

"I know," Marin said when he pulled back from the kiss. "You have to leave for your appointment. Go," she insisted. "I don't want you to be late, and you could end up hitting rush hour traffic on the drive to the base."

He could and would, but he still lingered a moment. "I'll talk to the sheriff," he repeated. "And I'll have Egan speak with the hands. They can keep an eye out if Brian tries to get onto the ranch. You should probably call Leo's teacher, too, just to let her know what's going on."

Marin nodded, and she seemed to settle even more now. Settle about Brian, anyway. Blue saw worry of a different kind in her eyes. And it was for him and this appointment.

"I'll let you know how the exam goes," he muttered, which was a stupid thing to say. Of course, he'd tell her, and she would no doubt be on pins and needles until she heard. Then, afterward, well...

They'd have to deal with what came after.

Blue didn't want to go there, not now, not when she was studying his eyes as intently as he was studying hers. Rather than say goodbye, he brushed another kiss on her mouth and managed a thin smile. Definitely not his usual, but then even his best smile wasn't going to fix this. Maybe nothing could fix it. And that ate away at him as much as the haunted look in Marin's eyes.

He gave Remi another goodbye hug. "Don't do anything I wouldn't do," he muttered to her. It was the customary farewell he always gave to Remi when they were saying goodbye—which happened a lot, what with them always heading off to various assignments.

Remi came back with her usual farewell, too. "Which means pretty much nothing is off-limits." She managed a thin smile, too. "Stay safe," they muttered at the same time.

After Blue went to his truck and drove away, he glanced in his rearview mirror and spotted Remi hugging Marin as well. He hoped his sister could say something, anything, that would make Marin feel better.

Since he wanted to be in uniform for the appointment, Blue had to stop by the house so he could shower and change. Still, he made good time, mainly because he didn't run into Effie, Egan, Alana or his dad. That was a huge bonus since he wasn't up to a face-to-face conversation with any of them. He just needed to get this physical over and done.

Since it would take him nearly an hour to get to the base, Blue used that time to deal with some of the things he had on his plate. He used the hands-free to send a text to Egan and Jesse to let them know about Brian's phone call and asked them to make sure Brian didn't get on the ranch.

The next text he sent was to Sheriff Jace Watson. Not exactly a friend, but in a small town like Emerald Creek where there weren't many degrees of separation, Jace had worked at Saddlebrook for a couple of summers when he was a teenager. Blue didn't get into the details of Brian's call, but asked the sheriff if they could arrange a meeting so they could talk. It was entirely possible that Egan would beat Blue to that meeting/talk since Egan would be pissed once he learned what Brian had tried to pull, but Blue still wanted to set things in motion.

Blue was about to text the PI next to give her an update, but his phone rang before he could do that, and he frowned when he didn't recognize the number that popped up on the screen.

"Hell," he growled.

His first thought was that Brian was using a different phone to call, and that caused some fresh anger to rip through him. Anger that no doubt came through loud and clear when he jabbed Accept Call. Blue didn't offer up any greeting and didn't voice the curse words that were on the tip of his tongue.

A good thing, too.

Because it wasn't Brian.

"Major Donnelly?" a woman asked.

Even though Blue had only spoken to her once, he instantly knew who this was. It was Airman Newell's mother, who he had met in the hospital.

"Yes," Blue managed to say. "How are you, Mrs. Newell?" And he prayed that she wasn't phoning him to let him know that her son had passed away.

"I'm wonderful," the woman said, her voice cracking on the last word. But it didn't seem to be cracking with sadness, but rather joy. "He's awake. Casey woke up."

The woman began to cry, but again this wasn't about sadness. Even though Blue could hear the joy and relief, it still took a few seconds for her words to sink in.

"He's awake," Blue finally got out. "When?" he managed to ask.

"About thirty minutes ago," she was quick to answer. "I know it's so early, and I was going to hold off calling you, but I thought—"

"I'm glad you called," Blue interrupted. And he was. He was so very glad to get this news.

For weeks, the guilt had been gnawing away at him, taking its toll. Crushing him. He wouldn't have cared if the call had come in the middle of the night because it was the answer to a lot of prayers.

Well, maybe.

"How is Casey?" Blue asked. He didn't spell out the fears that were threatening to overshadow the relief. He just waited for the airman's mother to answer.

"He's good," she was quick to assure him. "I mean, he's talking and he knows who I am. His voice is raspy because of the tube that had been in his throat, but I'm sure once that heals, I'll be able to have a real conversation with him. I'll be able to tell him how much we've all been praying for him."

"Yes," Blue muttered. He was having trouble speaking, too, because of the sudden lump in his throat.

"There doesn't seem to be any brain damage," the woman went on. "He can move his arms and legs. And the doctor says he's responding normally to things. I'm sure he'll want to see you if that's possible. I wasn't sure if you had gone back to your base in California or not."

"I'm still in Texas," Blue explained. "And I would love to see him."

That was mostly true. Blue did want to see the airman and tell him in person how sorry he was for what happened. He wasn't looking forward to that because it was possible that Casey Newell would aim a whole lot of anger and rage at him. If so, Blue would take it because he deserved it.

"I'm going to the base now for an appointment,"

Blue told her. "I'll call you after the appointment, and if Casey does want to see me, I can drop by then."

"Oh, that would be wonderful. He's going to be so happy to see you. Thank you, Major Donnelly."

Blue hadn't done a damn thing to deserve that thank-you, but for now, he'd take it. And he'd take anything else Airman Newell or his family doled out to him.

"I'll call you in a couple of hours," Blue assured Mrs. Newell, and he ended the call with the woman gushing out another thank-you.

Fortunately, he had to stop at a traffic light, and it gave him a moment just to sit there and take a breath. A breath that he desperately needed to tamp down his emotions. An entire mixed bag of them. But at the top of this particular heap was a biggie.

It was relief.

Finally, some good news. It didn't rid Blue of his guilt, but maybe this could be the start of it if Airman Newell did, indeed, make a full recovery.

For some reason that caused his brain to shift gears, and images of Marin and Leo flashed in his head. Not exactly a subtle message, either. Because while things were looking good on one front of his life, he was driving to an appointment that would mess up another aspect of it.

Because he would end up leaving Marin and Leo.

And that would be another fresh, deep cut of guilt. But Blue just couldn't see a way around it.

BLUE TRIED NOT to wince when he walked toward the elevator in the base hospital. Impossible to do, though, with the pain knifing through him. Still, he'd managed to get through the physical, and while he didn't know the results yet, he'd almost certainly passed. Not with flying colors.

But he would pass.

The flight surgeon and medical board would probably insist he continue physical therapy. And he would. The PT was helping, and he had to do something to try to lessen the pain. The medical powers that be would probably also suggest he get that dreaded DNIF status for a while once he returned to Edwards AFB. The "duties not involving flying" would be a hard pill to swallow, but it would only be temporary.

Soon, he'd be back in the cockpit of his Raptor.

Again, the image of Marin popped into his head. A really good image, not of her worrying about Leo, Brian, the horses. Or him. But an image of her in bed with him earlier that morning. Despite the throbbing pain in his knee, that mental picture caused Blue to smile, and instead of getting on the elevator, he stepped outside into a courtyard and called her. Either he caught her at a good time or she was waiting for his call because she answered on the first ring.

"Blue," she said, and there was a whole lot of emotion in her voice. So much that he got a third flash. Not of her, but of Brian.

"Brian didn't call you, did he?" Blue asked, feeling an instant jolt of fury.

"No," Marin was quick to say. "I was just worried about you. How did the physical go?"

"It went well." Not actually a lie, he assured himself, even though he had to lean against the courtyard wall to get some pressure off his knee. "I won't know the results for a couple of hours, maybe even days, but I was able to do all parts of the eval."

Not easily, but he hoped he hadn't damaged his knee even further when he'd been on the treadmill to test out his breathing and heart rate.

"Good," she said, and it sounded sincere.

Of course, it was. Marin wanted the best for him even if the best did a number on her heart. Blue could have told her that it'd do a number on his, too, but she didn't need the "misery loves company" slant here.

"There's more good news," he explained. "On the drive to the hospital, I got word that Airman Newell came out of the coma. I'm going up to see him before I head back to the ranch."

"Oh, Blue. That's wonderful." Plenty of sincerity in that as well, but he could almost feel her studying him, wondering how he was going to deal with seeing the airman awake.

"I'm not sure what he'll say to me," Blue added. "But I need to see him."

He needed to try to tell Casey how sorry he was. And, yeah, it would suck to own up to what he'd done, but it was necessary.

"How's everything at the ranch?" he asked.

"All right. Egan got the text you sent him about Brian, and the sheriff came out to talk to me."

That was fast, and Blue was thankful for it. He wanted this mess with Brian resolved in a hurry. Not only to lessen the stress for Marin, but because it was a loose end Blue wanted tied up.

"I told the sheriff about Brian's call," Marin went on, "and he was going to pay Brian a visit this morning."

More good news, and while Sheriff Watson wasn't the most intimidating guy on the planet, he wasn't a soft touch, either. The visit just might be enough to send Brian packing.

"I'll follow up with the sheriff after I get back to the ranch," Blue said. He checked the time. It was already noon. "I'm not sure how long this visit with Casey will go, but I should be back before Leo gets home from school."

"I'll see you soon," she said. Again, it wasn't all gushing relief in her voice, but her mind did seem to be eased somewhat.

Blue put away his phone, and bracing himself for the lightning bolts of pain, he went back inside to the elevator to ride it to Casey's floor. On the way up, it occurred to him that the medical staff might have moved him to another room since he was no longer in a coma, but Blue knew he had the right place when he spotted Mrs. Newell outside the door. She was talking to someone on the phone and smiling. She quickly ended the call, and with that bright smile on her face, she went to him.

"I'm so glad you're here," she greeted. "Casey will be thrilled to meet you."

Blue doubted that, but he pushed it aside and went with Mrs. Newell when she took him by the arm and led him into the room.

Casey Newell was indeed awake, and while Blue was betting he wouldn't be running a marathon anytime soon, he looked surprisingly healthy for someone who'd been in a coma for weeks. He was sitting up on the bed and going through something on a laptop. Casey looked up at Blue with eyes that were a genetic copy of his mother's.

"Major Donnelly," Casey said. Or rather he tried to say it. His mom had been right about the raspy voice.

"Blue," he offered.

Casey smiled. "Blue," he tested. "It's good to meet you."

Is it? Blue nearly asked, but thankfully, he bit that back. "It's good to meet you, too." He opened his mouth to launch into the rest of what he had to say, but Mrs. Newell spoke first.

"Casey doesn't recall the accident," she volunteered. "That could be temporary, but I've told him that he'll remember what he's supposed to remember."

That was definitely an optimistic slant on things. But it also felt a little like a caution for Blue not to press him on those memories.

"I don't recall some of it, either," Blue said. He decided against mentioning that he had viewed the footage of it, though.

Casey nodded, met his gaze. "Mom said you were hurt. Are you okay?"

"I'm all right. I just took a physical so I'm a bit stiff," he added since Casey had no doubt noticed the limp. "But everything else is fine," he lied.

Blue went closer and cleared his throat, ready to fall on his sword or do whatever else he needed to do.

"It was an accident," Casey said before Blue could speak. "Mom also told me how sorry you are, but it was an accident."

"I am sorry." And he didn't want this automatic understanding and forgiveness. "I wish I'd done things differently. I wish I'd been able to bring down the Raptor in such a way that no one was injured."

Well, no one but himself. Since he had seen the footage, Blue knew there was no way around that. He was lucky to be alive.

"You're a damn good pilot so I'm sure you did everything you could do," Casey rasped out, smiling, and then he added to his mother, "Sorry about the cussing. She doesn't like it when I cuss," he muttered to Blue.

"It's fine," his mom quickly assured him. "For this one time, anyway. Don't make a habit of it." With her smile beaming, she brushed a kiss on her son's cheek, and then she turned to Blue. "But Casey's right in that you did everything possible to stop anyone from being hurt."

Blue still wasn't sure he believed that, but it was good to hear it. *Damn* good. Maybe one day he'd even believe it.

He said his goodbyes to Casey and his mother, and Blue headed out to start the drive back home. On the walk to the elevator, he checked his email.

And froze.

He saw the message was from Rowan4321. Once he got past the initial jolt of shock, he read it.

Hi, this is Dawn Joyner, a friend of Rowan's. He's on a deployment so he asked me to keep an eye out for messages coming from the ancestry site. You didn't say much in your email, but I'll pass it along to Rowan. Do you know him?

Blue read the message three times and had a serious debate with himself as to how to answer. *Deployment* likely meant military. Ironic. Well, maybe not, considering all the other Donnelly siblings were currently in uniform.

The other thing that caught Blue's attention was that Rowan had asked a friend to check the messages. Maybe that meant his adoptive parents weren't alive? Or it could be that he just hadn't wanted them to know he had done the DNA test.

Blue was going with door number two on this.

The other thing that was missing was Rowan's surname, and that meant Blue couldn't do an immediate search on him. He would have loved to see a photo to check for any family resemblance.

He finally hit Reply and typed out a response to the email.

I don't think I've met Rowan, but it's possible he's a cousin. What's his last name?

Blue added his phone number to his signature and hit Send. He hoped he didn't have to wait too long for a response. But he rethought that. This could end up being a big-assed emotional deal for his family. Especially for his dad. No way to make that go away, but maybe the fallout wouldn't do more harm than good.

He finally made it out of the hospital and was on the way to his truck when his phone rang, the sound jolting through him. Because his first thought was this was Dawn Joyner or even Rowan responding. But no. It was the name of the flight surgeon's clinic that popped up on the screen.

Blue had to tamp down the kick that gave his heartbeat, and his hands weren't exactly steady when he answered.

"This is Lieutenant Colonel Markham," the caller said.

"Yes," Blue responded. Markham was the flight surgeon who'd authorized his physical. "I'm still on the grounds of the hospital if you need more lab work or something."

The doctor paused. And Blue tried not to believe that was a bad sign.

But it was.

"Major Donnelly, this is tough news, but I went over all the results of your physical and the reports from your surgeon and physical therapists." He paused again. "I'm afraid I'm going to have to recommend to the medical board that you not be approved to return to the cockpit."

Hell. Hell. Hell.

That sucked all the air out of his lungs, but Blue managed to stay on his feet. Managed to gather enough breath, too, to ask one huge question.

"For how long?" Blue demanded. "How long before you will approve me to return to flying?"

Another long, long pause. "Never. I'm sorry, Major Donnelly, but I don't believe your injuries will allow you to continue to be a pilot."

CHAPTER TWENTY-TWO

MARIN SHOWERED WHILE she kept an eye on her phone. Something she'd been doing all day since there was so much going on. She was always on alert for any calls from Leo's school, but this afternoon she was also looking for anything from Egan or the sheriff about Brian.

Blue as well.

Especially Blue.

He had stayed on her mind throughout the hot, sweaty training session she'd had with the rescued gelding and stallion. Hot and sweaty enough that she'd headed straight to the shower in the cabin before writing up any training reports. She'd focused on the training well enough, but she had also worried about Blue.

Marin had thought he would be back by now. Or that he would have maybe called or texted to let her know he'd be late. She tried to convince herself that the lateness was a good thing, that it meant the visit with Airman Newell went so well that he stayed longer than anticipated.

But she worried.

She tried to push that worry aside after she finished her shower. Marin wrapped the towel around her, grabbed some clean clothes and went back into her bedroom to dress. And she let out a garbled scream—followed by relief—when she saw the man sitting on the foot of her bed.

Blue.

Her relief didn't last long, though, when she took a better look at his expression. Mercy. Something was seriously wrong.

"Sorry," he said, scrubbing his hand over his face. He was still wearing his flight suit, but he'd unzipped the top of it some to expose a white T-shirt beneath. "I let myself in. I didn't mean to scare you."

Marin blew off the apology and went closer. "What happened? What's wrong?" She didn't dare spell out some of her fears. That maybe Airman Newell had had a relapse and was back in the coma.

Or worse.

But this could be about Brian, too. Or the physical, though Blue had said it could be days before he found out anything about that.

"Do me a favor and don't ask about…anything," he said.

Everything inside Marin tightened and it took every ounce of resolve inside her not to press and ask him what was wrong. She desperately wanted to know, but more than that, she just wanted to give Blue whatever comfort she could.

She sank down on the bed next to him, immediately sliding her hand behind the back of his neck and easing him to her for a kiss. She hoped it helped. Hoped that it fired up enough heat inside him that it made him forget whatever had put that sad look on his face. Except it was more than sadness she saw there. It was devastation. Whatever Blue had learned, it wasn't good.

Marin kissed him, and while he didn't actually resist, he didn't pour his entire self into it, either. So she tried harder by deepening the kiss, by pulling him even closer to her and adjusting their positions so that some of his chest was touching her breast. Only then did she remember she was just wearing a towel and was still damp from her shower.

"I don't want pity sex," he muttered after pulling away from her.

Marin eased him right back to her. "Good. Because this isn't about pity."

That was the truth. When she was with Blue, it was never about pity. It was about the heat, the attraction and all these heartfelt feelings she had for him.

It was about her falling in love with him.

She didn't want to burden him with that now, though. Not when he clearly had enough on his mind.

Marin got off the bed and stooped in front of him so that she could lower the zipper of his flight suit. Since the zipper went from neck to crotch, it wasn't a fast journey, but she added some flourishes along the way by kissing his neck.

And she finally heard something she wanted to hear.

Blue made a sound deep within his throat, a sound that was a mix of the lust and the need. It was still there. Still strong. And she would use it to try to soothe that devastation in his eyes.

She pulled him to his feet once she had the zipper down, and Marin shoved the top of the flight suit off his shoulders. She also got rid of that T-shirt so she could land some well-placed kisses on his chest. That was never a chore, never, and it amped up her own heat and need.

Blue amped up the kissing as well, taking her mouth in a long, hard, deep kiss that she felt in every inch of her body. Heat was helping her, too, and Marin's mind shifted from Blue's need to the need caused by this intensity.

He kept kissing her while she shoved down his flight suit, and once they had it and the boots off, that left him in only his boxers. Seeing him nearly naked never got old, either. Ditto for seeing him completely naked, which was what she got when she took off his boxers.

Yes, this amazing view never got old.

Marin slid her tongue down his chest. Down his stomach. And lower. He was huge and hard, and she took him into her mouth.

Blue made that sound again, that hoarse, needy groan. It was music to her ears, and she would've continued with what she was doing had Blue not taken hold of her shoulders and pulled her back up to face him.

This time, the kiss was even deeper. Even harder. And the urgency of it had her reaching over to the nightstand where she had put the condoms. Marin moved Blue back to a sitting position on the foot of her bed, got the condom on him and climbed onto his lap.

Blue took charge from there.

He thrust into her with that same ferocity of his kiss. It was exactly what she needed. Clearly, it was what he needed, too, because he began the fast and furious strokes inside.

She watched him. He was in the warrior mode now. The take and claim. And she was right there with him. She intended to do some taking and claiming of her own. This was a gift, a short interlude before what she figured was a fierce storm moving in. Not an actual one. But the release of the storm that was going on inside Blue.

Marin savored those intense thrusts. Savored the hungry way Blue continued to take her mouth as he took the rest of her. Of course, though, there was no way for that intensity to last, and she felt the climax rolling through her before she even knew it was going to happen. Like the rest of this, it was hard, fast and one of those moments that made her feel nothing but pleasure.

Leave it to Blue to accomplish something like that.

While the climax continued to ripple through her, Blue continued to push inside her. Taking her as if she were the cure for all that ailed him.

If only that were true.

When he finally reached his release, Blue gathered her into his arms and held her close.

BLUE WELCOMED THE mind-numbing that followed good sex. Welcomed it, embraced it, but then he silently cursed when it was gone in a flash.

Within seconds after Marin and he had finished each other off, the thoughts going through his head weren't anywhere near numb enough.

He fought through the tornado of images, bits of conversation and sickening dread and checked the time. A priority since he wanted to make sure Leo wouldn't come walking in on them after being dropped off from school by the car pool. But it was still an hour and a half before that happened.

Plenty long enough for him to talk to Marin.

Long enough for him to answer those questions that she clearly had for him. But ninety minutes wouldn't give him time to come to terms with what had happened. No, that was going to take a whole lot longer, and maybe it'd never happen.

"I'll be right back," he said, easing her off his lap. "Then, we can talk."

She didn't object. Marin just sat on the foot of the bed and watched him as he went into the bathroom. Part of him wanted to linger in there for a while, but lingering meant Marin would worry longer than necessary. No way did he want to add to that so he freshened up and went back into the bedroom to face her.

Marin hadn't put on the clothes she'd brought into the bedroom with her, but she had wrapped the towel around her again. She looked amazing, despite the worry on her face. Then again, she always looked amazing.

"First, I need to tell you I'm sorry," he said.

Her eyes narrowed a little. "You had better not be apologizing for having sex with me."

He shrugged. But he shouldn't have been surprised that she had just said that. However, he was sorry. Not for the sex, of course, but because he hadn't come to her in the right state of mind. He had needed her, and she'd had to fill those needs as only Marin could do.

"Is this about your visit with Airman Newell?" she asked.

"No." Blue took a moment to gather his breath and try to steady the nerves that had returned. "It's about my flight physical. The flight surgeon isn't going to recommend that I return to the cockpit."

He gave her some time to process that, but it didn't take long. Mere seconds before he saw a different emotion flash in her eyes. Not anger, but shock.

Yeah, that had been Blue's initial reaction, too.

"What does that mean?" she pressed. "Does that mean he can stop you from flying?"

That was exactly what it meant, but Blue didn't spell that out. It was still too painful to say it aloud. Instead, he went with a sanitized version that the flight surgeon had used.

"Flying can be a physical, draining experience," he explained, using the textbook version. "Especially in combat or test flight situations. There's constant stress on muscles and ligaments. Added to that, if a pilot is ever shot down in combat, he or she would need to be able to evade capture. In other words, run."

That was something he couldn't do. Ditto for not being able to climb the ladder to get into an F-22 cockpit.

"Basically, all parts of the body have to be at the highest level of functioning," Blue added. "It's the reason why standards and the selection process for being a pilot are so high."

As he'd done before, Blue gave her some time to process that, and there was no instant flash this time. Moments crawled by. And crawled. Before she finally muttered a single word.

"Shit," she said.

Again, that had also been his initial reaction. Well, after he'd gotten past the gut punch that had nearly brought him to his knees. After that, he'd done his own share of verbal and mental cursing while the flight surgeon had droned on about the reasoning he had for the decision that crushed Blue all the way to the bone.

"Can you appeal it?" she wanted to know.

He smiled a little because he'd already gone there, too. "I can and will, but the flight surgeon's opinion will carry huge weight with the medical board."

"Then, find another opinion," she blurted out, making him smile again.

Right now, she was thinking of him and only him. Of what this was doing to him. She hadn't taken the mental leap to see what was lying beyond this. That if he couldn't fly, what the hell else would he do?

Blue didn't have the answer to that.

Hell, he wasn't sure he could even consider answers. The flight surgeon had said the knee pain would always be there, that the ligaments and the kneecap were damaged enough that he'd never be 100 percent. Never. And that could be fatal in a combat situation. Not fatal just to himself, but to anyone else connected to that particular mission.

Blue couldn't just ignore that.

Especially not after dealing with the gut-wrenching guilt over the injuries he'd caused in that crash landing.

The pain would always be there, and it could affect him if he were in a combat situation. But he needed to figure out if the pain could be fixed enough to get the flight surgeon to change his mind.

That was a long shot.

If that didn't pan out… But he stopped. He didn't want to think about a future that didn't involve him flying. Even if that future had Marin and Leo in it.

"I need to tell my family," he said, trying to kiss some of that troubled look off her face. Then, he started putting on his clothes. "I came straight here from the base."

Well, almost. He'd gone to the cabin after he'd driven around aimlessly for a while, cursing and yelling at the top of his lungs.

She nodded, stood and began to dress as well. "Do you want me to go with?"

It was a generous offer, especially since she'd have to watch him pour out his crushed heart to his family. But he didn't want her to go through that. No need for both of them to go through another emotional draining.

"No, I'll tell them," he said. He finished putting on his flight suit and dragged on his combat boots. "I'll deal with their questions, try to reassure them that I'm not about to lose what mind I have left, and then I'll go for a ride on Iceman. After I've settled and done some thinking, I'll come back over."

Clearly, she was worried about him, and that worry showed on her face. Once she was dressed, she walked with him to the door.

"You know how you said not to tell you I was sorry about the sex?" Blue started. "Well, don't tell me you're sorry about this news from the flight surgeon. I don't have a strong hold on things right now."

And her sympathy and compassion might break him. He needed all the steel he could gather to tell his family.

Marin nodded, and when they reached the door, she kissed him. A damn good send-off because despite everything else, it helped ease some of those thoughts about his life going to hell in a handbasket.

Blue went to his truck and started the dreaded drive home. But he had barely made it out of Marin's driveway when he got a call. He groaned because he didn't recognize the number on the screen. Figuring it was Brian, his temper went through the roof, and he was primed for a fight when he answered.

The fight immediately went out of him, though.

"This is Dawn Joyner," the caller greeted.

The friend of Rowan's who was monitoring his emails while he was on deployment. Blue hadn't expected to hear from her. Not this soon, anyway.

"Blue Donnelly," he said, and he decided to wait to see what the woman had to say.

She huffed. That came through loud and clear. "Look, I'm not sure this call is a good idea, but I couldn't stop myself from making it. I care about Rowan. We've been best friends since kindergarten, and you should know I tried to talk him out of doing this."

"Out of doing the DNA thing?" Blue clarified.

"Yes." That was all she said for a long time. Then, she huffed again. "His mom and dad don't know. They aren't even aware that he knows he's adopted so that'll be one shitstorm for him to deal with. What I want to know is if you'll be causing a shitstorm for him as well?"

It was a good question, but Blue didn't have a good answer. "I don't know," he admitted, trying to shove away his own problems. Because this was a Texas-sized family problem, too. "I didn't know anything about Rowan until I saw the DNA results."

"Damn," she muttered. "I'm guessing you're his half brother?"

"I think I am." And he left it at that. It wasn't his place to spill the secret that Audrey had kept all these years. That'd be a possible shitstorm for down the road.

Well, if down the road actually happened.

"Does Rowan want to get in touch with his bio-family?" Blue came out and asked.

"He's not sure," Dawn was quick to say. "He did the test thing right before his latest deployment and said he'd deal with it when he got back."

"Deployment," Blue repeated. He had plenty of first-hand experience with those.

"Yes," she confirmed, but she didn't confirm anything else. Like where he was deployed or if he was there in a civilian or military capacity.

"When will he be back?" Blue finally settled for asking.

"At least three months. And I can't give you a number for him. He calls me sometimes, but he has to go through channels of wherever he happens to be."

So, he was possibly at a classified location.

"What about his surname?" Blue pressed. "Can you give me that?" So he could run a background check on the guy. Maybe it was his dealings with Brian, but Blue wanted to make sure this wasn't some ploy to get money out of the Donnellys or harm Audrey's career in some way.

"No," she said. "No surname without his permission, and I don't know when or if I'll get that."

"I understand," Blue assured her, and he did. If their situations were reversed, he wouldn't have wanted a stranger to know his surname, either.

"Look, I'll tell Rowan that you and I spoke," Dawn finally continued. "And I'll give him your number. But I'm also going to try to talk him out of contacting you. Rowan's dealt with enough shitstorms in his life, and he doesn't need another," she added just as she ended the call.

CHAPTER TWENTY-THREE

BLUE HAD PURPOSELY asked for all his family to be together so he wouldn't have to repeat what he had to tell them. It would be hard enough to say it once, to deal with the reactions once. And even though there'd be an aftermath for those reactions, this "no repeat" might help him get through the rest of the day.

After that, he'd work on getting through tomorrow.

It hadn't been easy to gather everyone together. He'd had to wait for Alana to get off from work and for Maybell to return home from a big grocery shopping trip. Now that they were all assembled, though, it was clear that Maybell, Effie, Egan, Alana and his dad knew something was up as they sat in the spacious family room. However, since Blue hadn't given them any clues, they might think this family meeting was about Rowan4321. Part of it would be. But first, Blue started with his own news.

"Is Marin pregnant?" Maybell asked. She immediately waved that off, though—after Blue's jaw nearly hit the floor. "Sorry, I just wanted to lighten the moment. The tension's kind of thick in here."

Yeah, it was thick, and it was going to get worse, but

Blue smiled at her to let her know he appreciated the effort.

"The flight surgeon isn't going to approve me staying in the cockpit," he said. He'd rehearsed the wording of that part. He'd wanted to start with the truth and then move on to the gray areas and the questions. "I'll fight it, but without his approval, my appeal won't get off the ground."

Blue hadn't rehearsed that last part, or he might not have used that flying term. Especially since his getting off the ground in a fighter jet wasn't looking very likely.

Could he come to terms with that?

Not at the moment he couldn't.

As expected, his family had stunned reactions. Maybe not as stunned, though, as he had expected. So, they had seen this coming. Or at least they had seen the possibility of it.

Blue hadn't.

That was why it had knocked him for a proverbial loop and was continuing to knock him.

"You got an actual report of the results of your flight physical?" Egan asked, sounding like both a commander and his big brother.

Blue nodded. "I read through it." He had stopped reading when he didn't see anything in there that was going to make him feel more positive about this situation. In fact, his mood had darkened with each word.

"And the knee?" his dad wanted to know. "Is it really that bad?"

It was, and Blue settled for another nod.

Effie looked at him. There weren't tears in her eyes,

but she looked on the verge of crying. Blue hoped she held back on those because he wasn't sure he could deal with them right now.

"So, what does this mean?" Effie wanted to know.

Blue figured she was asking about his plans. He didn't have any. And that seemed a problem far down the road as well. Right now, he was still living in the moment, and the moment was damn painful.

"That's still up in the air," he said, and he silently cursed yet another flying expression. He just couldn't get away from them, and each one yanked him back to the reality of the situation.

He didn't want the reality right now.

So, he went with another update since he had clearly given his family enough to think about when it came to his own life and career.

"In other news, I got a call from a woman named Dawn Joyner," he started. "She said she's a friend of Rowan4321 whose given name is actually Rowan, by the way. She wouldn't give me a surname, but did tell me that he was on deployment and couldn't be reached."

Blue watched that information sink in. It was one thing to know on paper that there was another Donnelly sibling out there. It was another thing to deal with the reality of it.

"He's in the military?" That came from his father.

"I think so, but the friend wouldn't confirm that."

His dad made a sound not of surprise. More like resignation. Maybe because it seemed as if all his offspring had been destined to be in the military.

Blue turned to Egan. "Do you think the PI should have a look at this Dawn Joyner to make sure she's legit?"

"Absolutely," Egan agreed, and he took out his phone, probably to get that started.

"Did this friend happen to say if Rowan wanted to meet us?" his dad asked a moment later.

"She didn't come out and say that." And Blue didn't want to get his father's hopes up about it, either. "Apparently, Rowan's adoptive parents didn't tell him he was adopted, and they don't know that he did this DNA test."

Alana grimaced because, yeah, she had no doubt figured out this could result in a, well, shitstorm. Dawn had nailed that part of it.

"Anyway, Dawn Joyner has my number, and she said she would pass along my message to Rowan," Blue explained. "It will be three months, though, before he gets back from deployment, and even then he might decide not to contact us."

Blue didn't mention what Dawn had said about Rowan already having been through so much. All of them in this room were in that same boat. And he was glad he had finally come up with a nautical reference instead of a damn flying one.

He glanced out the window when he saw movement out of the corner of his eye, and Blue managed a smile again when he spotted Marin and Leo. They wouldn't be able to fix this thudding ache in his chest, but Blue suddenly needed to see them. Maybe even steal a kiss or two from Marin. She had a way of leveling him out, and right now, he'd had all the peaking he could handle.

"Obviously, I'll let you all know what happens with

the medical board," Blue said. "And if Rowan does contact me, I'll tell you what he says." He didn't mutter a goodbye or anything, and he didn't wait around for what would be the inevitable sympathy hugs. Maybe even his grandmother's tears. "I need some fresh air," he added before heading out.

Blue went out the back door and straight to the corral. Marin must have heard him coming because she looked in his direction. Her initial reaction was a smile with, oh, so much joy in her eyes. But then she must have remembered his crap-filled day because the sadness came.

He decided to do something about that sadness. Both hers and his.

Even though Leo was right there, beaming out a big smile that was minus any sadness, Blue went straight to Marin and pulled her into his arms. To the sound of several whooping and cheering ranch hands, Blue kissed her.

MARIN HADN'T SEEN the kiss coming. She'd only seen a "down in the dumps" Blue as he made his way toward her. The kiss had been a surprise.

And very much welcomed.

Well, her mouth and mind welcomed it, anyway. Her body, too. But she knew they had an audience for this because one member of that audience—Leo—giggled.

With so much of her breath gone, she pulled away from Blue so she could study his face. It was there in his eyes. The deep hurt. So maybe he'd needed the kiss the way he'd needed sex with her after getting the devastating news from the flight surgeon. Marin would willingly give him whatever she could.

"Are you sure you're not gonna get married?" Leo asked. "Because people that kiss get married."

Oh, Leo certainly had a lot to learn once he got older. Plenty of people kissed without going on to marry.

"How did it go with your family?" she risked asking Blue.

"About as expected." Blue's gaze held hers for several moments.

"What did you do with your family?" Leo wanted to know.

Marin expected Blue to give the boy some kind of answer that wasn't anywhere close to the truth. But he didn't.

"Today, a doctor told me I might not be able to fly a fighter jet again," Blue said.

That caused Leo's eyes to widen, and Marin figured if Leo were older, he'd be cursing right about now. "But that's not fair."

"No," Blue agreed. He pointed to his knee. "Things got messed up in there when I crash-landed."

Leo's eyes widened even more, and she thought his young mind was trying to process that the man he idolized had just been crushed. "What you gonna do if you can't fly?" Leo pressed.

Blue worked up a smile and ruffled Leo's hair. "I'm not sure, but I was thinking about taking Iceman out for a ride. How about instead, I pick a more…friendly horse, and you could maybe get up in the saddle with me?"

That instantly brightened the boy's mood, and he whirled toward Marin. "Can I?" he asked.

No way would she tell him he couldn't go. Not when he was already so excited about it. And not when it might help Blue. At a minimum, it would distract Blue, but she didn't know if that was good or not. Eventually, Blue was going to have to face this head-on.

So would she.

Just because Blue might not be able to fly jets, it didn't mean he'd be getting out of the military. She suspected there were plenty of jobs he could still do. Maybe even a flight instructor.

The sound of her phone ringing cut off any thoughts of that, and Marin frowned when she saw the unfamiliar number on the screen. She wanted to curse the second she answered it.

"It's me," the man said.

Blue was watching her, and he must have picked up on her silent profanity and groaning. "Leo, why don't you go to the pasture fence and pick out which horse you want us to ride?"

That got Leo cheering and running. The boy immediately started toward the fence, and after he was out of earshot, Marin said, "It's Brian. I'm putting the call on speaker," she added so that Brian would know someone else was listening. "Neither Blue nor I are giving you money," she tacked on to that.

"No need," Brian replied, and while his voice was calm, there was also a taunting edge to it. "Aaron Wainwright. That's the name of my attorney. And, yeah, he's the real deal. Have your *boyfriend* check him out."

Marin bristled at the way Brian had said *boyfriend* because he'd made it sound sleazy, but the man had likely done that to provoke them. Blue clearly didn't fall for it, either.

"I'll text the lawyer's name to the PI," Blue whispered to her. "I'll ask her to verify if Brian truly is a client."

Good. They would need that info especially after the last ruse Brian had tried to pull on them. "What do you want?" Marin snapped at Brian.

"To let you know that this morning my lawyer filed the paperwork for me to get custody of Leo," Brian was quick to answer.

Even though Blue was still composing the text to the PI, Marin saw him pull back his shoulders. She was doing the same thing, and some of the color had likely drained from her face. This was all probably another empty threat on Brian's part, but it obviously still packed a punch. Of course, it did because it was a threat to Leo.

"My lawyer's walking the petition through to a judge as we speak," Brian went on, "and within the hour, I could possibly be granted emergency custody of my son."

"Emergency?" Marin snapped. "You trying to extort money from Blue is an emergency? Does your lawyer and the judge know that?"

"All a misunderstanding," Brian remarked.

It was just what Blue had figured he would do, and while Marin and he could tell a judge what Brian had said, it would still be their word against his. Of course, their word would hold more weight if Brian's background was taken into consideration—which it would be. But all of that took time, and right now, if Brian was to be believed, then he'd already set things in motion that would have to be challenged and fought.

"What's really important is the emergency situation," Brian went on. "That's what will give me back my son."

"There is no emergency situation," Marin was quick to say.

"Of course, there is. You created it when you started having sex in front of my son, when you exposed him to something his young eyes should have never seen."

"What?" Marin practically howled. "I didn't do that. I *wouldn't* do that," she emphasized. "And you and I both know what this is about. You don't want Leo. You want money, and this is your blackmailing way of trying to get it."

She'd opened her mouth to let loose a whole bunch of profanity. But she clamped her teeth over her bottom lip, trying to rein in her anger.

Blue was no doubt dealing with his own fury. And worry. A second later, Brian confirmed that worry.

"I have pictures of Blue's truck parked outside your cabin," Brian threw out there. "Judging from the hour, he stayed at least a good chunk of the night, and he did that while my son was there."

Marin's gaze flew to Blue's, and she saw some fresh anger in his eyes. She could tell Blue wanted to return verbal fire, but he didn't. He was thinking this through just as she was doing. It was possible Brian had in fact gotten those photos, but he would have had to trespass on the ranch to do it.

Maybe.

If he had access to a long-range camera, he maybe could have gotten the shots from the road. But if Marin or Blue pointed that out to him, it would confirm that

Blue had, indeed, spent a good chunk of the night in Marin's bed. Leo had been asleep and certainly hadn't witnessed any sex, but this seemed like something the lawyers were going to have to sort out.

"I'm sending a text to the ranch's lawyer to ask for a meeting," Blue relayed to her while he took out his phone again.

"I'll be over to get my boy when the judge gives me the green light," Brian taunted. "Pack his things so he'll be ready when I get there."

Brian ended the call just as Blue's phone dinged with a text from the PI. A text that caused Blue to mutter some ripe profanity under his breath.

"What now?" Marin asked, though she doubted she was anywhere near ready to hear any more bad news. Still, she didn't want Blue to keep it from her.

"Aaron Wainwright is a lawyer," Blue explained. "He heads up a nonprofit that helps fathers fight for custody of their kids. And the PI confirmed that Brian is his client."

Marin groaned and squeezed her eyes shut. "Is this Aaron Wainwright reputable? In other words, would a judge believe him to be credible?"

"I'm not sure," Blue admitted. "The PI will do some more digging, but she said that Wainwright is sort of a crusader and sees himself as a champion for fathers' rights."

That obviously wasn't what Marin wanted to hear, but it explained how Brian had managed to get the lawyer. Brian wouldn't have had to pony up any money. Added to that, since custody fights were Wainwright's specialty, it explained how he was able to get the petition in front of a judge so quickly.

"Am I gonna have to leave the ranch?" Blue heard Leo ask.

Blue and Marin reeled around to see the boy standing way too close to them. And since Marin had put Brian's call on speaker, Leo had possibly overheard every single word of the conversation.

Marin's forehead bunched up, and she went straight to Leo and pulled him into her arms. "No," she said. "You aren't going to leave the ranch."

Leo pulled back from her and shook his head. "But he said to pack my things. That was my dad, right? Is he coming to take me?"

That quiver in Leo's voice and the tears shimmering in his eyes broke her heart and probably did the same to Blue. He went closer to Leo, too, and even though it must have caused the pain to stab through his knee, Blue stooped down so he could look the boy straight in the eyes.

Marin hoped he didn't make a promise that he couldn't keep.

"Your aunt Marin and I are going to do everything humanly possible to make sure you stay at the ranch," Blue said. So, not a promise that Leo would never have to leave.

Leo stayed quiet a moment, staring at Blue. "Will you adopt me so he can't take me?" He turned to Marin, then. "You and Blue can both adopt me. Then, no one can take me away."

This had to be ripping Blue to pieces because it was

doing the same to her. Marin didn't put Blue on the spot. Instead, she jumped in to answer the boy.

"I am going to adopt you," she spelled out to Leo. "I was just waiting for you to get a little bit older so you could be sure that was what you wanted me to do."

"It's what I want," Leo was quick to say. "But Blue can adopt me, too. You know, so you'll both be my parents."

Again, Marin jumped in before Blue had to figure out how to deal with this. "Blue doesn't live here at the ranch."

"But he said he might not fly anymore," Leo argued.

"Yes, he might not be able to fly, but he could do another job in the Air Force. And his knee might get better."

Marin actually knew that last part was more than a slim possibility, and even though she'd been telling that to Leo, she could see that it struck home with Blue, too. His knee could definitely get better, no matter what the flight surgeon said. He could maybe ride this out with an instructor's job, work hard with the physical therapist and get back in the cockpit.

The relief eased the muscles in his face. She could see the hope return.

He'd been in such a dark place after what the flight surgeon had told him that he'd lost hope. Marin had just given it back to him. She was glad she was able to do that for him, but mercy, now she was battling her own dark place.

"So, Blue can't adopt me," Leo concluded, not only sounding worried but disappointed. "But you will so I can stay here," he added to Marin.

"I will," she assured him, and she managed to smile at the boy.

Her smile worked magic because some of the worry left Leo's face, and he glanced back at the horses. "Are we still gonna go for a ride?" he asked Blue.

"We are," Blue confirmed. "Have you picked out a horse yet?"

He nodded. "I think I want that one." Leo pointed to a mild-tempered mare, Snowball, and the horse was right up next to the pasture fence.

"Why don't you get a treat from the bin in the barn," Blue suggested, "and give it to Snowball so she'll have energy for the ride. Give her the treat the way I showed you. Open palm so she doesn't try to nibble on your fingers."

Leo giggled and held out his hand to prove he knew the correct way. "Can I give her one treat or two?"

"Two," Blue said.

Marin knew why he'd gone for the double treat. That would give a little extra time for Marin and him to "debrief" this situation with Brian.

As if the adoption/having to leave the ranch was no longer on his radar, Leo barreled toward the barn to get started on those treats. Blue quickly turned to Marin.

"The lawyer will fight anything Brian tries to throw at us," Blue spelled out. "And just because Wainwright feels this is the right thing, a judge probably won't agree."

She wished he could have substituted that *probably* for something that was a 100 percent guarantee. But as Blue had done with Leo, he obviously didn't want to promise Marin anything, either. Even if it was clear that her heart was breaking.

"I'll text the PI again and ask him to come out to the ranch right away," Blue offered. He did that and got an immediate response. "He'll be here soon."

Good. And Marin hoped the lawyer could do something to stop Brian.

She saw some movement from the corner of her eye and tensed. Then, relaxed a little when she saw it was Egan making his way toward them.

"Trouble?" Egan immediately asked, probably because he'd noticed Blue's and her dire expressions.

"Brian got a lawyer and he's pushing to get custody of Leo," Marin explained, and even though she'd tried to keep the emotion out of her voice, she'd failed big-time.

Egan groaned and shook his head. "Can we do anything to shut that down?"

"Our lawyer's on the way," Blue assured him, and he looked at his brother. "What's wrong?"

Marin had also picked up on the intense vibe from Egan, and she hoped this wasn't more bad news. Blue and she had had enough of that.

"The PI believes she's located the correct Dawn Joyner who you spoke to on the phone. She's a nurse at a hospital in Austin."

Austin was only an hour and a half drive from Emerald Creek. So close.

"The PI believes she's the correct Dawn Joyner because there are some photos on her social media pages," Egan went on. "Photos of a man who Dawn didn't tag or identify by name, but there's a resemblance. To us," he tacked on to that.

Egan held up his phone for them, and Marin saw the lanky dark-haired man with his arm looped around the pretty blonde woman's neck. Marin didn't recognize the blonde, but she could definitely see that the man did, indeed, look like Egan and Blue.

"That's Dawn," Egan said, tapping the woman's photo.

She watched as Blue took the phone and studied the couple. Marin didn't know what was going through his mind, but it had to be a jolt to see the face of the man who was almost certainly his half brother.

"Are you going to tell Audrey and Dad?" Blue asked.

"I already have. Dad doesn't want to contact Dawn. He wants to keep digging to find out Rowan's surname so he can get in touch with him personally and not use Dawn as a go-between." Egan paused, sighed. "Audrey didn't want to go that route. She wants to fly back to Texas and go see Dawn. I'm trying to talk her out of that. If we press too hard, it might put Dawn off, which in turn could put Rowan off."

It could, and when Audrey was in her general mode, she might come on so strong that Rowan could refuse to have anything to do with them. Which was still possible even without the strong-arm approach. It was possible Rowan would resent Derek and Audrey for giving him up.

"I think I can talk Audrey out of contacting Dawn," Egan went on. "But she's still insisting on coming back to the ranch this week."

Blue's eyebrow lifted. "That'd be a record for Audrey to come twice in the same month. If she's not going to try to see or speak to Dawn, then why is she coming back?"

"Because I think Audrey's planning on having some kind of showdown with Dad," Egan spelled out. "Audrey's had some time to think about this estrangement with Dad, and she told me she was going to fight for her marriage."

Clearly, that was a surprise to both Blue and Egan. Marin didn't know Audrey that well, but she must love her husband to come home and try to make things work.

Marin immediately thought of Blue, and she had a flash of her fighting to keep him. A flash that she quickly dismissed. He wasn't hers to fight for, and it wasn't a win she wanted. Not when it would end up making Blue miserable. If there was a chance, even a slim one, that he could fly again, then he needed to go for it.

That didn't help her already rock-bottom mood so when her phone rang, she instantly thought this would be more bad news, even though it wasn't a number she recognized.

"Marin Galloway," she answered.

"Miss Galloway," a man responded. "I'm Aaron Wainwright, the attorney for Brian Petty. I'm calling to let you know the judge has just come back with a decision on the custody petition."

CHAPTER TWENTY-FOUR

BLUE DIDN'T KNOW who'd just called Marin or what the caller had said to her, but he saw her knees buckle, and Blue hurried to take hold of her arm to keep her from stumbling or flat-out collapsing.

"It's the lawyer," Marin muttered, her voice a ragged whisper. "It's Brian's lawyer."

Blue took the phone from her and hit the speaker function. "This is Major Blue Donnelly. What do you want?" And he didn't add even a smidgen of friendliness to that demand.

The lawyer cleared his throat. "Judge Simon Mendoza just rendered a decision on the custody petition, and he advised me to contact Miss Galloway and let her know." Another throat clearing. "The judge denied it."

Even though Blue was listening carefully, it still took a few seconds for that to sink in. It must have taken Marin that time, too, because she didn't immediately relax. Then, she let out a sob of relief.

"Good for the judge," Blue told the lawyer, and yeah, he was gloating. "I'm guessing he didn't just deny it, he figured it was a waste of his time since your sleaze-ball client has a criminal record and a history of extorting money."

Wainwright didn't dispute a single word of that. The judge was probably pissed at what he would consider an outlandish petition by a man who had already signed away his parental rights, and Judge Mendoza had likely ordered Wainwright to let Marin know that.

"This is clearly a setback for my client," the lawyer said several moments later. "But he's not giving up. We intend to make a new request so he can have visitation with his son. Miss Galloway will be hearing from us soon about that...unless she wants to agree to go ahead and schedule the visitation."

"I do not," Marin was quick to say.

"Then, I'll be in touch." Wainwright's tone was crisp when he ended the call.

Marin immediately whooped with joy and launched herself into Blue's arms. Blue was doing some whooping of his own. After a day filled with crap news, this was a much-needed ray of sunshine. He might still have to make a tough decision, but Marin's life had just gotten a little easier.

"I can't imagine a judge granting visitation," Blue said to her. But he hoped Marin would talk to the lawyer about that, anyway.

"What's vis-tation mean?" Leo asked.

Once again, the kid had managed to sneak up on them. No surprise there, what with all the whooping and celebrating. Marin untangled herself from Blue's arms and turned to face Leo.

"It, uh, means when you see someone," she explained. "It's another way of saying visit."

Leo stared at her. "And that's what my real dad wants? He wants to see me?"

Marin nodded, but Blue could practically feel the hesitation coming off her. "Would you like that?"

"No," Leo was quick to say. He turned pleading eyes on Blue. "I don't want vis-tation because he might try to take me. I don't want to leave the ranch." He flung himself at Blue, much as Marin had done seconds earlier, but this wasn't because Leo was celebrating. He was scared. "Don't make me vis-tation," he pleaded, mispronouncing the word.

"I won't," Blue blurted out before he could think it through.

He probably shouldn't promise something like that since there was a slim chance that a judge might allow visitations. But if that happened, then Blue could hire a whole boatload of lawyers to fight it.

Leo continued to stare at Blue. Studying him. Then, Leo did the same to Marin. The boy was obviously trying to decide if they were telling the truth, and it was a relief when Leo finally nodded.

"The other horses by the pasture fence were sad when they didn't get treats. Can I give them some?" he asked Blue. "I'll do it right." He held out his palm to prove it.

"Yes," Blue agreed since he wanted to finish talking this out with Marin. "But only two treats per horse. No more. And stay away from Iceman and the rescue horses."

Blue didn't need to spell out to Leo which ones they were since he'd already pointed them out to the boy when they'd spent time together at the corrals and in the pastures.

"I will," Leo muttered, and he looked at Blue again. "How soon before you get your knee fixed up?"

The question threw Blue for a moment because he hadn't anticipated the shift in subject. "I'm not sure."

It was the truth. But it was a reminder that he needed to call his commander and fill him in on what was going on. He should also make a follow-up appointment with the flight surgeon and the head physical therapist to discuss being taken off medical leave. He might not accomplish much with those appointments, but the more information, the better. He was going to need all the help he could get to make his decision.

Whether to try for a shot at regaining his life.

Or...

Blue couldn't go there. Not yet. However, that decision was weighing hard and heavy on him.

"I'm not sure," Blue repeated to Leo when the boy just kept staring at him. He ruffled his fingers through Leo's hair. "But your aunt Marin, uncle Egan and I will keep you safe. That's a promise."

And it was a promise that Blue would make sure he kept.

Leo gave Marin and Blue one last glance before he headed toward the barn to get the treats so he could dole out more treats to the other horses. They watched him go, and once Leo was out of earshot, Egan turned to Marin.

"Take the rest of the day off," Egan insisted. "Step away from the day from hell and celebrate."

She nodded, and while Blue could tell she was somewhat relieved, the relief wasn't all the way there. That might not happen for a while. Because even if Brian's custody threat was completely shut down, Marin had to be worried about him, about what the future would hold.

Egan went back to the house, and Blue turned to her, pulling her into his arms. He also glanced at the barn to see if Leo was watching.

He wasn't.

The boy had already gone in to get the treats. Since Leo had already seen Marin and him kiss, this felt a little like shutting the barn door after the horses were out, but Blue didn't want Leo witnessing any more PDA between Marin and him. That, too, seemed like some kind of promise or assurance that the kissing and hugging would continue.

And it might not.

When he eased back from the kiss and looked into Marin's eyes, Blue realized that she was well aware of that, too. Of course, she was. They had grown close over these past few weeks. So very, very close. And she knew what was in his heart and in his head. Knew that this was a miserable decision for him to make.

"I know how much flying fighter jets means to you. I know that's the life you want. The life you need. So, whatever you decide to do about your career," Marin told him, "I'll be happy for you."

Blue's gaze stayed locked with hers. And he had no doubt that she meant every word of what she had just said. She would be happy for him if he got to do what he loved. She would be happy for him even at the cost of her own happiness.

"It'll be okay," she muttered, brushing a kiss on his cheek.

Blue tried to latch on to that reassurance. Just that. And because he couldn't stop himself, he kissed her again. He reminded his body it had to stay at just that. A kiss. But the heat—and so many other emotions— slid through him.

"Hey, Marin," someone called out.

Jesse.

Marin and Blue moved apart, both of them zooming in on Jesse as he stood in the doorway of the barn. "I was looking for Leo to give him some new treats to test out on the horses. Did he go in the house?"

"No," Marin answered. "He was going to get some treats from the barn and then give them to the horses at the pasture fence." She glanced around, looking for Leo who should have been exactly where she'd said.

He wasn't.

Blue hadn't seen Leo go past them, but since it was possible the kid had made his way to the house using the side yard, he called Maybell, who would no doubt be making dinner in the kitchen.

"Did Leo come inside?" Blue asked the moment Maybell answered.

"No." There was instant concern in the woman's voice. "I thought he was with Marin and you."

"He was. Do me a favor and check the house to see if he's there?" Blue asked, already heading toward the barn.

"Of course." Even more concern in Maybell's tone.

"You don't think his dad sneaked onto the ranch, do you?"

Blue didn't want to think that. But he did. "Just let me know if he's inside," he said, ending the call.

Marin was right on his heels as they made their way to the barn, and Jesse must have seen the alarm on their faces. "I'll look for him," Jesse volunteered, and he hurried toward the back of the barn where there were tack rooms and even an office.

"Leo could have gotten distracted and is playing in the stalls," Blue told Marin, trying to steady her. Trying to steady himself as well.

When they went inside the barn, Marin immediately called out, "Leo?" No response, but that didn't stop her from trying again.

Marin went to the left side of the barn. Blue took the right, and they began searching the stalls, even the ones that had horses in them. There was no sign of Leo, though. Nothing to indicate the boy had been there.

Blue's attention landed on the wooden ladder that led up to the hayloft. It wasn't anything like the ladder that led up to the cockpit of a Raptor, but he still got a flash memory of climbing those steps and taking his seat behind the controls. A place that had always felt like home, with the added bonus of an adrenaline rush. Until now, he hadn't given much thought to the effort it would take to climb those steps, but it was doable with his knee.

Probably.

However, it was going to hurt like hell.

Even though Blue had warned Leo about going up to

the hayloft, it might have been too irresistible. An adventure. Or a place to sit and think about the conversation he'd heard about visitations and custody. Leo hadn't walked away from that conversation with his usual rosy outlook. He'd been somewhat sad. Sad enough maybe to climb to a place he shouldn't be so he could have a moment to himself.

"Leo, are you up there in the hayloft?" Blue called out.

Again, no answer, so Blue dragged in a breath and started up the steps. The pain knifed through him. So sharp, so hard that it robbed him of his breath. Hell. This was worse than what he'd experienced right after he'd woken up from the crash landing.

Marin didn't notice what Blue was doing. She was focused on searching the rest of the barn, and she was calling out Leo's name as she looked in every corner and behind every shelf. Blue kept moving up the rungs of the ladder, the pain skyrocketing until his face was beaded with sweat and he thought he might puke. Still, he pushed and pushed until he made it far enough to peer into the loft.

There were some hay bales stored there and some feed sacks as a secondary storage area, but Blue looked down at the dusty floor. There were no footprints and no indication whatsoever that anyone had been up there in a long time.

"He's not up here," Blue relayed to Marin while he started the excruciating trip back down the ladder.

"He's not down here, either," Marin said, and despite his heartbeat thundering in his ears, Blue heard the fear in her voice.

Blue's own fear went up a significant notch when Jesse came rushing back in. "Delbert saw Leo running out the back of the barn and toward the pasture," Jesse explained, referring to one of the hands. "Delbert asked him where he was going, but Leo didn't answer. He just kept running."

MARIN FORCED HERSELF not to panic. Hard to do, though, when every cell in her body was screaming for her to find Leo. The pastures weren't safe since some of the horses and cattle could be aggressive. Plus, there were the multiple creeks and ponds on the ranch. But what was giving her the hardest jolt of fear was Leo himself.

Leo had maybe run away because he thought he might have to leave the ranch.

That was one theory, anyway, and at the moment it wasn't the worst-case scenario. Brian was. Because she couldn't rule out that Brian had sneaked onto the ranch and lured Leo out. Brian could have him right now.

"Leo went that way," Jesse said, snapping Marin's attention back to him. They were at the back barn door now, all of them scanning the pastures.

Leo was nowhere in sight.

Jesse pointed to the back pasture where the ranch kept the Angus cattle. "Has Leo been there with you?" he asked Blue.

Blue nodded. "Only to the fence, though. I told him not to go into the pasture since there are bulls." He cursed, clearly blaming himself, even though this wasn't his fault.

"It'll be faster if we ride," Jesse said, already saddling a horse.

While he did that, Marin continued to comb her gaze around the pastures and corrals while she took out her phone and made the call.

To Brian.

If he didn't answer, her next call would be to the sheriff, but Brian answered on the third ring, and she put her phone on speaker so Blue and Jesse could hear while they continued to saddle the horses.

"Calling to gloat, Marin?" Brian snarled. "Well, don't because it's a temporary setback, that's all. I'll start with visitation rights and then—"

"Is Leo with you?" Marin interrupted. "Did you kidnap him?"

"No," Brian was quick to say, and after several seconds, he repeated it, this time with what sounded to be concern in his voice. "Are you telling me that you don't know where he is?"

"We're looking for him now," Marin settled for saying.

Brian cursed. "You lost him. You lost my son," he spat out. "Oh, the judge is going to love hearing this. If he'd given Leo to me, this wouldn't have happened. Was Leo upset because he couldn't come with me?"

She ignored all of that. "Are you sure you don't have him?" she demanded, and Marin listened, waiting to hear any nuance in his voice to indicate he was lying.

"He's not with me," Brian insisted.

And her stomach sank. Because that didn't sound like a lie.

"Is he somewhere at the ranch?" Brian demanded. "I'll come over and help. And then I'll take him with me because you're obviously not fit to take care of my son."

Marin ended the call and looked at Blue. He'd heard every word, and he shook his head. "I don't think Brian has him. I think Leo ran away because I'm leaving the ranch."

Again, she heard the guilt, but Marin didn't have time to try to soothe that. Didn't have time to tell him this was her own fault, that she clearly hadn't handled it well, and that was because she'd been thinking about her own problems. About Brian. And about Blue.

While they rode out toward the back pasture, Blue called the sheriff and asked him to do a search of Brian's motel room. Something she should have thought of. Jesse didn't remain idle, either. He contacted one of the ranch hands and told him to put together a search team in case Leo had changed directions after he'd run.

And that was a possibility.

The ranch was huge, hundreds and hundreds of acres, and her little boy could be anywhere. He could be angry. Maybe even crying. If he'd run away of his own accord, then he had to be hurting. And she hadn't seen that.

"It'll be getting dark soon," she muttered and didn't want to think of the dangers that would bring.

But she thought of it, anyway. Of the coyotes that often prowled the pastures. Rattlesnakes—

"Don't go there," Blue said, not a snap but a calm insistence.

She doubted he'd read her mind. It wasn't necessary

for him to do that because she was wearing her heart and emotions on her sleeve.

Crossing all those acres took time because they had to search behind every tree and every outcropping of rocks. Marin tried to picture Leo running. He was fast, but he tired easily. She wasn't sure how far he could go without having to stop. Probably much farther than usual since his emotions would be driving him.

It took them about ten minutes to get to the gate for the pasture with the cattle. Even with the sunlight starting to go thin, she could see the cows grazing. Could see others at one of the ponds.

But she didn't spot Leo.

"Leo?" she called out, yelling so loud that it sent some of the cows scrambling away. Marin kept calling, until her voice broke, and she felt the tears spill down her cheeks.

"We'll find him," Blue repeated.

Jesse climbed down from the saddle so he could open the gate and let them through. She didn't ask if he could tell if the gate had been opened recently because if Leo had made it this far, he would have just climbed over it.

While they rode into the cattle pasture, Marin took out her phone again, and this time she called Aaron Wainwright. She wasn't sure what a call to Brian's lawyer would accomplish, but she was glad he answered right away.

"This is Marin Galloway," she said, putting this call on speaker as well. "I'm worried that Brian might have taken Leo," she blurted out.

"What? When?" the lawyer asked, and either he was genuinely concerned or he was good at faking it.

"Leo went missing about a half hour ago," Marin supplied. "I spoke to Brian, and he said Leo isn't with him, but he could be lying."

"He's not lying, not about that, anyway," Wainwright assured her with complete confidence. He paused. "Did Brian tell you what he did?"

That shot some alarm through her. "What?" she managed to say despite her throat snapping shut.

The lawyer muttered something she didn't catch, but it sounded like profanity. "Brian didn't take Leo because he was with me nearly all day, and right now, he's in his motel room. I'm in my car outside it, waiting for the cops to arrive."

"What?" Marin repeated. "You said Brian didn't take Leo."

"He didn't," Wainwright insisted. "And there's no one else in his motel room."

"Then why are you waiting for the cops?" she demanded.

The lawyer muttered something again, and this time Marin was certain he was cursing. "Because Brian is about to be arrested."

CHAPTER TWENTY-FIVE

EVEN THOUGH BLUE'S focus was on looking for Leo, he had no trouble hearing what the lawyer had just said. Apparently, neither had Marin.

"Brian's being arrested?" she demanded. "For something he did to Leo?"

"No," Wainwright was quick to answer. "For something he did to me. You said you called him. I guess he didn't mention what was going on?"

"No. What is going on?" And this time, there was even more urgency in Marin's voice.

There was more urgency inside Blue, too, and he was ready to rip Brian limb from limb if he'd done anything to harm Leo.

"Brian assaulted me," the lawyer explained. "I guess that's his way of repaying me for taking his case pro bono and working my butt off to do his petition. A petition I warned him was weak, and that the judge would probably deny it."

Marin shook her head, and like Blue, she quickly grasped what Wainwright was saying. "Brian didn't do anything to Leo, and he's about to be arrested."

"Right on both counts." There was some snark in the lawyer's voice now, but Blue was certain it wasn't aimed at them. "I'm having Brian arrested, and since he's already on parole, I intend to make sure he's put away for a long time. Maybe that'll teach him not to bite the hand that tried to feed him."

Brian was going to jail. That flashed like a huge welcome neon sign in Blue's head, and he would have wanted to celebrate had he not been worried sick about Leo.

"Trust me on this," the lawyer went on. "Brian won't be getting visitation rights with his son. He's a violent man with a mean streak, and I'll do everything possible to make sure he serves a maximum sentence for assault. No one dicks around with me and gets away with it," he added in a snarl. Then, he paused. "I hope you find Leo," he added before he ended the call.

Marin certainly wasn't celebrating, either, but she did look a little shell-shocked. After they found Leo and was certain he was safe, then, Blue thought, she might find a whole lot of comfort in knowing she wouldn't have to worry about Brian.

For now, though, they kept searching.

Kept praying.

He saw some movement ahead and spotted one of the bulls. Unlike the horses, they didn't name the cattle, but Blue figured this had to be the biggest bull on the ranch. And the meanest. The bull was clearly agitated and was pawing at the ground, his hooves throwing up dirt and grass into the air.

"There," Jesse said, pointing toward one of the many trees that dotted the pastures. This was a small oak only about a foot wide.

Blue had to pick through the cluster of cows and some

rocks, but he soon saw Leo. The relief came, punching into him. They'd found Leo.

But he wasn't safe.

The bull was getting ready to charge at him, and while Leo was next to the tree, the oak wasn't going to provide him protection.

Marin kneed her horse and bolted toward Leo. Blue went after the bull. Even in his best riding days, he hadn't been a "cutter," the cowboys who were trained to cull or "cut" livestock from the rest of the herd. It was definitely a specialty skill, one he didn't have, but that didn't stop him from racing his horse toward the nearly two-thousand-pound pissed-off bull.

"Hey, you!" Blue shouted to get the bull's attention.

And he got it, all right. The bull turned, lowering his head, and charged toward him.

"Shit," Jesse spat out, racing his own horse toward Blue and the bull. He started yelling, no doubt to divert the bull's attention to him.

It didn't work.

The bull focused on Blue, and even though he knew it was his imagination, Blue thought he saw red in the bull's rage-filled eyes. Either the bull was riled to the bone all the time or he considered this defending his territory.

Hoping the mare he was riding wouldn't rear up and toss him, Blue did a sharp maneuver to the right. And got a flash of an image in is head. Of him doing the same thing in the Raptor after the bird strike. It wasn't a solo memory. All the details came flooding back at what had to be the worst timing in history.

Cursing the memories and this damn persistent bull, Blue had to do another maneuver to avoid the bull ramming into them. The mare was scared, whinnying and squealing, and Blue couldn't blame her. If the bull did charge her, she could be killed. Both of them could be.

Blue had to fight to keep that thought at bay. Fight to try to ignore the god-awful pain in his knee, too. Thinking about those things wouldn't help.

Nothing would at this point except getting the bull away from Leo.

Jesse worked with him on that, and Blue had forgotten that Jesse actually did have some cutting skills. He worked his gelding in between Blue and the bull, following it with a quick slash of movement that had the bull veering off.

Blue picked up the rhythm and the pace and mimicked the move Jesse had made, pushing the bull back even farther from Leo and Marin. When it was Jesse's turn to cut, Blue risked looking over at Leo.

Marin had scooped Leo up into the saddle with her and was turning to ride toward the gate. Blue wanted to cheer her on, but he still had to focus on the bull. Jesse and he continued to take turns, cutting and pushing the Angus back until they either wore him down or the bull decided it wasn't worth it now that he no longer had an easy target in his sights. Since the bull could change his mind about that, it was time to get out of there.

"Ride like hell," Jesse told him.

Blue did. He pushed the mare into a full gallop, urging her to go as fast as she could. Because Blue was reasonably sure the bull was just as fast and might decide to go after them again.

Each thud of the galloping rammed his knee into the saddle and the horse. Each thud wracked him with pain after pain. But even through the pain, he saw something that made everything worth it.

Marin and Leo.

They were on the other side of the gate now, and Marin was sobbing with what he was certain were tears of happiness and relief while she cradled Leo in her arms.

Blue and Jesse sped toward them, and the moment they were out the gate, Blue barreled off the mare so he could hurry to shut it. When his feet landed on the ground, the pain flashed, causing a bright white light in his head. He tried to push it aside. Failed. And just had to lean against the fence for support.

Since the gate was metal, it would hold if the bull rammed into it. No holding was necessary, though, because the bull stopped, eyed them with what Blue was certain was contempt and then went back toward the rest of the herd.

"I'm sorry," Leo said, causing Blue to shift his attention to the boy.

Blue managed to hobble toward them, and he looked at Leo. There was a scratch on his cheek, but other than that, the boy didn't seem to be injured.

"I'm sorry," Leo repeated with tears in his eyes. "You hurt your knee making the bull not come after me."

No way did Blue want the kid carrying that kind of guilt. "My knee was already hurt." That was a "truer words had never been spoken" kind of moment that he needed to give some thought. For now, though, he focused on Leo.

"Why did you run away?" Blue asked the boy. It was a question he figured Marin would have voiced, but at the moment she was battling the adrenaline rush from hell and fighting tears.

"'Cause I didn't want vis-tation. I didn't want to leave the ranch." Leo's bottom lip quivered.

"You don't have to leave the ranch," Blue quickly assured him.

"And you won't have to do visitations with your father, either," Marin added. "You shouldn't have run. You should have come to talk to me about it."

Me. Not us. Marin was already mentally preparing Leo for when Blue wouldn't be around. But she was right to do that.

Blue just wished it hadn't felt so damn wrong.

MARIN STEPPED OUT of Leo's bedroom and immediately turned on the baby monitor she'd slipped into her pocket. She normally silenced it unless Leo was sick, but she'd be using it with audio tonight in case he had nightmares.

She figured she'd be having some nightmares of her own.

No way would she ever forget the terrifying race to get to him. And the relief she'd felt when she had scooped him up into her arms. She wouldn't forget the way Jesse and Blue had jumped in as well.

Or the pain that'd been on Blue's face.

The rescue had cost him, but she couldn't be sorry

he'd done it because now Leo was home safe and asleep in his own bed.

She went into the kitchen and saw Blue exactly where she'd left him a half hour earlier when she'd started getting Leo ready for bed. Before that, they'd had a pizza dinner together, and Marin had subtly questioned Leo to make sure he didn't have any more doubts about staying put at the ranch. When she'd been certain that he didn't, Marin had doled out some not so subtle warning about never ever, ever, going near the pasture with the bulls again. Thankfully, Leo seemed to have learned his lesson about that.

"Is Leo okay?" Blue asked. He was nursing the same beer he'd started a half hour ago.

She nodded, sank down beside him and finished the rest of her glass of wine. "He said he didn't know the bull was there when he climbed the fence, that he was just running."

Blue shook his head. "That pasture is nearly a third of a mile from the main barn. That's a long way for a kid his age to run."

"It is, but I think the fear was fueling him. I've convinced him there's no reason to be afraid. I didn't tell him that Brian was arrested. I just made it clear to Leo that he wouldn't have to see him, at least not for a long time." She paused, poured herself more wine. "If I have any say in it, that long time will turn into never."

Blue made a quick sound of agreement, and his gaze met hers. Studied her. Something he'd been doing since this whole ordeal had ended. He'd no doubt been watching to see if she was about to fall apart.

She wasn't.

And Marin had been watching Blue as well, to make sure the pain had lessened some. She thought maybe it had. Good. She didn't want him suffering.

"I can never thank Jesse and you enough," she said, not for the first time. "I'm so sorry—"

Blue leaned over and kissed her. Not a quick peck, either. He put some muscle into it, pressing hard and lingering a while. That melted some of the icy weariness that seemed to be in every muscle in her body.

"Why don't we call a cease-fire on the apologies?" Blue muttered when he eased his mouth from hers. "Just for tonight," he added.

Marin heard the shift in his tone and figured she knew what he meant by that. The cease-fire would end, maybe as early as tomorrow, when Blue would tell her that he was sorry, but he would have to leave Leo and her.

She didn't press him on what he was thinking. Or on his plans, though she did know he had indeed scheduled some meetings and appointments at the base for tomorrow. Decisions would be made there. Decisions that would put an end to this fling or whatever this was.

More than a fling, Marin decided.

For her, anyway.

But she'd known from the start that Blue wouldn't be staying, that he'd go back to his dream life. This knee injury was a hitch in that life, a huge one, but she had absolute confidence that Blue could overcome anything.

"Should I go so you can get to bed early?" he asked.

He hadn't drawled it, hadn't flashed that smile that always made her melt. In fact, he didn't do anything sexual. Well, except sit there and be himself. That was plenty sexual enough.

"No, don't go," she murmured and leaned in to return the kiss.

If he was going to leave tomorrow, then she wanted this one last night with him. It wasn't reckless because Marin knew it wouldn't cause her heart to break any more than it already would. Not exactly a pleasant thought, but Blue caused that thought to vanish when he boosted the kiss and went French.

His taste zinged through her, as it always did, but this time Marin cataloged it, sealing it firmly into her memory. It would be a way of hanging on to Blue a little bit longer.

He got up from the chair, somehow managing not to break the kiss, and he pulled her to her feet and into his arms. Everything stayed gentle. No urgency. No demands. And Marin could feel herself leveling down. Apparently, Blue was also the cure for a terrifying ordeal.

They didn't speak. They just kissed. And kissed.

It felt good to be here with him like this, but when the leveling down had finished, she felt the heat creep in. There was always heat with Blue, always. Tonight was no different. But instead of the slam of lust, it was more of a slow burn. And she knew exactly where this burn would lead.

With the baby monitor still gripped in her hand, Marin continued to kiss Blue as they backed toward the bedroom.

Her body revved up when he touched her. Revved even more as his hand slid between them and over her breasts, but they still managed to keep the unhurried pace. Even when they undressed each other, there was no frantic race to get to the bed. Only the touches. The gentle slide of his naked body against her.

The pace was maddening since parts of her were begging for the sex. For the release. Blue's body was probably doing the same because she sensed he was having an intense battle with himself. A battle he won because when they did make it to the bed, there was no heated rush to get on the condom she took from the nightstand.

Marin straddled him, a position that gave her the bonus of being able to kiss Blue when he slipped inside her. She kept up the kisses as the strokes began. And it was those strokes that snapped the temporary leash on the fire.

The need came. Mercy, did it. Clawing its way through her. Consuming her until Marin had to kiss him hard. Had to move fast. The speed mattered now as they raced toward the release that had to come.

And it did.

For her. For him. Together. And as the climax came, Blue kissed her again. It was ever so gentle compared to the spasms that were rippling through her.

Marin couldn't help but feel the kiss was Blue's way of saying goodbye.

CHAPTER TWENTY-SIX

BLUE WALKED OUT of the base hospital with answers. Something he'd very much wanted.

What he hadn't wanted were the still lingering questions.

But he'd deal with those later.

For now, he focused on what he did know. It had taken five hours of meetings, exams and conversations with his commander, the physical therapist and the flight surgeon, but he now knew there was a chance his knee would heal enough so he could get back in the cockpit. It might not be the cockpit of a Raptor or even a fighter jet because of the pressure that pulling Gs could cause, but he could maybe fly military cargo planes.

Not his dream job, but it could be a gateway to returning to fighters.

Another answer he had, and it was a particularly shitty one, was that the knee would always be painful. Not the excruciating throb like he'd had when they'd gone after Leo, but the pain wouldn't be going away. He could live with that. Live, too, with the intense physical therapy that the flight surgeon had recommended to try to give him as much mobility in the knee as possible.

A third answer had come from his commander. He

wouldn't be reassigned, not yet, anyway, since he'd have to face another medical board in a couple of months. During that time, Blue would get the dreaded DNIF status and would be relegated to planning other pilots' training missions and such. Basically, he'd become an instructor. Again, not his dream job, but he'd be in uniform.

The question was—would that be enough?

Would the possibility of his returning to the cockpit get him through what he had to do to stand a chance of that happening?

And the final question—and it was the biggest of them all—did he want to just change his dream to something else?

Of course, with that question the images of Marin and Leo popped into his head. Their images did that a lot. So did the ones of his family. And of the ranch. All things near and dear to him, but once upon a time flying fighters had been even more near and dear.

Was that still true?

Blue was debating that when he started the drive back to the ranch. He was still debating it forty-five minutes later when he took the turn off the interstate and his phone rang. His first thought was that it was Marin, and he felt the punch of disappointment when he saw Audrey's name on the screen.

"Audrey," he greeted when he took the call.

"How did your appointments go?" she asked right off.

Blue hadn't told her about the appointments, mainly because he hadn't spoken to her since she'd left the ranch, but it didn't surprise him that she knew. As a general, she had access to all sorts of information.

"Fine," he settled for saying, even though everything was still up in the air. "How are you?" he said to shift the conversation since he seriously doubted she was calling to ask for an update on his condition. Audrey and he didn't have that kind of relationship.

Which now struck him as sad.

She'd been his stepmom for over twenty-five years, and they'd never gotten past the "step" part. Blue thought he might do something to remedy that in the months to come.

"I'll be at the ranch in about an hour," she said. "And I don't plan on leaving until Derek and I have worked things out. I'm not giving up on this marriage, Blue."

Blue smiled. "Good for you. And I mean that," he added when he thought he heard her sigh.

"I still love Derek," she continued, and there was a little wobble in her voice. "But I might have messed things up for good."

"Rarely are things messed up for good," he heard himself say. Where the hell had that come from? And was it true?

In a way, yes.

Maybe in a very big way.

"Things just sometimes shift," he went on. "Priorities change. I think if you let Dad know how much you love him, that'll go a long way to mending things."

"I hope you're right," she muttered, not sounding totally convinced of that.

But Blue was convinced of it. His dad just needed

time. And, heck, maybe his dad just needed his anchor—
the ranch and his family. This could end up being a win-
win for Audrey and his father if they did get past the
mess and worked on the future.

"I won't ask you if you heard anything from Rowan,"
Audrey went on a few moments later. "Because if you
had, you'd have let me know."

"I would," he assured her. "And we still don't have
a surname for him. I did ask Dawn Joyner, but she said
she'd rather wait to get Rowan's approval on that." Blue
paused. "I'll be at the ranch in a few minutes," he let
Audrey know. "I'll see you when you get in."

Blue ended the call and finished the last part of his
drive. Which meant going past the pasture with the
cattle. He doubted he'd ever drive past it again without
thinking of Leo and how the boy could have been hurt.
It was definitely one of those hellish things he didn't
want to repeat.

Once he was at the house, he parked and glanced
around. And he immediately spotted Marin. She was
in the corral with the temperamental rescue gelding,
and it seemed to be a battle of wills as they faced each
other down.

Since Blue had studied up on her training techniques,
he thought this was the "pressure and release" tactic. It
involved Marin trying to get the horse to move, first by
tightening the reins and then easing up on the pressure
when the gelding took a step. It was a slow, tedious process, and Blue wasn't sure who was winning.

Since she seemed focused on the training, Blue decided to go inside, grab a Coke and watch her from

his bedroom window. That would give him some more thinking time. But the plan came to a quick halt when he went in the kitchen and saw Leo sitting at the table with Maybell and Effie.

Even though Blue knew the boy should be at school, he automatically checked the time. When he got confirmation that it was only one o'clock, he got an instant slam of worry.

"Are you okay?" Blue couldn't ask fast enough. He pressed his hand to the boy's head. No fever.

"I'm okay," Leo said around a mouthful of cookie. "My teacher puked all over the place, and that caused Brighton to puke. Then, Caleb. Then, everybody started gagging." He mimicked that in case Blue hadn't gotten the picture. He had.

"Did you puke, too?" Blue asked, though he thought he already knew the answer since, hey, he was chowing down on cookies.

"Nope," Leo proudly said. "But the room had to be cleaned, and the principal couldn't get a sub. That's somebody that teaches when the teacher can't," he spelled out.

"Yeah, I got that. So, they sent the students home early?"

"Yep, and I got cookies." Leo had another bite.

"How'd your appointments go?" Effie asked, and Blue could tell she was hesitant, maybe because of the answer he might give her or maybe she didn't want to put a damper on Leo's thrill over having school canceled and getting treats.

"I think they went fine," Blue settled for saying. "Oh, and Audrey will be here soon," he added in case Effie and Maybell didn't know. Judging from their reactions, they did.

"The doctor checked your knee?" Leo asked, pulling Blue's attention back to him.

"He did," Blue verified.

Leo stopped eating the cookie and stared at Blue. "You had to get your knee checked because of me? Because of what I did?"

"No." Blue said that as fast and firm as he could manage. No way did he want the kid to carry a shred of guilt over this. "But you won't be going back in that pasture with the cattle, right?" he tacked on to that.

"Right," Leo said, but he aimed another glance at Blue's leg. "Did your doctor make your knee all better?"

A tough question, and Blue dodged with an easy answer. "Some."

A whirl of emotions went over the boy's face. The first thing was what Blue thought was sadness, but then Leo seemed to try to push that aside. Or rather mask it. He plastered on a smile that didn't quite reach his eyes.

"You'll be happy now that you can get back to flying," Leo said.

Blue opened his mouth to say an automatic "yes." But the yes didn't come. Even more, he didn't feel that *yes* in the pit of his stomach. Or anywhere else for that matter.

"We'll see," Blue settled for saying, and he realized he'd just put a serious damper on his own mood. Not that it'd been stellar when he walked into the kitchen, but it felt as if he'd just hit rock bottom again.

And the one person he wanted to see was Marin.

He brushed a kiss on Leo's head and stole a bite of his cookie, which had Leo giggling. Then, Blue grabbed the Coke from the fridge, and decided to ditch that thinking time in his room and grabbed a second Coke for Marin before he headed out toward the corral. He stopped, though, under the big shade tree so he could watch her and try to figure out what the heck he was going to say to her. He didn't get much thinking time, though, because his phone rang.

Blue didn't recognize the number that popped up, but that didn't surprise him. He'd talked to a lot of different medical types today, and it could be one of them calling him with some follow-up questions.

"Major Donnelly," he answered.

And was met with silence. Just silence. For a moment, Blue thought this might be Brian trying to work up enough courage, or stupidity, to ask Blue to bail him out of jail. But it wasn't.

"Rowan Cullen," the man said.

Blue froze but damn near dropped both his open can of Coke and the unopened one he had tucked under his arm so he could answer the call. Man, he hadn't prepped nearly well enough for this.

"Thanks for getting in touch with me," Blue finally said, and then he rolled his eyes. Talk about a lame response.

"I can't talk long," Rowan was quick to say, and in the background Blue heard the chatter that flung him back to the days of his own deployments. "In fact, I'm not sure I want to talk at all," he added.

"I understand." Blue had considered Rowan might

want nothing to do with them. Still, he'd called so that meant he wanted something. "Do you have any questions for me?"

"No," Rowan insisted, but then he huffed. "You need to know that the DNA test thing was a…shock. Dawn gave me the kit because she joked that she wanted to confirm how much Neanderthal DNA I had. She figured I had plenty."

Blue smiled. But not for long. "I'm sorry about the shock. I only recently learned about you."

"Yeah," Rowan muttered after another pause. There was more chatter in the background, and someone called out "Vampire." "I'll be there in a second," Rowan said to whoever had spoken.

"Vampire?" Blue had to ask, wondering if that meant he had pointy teeth.

"Cullen," he grumbled. "My last name is the same as the sparkly vampires in those *Twilight* books."

So he had a call sign, which could mean he was a flyer or else special ops. But Blue didn't press him on it. Odds were if it was a classified deployment, Rowan wouldn't be able to say.

"Do me a favor, Major Donnelly," Rowan said, and he continued before Blue could offer for him to use his given name. "Don't tell anyone else in your family that I got in touch. I don't want anyone sitting around, waiting for me to call." He stopped, cursed, and it was a string of profanity that Blue would have used. "Look, I don't know what I'm going to do about this whole adoption thing. My folks… I've got to think of them. In fact, I need to do a lot of thinking."

"I understand." And he did. Blue had been on the "thinking" hamster wheel since his crash landing.

"Yeah, I'll bet you do." Someone called out "Vampire" again, and this time it had a more insistent tone. "I'll call you in a couple of months. Don't wait by the phone, though," he added, and Rowan ended the call.

Blue stood there and stared at the phone. He had a WTF moment, wondering how the hell he should feel about this. About this half brother who seemed as uncertain of them as Blue was of him.

Then, Blue smiled.

Uncertainty was okay. Now he had a voice to go along with the image of that photo he'd seen of Rowan on social media. A voice and a weird sort of camaraderie. Blue didn't believe in woo-woo stuff, but maybe DNA created some kind of connection. Maybe, he'd get to meet that connection in a couple of months. For now, that initial contact was enough.

He hadn't expected to tick Rowan4321 off his mental list, but Blue decided to do just that, and when he saw Marin heading into the barn, he knew he was ready to talk to her.

And, heck, he even knew what to say.

Still smiling, he walked to the barn and found her putting away the tack she'd used on the gelding. Marin must have heard his footsteps because she whirled around toward him. Blue enjoyed that unguarded look of surprise, and love, on her face before she managed to shut it down.

"How did the appointments go?" she asked, her voice filled with breath, and he could practically see her putting up a barrier so he wouldn't know how on edge she was about that.

"Good," he said.

And he meant it.

In fact, everything at the moment seemed to fall into that "good" category. Well, almost everything.

"I just got a call from Rowan," Blue said. "He doesn't want anyone in the family to know so we'll have to stay quiet about it for a while. But he said he'd maybe call again in a couple of months. Maybe," he emphasized.

Marin let out a long breath that she'd clearly been holding. "That's positive, right?"

"Damn straight, it is. I'd call it downright rosy, considering he could have just told me to go to hell." He set the Cokes on one of the racks outside a stall, and he picked up a saddle that had likely been set there for cleaning.

Blue tossed it at Marin.

Well, not at her exactly but *near* her. And then he smiled. She didn't. She just looked confused. So Blue retrieved the saddle and tossed it a little closer to her.

"What are you doing?" she asked as if he'd lost it.

"I took a page from your training, and I thought maybe the saddle would help you get used to having me nearby."

Marin shook her head, and some of the barrier went down. He saw some of what he wanted to see in her eyes. "I'm already used to that," she muttered.

He picked up the saddle again, and this time he brought it all the way to her and dropped it by her feet. "Well, I'd like for you to get used to it…permanently."

"Permanently?" she repeated, her voice cracking now.

"Yeah, I've decided to get out of the Air Force and move back to the ranch. I'll probably become one of those old farts who tells all those glory days stories. Except I think I've got plenty of glory days ahead of me. With Leo and you."

The remainder of the barrier vanished as if it'd evaporated, and a sound leaped from her throat. Happiness. Yep, that's what it was. Pure, unfiltered happiness.

And it was exactly the sound Blue had wanted her to make.

She threw her arms around him, but he was the one who made sure they landed body to body so he could kiss her. Mercy, he needed this, he needed her. But he also needed to give her the words. Of course, that meant breaking the kiss, but they could get right back to that.

"I'm in love with you, Marin," he said at the exact same moment that she said, "Blue, I'm in love with you."

Heck, they had always had good timing when it came to sex so it shouldn't have surprised him that the timing was spot-on now.

He yanked her back to him for another kiss, and he made this count. Well, he always tried to do that, but he put a whole lot of extra into this one. It was the kind of kiss that would lead to lots of groping.

And sex.

While he amped up the kiss, Blue was wondering if he could sneak Marin off to the office in the back of the barn and celebrate by getting naked.

"Are you two gonna get married?" Blue heard Leo ask.

That caused Marin and Blue to spring apart. Not completely, though. Blue kept one of his hands on her waist so she wouldn't go far. He had no idea when the boy had come into the barn, but the kid had just witnessed one very steamy kiss.

"Well, are you gonna get married?" Leo pressed.

Blue grinned at him. "The odds of that down the road are sky-high. If your aunt Marin says the one word I need to hear."

Leo beamed out a huge smile. "What word?" he asked, bobbling up and down on his toes.

But Marin thankfully didn't need any clarification.

"Yes," she said. "Yes, yes, yes."

And Marin pulled Blue back to her for a well-timed, scorching kiss.

* * * * *

Look for the next book in USA TODAY
bestselling author Delores Fossen's
Cowboy Brothers in Arms miniseries
coming soon from Canary Street Press!

And if you missed the first book in the series,
you'll find Heart Like a Cowboy *available now,*
wherever Canary Street Press books are sold.

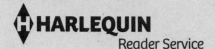

HARLEQUIN
Reader Service

Enjoyed your book?

Try the perfect subscription for Romance readers and get
more great books like this delivered right to your door.

See why over 10+ million readers have tried
Harlequin Reader Service.

**Start with a Free Welcome
Collection with free books and
a gift—valued over $20.**

Choose any series in print or ebook.
See website for details and order today:

TryReaderService.com/subscriptions